ROUX

A Novel

TAMIKA CHRISTY

BQB

North Carolina

Published in the United States by BQB Publishing
(Boutique of Quality Books Publishing Company)
www.bqbpublishing.com

ISBN 979-8-88633-019-9 (p)
ISBN 979-8-88633-020-5 (e)

Library of Congress Control Number: 2023949152

Book design by Robin Krauss, www.bookformatters.com
Cover design by Rebecca Lown, www.rebeccalowndesign.com

Editor: Allison Itterly

Chavis Family

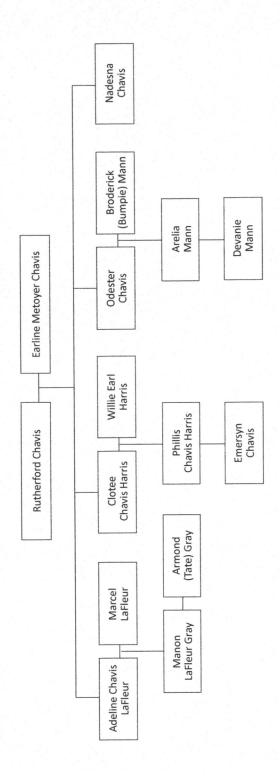

To My Daughters

Alegra, you taught me a depth of love that surpasses all boundaries. You will forever be in my heart.

Kamryn, your unconditional love and gentle soul taught me the beauty of compassion.. Your love fills my heart and inspires me to be better.

CHAPTER 1

Manon 2019

Manon rolled over and raked her fingers through her ginger-tinted waves. At forty-six years old, she was still childless and soon to be husband-less. She blinked against the bright Opelousas sunlight that filtered through her new plantation shutters. She was exhausted from a restless night of sleep, even more so lately because she still wasn't accustomed to sleeping in the house alone. She stretched her arms above her head and twisted her body from side to side. The first few minutes of the day were a bitter blend of brooding over her failing marriage and the dwindling hope that she'd ever be able to walk without pain again.

Last night, she'd dreamt of Leonard Dupree. Twenty years ago, little Leonard was just a week shy of his second birthday when he'd disappeared from his front porch on Bordelais Drive. Bordelais Drive was tucked away in the monied Clos Du Bois subdivision, close to I-10 and twenty minutes from the outlets. The families in Clos Du Bois were either old money or new money, but nothing in between. The police had arrived five minutes after Lulu Dupree reported her son was missing. No one knew Lulu was passed out drunk when her son toddled out the front door and across the street to the Lafleur house. Shortly after local authorities organized a search, Leonard showed up in Manon Lafleur's arms, giddy and clutching a chunk of pecan candy.

Leonard hadn't been missing long enough for the police to

arrest Manon, but certainly long enough that Lulu never looked Manon in the eyes again. Back then, folks rebuffed Lulu's claim that Manon had tried to steal her child, and twenty years later, mixed opinions still lingered about whether Manon tried to take little Leonard. A few folks from the neighborhood carried on the folktale that Manon kidnapped the curly-haired boy because she couldn't have children of her own. Others said Leonard's brief disappearance was a misunderstanding. After all, why would a light-skinned woman of Manon's prominence want a dark-skinned boy whose mama ran numbers at the juke joint? Leonard was in his mid-twenties by now, and he and his family had left Clos Du Bois long ago.

Some days, Manon would stay in bed for as long as she could hold her pee, like yesterday when she only got up because her personal assistant Celeste had forgotten her keys. Dr. Task called Manon's agonizing mornings "early morning paralysis," the period between latency and living where the unfulfilled psyche gets trapped. Whatever that meant. It was hard to keep up with all the diagnoses, afflictions, and medications her doctors hurled around these days. Manon missed pain-free Pilates and morning walks. She felt like a science experiment and didn't acquiesce to Dr. Task's depression diagnosis, and she outright rejected Dr. Boligard's prognosis that she'd never walk again. "This level of nerve damage is irreversible," Dr. Boligard had said after Manon's last surgery. "At best, you will use a walker for the rest of your life."

She sat at the edge of her bed and wiggled her toes. Her last pedicure was eight weeks ago, and her feet looked dreadful. Before the car accident, Manon never missed a routine maint-enance appointment: biweekly mani-pedis, Brazilian wax every six weeks, Botox every three months, monthly facials, and annual teeth whitening. She stretched her neck and saw the photo of her father on her nightstand. Manon missed Marcel: her best friend, greatest supporter, fellow documentary lover, and birthday twin. She shared his wide smile and warm undertones. Her father was the only person who understood her. She wasn't social like her peers, and she preferred books to people as a child. Marcel never berated Manon, and he enjoyed spending time with her. As a young girl, Manon would dash into her parents' bedroom in the morning and hop onto the bed. Marcel would sit up, open one eye, and say, "Now, here's the real sunshine."

She smothered a yawn and twisted the wedding ring on her finger. She and Tate were supposed to be together forever. Supposed to grow old and chill in the rockers on the porch. Now, they were strangers. The stench of crawfish cast veiled memories of last night's Netflix and Bordeaux binge. Whoever said one person couldn't finish a bottle of wine alone had lied or hadn't truly lived. *Laissez les bon temps rouler, let the good times roll.*

The phone rang, piercing Manon's ears. It would take too long to get out of bed to answer it. She had no doubt it was Serenity Village calling again. It was the third time this week the long-term care facility had reached out. Her mother, Addie, was probably requesting more thread count sheets or had another tantrum about the limited meal options. God bless the nurses who worked at the facility. Manon was never close to her mother, and their relationship further severed after Marcel died a year ago. Prior to the stroke, Addie was the epitome of a healthy geriatric: daily yoga, plant-based meals, and immense water consumption.

She made a mental note to call Serenity Village later in the day and half-listened to a news segment about the upcoming Assembly race. The current assemblyman had reached his term limit, and political aspirants were clamoring for his seat. The next year would be a revel of prideful, power-hungry locals touting their resumes and soliciting contributions. *Oh joy.*

Manon wrapped a kimono around her. Out of the corner of her eye, she saw someone standing in her bedroom doorway.

"Tate! How did you get in here?" she gasped, surprising herself at how quickly she sprang off the bed.

"You're walking." It was Tate's turn to gasp. His lean girth filled the doorway, and morning sun rays danced off his silver beard. His dark-framed eyeglasses and square chin reminded Manon of morning coffee chats and tiny kisses. How dare he come to her house unannounced looking fine as hell?

Manon frowned. "How did you get in here?"

"We designed this house together, remember?" He looked around the once familiar home. New floors. Modern window dressings. Knick-knacks that meant nothing to him. "Although it doesn't look like the house we designed. I can get in here with my eyes closed." Tate shoved his hands into his pockets.

Manon recalled the power of pause and deep breaths she'd learned in their many couple therapy sessions. *One. Two. Three.*

"Just because you can get in here"—she took another deep breath—"doesn't mean you can come in unannounced." She balled the edges of her kimono and stared at her estranged husband. The way his shoulders reared back was unfamiliar to her. He exuded more confidence, perhaps even a hint of pride. "And yes, I'm walking," she added.

"That's great." Tate's eyes passed from Manon to the gold-framed floor mirror and woven rattan chair. A canopy and ecru faux fur rug blended out the monotone of the remodeled bedroom they once shared. It was beautiful, resort-like.

"It looks good in here," Tate admitted. "Different, but good. You still have the best decorating taste of anyone I know."

Manon didn't share her redecorating plans with Tate, but that was par for the recent year. She also didn't share her recurrent nightmares about Leonard or that she was walking again. She didn't share much with Tate anymore, except to forward his mail and the recent exchange of financial information for tax-filing purposes. It was easier to pretend as if the last few decades never existed. Manon and Tate's mutual disillusion and matrimonial complacency led them to this place where even typical encounters like this were awkward.

"You can't just come here unannounced," Manon repeated.

"You're right, but you haven't returned my calls. I didn't know what was going on. Whether Betty was still coming to take care of you, or how you were getting along. I've been worried. I just wanted an update."

Manon's eyes traced Tate's bare ring finger.

"We're separated," she reminded him. "I didn't realize I needed to keep you apprised of my daily activities."

"That's not fair, and you know it," Tate said. "I still care about you. You can at least return my calls. We don't have to be enemies."

"Oh no?" Manon folded her arms. "So, do you propose we be best friends after your betrayal? That makes a lot of sense," she spat.

"Why are you so angry?"

That was the question of the year. In therapy, Manon had uncovered so many childhood traumas, she didn't know where to begin. She was angry for reasons that had little to do with Tate, yet he took the brunt of her fury. Manon liked to pretend she was unbothered by her father's death, her mother's indifference, and a secret that threatened her sanity. The accident was the rancid icing on a spoiled cake.

"I'm not." She pressed her palm to her forehead. "What did you want to talk about?"

"Well, among other things, Serenity Village called me."

"Why did they call *you*?" She looked into his brown eyes and remembered romantic walks on Jetty Beach for her fortieth birthday, and their tenth anniversary in Cannes. Their plan was happily ever after in a life with love, security, minimal family contact, and plenty of travel.

"I don't know. Maybe Addie added me to the emergency contact list." He shrugged.

"I'll check in with them," she said.

"The nurse said she tried calling you a few times. Something about Addie's progress."

"I'll call them," Manon said tightly.

"I understand." Tate's cologne folded the room like a warm blanket. "Just let me know if there's anything I can do to help. I'm still here for you, you know."

"Thank you, Tate." Manon ran her fingers through her waves. "I have to get ready for an appointment soon, so . . ." Her sentence trailed off to nothing, much like their communication over the years.

Tate focused on the music box on her nightstand, one of the few things he recognized. "I know you have a lot going on and we've had our issues, but you've never been cruel."

"So, I'm being cruel now? Manon rested her hands on her hips. "Because I'm setting boundaries?"

Tate sighed. "This is not about boundaries. It's about not returning my calls and treating me like a stranger. That's not us. It's never been us. But since the accident, we've—"

"I understand, Tate," Manon interrupted. She still wasn't ready to discuss the night of the accident. It was too much to digest.

"We need to talk," Tate matched her tone. "Even if we don't talk about the accident, we can't continue like this."

"Yes, of course." Manon walked toward the foyer. "Call Celeste and schedule a time this week. I simply can't today."

Tate followed Manon through the newly decorated home to the front door. They planned to retire, raise kids, and spoil grandchildren in this house. When Tate first found the house, Manon wasn't interested in a home that needed work. She didn't care about the "character" the real estate agent had gushed about. The double roof octagon gazebo was atrocious, and the window grilles were dated. Manon wanted to move into a new home with shiny, new appliances, where all she had to do was paint and decorate. But Tate wasn't having it. He insisted on purchasing a home together—one they could both afford, rather than relying on Manon's trust fund. And, to Manon's chagrin, the Bordelais house was in Tate's budget, so she reluctantly agreed. In the first few months, Manon sulked and complained about ripping out carpet and busting down walls. But the fixer-upper eventually became their dream home after a lot of work, time, and love. Now their dream home was Manon's personal utopia. Since Tate moved out, she had decorated the home yet again. Minimalism described Manon's updated décor. She replaced ornate accents, Marge Carson chairs, and heavy, luxurious fabrics with austere colors and laconism. Six months of selecting fabric, new paint, and sourcing unique pieces, Manon had transformed their former dream house with the decorative sorcery of a professional designer.

"Okay." Tate surveyed her legs again. "I'll call Celeste to schedule a time."

"Perfect," Manon softened her tone. "I have so many things going on and don't want to double-book." She opened the front door, and the warm morning greeted her.

"I understand," Tate said. "It's good to see you walking."

"Thanks." She ushered him out of the door. "We'll talk later this week."

She closed the door, relishing his dwindling scent. She missed him more than she cared to admit. His laugh, the way he tilted his head to the side when he was confused. He wasn't perfect, but he was her husband, and life was different without him around.

Her thoughts were interrupted by her cell. Manon hobbled to retrieve the call. The pain wasn't as excruciating but still very apparent. In the accident, her leg had been pinned between the door and her driver's seat, so even in moments of pain, she knew what the alternatives could have been. She was sad about her injuries and often frustrated, but she always tried to keep gratitude first.

"Morning, boo," Gwen said.

"Morning, boo," Manon said as she settled back onto her bed. She leaned back against her pillows. "Are you in town?"

"I am for now." Gwen sighed. "Trying to decide if I want to go to the Boule's Community Service Gala."

Gwendolyn Artiest was Manon's legacy friend. Their moms were best friends in high school and raised the girls together. Gwen and Manon were similarly close growing up. After high school, Gwen headed to the East Coast to pursue a career in design, and Manon stayed in Louisiana and married Tate. Gwen and her now ex-husband moved to Opelousas to care for Gwen's ailing mother and to be closer to his family.

"And why wouldn't you go?" Manon bit into a hangnail and tried to ignore the scent of Tate's cologne that lingered. "That event has been a staple on your calendar for years."

"You know why," Gwen said. "Tom will be there with that girl. It's traumatizing."

"That 'girl' is his wife," Manon reminded her friend.

"I know, Manon," Gwen seethed. "But why did he marry someone so much younger? It's degrading."

"Why is it degrading?"

"Uh, because I'm not a thirty-year-old woman, Manon."

"First of all, he's your ex," Manon said. "Second, who in their right mind would want to be thirty again? All of the insecurity and mediocre credit scores. Not me. Listen, G, if you spend your life comparing yourself to other people—especially a thirty-year-old—you will come up short every single time. You are a well-preserved forty-eight-year-old woman, and that's good enough. Besides, you didn't like Tom when he was your husband. You called him petty and controlling. You said his own kids didn't like to be around him."

"That's true," Gwen said. "He had to make them come visit."

"Well, there you have it. When your kids don't want to spend time with you, there's a problem far greater than you. You know this stuff, G. We've talked about it so many times. It's time to open yourself up to meet someone."

"I *have* someone." Gwen sucked her teeth. "Jason completes me."

"Jason? You need someone who knows what a sommelier is."

"He misheard the guy," Gwen defended. "I told you that. He knows what a sommelier is!"

"He knows *now*," Manon muttered and pulled the duvet over her feet. "My point is, don't settle out of desperation. You won't pine after Tom if you date men who are up to your standards."

"I don't have time to pine after Tom. Taking care of Ma takes up all of my time."

"And how's Miss Holly doing? I miss her."

"Good, I suppose," Gwen said. "She can't remember most of her problems these days. Namely me. The other day, our neighbor caught her walking down the street with the house phone and a butcher knife in her bag. Said she was going to see my grandmother. My grandmother has been dead for over thirty years."

"Oh, G. I'm so sorry. I know that's gotta be tough. Miss Holly was so feisty and strong. I remember how she and Addie wreaked havoc on our teenage lives." Manon let out a small laugh.

"I think it was the other way around," Gwen corrected. "Anyway. I can't leave her alone anymore because she's in the wandering stage. A nurse comes during the day, but I'm thinking about hiring someone full-time." Gwen sighed, then said, "But enough about my crazy life. How are you? Have you been able to get out of the house?"

"There have been opportunities, yes," Manon muttered. "Have I taken advantage of all of them? Not as much as I could, but I'm a work in progress. One day at a time. One step at a time."

"Therapy much?" Gwen said. "What time is Celeste coming? Maybe she can ride with you to run errands instead of doing them for you. You're cleared to drive, so get out of the house."

"Celeste will be here this afternoon, and driving is overrated. I hated driving before the accident. That hasn't changed."

"Fine. Just think about it," Gwen said. "I don't like you isolating like this. I'm surprised that head doctor of yours hasn't said anything about it."

"Speaking of my head doctor, I have an appointment in a few. I'll talk to you later."

"Love you, bye," Gwen said.

Manon hung up and lit a Newport. She tossed the lighter aside in mannered protest of her recurring habit. She turned on some jazz music and picked up the framed photo on her nightstand. Eight-year-old Manon, with a big, goofy smile, sat proudly on her daddy's lap. "Here's the real sunshine," she said to the photo. Soon, irritability was replaced with Monk's laconic improvisations. Manon recalled her father and her pépère's frequent disagreements about Thelonious Monk.

She smiled at the memory and made a quick call.

"Hi," she said into the phone. This is Manon Lafleur returning your call. I know my mom, Addie, is probably asking for new sheets, and I will get them there as soon as possible." Manon paused and listened as the nurse explained that Addie didn't need new sheets because she had progressed quicker than expected and would be ready for release soon. Manon hung up the phone dazed and scuttled to her laptop.

Two years ago, no one could have convinced her that she'd be doing online therapy with an Iranian woman from New York, but every Tuesday at noon, Manon logged in and let Dr. Task guide her through life issues.

"My apologies for being late," Manon turned on her laptop camera.

Dr. Task was the fourth therapist she interviewed. Initially, Manon was uncertain about doing therapy online, but Dr. Task made it worth it. Each week, she met with Manon from her home office. They started off talking about simple things—creating boundaries, getting organized, things that weren't too serious. It wasn't until recently that Manon decided she needed to take her life back and stop pretending that her life was perfect.

"No worries." Dr. Task's eyes were probing. "Is everything okay?" Dr. Task's small head briefly disappeared from her virtual background. The Zoom beauty filter softened her pasty skin, and she blinked a lot when she talked.

"I'm okay." Manon had stopped lying to Dr. Task months ago, but she revisited her old ways today. She didn't want to talk about Tate's visit or the call from Serenity Village. The last thing she wanted to hear was how she needed to care for her mother.

"This is a big week for you." Dr. Task sounded like a kindergarten teacher rewarding her student for reciting the alphabet.

Manon took a deep breath. In order to move forward, she needed to heal from the past. She hated thinking about what happened to her as a child, but she knew she had to address it to save herself and salvage what she could of her remaining relationships. It was the hardest thing she'd ever have to do, but she had no choice. Recuperating from the car accident isolated her in ways she'd never experienced, and she was forced to deal with her issues. She was angry at her mother, Addie, for not protecting her as a child, and angry at Tate for betraying their marriage.

"Beginning this week, the plan is for you to face yourself and deal with your pain. This is huge for you."

After the accident, Manon's resentment toward family and friends festered, and she cut most people out of her life. But working with Dr. Task allowed her to realize that her resentment was misplaced. She didn't like the isolation but didn't know how to reconnect.

"Okay." Manon rubbed her eyes. "Where do we start?"

CHAPTER 2

Odester 1967

O dester picked at her nail polish. Her older sister, Addie, was having another breakdown. *I can't do this. I can't do that. I'm tired. It's too much.* Odester tilted her neck as far as it would go and overexaggerated a sigh. She never understood how people with the greatest blessings yielded the most complaints. Odester could only wish for a percentage of Addie's beauty and smarts, yet there Addie was, slumped in the front seat, looking as beautiful as anyone could. Moulin Academy had plenty of rules, and one was that the drop-off lane was for dropping off students, not for coddling a spoiled high school senior who couldn't get over herself. Addie was holding up the line, making them the Negro family who couldn't follow the rules.

"Mama, we should go." Odester looked behind her. A few cars squeezed their way around Earline's yellow Chevrolet, but the others were too close and couldn't veer around.

"Hold on, Dette," Earline snapped, then turned to her oldest daughter. "Now, Addie, what's wrong?"

Odester scoffed and folded her arms across her chest. Addie was used to getting her way and being the best at everything. Now that she had competition at this all-white school, she finally felt intimidated and couldn't deal with it.

"I don't feel like it today," Addie whined. Her crimson waves cascaded over her shoulders, and her huge brown eyes were sad.

"I'm tired of people treating me like the representative for the entire Negro race!"

"You can do it," Clotee assured Addie. "You fixin' to be done soon. Don't give up now."

Clotee was the middle sister and shared Addie's incredible beauty and high academic accolades, but no matter how accomplished Clotee was, Addie always emerged ahead.

Odester looked at the cars waiting in line again. They needed to move before those white folks got antsy. "Every darn day we gotta go through this. Shoot!" she groaned.

"Dette, hush up!" Earline hissed.

Earline Metoyer Chavis was a bible-thumping Creole from Natchitoches, Louisiana. Originally, the term Creole meant a person was indigenous to Louisiana, indicating a Creole was nothing more than a geographical label. Over time, the term became racialized, wrongly implying that Creoles were exclusively white people. By the time Earline was born, the word changed to include mixed race or free race of people. Earline was often mistaken for white, with her straight hair and delicate features, but she never tried to pass for white, and she'd warned Addie and Clotee to never try either. "That there is dangerous," she would say. "You was born Black and gone die Black. I don' care how light you is."

Addie let her thin body go limp in the seat. "I can't go to school today."

Odester sucked her teeth. The morning pep talks were a weekly ritual: Addie protesting her attendance at the prestigious high school for the academically gifted, and Mama and Clotee talking her off the ledge. It was getting old. Odester didn't sympathize with her sister. Who could feel sorry for the prettiest and smartest girl in the Brickyard? The only Black girl in their town who was smart enough to attend a fancy white school for smart white people. Addie was annoying.

"Yes, you can, Addie." Clotee reached over the seat and held her sister's hand.

"It's too much pressure," Addie groaned.

Addie was almost eighteen, Clotee had just turned seventeen, and Odester was fourteen. Addie and Clotee were academically exceptional, but Addie outshined everyone, damaging grading curves and receiving top honors in all her classes, which was how she got the scholarship to Moulin.

Odester wasn't as academically gifted or as pretty as her sisters. She hated school and her mocha skin, plump lips, and wide-set eyes. She wanted to be light skinned, with wavy hair like her sisters and mama. She cursed her grandmother for passing down those nappy-headed genes. Her mediocre grades and minimal effort at school put her on her mother's radar. Odester couldn't catch a break. Sure, she was standing next to the fire alarm at school last week when it went off, but she wasn't the one who'd pulled it. And she'd skipped classes the week before because she was bored and hadn't finished her homework. The Chavis sisters woke up at the crack of dawn every weekday to take Addie to a school across town, only to listen to her complain.

"Then transfer to Beau Chêne." Odester rolled her eyes.

"That's not an option," Earline snapped.

"Of course, Beau Chêne is not an option," Odester said under her breath.

Earline whirled around and glared at Odester. "Dette, you watch your mouth and hush up. I hear you." Her mother's milky skin didn't reveal anything about her age, and her silky hair was pulled into a bun. "You think it's easy for Addie being the only one of us in this here school? Show some compassion, chile."

Earline shifted in her seat to face Addie again. "Now, Adeline, this your calling. I know it's rough, and we all tore up with how folks treat Dr. King, but you the top student at one of the best schools in the state of Louisiana. They chose you, baby. We are all rooting for ya. Our people rooting for ya. All this stuff happening around us, especially now. We gone need smart Black lawyers."

Odester kicked the back of the seat.

Addie turned around and shouted, "Stop it, Dette!"

"Then get out of the car," Odester said. "Me and Tee have school too. You ain't the only one. And Mama gotta get back to get Nadesna from Ms. Joubert." Odester had several bones to pick with Mama. Not only did she let Addie get away with whatever she wanted, but Mama gave birth to Nadesna last year and had even less time for Odester.

"It's not easy," Addie said. "You don't understand what it's like here. Y'all see how they treat Dr. King. I don't want that pressure."

"Dr. King is a legend, a civil rights activist who's changing the world. You a light-skinned girl from Opelousas. Ain't nobody gone do you nothing, Addie. And you sound just like them white folks. Go on and go to school so we won't be late again," Odester said. "I'm already in trouble for being late."

"No, Odester," Earline corrected. "You in trouble for skipping class. Remember?"

Odester slumped down in her seat. Nobody had asked why she wasn't in class. But even if they did, they wouldn't believe her. Odester's dishonesty preceded her, and her sanctimonious family never let her forget it. She wanted to do well in school, but she couldn't focus on the lessons no matter what she tried. She'd focus as hard as she could, but then she would get lost in thought or notice someone behind her sneezing. She just couldn't remain present. But her mama didn't want to hear it. "You can pay attention to them TV shows," Earline would argue when Odester talked about her attention issues.

"You gone be fine," Earline told Addie. "Dr. King leads the movement so y'all can have opportunities like this. To make something outcha yourselves. Not to be cleaning houses or scrubbing no floors. You destined for greatness, Adeline. The first lawyer in the family . . . but not the last."

"She been going to this school for four years now," Odester said. "I don't understand why we still gotta go through this here. She gone graduate in a few months, dang."

"Shut up, Odester," Addie snapped.

"You shut up. You think you can do what you want 'cause you Mama's favorite?"

"Like you ain't Daddy's favorite!" Addie said.

"Both of you stop it now!" Earline reprimanded. "Yo daddy and me ain't got favorites. We love all of you in different ways but no more than the other. Y'all got that?"

"Yes ma'am," the girls said in unison.

Addie continued to complain. "I wish Miss Thomas never recommended me for a scholarship here."

"Dontchu say that," Earline said. "That scholarship got you here tuition-free. Lord know me and your daddy would never have the money to send you to this fine school."

Odester sighed again. She didn't feel sorry for pretty, smart Addie, with her demure smile, long lashes, and hair she could untangle with her fingers. Odester never got attention from her mama the way Addie and Clotee did. Even when she was a kid, Odester was the odd one. When Earline read to the girls years ago, Addie and Clotee would laugh when appropriate, covering their mouths simultaneously, and nod in agreement. Odester could pay attention long enough to follow the stories, but as soon as Earline started reading, Odester's mind would wander to something else—a spider web in the corner, or the smell of dinner cooking. Her lack of focus extended to the classroom, where teachers labeled Odester as troublesome and attention-seeking. Odester wanted to learn; she just couldn't sit still. It wasn't her fault. Her father, Rutherford, wasn't like Earline; he always told Odester to keep doing her best.

"All right now, Addie," Earline said. "I gotta get these girls cross town to school. You have a good day, and say a prayer before you get to class. The good Lord got your back, chile."

Addie flung one leg out of the car. She blew Clotee a kiss and hoisted her backpack onto her shoulder.

"Remember the goal," Clotee said. "You gone be the best lawyer in Louisiana, big sis. Look at Thurgood Marshall. You next, boo. Love you."

"Love you too." Addie waved, finally walking onto campus.

Earline veered onto the highway back across town. She dropped Clotee off at Beau Chêne High, and five minutes later, she pulled in front of Booker T. Washington Junior High School.

"Now, Dette, you have a good day." Earline squinted her eyes. "Don't cut class, and you pay attention, hear? I don't want no phone calls, and I don't want you coming home talking 'bout how you don't have homework. Your teacher said you always have homework." Earline pointed a finger at Odester.

"Yes, Mama." Odester looked down. She wanted her mom to understand that she wanted to get scholarships like Addie and win debate contests like Clotee, but Odester's brain didn't work that way. She hated school and dreamed of being a dancer. Dancers didn't have to do algebra. She straightened the collar on the new dress Mama had made for her.

Odester swallowed her disappointment and hopped out of the car. Why were her parents so hung up on education and "making something out of life"? Odester didn't care about homework or college or using proper English.

"I love you, Odester. And I need you to take school seriously. This the only chance we got. Life only gets harder as you get older. Take advantage of your opportunities now."

Booker T. Washington Junior High School was a single-story building with peeling beige paint and white around the windows. The hallway was narrow and dimly lit, and the lockers were rusted and too damaged to repair. The basketball hoop was falling down, and there was no playground or recreation area. Most students walked miles to school. Odester was one of the few lucky ones who not only got a ride to school, but whose family had a car.

"Hey, baby," Regene said as she approached Odester at her locker. Regene was a mousy girl with bulging eyes and patchy skin. "My mama's working today. We can watch TV after second period. By then, nosey Mrs. Johnson will take them blue pills and be asleep," she snorted.

"I'm gone stay at school today." Odester pulled a book from her locker and sighed.

"Since when you wanna stay at school? Is you sick or something?" Regene put her hand to Odester's forehead.

"No." Odester swatted Regene's hand away. "I don't feel like cutting today, that's all. I'll be in ninth grade next year, and I need to focus on my schoolwork."

"Girl, please. Tim and Roderic coming. That's gone be fun, and you know Roderick like you." Regene flicked one of Odette's fluffy French braids.

"Stop saying that. Roderick don't like me," Odester said.

"He like you, yeah," Regene cooed over Odester's shoulder. "He told Tasha Stevens you look like Eartha Kitt."

"Don't lie," Odester challenged with squinted eyes.

"I'm not." Regene pushed her glasses up on her nose. "You *do* look like Eartha Kitt. Everybody say so. Just 'cause you ain't light-skinned like yo sisters don't mean you ain't beautiful, boo. I be telling you that all the time."

"I'm not talkin' 'bout how I look. Don't lie about Roderick liking me." Odester looked around sheepishly.

Regene's loud voice was drowned out by the roar of passing trains on the tracks adjacent to the school. The last thing Odester needed were more rumors swirling about her promiscuity. Roderick was captain of the football team, and all the girls in school liked him. There was no way he was interested in Odester, who barely went to class and didn't even make the cheerleading squad.

"You know nobody likes me since all that stuff with Bo-Peep," Odester said.

"To hell with Bo-Peep." Regene slapped her hands together. "I swear, I wish you let me tell my brothers so they can whoop Bo-Peep's ass for how he lied. Ugly ass goon."

"Well, that ain't gone happen because you swore you wouldn't mention it again," Odester said.

"Odester Chavis, we been friends since first grade. I don't tell yo secrets. But you should tell everybody the truth. Clear your name, girl."

Odester slammed her locker shut. "I tried. And nobody believes me, okay? I don't wanna talk about it no more."

"Fine." Regene rolled her eyes.

Odester had tried to clear her name after the incident last semester when she cut school and went for a ride with Bo-Peep. Bo-Peep was a Beau Chêne High dropout who liked to hang around campus and flirt with the junior high girls. Bo-Peep took Odester on a ride across the river after promising her dinner.

They kissed in the back seat of his car, and when he tried to put his hands down her pants, Odester refused and demanded he take her back to school. Bo-Peep called her a tease and barely stopped the car for her to get out when he dropped her off. The next day, a rumor started that Odester had had sex with Bo-Peep.

"See you later." Odester headed to class.

The classrooms were small with limited ventilation. Odester struggled to read the writing on the worn chalkboard. The letters all jumbled together, and she wondered how her classmates were able to ask questions when she could barely grasp the concepts. She wiggled in the uncomfortable chairs and prayed for the day to be over. How dare Addie complain about going to a school with decent food and air conditioning. How dare she act like she was struggling when Odester's school barely had books. By day's end, Odester was tired of pretending like she paid attention or learned anything.

When the last bell rang, she trudged to the front of the school feeling defeated and waited outside for Earline near the curb. A few guys headed toward the tattered football field. Earline was usually on time because she didn't want Odester to get into anymore "devilment" after school. But so far, she hadn't shown up.

"Look at him." Regene pointed to a tall boy with short hair who was jogging in place.

Odester hunted through her backpack. "I forgot my English book," she said.

"So what? You don't read," Regene declared. "I like that one right there who's stretching. You see one you like?"

"I won't be seeing nothing if I don't get my English book. You know I'm in the doghouse with my mama. I gotta get my book so I can get my schoolwork done. You coming?"

"Nah, I'mma wait here." Regene smeared shiny gloss on her lips.

Odester sprinted off to her locker. She was going to do all her homework tonight. She'd show her mom that she could be smart and disciplined like Addie and Clotee. All she had to do was put her mind to it. The hallway was dim and empty since most kids had a long walk home. She double-timed it to her locker so she could get outside before her mom arrived.

"Hey, slow down," a voice said from behind.

Odester turned to see a tall, slender boy with skin that matched hers. He had short hair with a small part on the right side, and peach fuzz lined his top lip. She knew most of the kids in the school, but she'd never seen him before. She looked around the hallway, but no one else was around.

"S'cuse me?" Odester frowned.

"I don't want you to hurt yourself."

"Oh, I won't hurt myself. I ain't cut like that."

She kept walking. His footsteps trailed behind her. She quickened her pace. So did he.

"Why you in such a rush, girl?"

"My name ain't girl. Ya heard me? And I have to get back outside to catch my ride." Odester stopped at her locker and pulled out her English book.

"Okay, if your name ain't 'girl,' then what is it?"

Odester considered this strange boy who may or may not be a student here. His brown-striped shirt was half-tucked into his starched jeans.

"I don't tell strangers my name," Odester softened her voice.

"I'm Bumpie." He extended his hand.

"What kind of name is that?" Odester frowned.

"That's what my friends call me." His smile revealed missed dental appointments and drinking too much Kool-Aid.

"Well, I don't know ya like that," Odester quipped. "What's ya government name?"

"Broderick Mann."

"Pleased to meet you, Broderick Mann. I'm Odester." She took her time shaking his hand. "Friends call me Dette." Her smile revealed scheduled dental appointments and very little sugar consumption. Earline was known for comparing sugar to Satan.

"Nice meeting you, Miss Odester. What grade you in?" Bumpie kept his distance, but his eyes bore into Odester's like he was looking for a secret.

"Eighth," she said, then quickly added, "almost ninth."

"Well, you the prettiest eighth grader I ever seen, ya heard?"

"You don't go to school here," Odester said. "You too old. You must go to Beau Chêne?"

"Something like that," Bumpie said.

Odester's heart skipped a beat. A high school boy thought she was pretty!

She heard a honk in the distance. "I gotta go. My mama waiting for me out front."

"Wait." Bumpie grabbed her hand. "Can I keep in touch with you? Can I call you sometime?" His smile was wide and dingy.

"I think so."

"Here." Bumpie handed her a piece of paper. "Won't you write yo number down."

Odester hesitated, then wrote her phone number on the piece of paper.

"You shole is fine." His eyes traced Odester's hips, and she melted beneath his gaze.

"Thank you." Odester blushed as she rushed down the hallway and outside. Luckily, Earline hadn't arrived.

"Guess what?" Odester gushed as she stood next to Regene.

"What?" Regene's eyes widened.

"I met a high school boy."

Regene looked around. "What? Where? Ain't no high schoolers s'posed to be on this campus."

"He was by the lockers. Said he's waiting for his brother or something. Anyway, he asked for my number!"

"For real?" Regina covered her mouth with her hand.

"Yeah." Odester couldn't stop smiling. She was still on cloud nine when Earline arrived.

"Hurry up," Earline said. "Gotta get back to get Addie."

Odester slid into the back seat.

"Why are you smiling so much," Clotee asked. Her sister didn't miss a beat. Clotee was nurturing and nosey, always asking about Odester's whereabouts and what she did in school, as if she were Earline's secret agent. Odester didn't mind because Clotee wasn't a snitch. Odester's secrets never got out when she told Clotee. Addie was another story; she couldn't hold water, but Clotee was loyal to the soil.

"I'm not smiling," Odester said.

"Actually, you are," Clotee said with a smirk.

"Well now." Earline looked at Odester from the rearview mirror. "Looks like your day got better."

"It sure did," Odester beamed.

CHAPTER 3

Emersyn 2019

Emersyn pulled the scale from under her desk, slid off her loafers, and stepped onto it. She stepped off again, took off her suit jacket, and stepped back on. There was no way on God's precious earth that she had *gained* three pounds in one day. She cursed the treasonous machine and recounted her calorie intake over the last twenty-four hours. *Water weight,* she reasoned. Her period was a week away, and she always retained water right before her cycle. Satisfied that she wasn't on track to becoming morbidly obese, she sat down at her desk.

"Good morning, Miss Emersyn." Sweat beads eclipsed Adam's forehead. Adam was a decent assistant, but a series of issues recently had affected his work and threatened his job. "Sorry, I'm late," he heaved. "I had car trouble, and you know I don't know anything about cars."

"Mm-hmm." Emersyn leaned back in her ergonomic chair with measured patience. Last week, Adam was late because of a plumbing issue, and his Chihuahua had a skin rash the week before. Adam's increasing ineptness was enough for a strongly worded email but not enough to be fired. Emersyn showed grace, as she wasn't ready to make significant employee decisions in the wake of her recent promotion.

"Usually, Brent takes care of that stuff." Adam fanned his face. "But he's traveling again, so I had to figure it out myself. And you know, I am not the one to be fixing a car."

Emersyn had a lot on her plate today: three new cases, a case management meeting, and the oncologist still hadn't called with her mother's test results. Emersyn had graduated at the top of her class, interned at some of the most respected PR firms in the country, and, at twenty-five, was the youngest associate at Bricks and Associates. The consummate perfectionist had a low tolerance for mindless errors. If overachieving were a person, it would resemble Emersyn Chavis, with shoulder-length coils conserved in a soft bun, five ear piercings, and donning smart workwear.

"I see," Emersyn said, hardly listening. "But I can't meet with you now. Our meeting was scheduled thirty-five minutes ago." She checked her watch. "And I have to be ready for my next one in ten minutes."

"I'm sorry." Adam looked down at his hands. "I know I've been a lot to deal with lately."

"I don't need you to be sorry, Adam. I need you to be punctual and efficient. Is that too much to ask?"

Adam diverted his eyes. "It's not too much to ask."

"Good. Did you make the changes to the Hawkins PowerPoint like I asked?"

"Yep. Sent it to you this morning."

"The one you sent me still had my comments on it." Emersyn scrunched her nose in confusion.

"Yeah, I made the edits you asked for."

"And left the comments in the presentation? For the client to see?"

Adam lowered his eyes. "I . . . uh, I'll resend it."

"If you need some time off, let me know. My caseload is increasing, as is my responsibility. I need you to be on it." Emersyn rested her forehead in her palm. "We can't keep making careless mistakes. If you need more time to address family issues, we can figure out a work plan, but this has to stop. Now."

"I know." Adam looked at the ceiling and blinked rapidly. "I have a lot going on. And you're right, I should have just taken leave. But things are better now. I'm on it. Now."

"I hope so." Emersyn placed her phone face down on the desk. Before Adam arrived, she was scrolling through her cousin Devanie's Instagram for a daily reminder of how much she wanted to meet her Opelousas family. Devanie's social media photos boasted holiday and birthday gatherings, with relatives laughing, posing, dancing in the kitchen, and holding up plates of food. Emersyn and her mother usually traveled for the holidays: Thanksgiving in the Maldives, Christmases in Hawaii, and birthday dinners at Michael Mina. "Traveling during the holidays isn't wrong," Phillis would say. "It's just different."

Matt peeked into her office and waved.

"We'll pick this up later, Adam," Emersyn said. "Please remove my comments and resend the presentation to me for a final review by close of business."

"Congratulations!" Matt sang after Adam sulked out of the office.

"Shhh, people don't know yet," Emersyn said.

"Paul already sent an email to the partners." Matt's blue eyes beamed. "Got it this morning. It's just a matter of time before it filters to staff. I'm proud of you."

"Thank you, Matt. And thank you for your support."

"Just think, you are the first Black associate at this firm." Matt held a fist in the air.

"Matt, put that white fist down."

"Why? You think I can't appreciate this moment because my fist is white? I love that Paul recognizes the talent of a Black woman. A bold, collard-green-eating Black woman. You can kill a revolutionary, but you can't kill a revolution." Matt flung his fist up again.

"All right, Afeni Shakur," Emersyn hissed. "I admit I was shocked when Paul called me into his office. I thought he was going to fire me after the Hamilton fiasco."

"Forget about Hamilton. Everybody makes mistakes. Don't talk about that right now. Let's talk about how you're a boss." Matt's eyes crinkled in the corners.

"How can I not talk about it? Did you see the press? I humiliated the firm. And you see the way Ted Hawkins looked at me in the case management meeting yesterday? Like I'm the biggest mistake this company has ever seen."

"Ted Hawkins hates his wife and his life. He looks at everybody like that. Besides, it wasn't your fault," Matt assured. "And Paul didn't think it was a big deal because he still promoted you."

The Hamilton case was a mark on Emersyn's perfect record. No one knew Winfred Hamilton had a boyfriend in Las Vegas that he was supporting for thirty years behind his wife's back. When Hamilton hired Bricks and Associates to represent him in a sexual harassment claim, certain information became public knowledge. The media backlash was horrendous, and the alleged victim's lawyer pounced on Hamilton's character. Ultimately, the case settled for an undisclosed amount, but the damage was done. Hamilton followed Emersyn's instructions to tone down his flashy clothes and stop spewing venom via email. He also took heed to refrain from tirades at the electric battery company he'd founded. However, he didn't take Emersyn's advice to disclose all pertinent information, and that single oversight cost him his reputation and what remained of his marriage. It was a lash to Emersyn's PR campaign, but it was beyond her control. Fortunately, the media headlines focused more on the sordid affair than the PR firm that was representing Hamilton.

"You might be right. I'm still so mad," Emersyn said.

"You are a perfectionist, Chavis. And you can't be a perfectionist in the PR world. Too many anomalies. Even at the best PR firm in Oakland, California."

Bricks earned its reputation for representing high-profile cases, with a firm full of white men. Some welcomed Emersyn when she arrived, while others were speculative. She was young and primarily focused on cases related to race and women's rights. Like the Spa case that caught Paul Brick's attention. Ten Black women in a spa were asked to leave for being "too loud." Emersyn had challenged the organization's policy and tolerances, the board of directors, and the city. The Spa case garnered national headlines when it settled for a staggering twenty million dollars.

"Did you bring lunch?" she asked.

"Nope," Matt said. "It's Wednesday, remember?"

"That's right." She fist-bumped him. "Day drinking?"

"Your rules, not mine." Matt shrugged.

"I have a conference call later, so I'll just meet you at the usual watering hole."

"All right. Do you have any clue what Paul's announcement will be at today's meeting?"

"Nope." Emersyn pulled a black wool blazer over her silk tank. "Maybe he has a new girlfriend."

"That wouldn't be a case announcement." Matt grinned. "That's a pending update."

Matt followed Emersyn to the massive boardroom, where they filled their assigned seats—Matt in the center of the room, and Emersyn at the end of the table next to Paul. Matt was Emersyn's first ally at the firm and became her de facto mentor. They began by chatting at the coffee machine, which then evolved to weekly lunch meetings and then Wednesday drinks. The Hoyas alums bonded over their love for the Notorious B.I.G. and Eritrean food.

"Morning, everybody," Paul drawled from his seat.

Paul, a burly Kentuckian, stood at five-four in his best Taft shoes. The remaining strands of his silver hair were plastered across his forehead. He founded Bricks and Associates forty-seven years ago. He became enamored with Emersyn after closely following the case of the unruly spa women. Paul was patient but determined when he recruited Emersyn to join his firm. At the time, Emersyn wasn't interested in working for a large PR firm with few women leaders and little diversity, but Paul's genuineness had sold her. Emersyn was impressed with the firm's commitment to the community, and the bonus structure didn't hurt either. Paul was a good guy. His farmland dialect was perfect for presenting the senior leaders with Pappy Van Winkle at holiday parties and telling inappropriate jokes. Paul had residences in Kentucky and Oakland, and while he left much to be desired in cultural competency, he was honest. He'd never win an award for being socially conscious, but he was generous, offering staff members a paid week off for Christmas, and sixteen weeks for maternity or paternity leave.

"I like you," Paul had told Emersyn just before he offered her the promotion. "You bring something to this firm that we ain't never seen before, and I'm not just talking about you being Black and them cornrow things you wear in your hair sometimes—I like all that stuff too. But I like that you aren't scared of nothing and nobody. You're smart and make decisions from your gut, which I admire. I need you on my A-team."

Emersyn thrived at Bricks. Everything in her life was coming together except for her desire to know her family and to find her father. Throughout the years, Emersyn's inquiries about her family were met with mired deflections from her mother. "A lot happened back in Louisiana, honey," Phillis said one day. "You'll understand when the time is right. It's better this way." Year after year, holiday after holiday, Phillis had made excuses about why they couldn't visit their family in Opelousas. The issue blew up in high school when Emersyn had to complete a project about familial generations.

"I'll need phone numbers, Mom," Emersyn had told Phillis with a mouthful of braces and an expectant heart. "And some stories."

"I'll see if I can find a few numbers," Phillis had said, but she never followed through. Instead, she complied with Emersyn's request to share a family story.

"I loved when my family had potlucks," Phillis had said with the faraway look she always had when she talked about home. "It meant I got to play with my cousins, Manon and Arelia. Nadesna was our aunt, but she was much younger than her sisters, so she mostly hung out with us. One day, we were all outside my mom's house, sitting on the grass, and I remember the sadness. Manon said her mother didn't love her, and Arelia had been abused by one of my aunt Odester's boyfriends. I remember feeling helpless and torn. And whenever I think about returning, the same feeling of helplessness creeps over me. There are some things we can't fix, and some trauma can't be helped. And I chose to stay away from it."

Emersyn's great-grandparents, Earline Metoyer and Rutherford Chavis, were Cane River Creoles. During the Colonial Era, planters were permitted to engage in relationships with African and Native American slaves. The children born from these unions were frequently granted their freedom and gave rise to a unique class of people, blending elements of French, Spanish, African, and Native American cultures. The descendants of these people in the Cane region came to be known as the Cane River Creoles. They were successful agriculturalists, business owners, and planters. Emersyn's grandparents, Clotee and Willie Earl Harris, weren't educated, but they'd successfully given Phillis a decent life.

Phillis also shared family recipes and scant stories of her childhood, but when Emersyn pressed for more information, her mother always deflected. Emersyn wondered why her mother never shared more stories. From what Emersyn saw on Instagram, their family in Opelousas didn't look damaged or dysfunctional. And if they were, so were most families.

Emersyn wanted to know about her history and her father. But these requests were met with more deflections and even less insight. It was as if Emersyn's father, Otis McGee, was a ghost, a made-up person with no online presence or living relatives. According to Phillis, Otis was from Opelousas and worked as a welder, and he wanted nothing to do with his daughter. Phillis had met Otis after she graduated college and fallen head over heels in love, but Otis's family didn't support an unwed pregnancy, so she'd left town. Never to return. That was all Emersyn knew about her father.

Emersyn wasn't totally convinced with her mother's version of the story, so she sought out Ike Tagamet. According to her sources, Ike was the best and cheapest private investigator in town. Emersyn was on the fence when she'd met Ike at his office in Solano County, just west of Oakland in the nondescript town of Benicia. Tagamet and Company was housed in a small storefront next to a row of medical office buildings. Ike's secretary was "out sick," and when Emersyn arrived, he'd grabbed a bunch of files from a nearby chair to let her sit. Manila envelopes lined the walls like bookshelves. His cell phone sat on the desk next to a cup of Peet's coffee and a half-eaten sesame seed bagel with a pile of scraped-off cream cheese.

"Don't sleep on Benicia, eh," Ike had advised. "If you ever need commercial space, come here. It's up-and-coming. Don't believe me, just watch." Emersyn didn't want to watch, nor did she want to be in Ike's creepy office. His demeanor was off-putting, and he chewed like a camel.

It took three weeks for something to turn up. Ike had sent her an email informing her that Otis was still living and provided the name of his last place of employment. Attached to the email was a grainy photograph of Otis, who looked to be in his twenties at the time the picture was taken. Emersyn studied his face, but she didn't recognize herself in his eyes or his smile. Now, she needed to figure out what to do with this information.

Emersyn refocused on Paul's announcement.

"I know we talked about it in our last meeting," Paul said, "but I want to formally introduce our newest promote, Emersyn Chavis." Paul's suit struggled around his belly, and he rested his fingertips on the table.

Mild applause rippled through the room. Emersyn thanked everyone briefly and turned the floor back to Paul. Matt beamed, and Ted furrowed his brow at his cell phone but didn't look up.

The team listened as Matt gave an update on an effective campaign for an NBA coach accused of cheating on his wife with one of the team dancers. Then there was an update regarding a local city attorney who gave terrible advice about the passing of a ballot initiative that cost the city millions of dollars in settlement costs. Finally, Paul got to new case announcements.

"Y'all know my friend Ben. I talk about him all the time. The CEO of that new self-driving car company in Silicon Valley? Well, his surrogate uncle is running for state office." Paul rested his hands on his belly. "And we all know that he's gotta do a sweep before an announcement like that." Paul looked at Emersyn.

Emersyn managed the firm's public, municipal, and legislative accounts. Her senior manager, Misty, did political sweeps all the time. This would be no problem. Misty was sharp, judicious, and ran political campaigns in DC before she relocated to the Bay Area.

"Emersyn, this is one for your team, and I know you'll assign someone capable to handle it. It's probably a two-week assignment. Just have your people do some research, turn over all the rocks, and get things cleaned up. According to my source, this guy's main issue is being a Class-A jackass. That shouldn't be too hard to manage, but he's my friend's uncle, so your best person and kiddie gloves are appreciated."

"Of course, Paul. No problem." Emersyn typed notes. This would be an easy case and a sure way to bounce back from the Hamilton fiasco. Issues were coming at her fast, but she took them all as opportunities to prove herself. A case like this would show her competence. Even if Matt didn't think the Hamilton case was a big deal, Emersyn wanted to prove it to herself that she was capable.

"The only problem might be the location." Paul cleared his throat and straightened his tie. "I know your team typically travels to more excitable locales, but this place isn't enticing unless you're looking for some good eating."

"Oh?" Emersyn stopped typing. "Where is it?"

"Opelousas, Louisiana."

CHAPTER 4
Manon 2019

Manon sat cross-legged in her living room with her hands pressed together. One year ago, she would have rather swallowed sandpaper whole than practice yoga. But one year ago, she lived a full life and walked effortlessly. Fascinating how single living and severe nerve damage could change your mindset. Now, Manon Hatha-flowed to peace and detoxified in asana every day. She folded her legs and rolled her spine toward her yoga mat, allowing deep breaths to guide her. Afterward, she shuffled to the kitchen and left a note for Celeste. She'd hired Celeste after firing Betty—the home health nurse who smelled like pickles and talked with food in her mouth. Manon's dependence on Betty tapered off six months after she was released from the hospital, as did her need for a cocktail of pain meds. As her strength increased, she bid farewell to Betty and reduced her prescription intake to the occasional anxiety pill. But she still let Celeste help with menial tasks.

She showered and slid into a Taylor Jay jumper. It was similar to the jumper she was wearing on the day of the incident with Leonard twenty years ago. Manon's chin quivered. She'd explained the incident to Dr. Task the same way she recited it to the authorities back then: Leonard had walked over to Manon and Tate's yard with a soaking wet diaper and a binkie dangling from his mouth. Leonard's parents weren't friendly—they never spoke or participated in neighborhood activities. The neighbors didn't talk to them because of their suspicious guests and vicious-looking pit bulls. The last time Leonard had wandered over, Manon played with him for ten minutes and gave him a cherry popsicle before carting him back home, where his mom hadn't noticed his absence. The time before that, he'd wandered over with scruffy plaits, and Manon had given him a bag of grapes and carted him home again. But on the day of the incident, Leonard had wandered over and gotten stuck trying to climb up the porch steps, and Manon, who was nearby pruning roses, smiled at the struggling tot before coming to his rescue. Just like the other times, Leonard's parents were nowhere to be seen.

"Good afternoon, Miss Manon," Celeste called, interrupting Manon's thoughts.

Celeste was cradling a small pile of mail in her skinny arms that were stacked with clanking gold bracelets.

"Hey, Celeste." Manon took in Celeste's thin frame. She couldn't ever recall seeing Celeste eat anything.

Celeste sipped her iced pecan latte and sat across from Manon, who was sitting in her chaise. Celeste wasn't the prettiest girl Manon had ever seen, but she'd fare much better without so much makeup. She could accent those high cheekbones and tiny eyes with concealer and highlighter. The foundation she wore didn't match her skin tone, and her eyelashes looked like tarantulas.

"So, I met a guy last night," Celeste said randomly as she sipped her latte and sorted through the piles of mail: bills, invitations, greeting cards, things for the shredder.

Manon yawned. Celeste was entertaining with her first-world problems, complaining about things that most twenty-somethings could only dream about.

"And I mean, he was sexy AF." Celeste tossed her hair in her native Californian style. "But I'm not looking for a boyfriend right now. I need to find a real job so I can pay my rent because my parents are so primitive. 'Earn your living. We can't take care of you forever.' Why not? I didn't ask to be born; they had *me*. And they act like they don't want to take care of me."

Manon pursed her mouth. "What does 'AF' mean?"

Celeste frowned. "As fuck."

"Ah." Manon leaned back in her chaise. Why hadn't she ever thought to use that? *These young people are geniuses,* she thought.

"Excuse my French, but you asked. Anyway, I told him I wasn't ready to date. So we talked on the phone a few times, and he invited me to the Blue Face concert. He must have figured I like Blue Face because I'm from SoCal, which isn't cool. You know?"

Manon shook her head. She had no idea why anyone would paint their face blue, but she didn't care. She also didn't care that Celeste had forgotten again to put her coffee cup on a coaster.

"Mm-hmm," Manon half-listened while picking a hangnail. She needed to call Serenity Village, but she wasn't ready to hear anything they would say. For the first time in a long time, she didn't have anyone to take care of, not her parents or a husband. It was just her in her newly remodeled home, studio-sized closet, and an assistant who thought iced coffee was a meal.

"Miss Manon, are you okay?" Celeste raised her lip on one side.

"I'm fine." She shifted in her chaise.

"Good." Celeste stared at Manon's laptop as if she were doing rocket science even though her job duties were basic. Manon didn't need Celeste; she kept her around for selfish reasons, one of which was Celeste's access to elite gossip from her socialite mother.

Celeste asked how to reply to various communications, and Manon nodded accordingly—yes, pay her Amex; no, she wasn't supporting that bigoted Republican candidate from across the river; and, please, please, reorder her face cream because she was almost out. She examined her cuticles while Celeste called out events that Manon had been invited to. There was a time when Manon wouldn't dream of missing those events. Now she couldn't care less.

"Would you like to go to the One Hundred Black Women luncheon?" Celeste asked.

"When?" Manon pulled at a strand of hair and examined the ends. She needed a deep condition.

"Third Friday in April." Celeste frowned at the screen.

"Fine." Manon yawned. "Add it to my calendar."

"Cool. Vieux Carre House fashion fundraiser?"

"Add it." Manon flicked a piece of lint from her jumper.

"That's a good one. I love that organization," Celeste beamed. "They have plenty of money. I don't know why they keep having fundraisers. Too many fundraisers aren't cool."

There were multiple events, causes, and people that Celeste didn't deem "cool." Poor thing couldn't recognize the Secretary of State, and she struggled with simple math, but she could identify anything that "wasn't cool." Go figure.

"Alrighty, I think that's it for calendaring." Celeste flashed dramatically sculpted nails. The nail on her ring finger was painted gold, and the rest were matte pink, the perfect set for a pampered princess. "I'm here twice more before vacay, and you said you wanted to clean out your closet, right?"

"Right. It can wait until you return," Manon dismissed with a wave of her hand. Cleaning her closet was on the bottom of her list because she never got rid of anything. She'd start to purge with the best intentions but couldn't let anything go except for her marriage. She and Tate started growing apart years ago after her last miscarriage. They were both frustrated and hurt, but neither could find the words to share their feelings. Instead, he dove into work, and she took on projects to occupy her time. When she confronted him about his infidelity, they had an argument, and he booked a hotel for the night. That was the last time Tate had spent a night in their home. She fought harder for a parking spot than she did for her marriage.

"What else do you have for me?" Manon closed one eye.

"Um, I guess any other big projects can wait until I get back. Should I have Miss Tilly come an extra day and clean the house while I'm gone? I mean, I know you're a neat freak, but it might be good company for you," Celeste said.

"That's fine," Manon said.

"Okay. Pierre is coming to do the yard on Tuesday. I know you are still upset that he cut that tree too far back, so I told him to send the invoice and I'll pay it when I return, unless you want to pay him when he's here. Did you want to do that?"

"Do what?" Manon blinked a few times.

"Pay Pierre while I'm on vacay."

"Okay." Manon wiggled her toes.

"Wanna hear about my trip?"

"Sure." Manon had already heard about the upcoming Dubai trip four times, but if it meant a few more minutes of company, she could endure it. Manon pretended to listen while Celeste gabbed about Dubai. Celeste and her girlfriends were staying at Burj Al Arab—*it's a zillion dollars, her parents are triggered about it, yadda yadda.* It wasn't clear if Celeste liked repeating herself or if she had short-term memory loss, a side effect of those green gummy bears she frequently snacked on.

"So, my friends and I will stay two nights at the Burj Al Arab. I know, I know. It's like a zillion dollars a night, but you know what? Life's short. So, we'll split it four ways and then stay at a Marriott on Jumeriah Beach afterward. I know, right? *Marriott.* Ugh. My parents are tripping out about the cost, so I have to stay at a Marriott and use my points. It's not *eeeeven* cool. They don't understand what it is to be young and want to travel. They want me to be all serious-minded. Yeah, my dad was a lawyer at my age, and my mom started her first business before she was thirty. Good for them, but that's not me. I need to find my passion and purpose. I'm tired of them constantly comparing me to their friends' kids and my mom insisting I learn her pie recipes."

Manon closed her eyes. Addie hadn't taught Manon how to bake. Between board meetings and Jack and Jill obligations, Addie didn't have time to be a mother. Instead, she spewed innuendos doused in comparison, making sure Manon was perfectly groomed with a packed schedule.

"Your cousin Gilda is the class president of her middle school," Addie had reminded Manon one day. Manon was in high school at the time, and while she wasn't the class president, she was the student council treasurer and was featured in her school's theater production three years in a row. Manon also graduated salutatorian, but that wasn't good enough. Nothing Manon did was ever good enough for Addie.

One day in sixth grade, Manon had rushed home, brandishing her report card of four A's and a B. Addie tossed the grade report to the side and said, "Next time, bring home all A's."

Her aunt Odester once told Manon that Addie projected her insecurities onto her because of how she was treated in high school. "Your mama was the only Black girl in the school, and all the white kids either hated her or ignored her," Aunt Odester had said. Addie's continuing ridicule and her penchant for blaming Manon for everything that went wrong in her life caused continual rifts in the mother-daughter relationship.

"Are you listening to me?" Celeste whisked her nails in the air.

Manon muttered, "Yep. Sounds divine."

"It will be. Anyway, I got three free nights because the front desk receptionist mixed up my reservation on my last trip to Paris and gave me a key to another guest's room! Can you imagine? It was a couple on their honeymoon. That wasn't cool. I walked in, and the wife was on top and . . . well, you get the picture. Anywho, that's how I was able to extend the trip. Unbelievable, right?"

"Mm-hmm." Manon rested her chin in her hand. She and Tate discussed visiting the Emirates years ago. Manon wanted to see the spice souks, and Tate wanted to experience the desert safari.

"Are you okay, Miss Manon?"

"Huh? Yes, I'm fine. Why?"

"Well, I don't mean to pry, but you asked me to register you for the Mayor's Scholarship Gala last week. My mom and I were there, and I didn't see you."

"I decided not to go at the last minute," Manon said dismissively.

Before the accident, Manon and Tate cavorted with the who's who of Opelousas, so-called dignitaries, socialites, professionals, church clergy, and politicians. She'd invited them into her home, shared their lives, and even vacationed with some of them. Yet most of them didn't even bother to attend her father's funeral, let alone send a card or text. Same with the accident. She'd heard from the same four people. Manon was tired of surface friendships with fake people who had the emotional capacity of a zombie. *Good riddance.* Sitting at home alone for months recovering from the accident gave her ample time to realize that she didn't like most of them anyway.

Celeste flapped her lashes again. "Well, I didn't see you at the Link's fashion show and the inaugural egg hunt for Higher Heights either. Have you been getting out of the house, Miss Manon?"

Manon frowned at the Gen-Z scheduler who attended every event in St. Landry's parish wearing shoes that cost more than her refrigerator. Celeste reminded Manon of herself as a young debutante who was trying to fit in and be perfect at everything in order to please Addie.

Manon pursed her lips. "I still get a little tired here and there and don't feel like attending as many events." *Just manage my calendar and shut up.* "Nothing for you to concern yourself with."

"Maybe you should try a wellness retreat. My mom lives for those. I actually think she goes just to get away from my dad. Or you could try seeing a hypnotherapist. Remember I told you about my friend Beck? The one with the Nipsey Hussle tattoo on her back? Well, she hired a hypnotherapist, and she's much better."

Who is Nipsey Hussle?

"So, there's one more thing." Celeste took a deep breath.

"Okay," Manon asked as she played with a strand of gray hair.

"Don't get all crazy on me."

"Do I ever?"

Celeste glared at Manon. "Actually—"

"Never mind," Manon interrupted. "Just tell me."

Celeste cleared her throat. "Well, your aunt Nadesna sent an invitation to a party next week." She turned the laptop screen to show her the invitation. "Anyway, I presume the answer is no, just like the last twenty times she invited you to something, but I thought I'd ask."

Manon hadn't spoken to her family in years, and with good reason. She didn't have time for the drama. But it was time for things to change. Manon would no longer hide the truth. If her family wanted her to attend an event, then that was just what she would do. And she'd do it with a bang.

"I'm going."

"What did you say?" Celeste asked.

"I'm going," Manon repeated.

Wide-eyed, Celeste RSVP'd before Manon could change her mind.

CHAPTER 5

Odester 1967

"**A**ddie, hurry up," Clotee hissed at the bathroom door before marching back to the kitchen where Odester was peeling potatoes. Odester and Clotee did most of the cooking and other chores because Addie had too much schoolwork. Odester didn't think it made sense for Mama to let Addie off the hook because of homework, but it didn't matter. Addie could do what she wanted because she was smart, pretty, and looked white. Their father hadn't made it home from work yet, and their mother was working on a dress while the girls cooked. When Clotee and Odester weren't talking or laughing, the quiet hum of the sewing machine and gospel music filled the air.

Odester sat at the kitchen table begrudgingly peeling potatoes. "Addie don't care nothing 'bout nobody else having to use the bathroom," she huffed. "Ain't good enough she don't have to cook dinner, but she get to take all the time she want in the bathroom too? Probably trying to look good for that snooty white-looking Marcel."

"Dette, hush. Why do you always give Marcel such a hard time? He a nice fellow and always buying her nice things. And you know he ain't white! His family is French Creole."

"I don't trust him." Odester waved the potato peeler in the air. "Something 'bout him ain't right. He wanna be white if you ask me."

"Well, ain't nobody asked you. Hurry up with them potatoes and clean the greens next," Clotee snapped.

"All we do is cook, and Addie ain't never gotta do nothing," Odester whined.

She got up and stormed through the living room to the bathroom. The one-story house, with yellow siding and a low-pitched roof, was one of the nicest on the block. Rutherford had extended the wooden porch, and it was now big enough for two rocking chairs instead of one. The wooden screen door was the sturdiest Rutherford could afford, but it still clattered against the doorframe during thunderstorms. The hardwood floors were partially covered with Oriental area rugs that were handed down from Rutherford's boss. Earline added lining to the flowered curtains, and framed photos lined every available surface.

Odester banged on the bathroom door. "Get on outta that bathroom, Addie! Tee gotta pee!"

"Dette!" Clotee hissed when Odester trampled back to the kitchen. "You crazy? Mama gone hear you."

And Mama did.

"What in the good Lord's name is all this fussin' about?" Earline appeared in the kitchen looking like she swallowed sour milk. Her skin was flawless. If Earline had a dime for every time someone confused her for her daughters' sibling instead of their mother, she'd be a rich woman. Her shiny hair was pulled back in a low bun, the strands of gray at her edges. "Ain't no time limit on the bathroom. Now, Addie got a big exam comin' up. Y'all know that. Been knowin' that. Go on and finish dinner 'cause ya daddy be home soon."

"But Addie is hogging the bathroom!" Odester shouted.

"Don't you sass me." Earline pointed the finger at Odester and raised an eyebrow. "Now go on and do what I said."

"Yes, ma'am." Odester lowered her eyes and puffed out her

cheeks. How did she get in trouble for trying to help Clotee? Probably for the same reasons she was blamed for everything and got stuck with most of the chores. Nothing in this house was fair, and no one cared about Odester's feelings.

"I told you," Clotee whispered when Earline disappeared into the living room.

"Told me what?" Odester grabbed a towel and wiped the linoleum counter.

"You need to calm down. And you need to stop upsetting Mama. She got a lot going on. Especially since she had Nadesna."

"Ain't nobody told her to have a baby at this age. And she ain't got nothin' going on. We do all the work round here. She hate me. That's all there is to it."

"Dette, stop that foolish talk." Clotee checked the oven. "Mama don't hate you. But you gotta admit you gave her and Daddy grief that time you ran away and we couldn't find you for two days. And all that cutting class. Dette, you can't keep acting up like that. You gotta start taking life and school seriously."

Odester sucked her teeth. If she hadn't cut school or run away, Mama wouldn't know she existed.

"Take that trash out." Clotee pointed to the overflowing container near the back door.

Odester sighed, grabbed the bag, and headed outside to a small space on the side of the house where garbage cans waited for Tuesday morning pickup.

The evening was warm, and the cicadas were doing their thing. Thick brush and a huge magnolia tree spread across the backyard the Chavises shared with their neighbors. Odester walked toward the garbage, careful to avoid the red ant beds. She neared the garbage cans and peered at the street. Some of the neighborhood kids were sitting outside. A couple of them had popsicles.

"Hey there, beautiful."

Odester jumped. She knew everyone in this neighborhood. It didn't take her long to realize it wasn't one of her neighbors, but it took her a few seconds to register who the person was.

"Broderick?" She squinted. "Whatchu doin' round here?" She lowered her voice. "You don't live in the Brickyard." Odester looked around and fussed with her bangs.

The Brickyard was where Black families lived who preferred peace over breaking racial barriers. The Johnsons had attempted to move to Plaquemines Parish but returned to the Brickyard after their son, Julius, was arrested for trying to break up a fight between white and black teenagers. The story made headlines because the police burst into the Johnsons' new home after the fight and arrested Julius for assault. The Johnsons moved back in with a moving van and a Buick because Mr. Johnson's truck had been burned to char.

The Brickyard wasn't perfect, but it was safe. Families looked out for one another. Children played on the asphalt roads until the streetlights came on, careful not to fall into the drainage ditches. The fish man came through every week selling catfish from the back of his pickup, and he was almost always followed by the ice cream truck. The neighborhood was comprised of shotgun homes with varying forms of siding and graveled front yards. At first glance, the community looked comfortable, but it was hard to see hunger and poverty with the naked eye. Some families, like the Nelsons, had three generations living in a two-bedroom home.

Rutherford and Earline arrived in the Brickyard from Natchitoches in his father's Buick Electra with a dented fender and a passenger door that wouldn't open. Their family lived on Le Grange Street across from Miss Cletus and next to Dr. and Mrs. Joubert, who were the first family to add additional rooms to their home. Property crime was low, schools were subpar, and most residents were still afraid to vote. On Halloween, families set up a table with bowls of candy for costumed candy seekers to pick from, and during the Christmas season, everyone, except for Miss Cletus, decked out their homes with bright Christmas lights.

Rutherford worked for a local developer and made a good living for a man with a sixth-grade education. Earline, the best dressmaker in town, picked up the slack with a three-month waiting list. Even white women trekked across town for Earline's superior dress-making skills. With three teenage girls, a new baby, and a husband who worked long hours, Earline ran a well-oiled machine of homework, house chores, and church.

"I told you my friends call me Bumpie."

"Well, we ain't friends," Odester sassed as she dropped the trash into the bin.

Bumpie watched her every move. "Aw, come on now. Course we is." He twirled a toothpick between his lips.

"We'll see 'bout that," Odester said. "Whatchu doing round here?"

"Came round here looking for yo fine ass." His eyes traced her hips.

Odester swayed under his gaze. She'd been around plenty of high school boys, but no one like Bumpie. "Hush on up. You ain't lookin' for me. Must have family round here or something."

"Naw." He twirled the toothpick. "I came looking for you. Wontchu gimme a lil kiss?"

"Kiss? I ain't that kinda girl. I don't know what you heard. And who told you where I lived?"

"Ain't heard nothing. Just like what I see." His eyes retraced her hips. "And when a man like what he see, he go after it. Can't stop thinkin' 'bout you since I met you the other day."

Odester's insides flushed. Bumpie had come over here just to see her. No boy ever cared that much. Not even Bo-Peep's bucktooth, lying ass. Odester was flattered, but then she remembered Clotee's warning and the backlash from Bo-Peep's lies.

"That's fine and dandy," Odester said, "but what exactly you looking for?"

"Lookin' for a fine gal like you." He moved closer.

"Bumpie, you too much." Odester said.

Bumpie wasn't the kind of boy her sisters would fancy. Addie liked stuffy, rich Marcel, who laughed like a hyena and told stupid jokes. And Clotee wouldn't be caught with any boy who didn't speak in tongues, bless her Jesus-loving heart. If Clotee kept giving Willie Earl goo-goo eyes at Sunday school, he'd probably propose sooner rather than later.

"Oh," he said. "You ain't seen nothing." Bumpie wrapped his arms around Odester's waist. "You the prettiest one in the family."

"Stop, Bumpie. You know that ain't true. I'm dark. Tee and Addie both light. Got that white-girl hair."

"Ain't nothing for me to stop about. I'm a man who takes chocolate over vanilla any day." He rubbed her cheek. "And this here hair"—he touched her stiff bangs—"is the most beautiful hair I done seen."

"Sho nuff?" Odester asked.

"Sho nuff," Bumpie confirmed.

She never got compliments like Clotee and Addie. Nobody but her daddy saw the beauty or the positive in Odester. But Bumpie thought she was pretty, even with her dark skin.

Odester felt like one of the ladies in those movies Clotee watched, except her hair didn't swing when she turned her head, and her eyes were brown. She didn't feel like the ugly, dark, dumb sister for once. This time, someone was interested in her for who she was. And it felt good.

"Dette?" Clotee's voice called from a distance.

"Tee callin' me." Odester lowered her eyes. "I gots to get back inside to help with dinner."

"When can I see yo fine ass again?" Bumpie moved so close that Odester could smell the pig lip he had eaten for lunch.

Odester hunched her shoulders. "I don't get out much these days. Mama be watching me like a hawk."

"Dette?" Clotee called again.

"I gotta go," Odester said quietly. "I'm already in trouble. If I do one more thing, Mama won't let me out the house for the rest of the year."

"Shoot, I'll wait a lifetime for you, gal." Bumpie moved even closer.

"Say what now?" Odester tilted her head to the side. "Lifetime might be a long time, Bumpie. Don't be making no promises you don't tend to keep."

"Oh, I keep all my promises, ya heard?"

His smile paralyzed Odester.

"Guess we see 'bout that, huh?" She grinned.

"Guess so."

She quickly trotted back to her house and disappeared through the back door.

Clotee turned from the stove and glared at Odester. "You got lost or somethin'?" she hissed. "Help me finish up. You know Daddy be home soon."

"Tee, you always tryin' to act like somebody mama," Odester complained, though she wasn't as irritated as she typically would be. That bald fade, that smile, and that thing Bumpie did with the toothpick drove her crazy! She couldn't get Bumpie off her mind.

"And what done got into you?" Clotee put her hand on her hip and studied her.

"Ain't nothing got into me." Odester turned up her lip.

"Don't lie to me. You got that same look you had the other day when Mama picked you up from school. Hope it ain't one of them nappy-headed boys got you acting like that."

Odester hesitated, then said, "Tee, can you keep a secret?"

"Dette, what?"

"A high school boy like me."

"High school? What a high school boy doing interested in a little girl like you?" Clotee's eyes were wider than the skillet she used for the fried liver.

"Little girl? I ain't no little girl," Odester huffed.

"Who is it?"

"His name is Broderick. He like me."

Clotee pursed her lips. "Broderick Mann?"

"Where you know him from?" Odester moved closer to Clotee.

"Don't worry 'bout it. You best be careful. Them Manns is crazy. His brother got five kids—don't take care of none of 'em."

"Bumpie ain't like that," Odester said defensively. "He like me."

"He chasing tail, like most boys."

Odester ignored her sister as she spread the rooster tablecloth across the table and placed the serving dishes in the center. Regene always teased Odester, saying her family thought they were fancy because they ate dinner together every night. Odester didn't think it was fancy. It got on her nerves.

Rutherford arrived home as jovial as always. His eyes were large, and his mustache covered his top lip. He removed his work cap, revealing shiny black curls. He was always filled with gratitude, no matter the circumstances. He once told Odester, "When you experience a lot of loss, you learn to appreciate what you have and spend less time focusing on what you don't have."

The Chavis family gathered around the dinner table, and Rutherford blessed the food. Rutherford and Earline sat at the opposite ends of the table and the girls sat in the middle. The table barely fit in the space between the kitchen and the living room, but Earline insisted on a formal dining table. The dishes were so close to one another that there was hardly any room for their plates. A large canvas print of *The Last Supper* hung on the wall behind Rutherford.

"Amen," the family echoed. Rutherford piled his plate, careful not to elbow Clotee, who was seated next to him. Earline was feeding Nadesna, who shrieked when the sweet potatoes didn't get into her mouth fast enough.

"Dinner looks good, girls," Earline said.

"Sure is, I tell ya." Rutherford slopped hot sauce on his greens. "Best dinner yet." Rutherford said the same thing at every meal.

"How'd you do on that math quiz?" Earline probed Odester.

Odester squinted her eyes and looked at the ceiling. Was that a trick question? And why did her mama always discuss academics at the dinner table? Odester felt embarrassed that everyone would hear how horribly she was doing in school. She did her best, but that wasn't good enough for Earline. Nothing Odester did was good enough for Earline.

"Did fine," Odester lied. She had been the first one to finish the test and hadn't bothered to check her work. Not that it mattered. None of it made sense, and it never would. She wondered if Bumpie was good at math.

"Good," Earline said. "Education takes you far. Will help you make a mark in this world, like Dorothy Height and Fannie Lou Hamer."

"Yes, ma'am," the girls said.

Earline turned her attention to Addie and asked, "How's Marcel?"

"He's good, Mama." Addie beamed whenever anyone mentioned Marcel.

Odester wanted to gag, but she knew she'd get in trouble. How was it that some people were born with everything? Addie tossed her hair over her shoulder when she talked about Marcel, her eyes glazing over. Odester seethed on the inside.

"Y'all serious now?"

"Yes, ma'am, we are getting there," Addie said.

"Just be careful, and remember, you are just as smart and important as anybody else. You got that?" Earline said, and Addie nodded. "Education is the most important. Don't rush into no marriages, and don't let these boys get in ya head. And don't brang no babies round here if you ain't finished school and married."

"I'm going to college and then law school," Addie said. "No doubt about that. I'm not sure I want to have babies. I heard they do terrible things to your body."

Like she has to worry, Odester thought. Of course, Addie wouldn't want to ruin her perfect figure by having children.

Earline looked at Clotee. "I see you and Willie Earl made snack bags for the fall festival at church."

"Yes, ma'am," Clotee said.

"I'm proud of you girls—all of you. Just make sure to put yourself first. Accomplish your dreams and focus on yourself while you young. You got plenty of life to live. Don't rush nothing."

"They gone be fine," Rutherford said. He sat back in his chair and rubbed his belly. "They gone be fine 'cause you they mama." He grinned at Earline, who pursed her lips.

Earline didn't make much time for smiling and kind sentiments. She expressed her love through actions and advice. She hugged seldom and quickly, and she fussed more than she needed to.

"What do you know?" Earline asked Rutherford.

"I know these here girls gone be all right." Rutherford smiled again. "Ain't that right, girls?"

"Yes, Daddy," the girls said in unison.

The next day, Bumpie met Odester after school. They had three minutes to talk before Earline arrived, but it was enough to boost Odester's spirit. She was growing increasingly frustrated. No matter how hard she tried, her efforts to succeed in school were not working. She was still struggling with math, and when she asked for help, the teachers labeled her as lazy or accused her of not listening. In the little time she'd spent with Bumpie, she felt smart and beautiful—something she'd never felt before.

Over the next few weeks, Odester took babysitting jobs to get out of the house. She'd lie to Earline about the babysitting jobs ending an hour later than they actually did so she could sneak off with Bumpie. They would hang out in the apartment Bumpie shared with his sister, Doretha. Although Doretha would disagree, since that word "share" suggested that Bumpie took responsibility for something in the house other than eating her food and taking up space from her kids. Doretha was at her wit's end with Bumpie's laziness, but he babysat whenever she asked, which allowed her to pick up extra shifts at the warehouse, and since her no-good baby daddy wouldn't help, she tolerated Bumpie.

"I ain't ready for this, Bumpie," Odester said one afternoon when Bumpie's kisses grew more aggressive, and he fumbled with the buckle on her Wrangler jeans. They were lying on the tattered brown couch in the living room. Doretha's apartment had two windows: one in the bathroom and one in the living room. The kids slept in the middle room on two twin-sized beds, and Doretha's living room doubled as her bedroom. The air conditioner was broken, so it was hot and smelled like tomato sauce. Odester was getting nauseous and nervous. She was supposed to be home soon, and Bumpie started kissing her harder.

"Hush, nah," he said, breathing heavily in her ear.

She could smell whatever was left of his lunch and the weed he'd smoked all day. Odester stiffened. She knew what Bumpie wanted. Clotee had warned Odester about sex. She said it didn't feel good, it made you bleed, and if you had sex and weren't married, you'd get sick and others would shame you. Odester didn't ask Clotee how she knew all that since she'd never even kissed Henry, but maybe her sister was right. Bumpie breathing all hard and grinding didn't feel good at all. So whatever was supposed to come next wouldn't feel any better.

"I said no!" Odester shoved Bumpie off her so hard he rolled to the floor.

"That's how you gone act?" Bumpie jumped up and leapt toward Odester, who reared back. Mama was strict, but she never hit the girls, and Daddy never even raised his voice at them. Odester's heart raced as she saw the rage in Bumpie's eyes. Maybe it was the weed.

Before Odester had a chance to process Bumpie's anger, he unclasped the silver cross necklace from his own neck and placed it around Odester's.

"I'm sorry." He sat down next to her. "My daddy used to get real mad at me. Couldn't do shit right for that nigga." He looked in Odester's eyes. "Used to beat the shit outta my mama. That look you just gave me is the same look my mama used to have. I don't ever wanna do you like that. Never, you hear me?" He held her hand.

"Yes, Bumpie." Odester fingered the necklace.

"You is important to me, hear?"

"Yes, Bumpie."

"You belong to me."

Odester hurried home, her fingers tracing the silver cross. She finally belonged to someone. She finally mattered.

CHAPTER 6
Emersyn 2019

The Opelousas political sweep was far below Emersyn's paygrade, but so was micromanaging Adam and placating old white men who questioned her capabilities. She finally had the opportunity and a reason to travel to her mother's hometown. She loved that her new role would allow her to focus on strategy instead of day-to-day combat with the media, hard-nosed staffers, and arrogant politicians. She'd more than paid her dues. She was ready for the big leagues.

Her professional life fared better than her personal one. Amid the most important jump in her career—and her bank account—Emersyn now had to balance the aftermath of Phillis's cancer diagnosis. She and her mom did everything together. They often said, "We are all we got." Emersyn couldn't imagine being closer to anyone than she was with her mom. But she also couldn't shake the need to find her father.

Growing up, she always felt like something was missing. She knew other kids who didn't have a father, but there was always a reason for their father's absence. Emersyn didn't have a reason, unless she believed Phillis's explanation that Emersyn's father didn't want to be bothered. Phillis wasn't the kind of person who would have been in a relationship with someone so irresponsible, even in her younger years. It just didn't align with the image of the woman Emersyn had known her whole life. She tried not to have grand expectations about meeting her father and promised herself she wouldn't be disappointed.

"Mom?" Emersyn called out as she let herself into Phillis's renovated Victorian in the lower bottoms of West Oakland. On the outside, it looked like the other houses, but the luxurious neutral-colored décor, heated cement floors, inside courtyard, and gourmet Viking appliances made it a personal oasis. Phillis's Siamese cat pranced past Emersyn like she'd never seen her before.

"In here!"

Emersyn followed her mother's voice into the kitchen, where she saw her standing over a huge pot, smoke billowing in her thin face.

"Are you making what I think you're making?" Emersyn sniffed the air. She loved it when her mother cooked.

"Sure am." Phillis stuck out her cheek, and Emersyn planted a kiss. Jazz played softly in the background, reminding Emersyn of rainy days when she did homework while Phillis worked on financial plans for her clients.

"And since you're here, go ahead and put those onions and green peppers into the food processor and finish cleaning the shrimp." Phillis pointed to a plastic bag filled with fresh tiger shrimp.

"You need me to stir for you?" Emersyn offered. Phillis was always tired in the first couple of days after chemo.

"Nope," Phillis said. "You know the roux is the most important part of the gumbo."

"I know. And if the roux isn't right—"

"The gumbo won't be right," a voice said.

Emersyn turned and smiled at Amal Kahn, her best friend from childhood. "Amal, when did you get here?" She pulled her into a hug. Amal's skin was the color of copper, and her thick black hair hung to her waist. A nose ring adorned one of her nostrils. Amal always hated her eyebrows, but Emersyn envied the thick patches above Amal's deep brown eyes.

"Um, where do you think those fresh shrimp came from? You can't get those from Instacart, darling."

"Where are the kids?"

"With Brian." Amal rolled her eyes.

"Oh, he finally wants to spend more time with the kids?"

"Uh, no." Amal popped a dried shrimp into her mouth. "He's tired of sending me those hefty child support checks. You know how it goes. The more time he has them, the less he has to pay me. Little bitch."

"Hey." Phillis scrunched her eyebrows together.

"I'm sorry, Miss Phillis," Amal said. "Anyway, I should have followed your path."

"And what path is that?" Emersyn asked.

"The one where you are single and have it made," Amal said.

Emersyn's life was far from "made." She couldn't fit into the jeans she bought two weeks ago, she spent Valentine's Day at a press conference, and she recently found gray hair on her rarely used coochie. It was ironic that Amal perceived Emersyn as successful. The idea that a well-traveled, gainfully employed, childless, single woman in her twenties had it made was a misconception perpetuated by stay-at-home moms and bored housewives who believed the grass was greener on the other side. The grass was never greener on the other side. Emersyn longed for a partner to nurse her when she had a cold, to pick her up from the airport, and plan vacations with. Instead, her inveterate existence revolved around business trips, board meetings, monthly facials, and dates with unremarkable men she didn't connect with.

"I don't have it made, Amal. You have it made with three

amazing children and a body that refuses to reveal that you ever gave birth."

"Everything is not about weight, Em," Amal reminded her.

"All skinny people say that."

"Whatever," Amal said, not wanting to repeat another weight discussion with Emersyn. "Whatchu need help with, Auntie?"

"You can clean the crab. Make sure to get all the hair off. My mama never left any hair on her crab," Phillis said.

"Didn't you say Grandma Clotee was her parents' favorite daughter?" Emersyn asked.

"My grandmother didn't have favorites, but she preferred my mama's cooking over the other two," Phillis said with a laugh.

Gumbo wasn't just a meal for Phillis. The well-seasoned brew reflected the improvisational spirit of Opelousas and family. Opinions varied on preparation: okra, no okra; chicken, no chicken; flour, no flour. But there was no one perfect formula for gumbo, just like there was no perfect formula for family dynamics. The key to a good gumbo was a good roux stirred to blend the spices to an ideal consistency, making a spectacular base for the rest of the ingredients. One could never truly know the greatness of making gumbo until you made one. Phillis traveled for work a lot when Emersyn was younger, and the best memories Emersyn had with her mom were in the kitchen, where they would prepare dinner and talk about the day—much like it had been for Phillis when she was younger.

Emersyn leaned against the counter and watched her mom as she tried to build up the nerve to mention her trip to Opelousas. She hoped Amal's presence would lighten the blow. Phillis was always dismissive when Emersyn asked about their extended family. Phillis had a softer spot for her parents and grandparents, often citing how Earline and Rutherford provided Grandma Clotee and her siblings a life that most Black families in their neighborhood couldn't achieve. Phillis also took pride in how her mother taught her to manage money.

Emersyn took a deep breath. "Mom? Why don't you visit home more often?"

Amal shot Emersyn a glare, but Emersyn ignored her.

"Don't start that." Phillis sipped roux from a spoon and swayed from side to side, revealing the tiny heart tattoo on the inside of her wrist. "Mmmm, that's good," she moaned. "Now, tell me about work. How did it go today?"

Phillis was as invested in a perfect roux as Emersyn was in her professional endeavors. She'd sacrificed everything to ensure Emersyn attended the best schools and summer camps. As a child, any hole in Emersyn's schedule was when she was sleeping. And Phillis's efforts paid off. Emersyn excelled academically, earning all twelve full-ride scholarship offers to college.

"Yeah, Paul announced your promotion, right?" Amal chimed in.

"Today was okay," Emersyn said dismissively. "Paul announced me as an associate and asked me to do a new case."

"What?" Phillis stopped stirring. "Paul Bricks asked you personally to take a case? Em, that's better than okay. That's freaking awesome!" She threw her arms around her daughter.

"Yeah, I guess," Emersyn said. She was excited about her new role and proud to tell her mother about the announcement, but when Paul mentioned Opelousas, a familiar yearning resurfaced.

She remembered all the father-daughter dances she'd gone to with Amal's father and the feeling that something was missing in her life. Why was she so curvy when Phillis was so small? Was her father a big man? Was he good at math like Emersyn? What was his blood type? She had so many questions in high school that she'd written them down in a journal. She could face disappointment and hurt, but she didn't want to live the rest of her life without knowing her father. She couldn't do it anymore. As she looked at her mom, she almost lost her nerve.

"Em, what's wrong? This is amazing news, babe. Why the long face?" Phillis asked.

"I want to know who he is."

"Who you talkin' about?" Phillis busied herself cleaning the sink.

"You know who."

Phillis sighed and rested a palm on the counter. "Emersyn, if he wanted to be a father, he would have reached out to you by now."

"How can he reach out, Mom? He doesn't know where we are. What if he's tried to reach out?"

"Emersyn, we are not going to ruin this incredible day talking about this. It always brings you down." Phillis cupped Emersyn's face in her hands. "You are amazing, and you don't need anybody to affirm that, you hear me?" Emersyn nodded. "Good. Now where is this case?"

"South."

Phillis frowned. "Ew. Which part? I hope not Florida. Bless their hearts. They mean well, but Floridians always—"

"Opelousas," Emersyn cut in. No need to prolong the inevitable.

Amal dropped a crab leg on the floor. "My bad," she said.

Phillis's eyes were wide, her lips tight. She reacted similarly when Emersyn chose Georgetown over Stanford. Phillis stirred the roux in silence.

"So that's where this renewed interest in your father is coming from." Phillis held up her hand. "Emmie, it's a good day. My energy level is good, and I haven't been nauseous all day. Don't do this right now, please."

"Do what, Mom? Try to figure out who I am? Wanting to know

who my father is? What's wrong with that? What about Grandma Clotee? You always have such great things to say about her. Why didn't we visit her when I was growing up? Why don't you visit now?"

"Emersyn Chavis, I'm warning you. Stop it."

"Fine." Emersyn knew her mother's limit.

Phillis lowered the heat and placed a lid on the steaming pot. "Tell me about the assignment."

"Um, this guy is running for office . . . it's just a campaign sweep." Emersyn let her words run together.

"A campaign sweep? You're an associate now. You shouldn't be doing sweeps, for heaven's sake. You did those right out of college."

"Well, Paul knows the guy."

"Ah, that's right." Phillis sighed. "I chalk it up to chemo brain. Paul asked you to do it. That's quite the honor."

Emersyn nodded. Technically, she volunteered to go. "Yeah, it shouldn't be too stressful. And since I'll be there, I'll see what the family is up to."

"Family?" Phillis leaned her palms on the countertop and stared at the silver backsplash that had taken her three months to choose. "What family?"

"Uh, your family. Our family. The ones who live in Opelousas."

"Interesting."

"What?" Emersyn asked, ignoring Amal's attempts to get her attention. Amal had heard versions of this conversation, and she'd seen how upset Phillis could get with this topic.

"Nothing." Phillis alternated between leaning on the counter and resting a hand on her hip. She held her head proud as her sharp shoulder bones peeked beneath the natural fibers of her kaftan. Before cancer, Phillis was always on, never revealing weakness or showing fear. Ever resilient, even while battling an illness. The poised, petite powerhouse, who guided companies from financial ruins to earning consistent profits and mentored women CEOs, was Emersyn's hero.

"You knew about this?" Phillis asked Amal.

"No, I swear," Amal said. "I just think the last year has been hard on all of us. And I can understand why Em might want to find her father. Especially now."

"You say that as if I'm going to die. I plan on living a long time. I'm going to beat this illness," Phillis said.

"No, Auntie, that's not what I'm saying," Amal said, looking at Emersyn for help.

Emersyn sighed. "Mom, you can't hear anything when it comes to my father. You always find a way to talk me out of it or make me think he doesn't care. Whether he cares or not, I need to do this. Why can't you understand that?"

"I know things have been hard for you, Emmie," Phillis said slowly. "Our weekend trips to New York have been replaced with movie nights at home, and wine tastings along the Sonoma Coast have been replaced with in-home massages. But I don't want you going out and getting hurt. And trying to find your father will hurt you."

"Why? You always say that, but you never tell me why."

"Why don't we watch a movie while the gumbo simmers?" Amal grabbed a bottle of wine and two glasses. When Amal and Emersyn were kids, they would watch movies on Friday nights. It had been a long time since they'd done that.

Phillis slowly walked to the living room, passing framed photos of Emersyn and her many awards of excellence that hung on the wall.

Amal and Emersyn followed Phillis into the cream-colored living room with a plush white area rug, a sleek gas fireplace, and more than a dozen orchids. Phillis lay on her chaise, and Amal sat with Emersyn on the sofa.

"I love this room." Amal picked up a framed photo of her and Emersyn after a soccer game when they were six. "Remember we used to make a tent in here and pretend we were in Yosemite?"

"Yes," Emersyn laughed.

Phillis fell asleep on the chaise while Amal and Emersyn finished off the bottle of wine.

"Thank you for being here for us," Emersyn said. "It's hard not having any family."

"Excuse me?" Amal stretched her neck forward. "And who am I? And my parents? And my stupid brothers? I've known you since you came out of your mama's womb, little girl. We are family. Don't start that shit today."

Emersyn didn't intend to offend Amal. She loved Amal's family dearly, but she couldn't help but wonder what her blood relatives were like. Would they be as supportive as Amal and her family were? Would she have as much fun with them? Emersyn wasn't ungrateful, but there was a desire to fill the emptiness in her soul that longed to know where she came from.

"That's not what I'm saying," Emersyn said.

"You have a great life, Emersyn," Amal whispered so she didn't disturb Phillis. "You got your education, you travel, and you have a great career. Don't mess things up with a wild goose chase. If Otis intended to be in your life, he'd be here. Auntie is right."

"Amal, you have your parents and brothers and children, and even though you hate him right now, you have Brian. All I know is my mom and your family. I need to know my real family." Emersyn regretted the words as soon as she said them.

"I see." Amal blinked.

"It's not like that, Amal. I love you guys. I just need to know who my father is."

"All I know is my father has been there for you since before you could walk," Amal said. "You are my sister, and my parents don't think of you any differently than they do me and my brothers. But if you want to do this, I support you."

"Thank you. I love you so much," Emersyn said as she pulled Amal into a hug.

Emersyn grew up with no narrative for her father. She wouldn't have minded being like Sara Davis, whose father traveled a lot for work. Or like Luke Simmons, whose parents were divorced. Or even Travis Billings, whose father was a weekend dad and let Travis play video games the entire time he was there. This trip would be a reckoning. She'd impress Paul, visit family, and finally find her father. The stars were aligning.

"I love you too," Amal said. "Just don't go out there and get your feelings hurt."

"I won't. I promise."

CHAPTER 7

Manon 2019

Manon sprayed perfume on her wrist and dabbed concealer under her eyes. She caught sight of the mirror behind her, which reflected her walk-in closet with rows of Valentino, Miu Miu, Manolo Blahnik, and Gucci. Manon grew up with a silver spoon in her mouth, but the only thing she needed was the love and attention she received from her father. As an adult, Manon lived comfortably without a job and could do so for the rest of her life. But rows of designer shoes, luxury vacations, and a closet the size of a studio apartment didn't bring happiness. She would trade it all to have a loving relationship with Addie.

But life wasn't about wishes and hopes. The reality was that Manon was a middle-aged woman with thinning hair and estranged relatives. Years of grudges and secrecy were visible in the hollows of her eyes. She stared at the mirror and frowned. The first slap didn't hurt. Neither did the second one. The third one left a red mark on her face. As did the fourth one.

Manon started cutting herself after she returned home from camp one summer. She soon realized that cutting left marks, and some of the scars which she still had. She was able to hide her scars until Addie discovered the marks on her forearm. Manon lied and said her friend's cat had scratched her, but she knew Addie didn't believe her. That was when she started hitting herself instead of cutting. Slaps didn't leave scars.

She picked up her phone. Another missed call from Nadesna, two from Serenity Village, and one from Gwen.

There was a knock on the door, and Manon shuffled over to open it for Tate. Then she led him to the living room.

"How are you?" he asked. He sat on the edge of the sofa, as if it would swallow him whole.

"Doing good." Manon hunched her shoulders. "Taking things one day at a time."

"I'm proud of you," Tate said carefully. "You've come so far. Beat a lot of odds."

Manon blinked. "Thanks. What did you want to talk about?"

"Well, I think there are a few obvious things," Tate said.

"Can we do one thing at a time?" Manon wrung her hands together. She forgot to take an anxiety pill.

"Of course. Whatever you need." Tate was always amicable and reasonable. If he had his way, he'd live in the house with Manon to ensure she was okay. "What are you going to do about your mom?"

Manon flinched. "That's a good question. She's improving faster than the doctors anticipated. They think she'll be ready for release soon."

"If you need Addie to stay with me for a few weeks, it's fine." Tate witnessed the acrimony between Manon and Addie for years. The argument on Christmas morning because Manon had made croissants instead of buttermilk biscuits. Silent feuds that lasted for months. The distance at Marcel's funeral.

"Thank you." Manon rubbed her forehead. "But I have to figure this out on my own."

"You don't have to do everything alone," Tate said. "Let me help you."

"I appreciate the offer, but I don't need help. What's next on your list of discussion topics?"

"Our marriage. We can't keep living this way."

"Oh." Manon reared her shoulders. "And what way is that?"

"The limbo. It's been a year."

"You are the one who broke our vows and moved out of our home without warning."

"Stop throwing that in my face. You made it impossible for me to live here. I tried," Tate said.

"Oh? Tried to do what?"

"Tried to live with weeks of silence and closed-off emotions. You never let me in. You wouldn't let me be your husband. I never knew if you were happy or sad or frustrated. I lived with you for years and never knew you because you wouldn't let me."

"I gave you everything."

"I never asked you for anything. All I ever wanted was your heart. To be your partner and hold you when you hurt. To love you on the hard days and lift you up when you feel down. You equate things with love, and that's not how love works."

Manon scoffed. "Okay, so you're minimizing everything I did for you? Paying for you to go back to school and graduate debt-free? Adding the bulk of the money to our savings account. Paying for most of this house. I guess all that stuff means nothing. Now you are president of the largest union in the state and have your own consulting business. Didn't do so bad for not asking for anything, did ya?"

"I loved you," Tate said. "But I didn't feel love from you."

"What did you say?" Manon asked.

"Nothing."

"No. What did you say?"

"I shouldn't have said that. I'm sorry."

"You don't think I loved you, Tate? Is that what you really think?"

"No. I just think that sometimes we don't see ourselves. I know you love me in your own way."

"What does that mean?"

"Nothing. We just view marriage differently. I think you view marriage the way your parents interacted, where both people had roles and cared for each other and showed love to one another. I view marriage as a partnership filled with love and affection."

"Are you saying our marriage was transactional?"

"No." Tate looked down and sighed. "That's not what I said."

"Look, I'm not doing this. I have too much going on to fight with you," Manon said. "If you want to proceed with a dissolution, go ahead."

"I don't want anything from you."

"Oh no? Then why did you bring it up?" Manon seethed.

"Because I think that's the only reason you haven't wanted to move on. It's not about me. It's about your money."

"This visit is over." Manon stood up and showed Tate to the door.

After Tate left, Manon skirted to the bathroom and disrobed. It wasn't the six-inch scar on her hip from a seven-hour surgery that Manon focused on. It was the scars on her forearm. She shook her head to try to forget that horrible night at her summer camp when she was ten years old. One of the camp directors had taken a special interest in Manon. He let her lead the group songs and allowed her to help set up for circle time. But one night, he came into her cabin and tried to touch her. Manon punched and pushed him off her. She would never forget the look in his eyes when he told her that she couldn't tell anyone about what had happened. He said it was all a big misunderstanding, and Manon would get into trouble if she told anyone. Confused and ashamed, Manon spent the final few days of camp not making eye contact or participating in the camp activities.

When Manon came home that summer, she retreated to her room for a week, barely eating or talking to her parents. Nothing more than one-word answers. She felt shame, as if it was her fault. She didn't understand what she had done to make the camp counselor sneak into her cabin that night.

Finally, she'd mustered up the courage and told her mother what had happened. Addie pulled her into a hug, rocking her back and forth as if she were a baby.

"Now you listen to me. I'm sorry about what happened to you, and it wasn't your fault. Some men have a sickness that we can't explain. You are not to blame for this. But the truth is that you're a Black girl, and nobody is going to believe you. They will whisper about you behind your back. We need to keep this between us. Don't even tell your father. Nobody can know about this. This is the last time we speak of it, you hear me?"

Manon never spoke of the incident again. She stuffed down all those feelings of shame, regret, and guilt. Her confusion over the incident and her mother's reaction morphed into anger and resentment. That was when Manon vowed never to let anyone hurt her, and if anyone had a plan to hurt her, she'd get them first.

The irony was that almost forty years later, those quack doctors still had no idea what they were talking about. She was diagnosed with bipolar depression with intrusive thoughts. *Yeah right. Fuck them all.* She didn't suffer from depression back then, and she didn't suffer from it now. She suffered from a neglectful mother who seemed to care more about appearances than how her own daughter was feeling. She didn't like talking about her childhood. Tate used to ask all the time, but Manon only told him so much. Reliving her trauma through storytelling wasn't her forte. The constant judgment, unrealistic expectations, harsh words, and the institution were painful to recall. People assumed money insulated people from problems, but nothing could be further from the truth. If Manon could trade her trust fund to undo the emotional damage, heartache, and other internal scars, she would. The luxurious life her father provided for her didn't come without a cost.

She grabbed her cell phone and called Serenity Village.

"Hi, this is Manon Lafleur, Addie Lafleur's daughter. Please tell the administration that I'm working on arrangements for my mother, and I'll need a few more days."

CHAPTER 8
Odester 1970

"Just try it and stop being so damn scared." Bumpie pounded his palm against his chest to curb the choking.

Odester watched Bumpie smoke weed all the time, but she never tried it. She had no idea what the white stuff he sprinkled over the weed was, and she didn't want to know. Clotee said people who smoked reefer lost their hair, and Earline told Odester that drug abusers ended up in hell. Odester didn't want to meet either fate, but she loved Bumpie. They had their struggles over the last three years, but everyone had faults. Odester had given up thinking that she'd find someone like her father. Daddy was one of a kind, someone God had sent down to this earth for Mama and the girls. Bumpie tried to fight his own demons the best that he could. He had a hard life growing up and still tried to love Odester. He made her feel pretty when no one else did, and he understood her. He always wanted to be around her, and he even bought her a rose last week. He had a temper sometimes, but it was because he was under a lot of stress.

"It's just reefer, huh?" Odester asked when Bumpie shoved the joint in her face. "'Cause Tee said—"

"Stop talkin' 'bout what Clotee says all the time. You act like she yo mama. Do Clotee love you like I do? Make you feel good like I do? I wouldn't lie to you, baby girl. This here gone make everything all right." He blew a puff of smoke into the air. "Try it. It's gone make you forget all yo problems. Watch."

And it did.

That was months ago when Odester had smoked her first joint laced with cocaine. Since then, she'd spent most days getting high and trying to stay awake in class . . . when she attended class. Last week, Miss Daniels had sent Odester to the school nurse. "You sick, girl? Falling asleep every day like that." Odester's babysitting money trickled through her hands like faucet water, and Bumpie hustled whatever money he could to feed their habit: washing cars, cutting lawns, anything to make a quick dollar. She didn't ask Earline and Rutherford for money because they would harass her about college. Odester was an adult, and now that Addie and Clotee were away at college, Odester spent less time at home. Home wasn't fun anymore. Her parents always looked at her as if she were the worst disappointment of their lives, and Nadesna was too young to confide in.

Odester dreamed of the day when she and Bumpie could get an apartment of their own. She didn't mind Doretha's place, but sneaking around to have sex was getting to be too much. Odester still had a leg cramp from the night before. The tiny kitchen, with yellow walls and rusty tiles, was cluttered with appliances, kid science projects, and everything that didn't fit in the cupboard. Doretha worked ten hours and day and tried her best to keep the house as clean as possible.

"I'mma get us a crib soon," Bumpie said one day. "My boy Lando knows a cat who manages the apartments over there by the college."

Bumpie and Odester were high, munching on cold chicken that Doretha had fried the night before. Bumpie propped his foot up on the worn wooden table as Odester lay across his lap on the sofa.

"I can't wait." Odester folded her knees to her chest and snuggled closer to Bumpie. "I'm tired of it here. No privacy."

Bumpie jumped up. "Oh, you too good for my sister's place? Rather be over there where they don't have no respect for you?" he roared.

"Babe, please." Odester put her hands up. "Didn't mean it like that."

"Yes, you did!" Bumpie's belt buckle rattled as he paced back and forth. When his anger escalated, it was hard to bring it back down. The last time he got angry, Odester had to hide her left eye for three days, which was hard to do because Earline watched her like a hawk.

"Ain't shit good enough for you?" Bumpie snapped. "All you do is compare me to yo damn daddy. Think you too good for me?" He was so close that Odester could feel his warm breath float across her face.

"No," Odester pleaded with her eyes. "You always been enough for me, baby." She barely got the words out before she tasted blood in her mouth. Her face stung so much from Bumpie's fist that she almost thought she was dreaming. "Bumpie, please!"

She ran toward the back of the house, but Bumpie was too quick. He grabbed her by the hair and slammed her to the floor. She covered her head and balled up her body. The first blow to Odester's head made her ears ring. The second one knocked the wind out of her.

"Ungrateful, bitch," Bumpie roared as his foot landed on Odester's back. Her shriek shook him out of his rage. He looked down at Odester, her body rocking with anguish and pain.

Bumpie retrieved a wet towel from the bathroom and wiped the blood from her face. "Why you make me so mad? You know I don't ever want to hurt you like my daddy hurt me," he sobbed.

"I swore I would never be like that nigga, but look at me. I'm the same." He cried harder.

"You ain't like him," Odester said. Her head was spinning. "You a better man than him."

"I'm not," he hissed. "Ain't got no money. Ain't got nowhere for you to lay your head. I don't even deserve you."

"Bumpie, stop." Odester ignored the pain in her side and gently rubbed his face. She blamed herself for upsetting him. More than anything, she wanted him to calm down. His temper was getting worse. "It's okay. We gone be alright."

"Naw, you gone leave me," he cried. "I know it. I ain't like them dudes yo sisters date. I ain't nothing. I come from nothing."

"Bumpie, you stop that right now." Odester grabbed his face so she could look in his eyes. "We in this together, you hear me? You been here for me when nobody else has. We gone be alright."

"You promise?" Bumpie wiped his tears.

Odester nodded.

"You know I love you. I just get so mad. Things are hard for me right now, and all I wanna do is take care of you, baby."

"I know," Odester whimpered.

"Do you?" Bumpie laid her head on his chest. "You know how much I love you?"

"Yeah. I love you too." She swallowed the blood in her mouth.

Bumpie walked over to the table and picked up the joint. "Here." He lit the joint and handed it to her. "This will make you feel better."

And he was right. Odester's pain went away, and so did her fear. She sucked in the smoke and held it for as long as she could, then passed it to Bumpie.

"Will you marry me, Dette?"

"Really? You want me to be your wife?" The thought of being a wife made Odester giddy. She would finally be worthy like her sisters, not some stupid girl who couldn't get good grades and got into trouble. She would have a chance to raise her own family and her parents would respect her. Her heart quickened at the thought. She and Bumpie could talk to a minister at Clotee's church to help with his temper, and Bumpie would get a good job at the lumberyard. She would learn how to sew dresses like Earline, and she would cook dinner every night. She would be a wife. She would have a family. She would matter.

"Yeah, girl. Now answer me. Will you marry me?"

"Yes."

Odester 1971

"Be still!" Clotee moved Addie's head to the side and attached the white lacey veil to her hair with a bobby pin. They were in a dressing room with large windows, white curtains, and a vanity for the bride. In less than thirty minutes, Addie would be marrying Marcel, the wannabe white boy with parents as rich as the Kennedys. Lucky Addie.

"You are a beautiful bride." Earline's eyes beamed, and her bottom lip disappeared in her smile. Mama looked happy, but Odester wondered if she really was happy. Clotee got married before finishing college, and Addie was about to do the same thing, which was exactly what Mama had told them all not to do: put a man before education and career. Odester hoped that she and Bumpie would get married first, but he hadn't mentioned marriage since his proposal, and he got mad when she brought it up.

"Thank you, Mama," Addie said, looking angelic in an heirloom ivory silk organza gown. The venue at the Chapel at Le Vieux

Village was illuminated with dozens of string lights and floating magnolias lining the aisle. Addie and Marcel had opted for an evening wedding, and his parents spared no expense on details, from the best wedding planner in St. Landry's County and the exclusive guest list, to the live band and private transportation for the wedding party and parents of the bride and groom. When Marcel proposed, Addie was worried because her parents couldn't afford the kind of wedding Marcel's family would expect. But perfect Marcel and his rich parents offered to pay for everything. Problem solved. Lucky Addie again.

"She is a beautiful bride," Clotee said as she shot a look at Odester, who was slumped in a white cushioned chair. "Ain't that right, Dette?"

"Uh, yeah." Odester tugged the itchy dress that felt tighter than it did when she'd tried it on a month ago. "Just like Dorothy Dandridge."

"Let me go check on ya daddy," Earline said. "He nervous about walking you down the aisle. And I need to make sure Nadesna is ready for flower girl duties." Earline chuckled before disappearing from the dressing room.

"Mama is so happy." Addie smiled.

"Why wouldn't she be?" Clotee dabbed powder on Addie's face. "Her daughter is marrying the most eligible and rich man in the state of Louisiana. We all proud, ain't we, Dette?"

"Whoop-de-doo," Odester said, circling her finger in the air.

"You okay, Dette?" Clotee whispered. "You don't look well."

"I'm fine," Odester lied. It felt like rotten tomatoes were growing in her stomach, and she had spent most of the morning heaving over the toilet. Luckily, she and Bumpie had their own place now. Things weren't better between them, but at least she didn't have to worry about sleeping on Doretha's couch.

Whatever was left of Earline and Odester's relationship deteriorated further when Odester moved in with Bumpie after she graduated high school and got a job instead of going to college. Earline had begged her not to leave home, but Odester didn't listen. She wanted to be loved, and Bumpie loved her.

"I can't believe it," Addie said. "Soon I'll be married to the smartest and most handsome man in the world."

"Well, that huge ring on your finger should be confirmation," Odester mumbled.

"Dette, you eating salt?" Clotee placed her hand on the back of Odester's forehead.

Odester pushed her hand away. "I'm fine. I just get like this when I'm about to get my period. Stop meddling me and make sure this girl is ready to marry that rich man out there."

"Marcel is a dreamboat," Clotee said, ignoring Odester's rudeness. "Addie, this wedding is going to be beautiful, and you are perfect."

"Not as perfect as you were when you married Willie Earl." Addie stood and put her hand on Clotee's shoulders. "You were exquisite."

Clotee was beautiful on the day of her wedding, but Odester was convinced that Clotee and Willie Earl had a shotgun wedding. Why else would Clotee marry slow-ass Willie Earl before she graduated college? Odester was waiting for a baby bump to emerge. Clotee and Willie Earl's wedding was nothing like Addie's. It didn't have an ice sculpture, six bridesmaids and groomsmen, two dresses, and catered food. Reverend Adams had performed the ceremony at Bethesda Apostolic Church, and Addie and Clotee served as the wedding party because Willie Earl had no friends. Their reception was a potluck in the banquet hall of the church. They served gumbo, crawfish etouffee and fried oysters, and danced to zydeco all night. Odester never understood why Clotee agreed to marry ugly, broke Willie Earl, but Clotee seemed to love him.

"Y'all about ready?" Earline returned.

"Yes, Mama," Clotee said.

"Ah, my sweet girl. You make me so proud." Earline embraced Addie. "God is so good."

"Hallelujah! All the time." Clotee waved her hands in the air and her body jerked. Ever since marrying Willie Earl, Clotee "felt the spirit" often.

"Dette?" Earline looked over at Odester, who was slumped in a chair. "You all right? You gone wrinkle your dress balling it up like that."

"Oh, she's just getting her period, Mama," Addie offered.

"Yeah," Clotee chimed in. "She cranky and sick."

Earline squinted her eyes at Odester. "A woman's cycle don't make her sick. Not like that." She moved closer to Odester. "Dette, stand up."

"Mama, please," Odester pleaded. "These cramps killing me. Let me save my energy for the ceremony. Please."

"Cramps huh? Stand up."

Odester sighed and stood up.

Earline leaned closer. "Breathe."

"What?" Odester reared her head back. "Mama, what are you doing?"

"Breathe, girl. You heard me."

Odester exhaled a shallow breath.

Earline closed her eyes and stepped back, her eyes raking over Odester and stopping at her belly. The old wives' tale about a pregnant woman's breath was true, and no amount of hoping would bring a different result for Odester.

"Mama."

Earline held up her hand. "Shh. Today is Addie's day." She

turned back to the other girls. "I'mma go take my seat." Then she disappeared from the dressing room.

Addie and Clotee stood with their mouths open.

"Dette?" Clotee said.

"Not a word!" Odester spat. "Not a word."

"You let that man get you pregnant after all he done to you?" Clotee's eyes brimmed with tears. "Why, Dette?"

"Tee, stop," Odester said. "Addie getting married."

She'd regretted confiding in Clotee about her issues with Bumpie. Clotee meant well, but she shared too much of Odester's business with Mama and Addie. Now all three of them felt sorry for her, and Odester didn't need them now. She needed them when she struggled in school, and they kept telling her she was lazy. She needed them when the kids at school teased her, and they all said she was sensitive. She didn't care what any of them thought now. It was too late.

"You got something to say, Miss Perfect?" Odester snarled at Addie.

Addie looked at Odester's stomach. "Not a word," she said icily. "Not a single word."

Clotee could hardly contain her tears. "Dette, you gone be all right?"

"I'm always gone be all right, sister dear. You ain't never gotta worry about me."

An hour later, the reception was in full swing. The band Marcel's parents hired played all the top hits. Nadesna ran around passing out flowers, and the wedding party sat at the long table in the front of the ballroom. The music quieted, and Addie's best friend, Holly, tapped the side of her champagne glass with a fork.

"Good evening, everybody," Holly cleared her throat. "For those who don't know me, I'm Holly, and I've been friends with Addie since high school. Addie has always been one of my favorite people," she gushed. "These two are perfect together. Not only are they both beautiful and smart, but they are exceptionally kind people." Holly placed her hand over her chest. "This girl is the smartest chick I know. Marcel, you are lucky as shit to have her. Oops!" She covered her mouth. "I'm sorry, Miss Earline!"

Earline smiled. Some things never changed.

"Addie," Holly continued. "You are my very best friend in the world, and it warms my heart to see you happy. I know you've had some bumps in the road, but you overcame it all. You always have and will always be good enough." Holly and Addie both wiped away tears.

Odester cleared her throat and placed her hand on her belly. She dreamed of being a wife and mom, but not this soon. Bumpie still lost his temper too often, and neither of them had enough money to take care of themselves, let alone a baby. Clotee was still in school, but she attended those finance classes at church and learned about investing and saving, which made Odester's head hurt when Clotee talked about them. Addie was marrying money, so it didn't matter what she did with her future. But Odester's situation was different. She and Bumpie didn't have a plan, they weren't in school, and they didn't have money. Odester tried to stay positive though. If Earline was right, then God was in control, and everything would be all right. Odester and Bumpie would have their own wedding. She would wear white on her wedding day, and Bumpie would look at her the same way that Marcel looked at Addie, like there was no one else in the world. One day, she would have her life together like her sisters, with a loving husband and a safe home. Odester held on to hope.

CHAPTER 9
Emersyn 2012

"Emmie, what's up?" Amal dashed into Emersyn's room, which had pink walls adorned with posters and achievement awards. Her white vanity was neatly organized with jewelry cases, a purple oscillating fan, and a framed photo of Amal and Emersyn on their first day of preschool.

"Wait." Amal held up her hands and looked away. Her red fingernails matched her toes, and she wore as much makeup as she could get away with. "Where are you going in *that*?"

"What do you mean?" Emersyn stopped applying mascara long enough to look down at her black pleated slacks and platform sandals. The look was much better than her usual acid-washed jeans and dusty Converse. "I'm going to Amy's graduation party."

"Em, you wore those pants to the debate finals." Amal rolled her eyes.

"I know," Emersyn grinned. "And I won, remember?"

"Emersyn Chavis, will you pu-leeze stop dressing like Ms. Tisdale? I know you have a tank and a decent pair of jeans in this huge closet of yours." Amal stepped into Emersyn's closet and began sifting through her clothes.

Ms. Tisdale was Emersyn's favorite teacher. She explained organic chemistry like no other, and their sidebar about Le Chatelier's principle in class last week had put Emersyn's brain in a tailspin. Ms. Tisdale was a gem, and Emersyn loved her

AP chemistry class, but Amal's comment didn't seem like a compliment.

"Uh-uh, change." Amal swooped her raven mane across her shoulder, her full lips pinched in her signature pout.

"Into *what*?" Emersyn looked around the room as if an outfit would pop out of the air.

"This!" Amal plopped a white crop top on the bed.

"I'm not wearing that." The top was cute, but Emersyn preferred to keep her double Ds under wraps. Amal envied Emersyn's boobs, and Emersyn envied hers. If there was such a thing as a boob do-over, she would stand in the B-cup line. Emersyn didn't inherit her mother's petite stature.

In elementary school, Emersyn was in the eightieth percentile. Perhaps this was news to the pediatrician, but at the time, Phillis wasn't surprised. When Emersyn was in third grade, she had constantly tested in the highest percentile, particularly in math and science. She walked at nine months and was reading before she was potty trained. But being in the eightieth percentile in pediatrics was different from being in the eightieth percentile in academics. The eightieth percentile in pediatrics meant that out of one hundred kids, Emersyn was bigger than eighty of them.

This status plagued Emersyn throughout middle and high school, where guys like Tolando Travillion preferred smaller, thin girls. Young Emersyn didn't want to be bigger than the other girls. She wanted to be like Sally Sjolin, who wore plaid skirts and frilly T-shirts to school. Emersyn's round face and doe eyes didn't leave her unnoticed. She was a beautiful girl often described as "thick," "chunky," or "healthy," terms that made her cringe at the sight of a scale, and even more so at the sight of the tank top Amal suggested she wear.

"Emersyn Chavis, if you don't put on this tank top and stop

dressing like a pilgrim, I'm going to pull your hair out of that bun so it can flow beautifully like it's supposed to!"

Emersyn fingered her bun. She wasn't as keen on fashion like Amal, but no one ever accused her of being homely. She even added an extra swoop to her edges for the party.

"This is *the* party of the year. I heard Mistah FAB is going to be there." Amal wiggled her hips. "I can't show up with my best friend looking like a math teacher."

Ms. Tisdale taught chemistry, not math.

"Excuse me, Amal, but I won't even know anyone who will be at the party. You don't go to Mater, remember?"

"No, I don't go to the snotty school that costs more than tuition at San Jose State, but I heard y'all rich kids know how to throw a party."

"I'm not rich," Emersyn reminded Amal for the umpteenth time. Phillis did well as a financial consultant, but they weren't rich. At least not in comparison to the other kids at Mater whose parents had full-time housekeepers and vacation homes overseas. Phillis made wise investments and saved aggressively for Emersyn's education. Her goal was for Emersyn to graduate from college debt-free.

"Anyway, Michael is going to be there. He's the only person I need to know. I'm gonna do it to him tonight."

"Amal Khan!"

"Yep." Amal lifted her chin. "I can't turn eighteen and still be a virgin. That means I'm ugly."

"That makes absolutely no sense." Emersyn frowned. "And where will you have sex with Michael, and when? We have a curfew, remember?"

"You're so boring, Em. I don't have all that figured out, but I'll let him finger me if we can't go all the way."

"Amal, don't have sex with Michael. It's haram."

"Oh hush, everything isn't haram, Em. I hate that my parents ever taught you that. They've used that against me for years. You wanna know what's haram? Threatening your daughter and keeping her from having a social life. That's haram!"

"But Michael isn't even smart. He barely graduated and had to take summer classes." Emersyn shuddered at the thought of dating someone who wasn't on the dean's list.

"Em, nobody cares about that kind of stuff except for you. I don't care if he doesn't know his ABCs. He's cute, and I'mma do it to him."

"Amal, you just met him last week at my academic awards ceremony!"

Amal rolled onto Emersyn's bed, laughing. "I know. I wish you would have invited me to a Mater event before. People talk bad about y'all over at Mater Royce—about the snooty, rich, smart people that attend, but nobody said anything about how fine the boys are." Amal's bamboo earrings swung as she laughed.

"How about this?" Emersyn held up a black halter top.

"Perfecto," Amal said.

After Emersyn changed, Amal helped her put on a rhinestone choker, and they were ready to go. It was their first time going to a party without one of their parents driving them. It was also their last hangout before Emersyn went to study abroad in Spain.

"Well, hello there," Phillis said when the girls appeared in the living room. She was sitting on the sofa looking through the mail.

"Hey, Auntie!" Amal said.

"Hey, Mom." Emersyn noticed a yellow envelope in the pile of mail. "Paying bills?"

"Yes." Phillis sighed and tucked her hair behind her ears. "Gotta keep the lights on for the salutatorian of Mater Royce's newest graduating class."

"What's that yellow envelope?" Emersyn asked even though

she knew the envelope was from Phillis's aunt Nadesna in Opelousas. Emersyn had seen correspondence from her before, but Phillis never acknowledged it.

"Just an invitation," Phillis said. "You girls ready for the big party? Let me see those outfits."

Amal showed off her outfit, seemingly happy that her parents weren't there. They usually had wine with Phillis on Friday nights but had other plans that evening.

"An invite to what?" Emersyn probed.

Phillis opened her mouth then closed it.

"Em, we can't be late for the party," Amal said.

Emersyn stared at Phillis.

"I didn't look at it close enough to know," Phillis said with an awkward chuckle that Emersyn had never heard before. Why was her mother nervous?

Emersyn tried to maintain her cool. Year after year, she'd seen mail from Opelousas go unopened or unanswered. How could her mother just turn her back on her entire family? Emersyn wanted to know the contents of the envelope. Enough was enough.

"So, you are just going to ignore it? What if it's important?" Emersyn was tired of the deflections.

"Emersyn Chavis." Phillis pushed the mail to the side and stood up to face her daughter.

"How do you know it's not important?" Emersyn said. "You just dismiss everything that comes from the state of Louisiana like it's nothing. Like we don't have family there. Like my dad isn't there!"

"I see," Phillis said. "This is about your dad again. I can assure that nothing inside that yellow envelope contains information about Otis McGee."

Phillis was probably right, but it still bothered Emersyn that her mother didn't acknowledge their family or Emersyn's father.

He was the person who created her. She had a right to know who he was and where he was. The secrecy was too much. She wanted to know her history and where they were from. That wasn't an unreasonable request.

Phillis snapped her fingers and said, "I have something for both of you." Then she disappeared into the kitchen.

Emersyn's heart pounded as she quickly grabbed the envelope and pulled out the invitation.

"Em," Amal warned. "Don't make Auntie mad."

"I'm not," Emersyn said. She quickly scanned the invite, her eyes wide. According to the invite, Emersyn had a cousin named Devanie, who was graduating from high school as well. "Devanie," she whispered. "What a pretty name."

Emersyn replaced the invite just before Phillis returned.

"Here." Phillis handed each of them a small container.

"Pepper spray, Mom?" Emersyn frowned.

"Better safe than sorry."

"Thanks, Auntie," Amal said, hurrying Emersyn out of the door. She paused in the driveway and pulled out her phone.

"What are you doing?" Amal asked. "This party waits for no one. Let's go."

"Just a second," Emersyn said as she scrolled through social media. "That invitation said my cousin's name is Devanie. I'm looking for her Facebook account."

"Are you serious, Emersyn? Let's go to the party."

"Bam. Found her!" Emersyn grinned. "And I requested to follow her."

If Phillis wasn't going to allow Emersyn to get to know their family, then Emersyn would find a way to do it herself.

CHAPTER 10

Manon 2000

Manon looked out at the backyard, her hand resting on her stomach, as emptiness enveloped her. The tragedy from last week circled her mind like the particles in the snow globes she collected. Nurses whooshing around her bed, Tate pacing back and forth, the look in the doctor's eyes, and the tiny body wrapped in a pink blanket. Manon had known something was wrong when she saw the dark red blood trickling down her leg. Pregnant women didn't bleed. Tate had rushed her to the hospital, but it was too late by the time they'd arrived.

The trees needed trimming and the grass was too long, but she'd been too preoccupied to schedule an appointment. Tate used to handle those tasks, but he no longer had time since his recent promotion as union president. She caught a faint reflection of herself in the kitchen window. Her loose waves were piled at the top of her head, and the diamond pendant around her neck reflected in the morning sun.

She sipped black coffee and enjoyed the warm liquid sliding down her throat. If there was a bright side, it was being able to drink coffee again. She put Tate's lunch on the counter and filled his thermos with coffee. Plenty of cream, no sugar. Once he left, she'd crawl under her goose-down duvet and drown her sorrows in *The Oprah Winfrey Show*.

Manon eyed the small pill bottle near the windowsill. "These will help you get through your days," her doctor had claimed.

Manon wasn't one for false happiness. She preferred to heal naturally. She had miscarried so many times that grief felt natural. Suppressing grief did not. She chucked the pill bottle into the junk drawer, just in case. She could be a good mother. She was nurturing, and unlike Addie, Manon would protect her child. She'd witnessed people mistreat their children and abuse their privilege of motherhood time and time again. Wanting another person to love you unconditionally didn't seem like that much to ask.

Manon spent her entire existence trying to escape her mom's influence, and she was angry that Addie had silenced her after she'd been abused at camp. She only recently started working through those feelings in therapy—not only Addie's neglect but the assault. But no matter how much she tried to resist anything that resembled her childhood, her kitchen was almost identical to Addie's. Gourmet cookbooks, a recipe box, a glass cookie jar filled with Madeleines, and fresh flowers. If her refrigerator wasn't stainless steel, she might even have magnets hanging all over it.

The apple didn't fall far from the tree.

She glanced at the pile of mail on the counter. Her aunt Nadesna had invited her to a family gathering. Her estrangement from her family wasn't entirely her fault. She could accept more invites and communicate between holidays, but she wasn't interested. When Manon was young, Addie preferred spending time with Tate's family over her own, and the times they'd visited Addie's family were always short and hardly sweet. Addie called her siblings and cousins bothersome and unambitious, and she and Aunt Odester always argued.

Tate's footsteps interrupted her reverie.

"Good morning, beautiful." Tate inherited his father's curly hair and penetrating eyes.

"Morning," Manon said as she adjusted Tate's white dress shirt. "Looks like somebody has a big day today."

"Yeah. Trying to get salary increases for the workers. The railroad's labor negotiator is offering to raise salaries but reduce pension shares. I don't know who they think they are dealing with." Tate stuffed a homemade biscuit into his mouth. His appetite was that of a man twice his size.

"They are lucky to have you, Mr. Union President," Manon said.

"And how about you?" He took another bite. "What's on your agenda?"

"Not much." She looked down at her cotton lounge set. "I might try to get in the garden. I also need to clean out my closet."

"Just take it easy."

Manon reared her neck. "What does that mean?"

Tate lowered his head and sighed. "I want you to be okay, that's all."

"I'm fine," she said.

"Of course you are. You're my strong angel. But you've been through a lot recently and had a rough time with this one."

Things were always rough for her. Contrary to popular belief, Manon suffered just like everyone else. Just because she didn't struggle financially didn't mean she didn't have issues. She was always bloated, crampy, moody, or depressed from fertility drugs.

Tate folded her into his arms. "I love you," he said. "You are the strongest, most beautiful woman I know. I couldn't love you more than I do in this moment."

"You're too kind." She looked away.

"Hey." He pulled her face toward him. "You're amazing."

Tate kissed her again. There was a time when she couldn't dream about living without his kisses, his touch. Making love to

Tate had always been her absolute pleasure, until recently. Sex morphed from sensual intimacy to a chore, an act that served as the thing that would make her a mother.

"I'll be home late this evening. I'll stop by Blockbuster on the way home and get the new Tyler Perry movie. How does that sound?"

"Why will you be late?"

"Just work stuff." Tate searched her face. "Why are you giving me that look?"

"Nothing." She sipped more coffee.

Tate said his goodbyes, and Manon stood on the front porch and watched his truck disappear down the street.

"You not grounded," a voice came from the sidewalk.

"Miss Genessa," Manon gasped. "You nearly scared me to death."

Miss Genessa's dark glasses covered her eyes, and strands of her wiry white hair framed her mocha face. Her raisin-like hand wrapped tightly around her snakehead walking stick. In the other hand, she carried a plastic bag that swung as she walked. She wore a black and yellow kaftan and a ring on each finger. It wasn't apparent that Miss Genessa didn't have teeth until she started talking, and even then, only her rare smile revealed the whole truth. Manon befriended Miss Genessa despite rampant rumors about voodoo, Clo du Bois superstition, and Tate's objection. Manon returned a wave to a woman pushing a stroller, then to the gardener a few houses down as the old woman wobbled closer to her porch. The aroma of crawfish etouffee mixed with the rancid-smelling river filled the air.

Miss Genessa was the first to welcome Manon and Tate to the neighborhood. She had shown up with a pot of red beans and homemade pecan candy. Back then, she walked without a cane and had all of her teeth. Miss Genessa took an instant liking to light-skinned Manon and loyally defended her during the Leonard Dupree debacle. Manon and Miss Genessa were generations apart, but she valued their friendship. It wasn't uncommon for Miss Genessa to stroll across the street with a pot in one hand and unsolicited advice in the other.

A barefoot Manon waited patiently for the older woman, who paused a few times to rest her knees before finally reaching the front door. Manon led Miss Genessa inside, trying to forget the argument with Tate, because if she didn't, Miss Genessa would bring it up.

Miss Genessa knew things.

She knew things Manon hid from everyone. She even knew things Manon tried to keep from herself.

"I love this house." Miss Genessa looked around like she did every time she visited. "You got a real eye for decorating." She handed Manon a sagebrush. "You never know what is walking across your threshold." Miss Genessa frowned. "Gotta be careful. And keep your windows open when you burn this here sage. People be running around here burning sage with the windows closed— demon spirits just running around in a circle." She laughed. "Can't even much get out."

Miss Genessa settled into a chair and set her walking stick next to it. She never removed her dark frames. "You lost another one," she said.

Miss Genessa looked through Manon's eyes and into her soul. Manon looked away, not from the woman's glare but from the shame. What was wrong with her? Why didn't her body work properly? She maintained a healthy diet, exercised, drank water, and minded her business. What was the fate that doomed her to a life of misery? An agnostic mother, a busy father, estranged family, betrayal, and a barren womb.

Manon had never said a word about it, but Miss Genessa somehow always knew every time she miscarried.

"The universe will pull it all together, chile," Miss Genessa said. "I keep telling you that. Trust the timing. Trust what's supposed to be. Trust your body."

Manon bit back tears. The shameful misery of losing another baby pounded on her like an emotional tsunami. Her body shook with ripe pain, and she tried to catch her breath.

"Let it out." Miss Genessa lifted her head high and took deep breaths. Usually, their visits were less dramatic.

"The doctor said I may not be able to carry to full term," Manon finally managed to say, and the tears burst forth. She grabbed a tissue and blew her nose.

"Well, we can't listen to everything we hear, can we? Six months ago, they had us thinking the world was gone end, and look." Miss Genessa waved her hands about the room. "We still here."

The Y2K scare was as palpable as the cottonmouth Manon would get from the fertility cocktail. People started putting many things into perspective when they thought the world was going to end. Government agencies and programmers scrambled to repair software while Manon examined her faith and the hereafter. Manon's parents weren't religious. Addie thought it was preposterous to teach people that they could end up in a fiery inferno for minor infractions.

"I feel like giving up," Manon said truthfully. She was emotionally exhausted, and her body was constantly swollen and stiff, preparing to be pregnant. Her barren womb was just another disappointment. If Manon wanted to truly heal, she needed to face her past—not just the pain inflicted on her, but the pain she caused others.

Addie had convinced Manon to keep the sexual assault a secret, and despite Manon's attempts to live a normal life, she couldn't escape the past. Addie was from a different generation, and even though she was trying to protect Manon, the secret did Manon more harm than good. Addie had since apologized, but the damage was already done. Now, Manon wondered if her marriage would have survived if Addie had given Manon different advice.

"Did you hear me?" Miss Genessa frowned.

Manon shook her head.

"What's got you all upset?" Miss Genessa asked.

"I'm fine," Manon said.

"No, you ain't. And that's fine. People think they gotta be fine all the time. Give yourself some grace, you hear?"

Manon nodded.

"You met the new people?" Miss Genessa motioned toward the back door and the new neighbors' backyard.

"Not yet. I saw the moving trucks and waved in passing, but I haven't had a chance to talk to them. They are white, though."

"I don't care what color they are as long as they stay out of my roses," Miss Genessa grunted, trying to stand. "You know how I get about my roses."

CHAPTER 11
Odester 1972

"How do you go from wanting to be the first Black Supreme Court Justice to lining cabinets and cutting recipes from *Ebony* magazine?" Odester passed Addie a piece of checkered liner.

"I still have time." Addie frowned as she stretched to line the highest shelf in her kitchen.

A year after her extravagant wedding to Marcel, Addie was almost finished decorating the house Marcel's parents had gifted to them. Odester saw a change in her sister. Addie hadn't mentioned law school since she got married.

"How much time do you have exactly?" Odester cut another piece of liner.

Addie sighed. "Can't I settle into my new life?" She waved her hands at the gourmet kitchen and almost lost her balance. "Law school is a huge undertaking. I need to focus solely on law school and nothing else. There's too much going on right now."

"Seems to me like Marcel's got too much going on," Odester said.

"What did you say?"

"I'm just saying, Addie. We ain't pressing you for nothing on this side of the family. Seems like something always comes up with Marcel or his family when you wanna get to law school. First his mama got sick, then his job took him to Dallas for four months. Ain't none of that your mind."

"Marcel is my husband!" Addie hopped down from the counter and glared at her. "What he goes through, I go through. We are a team."

"Look like a team of one to me," Odester said under her breath.

"What did you say?" Addie challenged again.

"Y'all cut that out," Clotee walked back from her third trip to the bathroom. "Still acting like little girls. Dette, let Addie be. She can figure out her own life, just like you gotta figure out yours."

"Oh Tee, you always defending Addie." Odester placed a pacifier in Arelia's mouth. When Arelia was born six months ago, Bumpie renewed his promise to marry Odester. The promise came without a date or a ring, so Odester didn't hold her breath like the other times he'd promised to marry her.

"She's so cute, Dette," Clotee cooed at Arelia. "How's Bumpie doing?"

Odester shrugged. "He back home."

Addie and Clotee exchanged looks.

"For good this time?" Addie asked quietly.

"Well, he finally off parole, if that's what you mean. And he trying to get a job. We getting another place soon."

They had gotten their own place, and Odester had given birth to her beautiful daughter. But everything had gone downhill. Bumpie had been in and out of jail, mostly for petty theft. Sometimes it was to support his habit, but the last time he had been arrested was for stealing a package of turkey legs for Odester to cook. Another time, they had a big fight, the neighbor called the police, and Bumpie was arrested. Odester didn't press charges, but the judge mandated Bumpie to anger management classes. The classes seemed to help, but Bumpie still got frustrated over money, and instead of lacing his weed with cocaine, he snorted it instead.

She wanted to explain everything to her sisters, but her

conversations about Bumpie often left her feeling ashamed. He wasn't like her brothers-in law, and Odester didn't want anyone judging him any more than they already did. Especially after they were evicted from their place a few months ago and Odester had to move back in with Mama.

"I agree that all grown folks need their own place, Dette," Clotee said. "But can you afford it? And if you move out again, who gone babysit Arelia while you work?"

"Mama will still babysit," Odester informed her sisters. "I gotta get out of there, y'all. I'm a grown woman with a child, and I'm used to having my own place. I can't have Mama looking at me every day with disappointment in her eyes and tellin' me what to do. She always tellin' me how to bathe Arelia, and what books to read, and not to let her listen to certain music. I ain't got time for all that." Odester looked down at her feet.

Her sisters were silent.

"When are you two having babies?" Odester deflected.

"I don't know," Addie said. "There's no rush for me. I don't even know if want children. They are messy and needy."

"Oh. No rush, huh?" Clotee tilted her head to the side. "Then our kids won't be able to grow up together like we always planned." She rested her palm on her flat belly.

Addie covered her hands over her mouth. "Tee! What are you saying?"

"I think she saying that Arelia gonna have a baby cousin soon." Odester smiled. One of her front teeth had decayed. Addie had given her money three times to get the tooth fixed, but Odester never did, and Addie was tired of asking why.

"Me and Willie Earl are expecting," Clotee announced.

Odester and Addie put their arms around Clotee.

"That's why you been running to the bathroom all day," Odester said.

Clotee lowered her eyes. "Yes. That's why."

"They gone to be close just like us," Odester said excitedly. "They gone be best cousins."

"Oh, Tee, I'm so happy for you," Addie said with less enthusiasm. She hugged her sister again, then quickly pulled away.

"I'm happy too," Clotee said. "I think this might give us the boost we need."

"Whatchu you mean, 'boost'?" Odester asked.

Clotee sighed. "Willie Earl is drinking. He works every day, then comes home and drinks. I don't know what to do most days, but I think this baby will help. Give us hope. You know what I mean?"

Addie and Odester exchanged looks.

"When he start drinking again?" Odester asked, her eyebrows furrowed with concern. She hated for Clotee to endure anything hard. If anyone deserved a good, easy life, it was Clotee. She never did anything to anyone. And why did Willie Earl need to drink? He had a job and a beautiful wife. Some people were never thankful for what they had.

Clotee pursed her lips. "Now, ya'll know the devil is busy trying to bring God's people down."

Odester rolled her eyes. "Clotee, stop blaming everything on the damn devil. He ain't that busy. Some of this stuff be our fault. The devil ain't got time to make Willie Earl drink when he busy making white folks hang Black folks."

"Anyway," Clotee picked up her purse. "Willie Earl is excited about the baby. I'm praying this will make a difference."

"Well, let's hope so." Addie smoothed out her dress and cleared her throat. "But if he doesn't stop, you have to make him get help." She looked Clotee in the eyes.

"Or leave," Odester said quickly. "And where are you going?"

"Down to the church," Clotee responded. Deacon Raines is having another seminar tonight."

"Why you always running down to them seminars?" Odester frowned. "They ain't gone make you have more money."

"Odester Chavis, you choose to spend your time at the gambling shack. I choose to spend mine learning about money. How you think these babies gonna go to college if we don't prepare?"

"Aw shit, now you sound like them white folks at the county building," Odester sighed.

"Dette, stop it," Addie said. "Clotee is doing the right thing."

"Thank you, Addie." Clotee kissed her sisters on their cheeks. "The Bible says a wise woman buildeth her house."

"Clotee, shut up," Odester chuckled. "Ask Deacon Raines 'bout my money when you get to the church."

CHAPTER 12

Emersyn 2019

Sunrays beamed on a highway flanked by patches of the bayou. Cicadas caroled off the fetid river, and sultry Spanish moss hung down with dignity. Emersyn was finally in Opelousas, the land of zydeco festivals, Black Creoles, and history as rich as its storied seasonings. And, she hoped, where she would find Otis McGee. She didn't know what to expect when she embarked on a trip to see her estranged father. There was a strong possibility there wouldn't be a happy ending, but at least there could be closure. He would never be Father of the Year, but maybe an acknowledgment would be nice. Or maybe Otis would see how accomplished she was—perhaps even how much she reminded him of himself—and they could be cordial.

Emersyn met Billy Ray's eyes through the rearview mirror. Billy Ray was a decent driver. He boasted that he had only one head-on collision since he started driving rideshares two years ago. His Corolla smelled like pine trees. Apparently, stop signs were suggestions in Opelousas. Billy Ray's dark eyes darted back and forth from the road to the rearview mirror at Emersyn. Shimmering rays of light pranced off his blond ponytail. He was cheerful, offering his account of the city's highlights: City Hall recently remodeled after a fire, Mama's Fried Chicken restaurant, and finding the best fish truck. "They only drive through certain neighborhoods now," he informed Emersyn. "You gotta know where to find 'em," Billy Ray winked, as if Emersyn would actually buy fish from the back of a car.

"You all right, ma'am?" Billy Ray adjusted his rearview mirror. "You ain't said much since I picked you up from the airport. And that was about twenty minutes ago."

"You don't have to call me 'ma'am,'" Emersyn told him for the third time.

The car tires screeched, and Emersyn grabbed the back of her neck.

"My bad, ma'am," Billy Ray chuckled. "The signals so low round these parts, I forget they there."

"Let's try not to forget the signal lights, Billy Ray." Emersyn texted Phillis to let her know she had arrived safely.

"No, ma'am. You right." Billy Ray chuckled.

Thirty minutes later, Emersyn scrambled out of Billy Ray's Corolla near downtown Opelousas. She hoisted her tote over her shoulder and rushed past an out-of-service parking meter and random shops: Ella Mae's Pies, Brother Ron's automotive, Ruth's Diner, and an abandoned storefront.

She stopped in front of a two-story building nestled between a used car lot and a personal injury lawyer. The elevator was out of order, so Emersyn tackled a flight of creaky stairs to Room 202. She wasn't accustomed to such circumspect assignments and texted Matt the address just in case. Emersyn opened the door of Room 202 and discovered a man with cocoa skin and a neatly trimmed silver beard tapping furiously on his cell phone. The room was less appealing inside, with faded industrial carpets and beige walls the color of brown eggs.

"Hi, I'm Emersyn Chavis," she greeted the man who could potentially represent the largest geographic district in Louisiana if he were elected. It was a community that demographically extended through small towns mired with poverty with little chance of economic growth.

"Armand T. Gray." He held out a hand. His friendly eyes crinkled when he smiled. His voice was like velvet, and he had the "thing" that one needed to be a successful candidate: charisma and looks. The self-proclaimed Son of Opelousas was a potential assembly candidate and one of the most successful businessmen in town. His reputation as a philanthropist and entrepreneur preceded him, and he was one of the more promising candidates in the upcoming race. He didn't have a long list of salacious social media posts, he married only once and didn't have children, and he was an avid mentor and sponsored several little league teams.

The campaign sweep should be a cakewalk, giving Emersyn plenty of time to hang out with her family and find her father.

"Nice to finally meet you," Emersyn shook his hand.

"Have we met?" He searched her face.

"No." Emersyn scanned the room. "Is this where we will be meeting?" Before leaving town, she'd attended a Weight Watcher's meeting in a room that looked like this. She half-expected a woman in pink leggings to emerge from behind the door and ask about her daily calorie points.

"Yes and no," he said, still searching her face. "This office belongs to a good friend. He's a consultant and uses this office to meet clients. You said we should meet someplace private to avoid the public knowing about my candidacy, and this is what I found." He held his arms in the air as if to display the room. "Hope it works."

"Should be fine." Emersyn sat down across from him on the couch and pulled out her laptop. "I won't regurgitate my bio, but I want to remind you that I started my career doing political sweeps, so you are in good hands."

"Are you sure we haven't met? Do you have family here?" Armand sucked in his bottom lip.

Emersyn blinked. She didn't want Armand to know that she had family in town, and her family didn't need to know about Armand's campaign either. No one would know Emersyn was trying to find her father.

"They say everybody has family in the South," Emersyn deflected.

"I guess you're right," he said, studying her face.

"Thank you for filling out the questionnaire." Emersyn looked at her notes.

"Anything I can do to help," he said.

Armand had an impressive background. His parents died when he was a boy, and an aunt had stepped in to raise him. He had a string of misdemeanors as a juvenile; he goofed off early in high school but got serious in his junior and senior years. He went to Grambling University and graduated at the top of his class. He owned several small businesses and was quite a community activist.

He sat back and rested his arm on the back of the couch. "I'm ready to lead this district to places it's never been. None of my opponents can touch me in community service or provide jobs to the people. None of them."

Armand T. Gray wasn't short on confidence, but confidence didn't win campaigns. Strategy did. Emersyn's job was to sweep out any cobwebs so his opponents couldn't pull them out and use them against him, and to develop a strategy to get his campaign started. Once she put his strategic plan together, his campaign team could take it from there. Armand could use the childhood misdemeanors to his favor: a young foster boy made mistakes and became an astute businessman and community servant. People loved success stories. They lend credence to the American Dream.

"All right." Emersyn cleared her throat. "What about your support of the police chief who wouldn't reveal the name of the officer who killed an unarmed Black man last year?"

"Oh, you just want to jump right in, huh?"

"That's the goal," Emersyn said.

"Foolishness," he spat. "That officer's family received death threats. The chief was trying to protect the officer's family, as any good leader would."

"Okay," Emersyn said. "And what about your district attorney friend who failed to bring charges against a local businessman for a sexual relationship with a minor?"

Armand stared at her for a few moments. "Who told you that?"

"Are those allegations true?"

"Absolutely not." He sighed. "That stuff is nonsense. I will be a partner to this district, an ally, and an advocate for the people of the fifth congressional district. That little stuff won't make or break my campaign."

"Mr. Gray—"

"Armand," he interrupted. "Please call me Armand."

"Armand, if we don't manage these fine details before you pull papers to file your candidacy, your campaign will be over before you start. Your opponents will use these things to crucify you. I need you to be honest so I can help you."

"It's all lies," he said, waving a hand in the air. "Mere misunderstandings."

Ah, so they weren't lies; they were misunderstandings. At least they were getting somewhere. Slow progress was better than no progress. Emersyn danced to this music a thousand times. Whether Mr. I-Will-Be-an-Ally-to-the-District knew it or not, as soon as he announced his candidacy, his opponents would dig into his past like ground squirrels and bury him.

"Look, young lady, I know you think you know a lot about

campaigns, but things are different here. That kind of stuff isn't a big deal here in the South. I'm the Son of Opelousas. That stuff won't matter."

Young lady? Emersyn leaned forward in her seat and covered her mouth with her fingertips. Another candidate sitting high on the hog must be knocked down to reality. This case would redeem her reputation, but the political punditry was nauseating.

"The first campaign filing deadline is in seventy-two days. Fourteen people pulled papers to run for this seat so far. The first group will get wiped out within a week of the filing deadline due to scandal, lack of financial support, or inadequate planning. Do you want to be in that first group?"

Emersyn took a breath. She'd given this spiel a million times, but most of her clients didn't get it until they got it. She didn't want to spend time extracting information from the Son of Opelousas's past transgressions. She wanted to find her father.

"That won't happen to me," Armand said.

"It could." She tapped her fingers on the top of her laptop. So this was how it was going to be.

"No, it can't." Armand leaned forward as if he were explaining to a toddler. "Look, I'm from here. I know these people. We aren't gossip-hungry folk who are bent on destroying one another. We want to do right by the citizens of this district, and I trust all the candidates will run clean, honest campaigns."

"Mr. Gray—"

"Please call me Armand," he interrupted.

"Armand, let me do my job. I'm here to make sure you can get to the polls. The rest is up to you and your campaign team, but I am here to ensure that you don't get wiped out of the race before the primary. And trust me, if we don't cover these issues, they could prove to be a barrier for you. I've seen it a thousand times before."

Armand looked past Emersyn through the small window covered by half-open mini blinds.

"We also need to talk about your wife," Emersyn added.

Armand stood up, his voice low and throaty. "We don't need to go into that. I think you are making this all a bigger deal than it needs to be. I know you want to impress Paul, and I promise to tell him how great you are. But it's not that serious."

"Yes, it is." Emersyn sighed.

"I don't think so." Armand pointed at Emersyn with a steady finger. "My wife will not be part of my campaign, so you don't need to speak to her. I'm sure my assistant made that clear early on."

Emersyn furrowed her brow. She'd known candidates who wanted to protect their spouse, but she never encountered such a strong reaction. What was the Son of Opelousas hiding?

CHAPTER 13

Manon 2019

The paramedics rolled down Bordelais Drive with Miss Genessa in tow. Manon sipped coffee and watched from her living room window. Hopefully, Miss Genessa hadn't fallen again. But then again, a fall would fare better than another stroke. The last one had left her on that walking stick.

Families moved in and out of Bordelais over the years. Some downsized after their children moved out, while others moved to Baton Rouge or Lafayette for job opportunities. And some, like Manon and Tate, and Miss Genessa and her husband, stayed for the long haul.

The Bordelais gossip mill would have everyone believe that Miss Genessa carried a talisman in one hand and a vial of blood in the other. Objectivity in Clos du Bois was as dead as the exotic fish that once lived in the pond near the security gate. Old superstitions eclipsed Miss Genessa's better qualities, but Manon stayed away from neighborhood gossip. She'd been the brunt of such talk years ago with Leonard Dupree. But if the rumors were true—that the medallion around Miss Genessa's neck was *gris-gris*—then Manon dared to stay on Miss Genessa's right side. A wise woman once said it was the sweetest taboo to have a friend in the hoodoo world, and Manon considered Miss Genessa a friend.

Manon should have checked on Mr. Genessa the way Miss Genessa checked on her in times past. "Chile, it's gone be fine," Miss Genessa had said one day, spitting tobacco into a Folger's can.

"When it's meant to be, it will be." Even with her peculiarities and unconventional beliefs, Miss Genessa was more of a maternal figure than Addie.

Instead of checking on Mr. Genessa like she should have, Manon moved to the back porch, ignoring another call from Serenity Village. She lit a Newport. The carcinogens filled her lungs, and cicadas serenaded the morning dew. Manon blew smoke rings and watched the Kruger children playing in their yard. The little one—Manon could never remember their names—wanted to swing like his big brother, but he couldn't get his leg high enough. Their mom tried to coerce him to the small swing and waved when she saw Manon.

"How y'all doin' over there?" Emily's blonde ponytail swung as she waved with one hand and pushed a tire swing with the other.

Manon waved back, silently cursing Pierre for overcutting the tree. She liked people-watching in private. "Doing good," Manon called. "Thank you." She prayed Emily kept her distance this time.

Emily and Sean started having kids a few years after they moved to Bordelais. Emily was a decent neighbor but overshared Sean's shortcomings in the bedroom and insisted on giving Manon and Tate pumpkin pies during the holidays. Tate indulged their Kentucky-bred neighbors, but Manon often steered her conversations with Emily to topics such as the overgrown planter in their front yard or their dog's poop that Emily and Sean never discarded. Perhaps Emily wouldn't mind discussing the oil stains in her driveway that were strictly prohibited by Neighborhood Association rules.

Emily motioned Manon to the fence they shared, and Manon obliged, silently cursing Pierre again.

"Well, I do declare. You're walking," Emily exclaimed in her native Kentucky drawl. Her *i*'s sounded like *a*'s and her *o*'s like *u*'s.

In these moments, Manon appreciated her healing progress, even if it meant chatting with Emily Kruger.

"They're growing up fast." Manon nodded toward the boys.

"Faster than weeds. They're eating Sean and me out of house and home. Thank goodness he works harder at his job than in the bedroom or we wouldn't be able to afford these rascals," Emily laughed. "You heard about Miss Genessa, huh?" She lowered her voice and glanced at her kids.

Manon shook her head. It was shameful that she'd find out what happened to Miss Genessa from Emily Kruger, whom Miss Genessa never liked. "I saw the ambulance. What happened?" she asked.

"I guess she had some sort of stroke." Emily looked around again. "But I'll tell you one more thang: God don't like ugly." She pruned her thin lips and told Manon that Miss Genessa had showed up at her door the other day. "She right scared me out of my mind," Emily exclaimed. "Standing at my front door in a long robe and those scary, dark glasses she wears . . . you know the ones I'm talking about?"

"Yeah." Manon leaned on the fence for support. She still couldn't stand for long periods without support. "They aren't the most fly glasses I've ever seen, but I wouldn't call them scary."

"After a few too many times of her accusing my boy, I asked her to leave," Emily said.

"Wait." Manon held up her hand. "You kicked Miss Genessa off your property?" She shifted her body so she was standing under the partial shade of the tree.

"I didn't kick her off my property!" Emily exclaimed. "I asked her very nicely to leave. She accused my boy of doing something he didn't do. He didn't do anything to her dang roses. All he did was get his ball! Can you imagine?"

The irony was overwhelming, but Manon digressed. Emily was the poster child for white privilege and didn't realize it. Manon would verbally reprimand Emily about white privilege and being falsely accused later. Today wasn't the day.

"She turned away really slowly like this." Emily moved her body in a deliberate semi-circle. "She said my boy would pay for what he did to her roses. I was scared right outta my mind. And, of course, Big Sean is traveling."

"So what happened?"

"Next thing you know, Sean Jr. caught some stomach bug and vomited all over the house. I declare I didn't think he would make it through the night." Emily held her hand over her heart and took deep breaths.

"Wow," Manon sighed. "What a coincidence."

"Coincidence!" Emily exclaimed. "That ain't no coincidence. That there is some straight-up witch spells or whatever that stuff is called. Plus, I've been to Bourbon Street, and I have seen them witch shops. Mary Anderson told me about some doll Miss Genessa carries under her robe. Something ain't right with her, Manon." Emily pronounced Manon's name like *cannon*. "And I heard she put a spell on the person who lived in the house before her!"

Manon heard false stories about how Miss Genessa got her home. Similar to the varied stories about Leonard. People speculated when they didn't know the truth. Granted, Mr. and Miss Genessa didn't appear to be the type to own a home that was worth a million dollars in today's market, but they did.

"Well, I hope Sean Jr. is feeling better," Manon said. Someone should have warned Miss Kentucky to be kind to an elderly Black woman from Louisiana who carried a snakehead cane. Hopefully, Emily learned her lesson or little Sean Jr. might not fare well the next time he trampled Miss Genessa's roses.

"Well, he is feeling better," Emily said, as if Manon hadn't heard her correctly. "But we don't want to live next door to a witch!"

Emily and her family were as safe on Bordelais as they would be anywhere else in Opelousas. Miss Genessa had a peculiarity to her: that wiry hair, penetrating stare, and slow, methodical movements. Still, Manon preferred a crotchety clairvoyant to the rash of property crimes in neighboring communities. After many stories about witchcraft and poop diapers, Manon assured Emily that her family was safe, then dodged probing questions about Tate.

"Just haven't seen him much lately, that's all," nosey-ass Emily inquired. "Especially with your recovery and all. Bet y'all can't wait to start traveling again, huh?"

"Yep," Manon said before she shambled back to the porch, cursing herself along the way for standing so long. She lit another Newport and scrolled through Facebook, ignoring friend requests from people who didn't speak to her in real life. Manon turned the porch fan on as the warm morning dampness reached her armpits. It was muggy, yet clouds hovered like gang members at a brawl. The stale gray sky's congruency and sweltering heat made Louisiana's climate a geological Rubik's Cube. She heard rustling from the side of the house.

"G, you scared me!" Manon pressed her hand over her chest. "I thought you couldn't come by today."

Gwen swung a bottle of Veuve Clicquot back and forth. "Mimosas anyone?"

"Always," Manon cooed. She was grateful for Gwen's company.

Gwen looked like a desperate housewife in a silk tank, white cropped jeans, and studded slides. She went to the kitchen and grabbed two champagne flutes.

They settled on the plush cushions in Manon's gazebo.

Manon folded her legs beneath her and looked at the oak tree while Gwen talked. When Manon was little, she was afraid of trees. Addie would say, "Trees are sneaky. Stay away from those sneaky trees." Manon never asked Addie why she didn't trust trees, but she grew to have the same disdain.

When Manon and Tate moved to Bordelais, she'd asked him to cut down the huge oak, but Tate refused. It was one of the first times he stood up to Manon, and one of the many contributions to the demise of their marriage. Tate was easily persuaded when they first married, but then he changed. He didn't have the same adoration for Manon that he once had. He made new connections and was invited to host community meetings. Tate was no longer the uncertain young man who didn't know which fork to use. He acted as if he'd outgrown Manon's advice. He also seemed to ignore the fact that Manon had helped get him to where he was today. She'd never make that mistake again.

"And that's why the Wilsons sold that land over there in Hyde Park." Gwen refilled her glass.

"So, he lost all of their money?" Manon asked as if she'd been listening.

"Yep." Gwen popped her lips. "Gambled it all away."

"Oh, poor Sheila. I hate to hear that. She's always so nice. She would bring those fruit cakes to my Fourth of July parties. Remember that?"

"You hate fruitcake." Gwen frowned.

"I didn't say I ate them; I just said it was nice of her. I used to take them to Miss Genessa."

"How is Miss Genessa?" Gwen asked. Manon knew she didn't really care how Miss Genessa was doing; she was just being polite because Manon and Miss Genessa were friends.

"The paramedics took her away to the hospital earlier, but I'm not sure what happened. Emily said it was a stroke."

"Emily Kruger?" Gwen lowered her chin. "She needs to pick up the dog shit in her yard and mind her business."

Manon doubled over in laughter. "I'm going to go over and check to see how she's doing later today."

"So, how are you doing?"

"Before you got here, I was thinking about how I used to sit out here with Tate in the mornings."

"You miss him, don't you?"

That was a loaded question. Manon missed companionship. She missed having a perpetual plus-one, someone to bring her tea when she was sick. She didn't miss the silence and awful communication. She didn't like living in a partnership rather than a marriage.

"I miss what we used to be. I can do without the rest."

"And counseling?"

"He won't do it. I've been in therapy for years. I guess he figures it hasn't done me any good, so why torture himself." Manon tried to laugh.

"You guys need each other. You just have to give it another try."

Gwen didn't know about the many tries Manon and Tate shared. They tried communicating better. They tried to check in more during the day, go away on trips, have couples' massages, and more sex, less sex. Manon and Tate looked good on paper but not in real life. She struggled to accept whether she found that out later in their marriage or if she knew it all along.

From the outside, it appeared Manon Lafleur had it all: handsome husband, beautiful home, lavish wardrobe, influential friends. Before the accident, Manon served as Board President of the Lady League and the Mayor's Ball planning committee.

Manon enjoyed the luxuries of being wealthy, but beyond social status and financial freedom, she also longed for peace. And she and Tate hadn't had peace in years. She missed him, but she liked getting her joy back.

"I don't know, G," Manon said. "I think I'm all tried out."

CHAPTER 14
Odester 1982

"Dette, hand me those chopped onions," Clotee said.

"Anything you need." Odester sat the bowl of onions on the counter.

"Whatchu got in that red cup?" Clotee eyed Odester as she stirred her roux with vigor.

"Ain't none of yo business," Odester challenged. "You mind what Willie Earl out there drankin' in *his* red cup."

Sunday dinners at Earline and Rutherford's house boasted plenty of food and alcohol. Odester and Arelia were the first to arrive as they lived closest, followed by Clotee, Willie Earl, and their daughter, Phillis.

"What time is Addie supposed to get here?" Earline stood at the kitchen door. Her all-white hair was pulled back into a bun.

"Mama, you know Addie take colored people standard time to new levels," Odester said. "Probably have to wait for Manon to finish one of her thousand extracurricular activities."

"That girl sure keep my grandbaby busy."

"Yeah, so she doesn't have to raise her," Odester said under her breath.

"Hope she get here before your father," Earline said, not hearing Odester's comment.

Odester giggled. "Daddy will be ready to eat as soon as his foot hit the porch."

"Aw, Mama, I love how you and Daddy still take care of each other after all these years," Clotee said.

"That's my boyfriend." Earline laughed.

"I hope to find a love like that one day," Odester said.

Earline frowned. "First thang you need to do is get yourself togther," she said. "Then you might have time for love."

"Mama!" Odester wailed. "Why you always gotta put me down?"

"Girl, ain't nobody putting you down. You put yourself down. Not going to college, not giving that gal a chance like the other girls."

"That *gal* is your granddaughter too, Mama!" Odester said. "Why you treat us like that?"

Earline ignored Odester's comment as she turned to Clotee. "Let me know if you need anything. I'mma go out here and check on these girls," she said.

"Okay, Mama," Clotee said quietly. "Dette, come stir this roux for me," she said when Earline was gone.

"Fuck that roux, and fuck Sunday dinner." Odester finished the contents of her red cup and refilled it. "I'm tired of Mama treating me like shit 'cause I ain't go to college. I'm sick of this."

"Dette, now you know that's not true. Mama love you—"

"Hush up, Tee. You always trying to keep the peace. Mama act like Addie a queen, and Addie ain't never done shit but married rich and treat Manon like a stepchild."

"Dette!" Clotee's eyes widened like a startled deer. "Why you talk about our sister like that? And why you sweating like that?"

"You know it's true." Odester twisted her lips. "Everybody wanna talk about me and what I ain't did, but nobody talk about Addie. Her shit stank too. And it's hot in here."

Clotee examined her sister slowly. "Mama got the air on, so

it ain't hot in here. Dette, are you and Bumpie still using that . . . stuff?" Her eyes lowered.

Just then, a girl with fair skin and Clotee's features peered through the back door and said, "Mama, is Auntie Addie coming?"

"Don't hang in the door like that, Phillis," Clotee said. "You letting all the air out. And yes, Auntie Addie will be here soon. I know you want to see Manon."

"Cool!" Phillis screamed, then shut the back door.

The Chavis sisters all had daughters. Arelia was the oldest at eleven, Phillis was ten and Manon was nine.

"I see Willie Earl refilled his cup, and it don't look like a cold drink," Odester said.

"God is still in the miracle-working business, Dette. I tell you that all the time. And don't try to change the subject."

"Bumpie and me party a little bit here and there." Odester scrunched her face.

"Y'all need to stop partying and start praying. You over here looking like you just ran around a track field. What's Mama gone say?"

"Mama ain't gone say shit because it ain't her business. Ain't yours either."

"Fine," Clotee surrendered. "Bumpie working yet?"

"God ain't made it to my part of town yet." Odester took a swig of her beer.

"God is everywhere, Dette, and you know it. It's hard out here for our men. Give it some time."

"How much damn time does he need, Tee? The bills don't give us time. They have to be paid."

Addie entered the kitchen and kissed her sisters on the cheek.

"Well, well, well," Odester said. "Look at what the cat dragged in."

"Did I make it before Daddy?" Addie asked. "I don't want him to see my banana pudding. It's a surprise."

"The surprise will be if he eats it." Odester pursed her lips. "Daddy is picky. He likes good food."

"He ate it the last time," Addie said.

"He was trying to be nice." Odester laughed.

"Addie, we told you to bring forks and napkins," Clotee said over her shoulder.

"I brought my banana pudding. As of today, I'm relinquishing my role of bringing utensils to family dinners. I'm going to start making desserts."

"Interesting," Odester said, then folded Manon into her arms and kissed the miniature version of Addie all over her cheeks. Manon was every bit as beautiful as Addie. Manon was high achieving and well-behaved. Addie got pregnant soon after Clotee, but she never seemed happy about being a mother.

"Now, what took y'all so long to get here?" Odester bounced Manon in her arms.

"I had homework," Manon said.

"On a Sunday?" Odester eyeballed Addie, who raised her chin in defiance.

"Smells good in here," Addie said.

"Addie, it's so good to see you," Clotee said. "Did you bring me any fine dresses you don't want anymore?"

"Sure did." Addie grinned. "They're in the car."

"Oh, good. The women's auxiliary members loved the last ones you gave me. They gonna be jealous when I get the new ones."

"Yeah," Odester snorted. "She's the best-dressed Sunday school teacher at New Hope Fellowship Apostolic Church."

"You got that right." Clotee turned back to the stove as the phone rang.

"That's probably Daddy calling now," Addie said as she put her banana pudding into the refrigerator.

"Daddy wouldn't be calling when he knows dinner is soon. You know he's never late," Clotee reminded her sisters.

"I don't know anybody more punctual than Daddy," Odester smiled.

Rutherford balanced the houseful of women with a calm demeanor, good nature, and incredible patience. He never took sides when the girls disagreed, and he always reminded his girls how special they were. He was proud of his girls and loved his wife. His bright smile followed him wherever he went.

Earline walked into the kitchen. She held the doorframe with one hand, and her other hand was clutching her stomach.

"Was that Daddy calling?" Clotee asked.

"I know he's not late," Addie chimed in. "That would mean the good Lord is coming back sooner than we thought."

Earline was still standing in the doorway. The color had drained from her face, and her eyes seemed to be looking at something that wasn't there.

"Mama wasn't wrong?" Odester walked toward her mother. "Please don't tell me those folks from the church are bothering you again."

Earline was silent as she stared into the distance.

"Mama, what's wrong?" Clotee approached a feeble-looking Earline.

The girls helped her sit at the kitchen table.

"That . . . was the hospital. Your daddy's been in a car accident," Earline whispered.

Odester swallowed the lump in her throat. "What?" Her legs felt weak. What had she just heard? They needed to get to the hospital right away. Her daddy needed her.

Addie jumped into fix-it mode like she always did, as if the others weren't capable. "Let me grab my keys. Which hospital, Mama? I'll take you. Clotee, you finish the food. Dette, you keep the girls distracted."

"Can we hear what Mama wants first?" Odester grumbled. "Always trying to boss everybody around but can't stand up to your husband."

"Dette, this ain't the time," Clotee snapped.

Earline sat at the table and cradled her forehead in the palm of her hand.

Clotee kneeled next to Earline. "What happened?"

"Is it bad, Mama?" Odester asked.

Earline raised her head and looked at her daughters. They each resembled Rutherford in different ways: Odester's skin tone, Addie's mouth, and Clotee's dimples.

"Ain't no need to get to the hospital right away." Earline sucked in air as if she were struggling to breathe. "Your daddy is dead."

"Odester, sit down," a tall woman with thick glasses ordered. "We here to take care of you and your family today. You don't need to cook."

Rutherford Chavis's funeral was over. A soloist from Clotee's church sang. Everyone from the Brickyard was there. Earline and the girls wore blue dresses—Rutherford's favorite color—and their husbands wore dark suits with blue ties.

Earline's grandchildren surrounded her at a circular table. She didn't touch the food Clotee's church had provided. Instead, she looked straight ahead with her ankles crossed. Manon said something, smiled, and then looked across the banquet hall at Odester.

Odester hadn't slept in days. She couldn't stop the emptiness that boiled in the pit of her stomach and then etched around her heart. Her hero was gone. The last conversation she'd had with her father, she promised to visit him more, but she never did. She was too busy fighting and chasing Bumpie. The last time she saw her father was at a gas station where he gave her money. He said he was worried about her, but she assured him that she would be fine. She also made him promise not to tell Earline about the money, and he promised he wouldn't.

"Mama looks so sad," Odester whispered. She, Clotee, and Addie sat at a table near Earline.

"She lost her soulmate," Clotee said.

"We will have to be here for each other more than ever," Addie said.

"I agree." Odester sipped from a small blue flask.

"Dette, is that alcohol?" Clotee hissed. "You can't drink alcohol in God's house!"

"Look, Jesus's auntie," Odester slurred. "I just lost my daddy. I can drink what I want. God knows my heart."

"I know you are grieving, Dette. We all are. You have to get yourself and Arelia home. How can you make it in that condition?" Addie asked.

"I will make it just like I always do." Odester blinked fast. "Except now I have to do it without anybody telling me how great and smart I am. Daddy never judged me, and he loved me for who I am." Tears filled her eyes and trickled down her cheeks.

Addie sighed. "I'm gonna miss him. His laugh."

"Oh my goodness," Clotee sniffled. "That loud laugh. You could hear him through the entire house."

"Remember how he said he should have been a member of the Temptations?" Odester laughed through tears.

"He was such a good man." Addie wiped her face.

"Things will never be the same," Odester said.

Odester buried her face in her hands. Her father, who'd shared the same look and sense of humor, was gone forever. Odester relied on Rutherford for advice. He and Odester would go to dinner, and he'd have a glass of wine. He never drank in front of Earline because she said alcohol wasn't good for his blood pressure. Odester kept his secret. He made Odester feel complete, worthy, and loved. Even though she made bad choices, her daddy never made her feel like a bad person. She'd never have that again. Her body rocked with grief.

"It's okay, Dette." Clotee rubbed Odester's back. "Let it out."

Odester picked up her cup.

"Dette, you can't grieve drunk," Addie said. "You can't keep drinking like this."

"I just lost the only person who understood me," Odester said through her tears. "Y'all smart like Mama. Pretty, light skinned. Everybody likes y'all. Always have. You don't know what it's like for me. I always got in trouble and got bad grades. Never understood school assignments. Impulsive and flip-mouthed. Mama has never looked at me with pride the way she looks at you two. But Daddy always told me that no matter what I did—right or wrong—I was a good person, and he wouldn't change me if he could." Odester wiped her nose. "Where will I get that kind of support again? Who gone love me like that, Addie? Who?"

Addie dabbed her eyes, and Clotee draped her arm across Odester's shoulder.

"It's gone be all right, Dette."

"But it's not, Tee," Odester cried. "Nothing ever gone be all right again."

CHAPTER 15

Emersyn 2019

Emersyn stood in Devanie's apartment, thirty minutes from her hotel and forty minutes from where she'd met Armand. Even though they were the same age, they didn't share the same fashion sense. Emersyn's khakis and loafers paled in comparison to her cousin's white crop top, high-waisted shorts, and sandals.

"I'm so glad you made it!" Devanie cleared a pile of books from the couch and tossed a Delaware Punch can into the trash. "My place is usually tidy, but my mama spent the last two nights with me."

"No worries. I'm glad we finally got to connect."

"Me too, girl," Devanie smiled. "All that social media and texting is cool, but it's good to see you in the flesh, cousin."

"Same," Emersyn said with a smile.

Emersyn found a seat on the mustard-colored couch. Devanie's one-bedroom apartment was decorated in lively colors with white wooden accents and shutters. A large mirror hung on the wall across from the couch. The deep-plum rug and large plants made the room cozy.

"I invited y'all down a few times for some of our big family gatherings. Shame y'all couldn't make it."

"Yeah, shame." Emersyn picked up a local newspaper with the headline: "Locals Fend for Assembly Seat." She held up the paper. "It's going be pretty active around here."

"Chile, it's gone be a shit show. Some of these folks can't manage their lives but want to run an entire parish." Devanie dabbed powder on her face. "Most of 'em don't even like to read," she chuckled. "How you don't like to read but want to work in politics?"

"Sounds about right," Emersyn laughed. "But in all of your posts, you seem to really like your job."

"Well, my job is demanding, public-facing, stressful, and will never afford to pay me a worthy wage, but I wouldn't change it for the world." Devanie looked at Emersyn through the reflection in the mirror and made a face.

"You are something else." Emersyn laughed.

"I mean it." Devanie pointed to the bookshelf across the room. "Those are land relics from some of my trips. I went to South Africa with the Calcasieu Parish delegation and did community service with the Atchafalaya Trade Commission. The rest are photos with some of my local favorites: Cedric Richmond and Mayors Alsandor and Davis."

Emersyn raised her eyebrows. "Wow."

"Yeah, it don't give Google perks, but there is a pretty good payoff sometimes."

"You hang out with the fancy people, I see."

"Now, you know those people ain't fancy. But I do know almost everybody in town. You're the one with the connections in high places, I hear." Devanie's laugh was deep.

Emersyn bit the inside of her cheek. It could be good and bad if Devanie knew everyone. Emersyn was proud of her cousin's accomplishments in local politics. This area wasn't friendly to help young Black professionals, and Devanie had broken ceilings to earn her role, but being that close to politics meant she might know about Armand's bid for Assembly.

"Did you find my place okay?" Devanie pulled her curls into a massive bun on top of her head, revealing flawless cocoa skin and perfectly lined lips.

"It was fine finding it. But my weather app said it would rain," Emersyn said. "It didn't say anything about a tsunami!"

"Welcome to Louisiana, baby." Devanie chuckled, swirling her baby hairs with a toothbrush. "I'm glad you made it. You here for two weeks, right?"

"Nine days." Emersyn had requested Otis's records from the county clerk's office and was told to pick them up in three to five business days. Hopefully, she could get Armand's sweep finished by then.

"Good. Because that's how long I'll need to tell you about your relatives." Devanie chuckled again. "Wait." Her eyes raked over Emersyn's khakis and loafers. "Do you need to change?"

"No," Emersyn said. She wished she had enough confidence to wear crop tops like Devanie. Instead, she snaked herself into body shapers and super support bras every day.

"Oh." Devanie squinted like she was trying to understand something. "Did Cousin Phillis come?"

"No." Emersyn avoided eye contact. "I'll be working, and she didn't want to be in the way."

"Be in the way?" Devanie raised a perfectly curated eyebrow as she applied gloss to her lips. "With all this family here? They would love to see her."

The last time Phillis visited Opelousas, she'd left Emersyn in California with a family friend.

Emersyn shrugged. "She worries about stuff like that."

"I see." Devanie nodded.

"Now, tell me about everybody." Emersyn concealed her excitement. She was finally going to meet her family—not friends who turned family or pretend cousins, but her own flesh and blood. The goose bumps wouldn't stay idle. "Who's the woman who wears the short blonde wig? And who is the man who wears the Tupac T-shirts? And that little boy with the long braids?"

"Whew, chile. I'mma let you settle in first," Devanie resigned. "Where are you staying?"

"At a hotel downtown," Emersyn said. "Close to my client."

"You're more than welcome to stay here. I can crash on the couch and give you the bed. The elevator shrieks, and the couple next door gets drunk and fights, but otherwise it's comfortable, and I haven't seen a stray pit bull in weeks," Devanie said.

Emersyn shook her head. "No, but thank you. My hotel is closer to where I meet my client."

"I was kidding about the pit bull," Devanie said.

"No, that's not it," Emersyn said. "This is a work trip, so I must prioritize time with my client. Otherwise, I'd love to stay here."

"Well, if anybody in the family asks, you might wanna say you are staying with me. Folks get offended when family comes to town and stays at a hotel. It's an abomination."

"Seriously?"

"Girl, yes." Devanie checked her cell phone. "People in this family get offended about everything and nothing at all. You in the Petty Capital of the world, baby." Devanie tossed a few things into her purse. "So, I know we talked about this before, but tell me, what do you do again? You help people hide secrets or something like that, right?"

"Not exactly." The PR business was interesting that way. Emersyn was accustomed to people not knowing her occupation. She often couldn't reveal her clients' identities, so she was okay with letting people assume whatever they wanted. She could give Devanie her standard spiel about delivering measurable results for clients in diverse categories like the government, entertainment, and transportation, but that was no fun.

"I help clients with strategic communication and planning."

"Well, Nadesna told everybody you are the Secretary of State in California, so be prepared for *that* conversation."

"Secretary of State?!"

"Well, that's better than the CIA, which is who Uncle Buster says you work for."

"I don't even know Buster."

"Yeah." Devanie shrugged. "Well, he doesn't know you either. But y'all family, and that doesn't stop him from telling people about your job, baby. So, who is this client? Do I know them? You know I know everybody in the parish."

Emersyn had to be careful. Her assignment to preempt potential casualties surrounding Armand's campaign announcement was confidential.

"Just a local businessman." Emersyn hunched her shoulders and looked at her reflection.

"Excuse me." Devanie slapped her hands together. "I know every businessman in town. Who is it? Gerald Toussaint? Léonard Longfellow? Please don't tell me it's Rodney Criss. That boy uses those laundromats as a cover-up for the seasoned greens he sells. It's legal in California but not in Louisiana."

"Nope." Emersyn ran her finger through a shimmery blush palette on Devanie's table and dabbed it on her cheeks. "I can't tell you." She tilted her head to the side and checked the mirror.

Devanie's eyes didn't match the smile on her face. "Okay, I get it if you don't trust me."

"It's not that." Emersyn felt terrible. This wasn't a good start. "The client asked for anonymity. If I could, I would. I promise."

"I'm not going to say anything," Devanie held her palms toward the ceiling.

"I can't tell you." Emersyn shifted her eyes. The last thing she wanted was for her cousin to think she didn't trust her, but she'd caused enough stink with the Hamilton case and didn't want to risk anything with this one.

Emersyn was thankful for the knock at the door.

"Anyway, Nadesna is cooking a welcome dinner for you, and everybody will ask you about covert operations. Welcome to the family," Devanie said.

She opened the door and in walked the most beautiful creature Emersyn had ever seen. Mocha skin with deep, brown eyes, a trim beard, and at least six feet tall. Emersyn sucked in her stomach.

"Hey, boo," Devanie said as she let the gorgeous man in. "This is my best friend, Rico. We've known each other since third grade."

"Yeah, she didn't have any friends, and I felt sorry for her," Rico said with a laugh.

"He's not telling the truth." Devanie swatted Rico's arm. "Rico, this is my cousin Emersyn from California."

"Aw, I love Cali." Rico talked like he pondered each word before speaking. "I heard the women out there are bougee."

"Not true," Emersyn confirmed.

"I'm just repeating what I heard. Are the rumors incorrect?"

"Yes, they are," Emersyn said. "We California girls come in all varieties. You can find a bougee girl in any state."

"Ya heard." Devanie snapped her fingers in the air. "Don't try and come for my cousin, Rico."

"I'm just kidding." He grinned. "Pleasure to meet you."

"It's a pleasure," Emersyn accepted his hand.

Devanie relieved Rico of the plastic bag he held.

"Rico is dropping off some blue crab," Devanie explained. "Nadesna is cooking gumbo, and I didn't have time to get any."

"My uncle owns a fish market," Rico explained.

"That too," Devanie chuckled. "We are heading out. You wanna come by Nadesna's?"

"I just might do that." Rico looked at Emersyn again.

"Cool, text me if you are."

"All right," Rico said. "I might see y'all later."

Emersyn melted onto the sofa after Rico left. "How have I not heard about him?"

"Girl, we just met in person today," Devanie said.

"Well, I need you to move faster." Emersyn joked. When she stood up, the photo of her father slipped out.

"Girl, you some silly." Devanie picked up the photo that fell next to Emersyn. "Who is this man? This your client?"

Emersyn tried to grab the photo, but Devanie pulled it away.

"He's part of the assignment I'm working on." Emersyn studied Devanie's face. "But he's not my client."

"Ah. Well, you don't have anything to worry about. I've never seen this man in my life."

CHAPTER 16

Manon 2009

Tate intertwined his fingers with Manon's as they entered the mahogany double doors. Manon straightened her wedding ring and pulled her shoulders back. She looked beautiful, with her hair pulled high on her head, and thanks to Leilani, her makeup was flawless. The last time she got her face done was six months ago for her thirty-sixth birthday.

"Hello," a man in a tuxedo greeted them with champagne.

"Thank you." Tate took a glass and handed it to Manon, then took one himself. The couple kept their circle tight and their lips tighter. Tate was always the gentleman—doting and attentive even. One would never know they just had a massive argument in the car and miscarried the week prior. Not even Manon's parents knew the specifics of their marriage. Pregnancy was something Manon failed at, and she refused to make it public.

Fireside Plantation was perfect for the Community Service Awards. It lay empty for years before the West family purchased and gutted the main house. It stood at the end of Fireside Road, the most serene and graceful home on the road. The three-story brick home boasted floor-to-ceiling windows and wrapping balconies. The circular driveway was perfect for valet parking and those with the fanciest cars to show off. From the outside, it looked like a large home with family members attending a soiree. Inside was filled with decadence: string lights, flower walls, crimson carpet, and extravagant dining place settings. A violinist served soft sounds, and servers passed out champagne and small bites. Opelousas high society was a small circle of dignitaries, community servants, business owners, and legacies—an extended family. They attended the same events, donated to similar causes, and sent their children to the same elite schools and summer camps.

Manon and Tate made the rounds, greeting acquaintances and posing for photos with some of their favorites. Most of the people here attended their Mardi Gras party last year.

Eugenia Beekirk waved from across the room. If the folks in the room were considered extended family, Eugenia would be the godmother. Eugenia's kind heart, large pocketbook, and sincerity made her a favorite among the Opelousas elite. But there were other reasons. She spoke three languages, her Birdies flats touched every continent at least twice, and she was politically connected. She played an active role in getting political hopefuls elected in local and state races. Traditionally, it was hard to get African Americans elected in their district, but people got elected when Eugenia Beekirk was involved. No one except for Eugenia's late husband knew her actual age, and he took the secret with him to his grave.

Eugenie approached Manon and Tate in a silver beaded gown. A mousy gentleman with thick glasses pulled up the rear. As Eugenia socialized, he pushed his glasses on his nose and stood close, but not too close. An array of diamonds splattered across her chest like fine art. Her bespoke accent oozed Southern comfort and privilege.

"Well, if it isn't Clos Du Bois royalty," Eugenie said in French as she air-kissed Manon's cheeks, then stood back and held Manon's hands. "The most beautiful thing ever to walk across the St. Landry County line."

"It's so good to see you, Miss B," Manon responded in equally flawless French.

"And this man right here," Eugenia said in English as she enveloped Tate in her arms. "If I were forty years younger, you'd be in trouble."

"You might be right." Tate smiled.

The discerning eye might notice that Manon and Tate weren't the same couple from a decade ago, with their shared inside jokes and constant display of affection. Lazy weekends in bed, making love all night. If anyone paid close enough attention, they'd notice how Manon tensed at his slightest touch and slid her hand from his at any given opportunity. But who would see such trivial body language? People dealt with their issues: aging parents, disobedient children, and vesting pensions. But a closer look at the most handsome couple would discover dimness in Manon's eyes and disappointment shrouding Tate's shoulders.

"Can I steal your husband for one moment?" Eugenia held up a thick forefinger. "There's someone I want him to meet."

"Of course." Manon flashed her best Mona Lisa smile and watched as Eugenia led a hesitant Tate through the crowd. The mousy man tagged behind.

Manon accepted another glass of champagne when she felt hands on her shoulders.

"You gone drink all of that?" Gwen looked dazzling in a satin halter dress. Her hair was pulled back in a low bun with a middle part. Her minimal makeup was a cheek highlight and a stark red lip, and her drop diamond earrings were blinding.

"Gwen." Manon shifted her eyes across the room. "I'm so glad to see you."

"Well, it's good to be seen." Gwen nodded to a passing couple. "Of course, I don't know why I bother hanging out with these stuffy rich people."

"Probably because you're one of the stuffy rich people." Manon chugged her champagne.

"Whoa there, Nellie." Gwen placed her hand atop Manon's. "Slow down on that drink."

Manon pressed her lips together.

"Are you okay?" Gwen asked.

Manon nodded. "Yes, I'm fine."

"I know you better than you know yourself." Gwen looked over her shoulder. "Another fight?"

"I can't pretend anymore, G," Manon admitted. "I don't think it's going to work."

"And it might not." Gwen giggled. "But we won't let everybody here know that. Come on." She held Manon's hand. "Give me a little laugh. Let's make this conversation appear light."

Manon mustered a chuckle.

"There you go." Gwen tossed her head to the side. "The last thing you need are these people all up in your business. Give me another laugh, boo."

"G, you are nuts," Manon laughed.

"That's why you love me." Gwen folded her arm through Manon's.

A tall man approached. "Hi, Manon." Tom leaned in and kissed Manon on the cheek.

"Tom. Good to see you."

Manon grew fond of Tom over the years. He was quirky and blond and a good guy. Manon had never seen a man love a woman the way Tom loved Gwen. He did everything he could to make Gwen happy, and according to Gwen, nothing was enough, but he kept trying.

"Well, it's good to see you." Tom put his arm around Gwen's waist.

"You're adorable, Tom." Manon raised an eyebrow at Gwen.

"I'm nothing without this woman right here."

Some might attest that Tom was correct, particularly Gwen.

Before meeting Gwen, Tom was a successful financier but had little regard for appearance or social status. Gwen encouraged him to ditch his signature brim hat and lose twenty pounds. She styled him, and he joined her in the Opelousas elite social circle. Gwen often joked that Tom morphed from Jed Clampett to George Clooney.

The emcee summoned the guests. Tate joined them, and the couples separated to their respective tables.

"So good to see you," Robin said when Manon approached their table. "Thank you for inviting us to sit at your table. We haven't been out to an adult event in so long." The woman smiled at her husband.

"Well, we are glad you could join us this year," Manon said.

"Same with us," Tammy chimed in from the other side of the table. "Since we started having children, it's all playdates, snacks, and cleaning up!" The group laughed.

"I know," Robin agreed. "I can't remember the last time I dressed up."

"Right?" Tammy. "Why get dressed up if you'll just have juice spilled on you?"

The group broke into conversation about minivans and waiting lists for schools.

Manon ordered another drink and focused on the slideshow.

"In college, we all said we'd never have children," Robin said. "Remember, Manon?"

Manon cleared her throat and nodded. "I do."

"Well, Manon was the only one who stayed true to that," Tammy said. "It must be so nice to travel the world and hang out with your husband whenever you want. I might scream if I have to watch one more episode of *The Backyardigans*."

Manon looked around the table at the women who thought she had a perfect life. The women she'd pledged with in college.

The women who didn't know that she had infertility issues. They all graduated and got married within ten years of one another. The others started having babies six years ago. Manon felt Tate's hand on her thigh. Her throat was tight. It could have been the champagne, but it was likely the hormones. She was always filled up on hormones, bloated, grumpy, or bleeding at the wrong time. It was exhausting.

"Yeah," she finally said. "It's quite the life." She sipped champagne.

"I mean, it's just awesome the way you don't care about tradition and what people say," Robin said. "Because my mama has been asking for grandbabies since I was a junior in college."

"Girl, mine too," Tammy said. "My mama always said I needed to get my act together so I wouldn't die an old maid. I was like, 'I'm twenty-six, Ma!'" The group laughed.

Manon felt a wave of relief when the emcee approached the podium. He gave a brief history of the community service awards and announced the chaplain, followed by the first presenter. Awardees came to the stage and thanked everyone for everything. The crowd clapped and smiled. Soon, Manon watched photo after photo of her delivering checks to local organizations and schools in the county. Her bio always sounded better when someone announced it over a microphone.

"And this year's recipient for the Community Service Awards needs no introduction." The emcee talked more about Manon's accomplishments and service to the community as she made her way to the stage.

After the gala, tucked safely behind the confines of her home, Manon poured a glass of wine and brought it to the bedroom.

"Did you have a good time?" Tate removed his necktie.

"Yes, it was a nice event." Manon slid out of her dress. She still had the body of a twenty-year-old and worked hard to keep it that way. If she couldn't have babies, she could at least look good.

"I'm proud of you." Tate tugged at his tie.

"What did Eugenia want?"

"Ah, she wanted to introduce me to a few people. You know how she is. Always the connector."

"Yeah," Manon said as she watched Tate undress. He caught her eye and sauntered over, pulling her close to him. "I'm tired." She pulled away.

"Come on, babe. We had a good night. You don't expect me to just let you go to bed looking this good, do you?"

"Tate, please. I have a headache." She rubbed her forehead. "And I'm bloated from the injections."

Tate sighed. "Come on, babe. I need you. It's been too long."

"Tate, seriously. I have a headache."

"You had a headache yesterday, and the day before that, and the day before that. In fact, you had a headache this month and all of last month too." Tate bit his bottom lip. "Please."

She furrowed her brow. "I'd expect you to be more under-standing. I've been through a lot."

"I'm not trying to be insensitive. I know you've been through a lot. I thought since we've passed the period where the doctor said we couldn't . . . maybe we could. I need you, babe." He nuzzled her neck. "I miss you so much. I miss us."

She pulled back and stared at him. All her life, she did precisely what she was supposed to do. She made the best grades, won horse shows, and was voted Best Dressed in high school. And now, she couldn't give her husband the thing he wanted more than anything. She was insufficient. She once attended church with Gwen and her mother, Holly. The preacher gave a sermon about a woman in the Bible named Sarah, who didn't have her first child until she was ninety years old. "Sarah was barren!" the crochety preacher shouted. After church, Manon had asked Holly what barren meant. "It refers to a woman who can't have children," Holly explained.

Manon was barren.

"I miss you too, Tate, but I just can't. Not yet."

"I'm worried about our marriage," Tate said.

So was Manon.

CHAPTER 17

Odester 1993

"D ette?" Addie opened her front door and blinked. "What are you doing here?"

"Is that any way to greet your sister?" Odester stood at the door with her hand on her hip.

"If that's how my sister deserves to be greeted." Addie ushered her inside and led her into the kitchen. "But since you're here, I have a little something for you." Addie pulled out a Tupperware bowl from the refrigerator.

Odester had her issues with Addie throughout the years, and though Addie was entitled and spoiled, they were sisters. Rutherford would often remind Odester to be kind to her sisters. "Family first," he'd say to a teenaged Odester when she complained about Addie or Clotee.

Odester's eyes lit up when she opened the container. She sat down at the table. "Who made these?"

"Tee. We celebrated Daddy's birthday yesterday. We tried to bring them by your house last night, but you didn't answer the door."

"He always did love Clotee's chitterlings." Odester's eyes teared up. Each sister grieved their father's death differently. Odester fell into depression and tried to drink her way through the grief. After three drinking and driving offenses, she lost her license for six months. Addie and Clotee tried to help, but Odester didn't conform to the rules, and she did what she wanted.

"Yeah, we all went to the cemetery. Even Manon and Phillis joined us. It was nice. You should have come." Addie looked into her eyes. "Arelia was there too."

Odester winced at the sound of her daughter's name. She and Arelia had been estranged because of Odester's drug addiction. Odester had tried to hide her addiction for as long as she could, but the weight loss and borrowing money alerted her sisters. Odester tried to get her daughter to understand that she was grieving, and that grief took time, but Arelia didn't want to hear it. She wanted Odester to be like Addie and Clotee, but Odester could never be like her sisters. It stung to hear that Arelia and the family were there for Daddy's birthday and Odester wasn't there.

"How was Mama?" Odester asked.

"She was okay." Addie lit a candle and warmed the chitterlings in a small pot. "Says she's been calling you. You know how she worries when she can't reach you."

"I know." Odester played with her fingers. "I was busy."

"Same thing for Mother's Day?"

"Addie, look, I said I was busy." Odester crossed one leg over the other and uncrossed it.

"Dette, what's going on?" Addie slopped the chitterlings in a bowl for her sister.

"Thank you." Odester avoided eye contact. She missed her father, bills were piling up, and Arelia hated her. She wanted to visit her sister and eat chitterlings without being interrogated. But that was asking too much. If her sisters didn't intrude so much, Odester would come around more.

"So," Addie sat across from Odester. "Why are you here in the middle of the afternoon?"

"I came to see my sister," Odester said. "And eat chitterlings."

"That's a new one." Addie said. "A visit with no strings attached? I'm shocked."

"Don't be sarcastic." Odester looked toward the bedrooms. "Is Manon coming for Mama's birthday? Clotee said Phillis was coming down. I know those two synchronize everything. Sometimes I swear they were supposed to be sisters."

"Yes, Manon and Phillis spend a lot of time together. Though I suspect some jealousy on Phillis's side. You heard she's looking at grad schools in California, right?"

Odester looked down at her lap. "You always think people are jealous of Manon. Phillis loves Manon like a sister. And the last time I checked, Manon kept up with Phillis, not the other way around. And, yes, Tee told me that Phillis was applying to one of those fancy master's programs in California."

"Yeah, well, I can assure you, Manon is too busy to run behind Phillis," Addie said.

"Shame you don't know your daughter." Odester shook her head. "Y'all got this fancy house and more money than you ever need, but you don't know your child. That don't make sense to me."

"Why you like that toward your own daughter?" Odester continued. "Manon is a good girl. Got a bad attitude like you did growing up, but she's a good girl. Why you always so mean to her?"

"Mean?" Addie scoffed. "Life is hard for Black women. We must be stronger, smarter, and better prepared than everyone else. That's just how it is."

"Is that how it is for Manon or for you?" Odester slurped a chitterling into her mouth.

"For her!" Addie insisted. "Manon needs to be strong and not let some man swoop her off her feet so she forgets who she is and all of her dreams and aspirations, only to be cooking his meals and to be arm candy, while he works late, forgets anniversaries, and gets too friendly with the nanny."

"Whoa," Odester said. "Did something happen?"

"No," Addie said.

"I know Marcel ain't stepped out on you. Pretty as you is."

"Dette, looks ain't everything, okay?"

"I see what this is." Odester sank back in her seat. "This ain't about Manon. You mad because you didn't go to law school like you wanted. Instead, you got married and became a housewife. All your friends got fancy careers, and you don't. Now you taking it out on Manon because you worried she gone follow your footsteps."

"That's absolutely ridiculous," Addie said. "Ridiculous."

"Is it, Addie? I ain't got to have no college degree to know that."

Addie rested her chin in her palm and watched her sister eat. "I just want Manon to have opportunities that I didn't. Being pretty can only get you so far." She reared her shoulders back. "Anyway," she said with a faraway look in her eyes. "You came to see me for a reason. What's up?"

"I'm pregnant."

Addie's eyes widened. "Pregnant? Dette, you're almost forty years old!" she exclaimed.

"Guess that's why you're the family genius," Odester retorted. "I know how old I am, Adeline."

"I thought you and Bumpie weren't doing good. Why have another baby? And not to pry, but when I saw Arelia for Daddy's birthday, she mentioned that she hadn't spoken to you in a couple of weeks."

"For somebody who doesn't mean to pry, you are prying pretty hard." Odester folded her arms across her chest. "And it ain't Bumpie's baby."

"Dette!" Addie exclaimed. "What are you saying?"

"I'm pregnant, and it's not Bumpie's baby. I just said that."

"How did this happen?"

"Well, let's see. I opened my legs, a man got on top of me—"

"Don't be crass, Odester," Addie interrupted. "You know what I mean. What are you going to tell Bumpie?"

"Tell Bumpie? The man who messed around with that big-boned girl from the Dixon, and who ain't had a steady job since Arelia was in middle school? I ain't telling him a damn thing."

"But when you have the baby, he will know it's not his." Addie caught Odester's eyes. "Oh, Dette. No. No, no, no . . ."

"Addie, shut up," Odester said with a huff. "This isn't the time. I can't have another baby. I can barely afford to help Arelia. And I'm tired."

"You are an adult, Dette. You were just a child yourself when you had Arelia. You have an opportunity to be a good mom this time."

"What the hell does that mean, Addie? Am I not a good mom? What, because Arelia didn't go to college like Manon and Phillis?"

"Odester, please. This has nothing to do with Arelia, and you know it."

Odester leaned back in her seat. "I'm trying, Addie. I swear I am. Just seems like everything I do ends up going the wrong way. God don't smile on me the way he do with you and Tee. It's like I was doomed from the start."

"Dette, don't do that. You are not doomed, and God loves you. We have to lean on our faith sometimes and believe there is a reason why things happen the way they do."

"A reason? I don't know about a reason, but I know about solutions. I'm going to Miss Cane."

"Miss Cane! You will do no such thing. That old woman is a witch doctor," Addie hissed. "And that's not safe."

"Addie, please. She ain't into voodoo, and even if she is, I'm not having this baby. No way."

"And what about Marchanette?" Addie asked. A family friend,

Marchanette, had visited Miss Cane years ago for the same issue. Marchanette went home that evening to rest, and when she woke up, she was bleeding uncontrollably. The doctors said it was too late to save her when she arrived at the hospital.

"Odester, I disagree with what you are planning, but if you insist on doing it, at least do it right."

"What does that mean?" Odester leaned forward.

"Go to a real doctor."

"A real doctor? No way. I saw a *Geraldo Rivera* episode about this. I'm not going to some clinic so those protestors can yell at me. Plus, I heard about that new law they tryin' to pass. I ain't going to jail over no abortion. I'll take my chances with Miss Cane."

"Then I'll ask Marcel. Several of his fraternity brothers are doctors. I'm sure he can refer you to someone who can help you."

Odester jumped up. "Really? Addie, thank you! I knew I could count on you."

Addie pursed her lips. "I am not making any promises. I said I'd ask. Dette, did you pray about this?"

"Pray about whether or not to keep my brother-in-law's baby? Um, no."

"Odester Harriet Chavis! You carrying Lenny's baby?"

Odester hiked her purse across her shoulder. "Everybody isn't as perfect as you, Adeline. Some of us make bad choices every once in a while."

Odester had tried to make better decisions but kept getting caught up. Lenny wasn't her ideal man. She wouldn't have given him the time of day if she were sober that night.

"This is not about being perfect, and you know it." Addie pointed a finger.

"Then what is it about? Me deciding to work at Dillard's instead of going to college? Me having a baby with no husband? Or me drinking too much? Because I know y'all talk about all of it."

Addie opened her mouth.

"Cat gotcha tongue?"

"I just want the best for you and Arelia. None of us judge you. We love you."

"The best according to whom, Addie? You?"

Addie's life of privilege, sorority meetings, and board memberships meant nothing to Odester, who lived paycheck to paycheck, juggling her job at Wendy's and with housecleaning gigs. She spent the bulk of her earnings on bills and the rest at the gambling shack. Pain pills offered temporary relief, and alcohol made up for the rest. Addie provided Manon with the best academic and social opportunities, while Odester recently insisted that Arelia contributed to the household bills.

"To you, of course." Addie's eyes searched the ceiling. "Dette, is everything okay with you?" She looked at her sister's thinning frame and unkempt hair. Odester used to be particular about her appearance. There was a time when she'd never leave the house with her hair uncombed.

"I'm fine." Odester waved her hand. "Nothing I can't handle."

"And Bumpie? What are you going to do?"

"Well, I just told you his brother got me pregnant, if that's any indication of what's next for us."

Addie took a long breath. "Good Lord, Dette. You sure you're okay?" She tried to catch Odester's eyes, which wandered everywhere except for Addie's.

"I'm fine, Addie. And I'll be even better once I take care of this situation," Odester said.

"Okay," Addie sighed. "I'll call you after I talk to Marcel."

Odester hugged Addie and left, leaving the chitterlings behind.

"Where you been?" Bumpie asked without looking up from the television. His coarse beard covered the dimples Odester used to love so much. He was slouched on the leather chair Addie had given them, holding a Michelob Light in one hand while the other hand was shoved down his jeans. The television was loud enough that Odester could pretend not to hear him.

Odester and Bumpie lived in Easy Town, the place where people lost family members in plain sight, and the area flooded faster than any other part of the city. Boarded-up homes stood idly next to fully inhabited homes. The majority of the community were renters, and despite the strategically placed Neighborhood Watch signs, property crimes were common.

She walked into the kitchen and swore under her breath. She'd cleaned the kitchen before she left. How had one person accumulated so many dishes in a few hours? She washed the dishes with lukewarm water, making a mental note to add plumbing to the fix-it list for the landlord, who still hadn't replaced the screen door or the second porch step. Odester didn't want to press the issue because repairs meant her rent would slowly inch up like the hairy worms that used to terrorize her as a child. Her jobs covered half of the rent, but Bumpie couldn't always come up with his half. She survived off payday loans and small bonuses from the lady she cleaned for. Last week, she gave Odester an extra seventy-five dollars for staying late while she entertained guests.

Odester popped a pill into her mouth. She'd run out of pain pills for her sprained ankle, and she used the ones Arelia had been prescribed when she had her wisdom tooth pulled. Luckily, Arelia didn't take pain pills, so she didn't notice. But after those were finished, Miss Audrey from next door had sold her a few of her pills.

"You ain't talking to me?" Bumpie looked at Odester, who was now wiping the kitchen counter.

"I'm talking to you. Just don't have much to say." She waited for the calm that the pill gave her.

"You haven't had much to say to me lately. Why is that?" Bumpie removed his hand from his pants and sat on the edge of the chair.

She wasn't in the mood for an argument. Fortunately, Bumpie picked his battles with Odester when Arelia wasn't around, which was probably why Arelia seemed to favor Bumpie over Odester.

"Bumpie, don't start today. I'm not in the mood." Odester walked toward her bedroom, but Bumpie hopped up and blocked it. Odester didn't know he could still move that fast.

"You ain't in the mood for what? To talk to your man?"

"What is wrong with you now? Do you need me to get you more beer? I cooked before I left, and the kitchen is clean. Just get out my face, Bumpie."

He moved so close she could almost taste the beer he'd been drinking since this morning. "I don't need nothing from you," he said, leaving spittle on Odester's face.

Odester turned away, but Bumpie grabbed her chin and yanked her face back so she could look at him.

"I got the worst Chavis sister. You ain't half as pretty as your sisters. The one who runs to the church three or four times a week is the prettiest thing I have ever seen. That other one is fine, but she uppity. And then you, dark brown with them alien eyes and funny-looking lips. You didn't even go to college. Everything you have you got from your sisters. Even this furniture. And you have the nerve to ask me what I need from you? I don't need shit from you." He tossed his beer can to the side, and the liquid spread across the carpet. Bumpie walked out of the house, slamming the door behind him.

After cleaning the carpet, Odester grabbed a beer from the refrigerator and took another pill.

CHAPTER 18

Emersyn 2019

"Y'all get on in here!" Nadesna yelped and threw her arms in the air. She smelled like mothballs and cucumber shower gel. Cool air trailed behind her. She looked the same on Devanie's Instagram, except Emersyn imagined she had a much deeper voice.

"Hi, Nadesna." Devanie hugged her.

"Hey, baby." She held out her cheek for Devanie to kiss, then popped her hand over her mouth. Tears formed at the rims of her eyes, and she wrapped Emersyn in her arms. As she embraced Nadesna, Emersyn stared at the black-and-white photo on the wall of three young women in white dresses and gloves.

"You look so much like my mama." Nadesna held Emersyn tighter. "And your mama, too, of course. She was always so beautiful. And smart too. We Chavis women are smart." Nadesna pulled back from Emersyn and straightened her collar, as if she needed to gather herself from too much emotion.

"Nice to meet you." Emersyn blushed. She recalled the years she longed for a day like this, to be among family in the home where they all gathered. It felt surreal, like a still breeze gently blowing time back into place.

Nadesna was the family matriarch. She wasn't the oldest Chavis sister, but she'd been holding family gatherings after Earline passed away. She admitted that she wasn't the best cook, but she was the only one with enough patience to tolerate the entire family in her home all at once. Before she knew it, she was hosting birthday parties, baby showers, and holidays for the family.

"So, your mama is my niece," Nadesna told Emersyn. "My sisters were in college by the time I was born, so I grew up with Phillis, Manon, and Arelia. Always been closer to them than my own sisters. Shame, ain't it?"

Nadesna's short hair made her large brown eyes look more prominent. She looked comfortable in a linen tank dress and bare feet. She led Emersyn through the house, which was crammed with photos, houseplants, and family. A wood-burning fireplace was used as decoration for brass fireplace tools. A framed photo of white Jesus hung over the fireplace, and a massive cross hung over the doorway. Interesting how much religion was in this one room; Emersyn had only been to church a few times in her life.

They entered the dining room where people were sitting around a table. Emersyn held her breath. Here they were, a roomful of people who shared her DNA. She searched their faces for resemblances, a soul connection or anything that felt familiar. She tried to identify people from Devanie's Instagram. The dining room table was formally decorated with chargers, champagne flutes, and linen napkins.

"This here is ya family." Nadesna held out her arms as if presenting the family to Emersyn. "That's cousin Doosie with the buckteeth." She pointed to a man with a bald spot in his afro. "And those are his two boys playing that darn video game."

Nadesna walked over to a demure woman with dark, sparkling eyes. "This here is my dearest friend, Womelda." Womelda stopped rocking long enough to shake Emersyn's hand. "Melda and me been friends forever. And that's our cousin Detra over there by the TV." Nadesna nodded to a woman with familiar eyes rocking in a chair. "Don't mind her for not speaking. Her mama took those red pills and drank Cisco the entire time she was pregnant. Now the poor thing is like a four-year-old. Gotta watch her all the time."

Nadesna led Emersyn to the next room. "That's our cousin Pat." She pointed to a round woman wearing a Saints cap with her arm draped on a man's lap. "And that there is her new boyfriend, Greg."

"Fred!" Pat corrected.

"Fred, Greg . . . I can't remember," Nadesna whispered as she led Emersyn away. "She was over here last week with her fiancé." Nadesna used air quotes. "You could have sold me for two cents when she walked in with this one today. I don't try to keep up no more."

As they walked down the hallway, Emersyn slowed to look at more black-and-white photos on the wall. Who were these people? She was just about to ask when a buzzing sound distracted her.

"And that's Jon-Jon," Nadesna said as a small boy zoomed past them in the hallway. "He doesn't listen to instructions, I'll tell you that now. So, don't be offended if he ignores you."

Nadesna picked up a toy car from the floor, then led Emersyn to the kitchen, where people milled in and out, helping themselves to food. The kitchen smelled like cake mix, pots were half-covered on the stove, and the counter was filled with serving dishes, paper plates, and plastic utensils. At the small table near the door, three men played dominoes.

"Now, this here is your uncle Buster." Nadesna introduced a man with suspicious eyes and a deep scar on his cheek. "He crazy as the ace of spades, but that's my heart right there."

Buster's belly rested in his lap, and he methodically tapped his sneaker on the floor. Emersyn smiled at him. So, this was the infamous Buster who told everyone that Emersyn worked for the CIA. Her heart raced with each introduction. She didn't know

these people, but she belonged to them. They belonged to her.
They were family.

"You here on a covert operation, ain't ya?" Buster lowered his
chin and looked at Emersyn. A tuft of white hair threatened his
right eye. He looked like Colonel Sanders in a Pelicans cap.

"Hush with all that crazy talk." Nadesna popped Buster on the
back of the head.

"It ain't crazy talk," Buster said. "I know you can't tell nobody."
He held two fingers to his eyes. "Just know that I know."

"Boy, hush," Nadesna admonished. "I told you this girl works
for the government!"

"The CIA *is* the government!" Buster argued. "I done already
told you that. And all the agents are part of the Illuminati." He
tapped his shoe against the floor and nodded knowingly. "Whatchu
do to get in? Sell a vital organ? Sacrifice your firstborn? You can
tell me. You amongst family."

"Ignore him, Emersyn," Nadesna said. "You ready to eat?"

Emersyn nodded as she stared at the food that was lined up
on the counter. There were numerous serving dishes filled with
sweet potato casserole, macaroni and cheese, black-eyed peas,
potato salad, cucumber salad, and, of course, a big pot of gumbo
was simmering on the stove. The paper plates and bowls were
stacked at the edge of the counter with utensils and napkins. All
the food that most people loved.

"Something wrong? Now, my food ain't California fancy, but
I'm good in the kitchen."

"Oh, no!" Emersyn bit the inside of her cheek. "Not at all. I
have no issue."

"Good, then grab ya plate."

"Emersyn is vegetarian," Devanie announced out of nowhere.
She disappeared during the house tour but showed up just in time
to embarrass her.

The room was momentarily silent.

"Aw, hell. Here we go." Buster threw his hands in the air and broke the silence. "Bringing all that California shit down here. Now, this the kind of stuff I'm talking about. So, do this mean you like men *and* women? Are you she/her, him/he, or them/they?"

Emersyn stared open-mouthed. She was mortified. The last thing she wanted to do was offend anybody. She had just met her family and now she felt like an outcast. Darn Devanie.

"I . . . uh . . ." Emersyn stammered.

"Didn't thank I knew 'bout that, huh?" Buster leaned back in his chair. "Oh yeah, Buster know all about the alphabet community and the pronouns. I ain't no bigot. I watch *Ellen*. The only problem is, I didn't think the CIA allowed that kinda confusion among the ranks."

"Buster! You stop that crazy talk!" Nadesna exclaimed. "I done told you already!"

"She the one who came in here with them California labels," Buster huffed. "Y'all really a state of crazies, and y'all got more money than most countries. Might as well make it official and separate from the rest of us."

"Buster, just be quiet." Nadesna turned her attention back to Emersyn. "You can have some of that cornbread. I made some greens—just a little salt pork in there that won't hurt your vegetarian diet. Get you some of that mac and cheese and some of that sweet potato casserole. Nadesna got you, baby. You ain't got to eat no meat if you don't want to. I need to start eating healthier myself." She patted her hand across her belly.

Emersyn and Devanie exchanged looks.

"Where ya mama at?" Buster asked Emersyn.

Nadesna popped Buster on the back of the head again.

This time, Buster sat up. "Nadesna, you got one more time to pop me in my head."

"She couldn't make it," Emersyn said quickly. Phillis was always so coy about her family. Was there a mutual distance? She didn't know how much to say.

"Stop asking so many questions and just greet my great-niece," Nadesna warned.

"I'm trying to figure out what's going on. Phillis ain't been here since this girl was a baby. Ain't nobody wondering why?"

"Buster, why don't you just hush up?" Nadesna raised her voice. "For the love of sweet Jesus."

Emersyn shifted her eyes, but no one was paying attention to Buster except her and Nadesna. The rest resumed eating or making up plates. Thank goodness.

Devanie led Emersyn to the backyard, and they sat on two chairs near Nadesna's storage shed.

"Welcome to the family, girl." Devanie grinned when she and Emersyn were safely out of hearing distance from the rest. Nadesna and Buster were still arguing in the kitchen. "Uncle Buster is harmless if you don't mind raging conspiracy theorists."

"It's cool." Emersyn looked back toward the kitchen. "Guess I have a lot to learn."

"The first thing you probably learned is that you can be vegetarian and eat salt pork." Devanie doubled over with laughter.

Emersyn grinned. "Don't tease Nadesna. She means well. And I do eat fish."

"I know, girl. Let's find you some food to eat so you don't starve to death!"

A few hours later, without learning how to play Spades and trying to convince Buster that she wasn't part of the Illuminati, Emersyn called it an evening. When she got back to her hotel, she plopped on the sofa and called Armand Gray.

"Hello, Mr. Gray."

"Young lady, please call me Armand."

Emersyn cleared her throat. "Let's make a deal. I will stop calling you Mr. Gray if you stop calling me 'young lady.'"

"Ah," he said. "Deal."

"So, Armand, I need to chat with your wife."

"I told you speaking with her isn't necessary. She isn't a part of this campaign and won't make any statements. Let's leave her out of it."

If it were that easy, Emersyn wouldn't be here. She had to get a signed affidavit from Mrs. Gray. It shouldn't be a big deal if the two were as amicable as Armand claimed. Armand wasn't convincing.

"What are you hiding?" Emersyn said. She wasn't usually so blunt, at least not so early in a client relationship, but Armand was being evasive, which meant Emersyn would have to work longer and harder, and it would take time away from her finding Otis. She'd checked into three different leads and wasn't any closer to finding her father. After meeting her family, Emersyn was convinced that Phillis was hiding something. She was nervous about meeting everyone, but she actually liked them and wanted to get to know them, which made her want to find her father even more. What if Phillis was wrong about him too?

"My marriage isn't perfect, okay?"

"Most aren't," Emersyn said.

"Let me finish," Armand said. "My marriage wasn't perfect, and my wife may not have the most favorable opinion of me. I don't want her tainting my name."

"Well, that's why you hired me. Let me see what she has to say, and if she says anything potentially 'tainting,' I'll fix it. But like I said, we need to get these things out now, not later."

"I don't agree."

"I know. But unless you have a more compelling reason for me not to speak to her, I'll be reaching out to her very soon."

CHAPTER 19

Manon 2019

Miss Genessa's husband, Glenn, was a slight man with leathery skin and weary eyes. His oversized trousers were held up by suspenders, and his house slippers looked like they'd survived three presidential administrations. Glenn tilted forward when he walked, his slippers sweeping the floor like a push broom. Manon peeped around the house as she followed him. She'd only been here twice before. Their home was like a museum. Trinkets, photos, dolls, and antiques. Vaulted ceilings. Victorian-era paintings. Piles of classic literature occupied every available corner, and there was no indication that they'd ever owned a vacuum.

The sweeping of Glenn's slippers stopped. "In there," he said.

"Thank you." Manon peeked her head into the bedroom where Miss Genessa was hidden under a large rouge-colored duvet. Her long, white hair was separated into two French braids that lay at her sides. She perked up when she saw Manon.

"Come on in." She waved a feeble hand and pointed to a chair that had newspapers piled up.

Miss Genessa was only in the hospital overnight, but it was different to see the sassy woman with trembling hands. "You moving around a lot better, I see," she said. "But you still ain't happy."

"I'm fine, Miss Genessa," Manon said as she removed newspapers and sat down.

"Gal, don't come to my house lying to me." She frowned. "You ain't happy. I know it. That ain't nothing to be ashamed of. You a good wife and a good person. And don't you let nobody tell you no different. These people round here always talking 'bout other folks' business. If I gave an ounce of shit, I'd be sick by now. Don't let these gossips get to you."

Miss Genessa's clairvoyance would earn her a pretty penny if she'd put it on the market. Manon wasn't as concerned about the neighbors as she used to be. They gossiped about the car accident or how Manon never left the house anymore. She heard as much from Celeste. But it bothered Manon to hear that the neighbors were gossiping about Tate being gone.

"I just hate my business being out in the street. It's embarrassing."

"If anybody should be ashamed, it's that friend of yours." Miss Genessa bumped her gums together. She never had kind words for Gwen. Years ago, Gwen's mom, Holly, had rented a house to Miss Genessa and Glenn. Miss Genessa said Holly was a slumlord and would never forgive her. The disdain was passed down to Gwen as well.

Manon knew exactly who she was talking about but pretended she didn't. "What friend?"

"You know who I'm talking about. That blonde gal. The one who messed around on a *good* man." Miss Genessa broke into a fit of coughs. "He was a little goofy looking, but he was good. Now, she follows him and his new wife around town like a lost puppy. I heard the new wife is pretty too. And Black, dark chocolate. Good for him."

"And how did you know that?" Manon smirked. Gwen and Tom's marriage was nobody's business yet everybody's conversation.

"I knows it all, baby. I knows it all." Miss Genessa's lips collapsed into her mouth. "Just like I knew you was special the first time I met you. Standing on that front porch lookin' like an angel. Just as pretty as you wanna be. And you speak so grandly, too, just like the white women I used to work for." She sighed. "You know Glenn is in love with you, right? That old geezer. I told him the only chance he'll ever have with you is on the other side of heaven, and even then, he got some serious competition." Miss Genessa's throaty chuckle filled the air.

"Thank you." Manon squeezed Miss Genessa's hand.

"I also knew you didn't take that Dupree boy." Miss Genessa fixed her gaze.

Manon swallowed the lump in her throat. Any mention of Leonard always made her stomach tighten.

"Emily told me you stopped by," Manon deflected. It wasn't the first time Miss Genessa tried to bait Manon into talking about Leonard, and it wouldn't be the last. But Manon wasn't ready to discuss Leonard. She always said that she never intended to keep Leonard, but sometimes even she struggled to understand why she kept him for so long that day. And the way she was treated afterward was something she never wanted to relive. It took her years to rebuild her reputation in the community.

"Oh yeah?" Miss Genessa raised her sparse gray eyebrows.

"Said you accused her little one of stepping in your rose garden."

"I didn't *accuse* him of nothin'!" Miss Genessa's spat. "I stated a fact." She pursed her bottom lip in earnest. "Those kids are terrible. She don't teach 'em no manners. Don't no kids call me by my first name. I'm grown!" She turned her head in disgust. "Emily quit her job to stay home for what? To wear them skin-tight pants and be in everybody's business? Women who stay home 'posed to raise their children properly. Any woman who stay home all day and rears disrespectful kids fails as a wife and mother. That's why some people ain't meant to have children."

Manon winced.

"Not you." Miss Genessa was eerie that way, threading thoughts out of Manon's head, knowing her feelings without being told, predicting the demise of her marriage, sensing her sensitivity about being barren. As if she were privy to the countless meetings with the fertility specialist. "God got different plans for you, baby. Something beyond being a mama. I promise you. Besides, that husband of yours wasn't ready. He still ain't."

Miss Genessa had her doubts about Tate from the beginning. The first time she gave Manon a cooking lesson, she said. "Now, I'mma show you how to make this here jambalaya 'cause you need to know, but cooking ain't the way to your husband's heart. That man is drawn to something else, something in the distance." Back then, Manon was a starry-eyed bride and paid little attention to Miss Genessa's predilection.

The sun circled the earth three times, *A Different World* was renewed for another season, and the internet was finally considered a thing before Manon had mastered Miss Genessa's jambalaya. And while her macaroni and cheese and etouffee dishes were forces to be reckoned with, Miss Genessa's words about Tate rested with Manon more than she cared to admit.

He's drawn to something in the distance.

Manon's growing discontent with her emotional health was starting to take a toll. She avoided people who were once integral to her life and avoided necessary conversations. She became a hermit—resigned from boards, allowed relationships to fade, and stopped attending events. She allowed grief and resentment to consume her. The ghosts from her past were haunting her. She was frozen, like that night when she was a young girl at the summer camp. She'd buried that secret for years, but now it grasped at her like Leonard used to when he held her finger. Manon was also upset that she didn't spend more time with her father before he died. She had been so busy with auxiliary meetings, fundraising, and helping everyone else that she had neglected the parent she loved the most. And, on top of it all, her picture-perfect marriage was in shambles.

"You listen to me." Miss Genessa pulled Manon's face toward hers. "This gone work out for you. I promise. I can't tell you when, but it will."

"Miss Genessa, that's very kind of you."

Miss Genessa didn't know the secret that ate Manon alive, how Manon had betrayed Phillis. No one did.

CHAPTER 20

Odester 1993

O dester lifted her head but flopped it back down on the couch. Her shirt was half off, and one of her socks was at the end of the sofa. Cigarette butts overfilled the ashtray, and cans were strewn across the living room table and on the floor next to the couch. Her addiction was taking over everything she loved, yet she couldn't control it.

Odester sat up and waited for the room to stop spinning. She recalled her doctor's appointment a few months ago. She felt empty as she lay on the operating table with her legs spread apart, the vacuum sound filling the room. A nurse had held Odester's hand. "S'gone be all right," the nurse said. Odester reminded herself over and over again that she couldn't take care of another baby, but it didn't stop the aching feeling in her heart. "Make sure you rest," the doctor told her. "Don't lift anything over five pounds, and if you start to bleed heavily or get clots, see a doctor immediately."

Something special was happening today, but she couldn't remember what. Was someone getting married? She'd partied at Peggy's house the night before. Peggy was a dark-skinned woman with a missing front tooth who used to work at the bank with Odester before they were both fired. Peggy's fish fry parties were regular on Odester's calendar. The adults partied after Peggy's three children were asleep. They nibbled on salami and cheese, drank whiskey, and smoked crack. One of the kids peeked into the living room on a fake potty run. "Get the hell back in that room!" Peggy had yelled when she caught her daughter lingering.

Early morning humidity seeped through the house like a leaky sauna. Odester pulled her shirt over her shoulder, leaned her elbows on her knees, and dug through the ashtray for a smokable cigarette butt. The tattered wooden table was one of the few pieces of furniture Odester didn't sell. Odester's addiction soared over the years. She and Bumpie's drug of choice was barbiturates mixed with alcohol. Now, Odester only took pills when she couldn't get crack. Bumpie moved out three months ago, and the estranged couple tried to be cordial for the sake of Arelia. The first time he came to pick up his things, Odester noticed he looked rested. The next time she saw him, he told her that he'd changed and "accepted Christ as his personal savior." He had no interest in alcohol or partying. He got a job at the gas station and said he planned to get his teeth fixed with his new health benefits.

Each day, Odester became better at failing—her relationships, herself, and her daughter. Efforts to stay sober ended in relapse, and the need to get high was more vital than ever. She still dreamed of her father every night.

She peeled herself off the couch, straightened her clothes, and stumbled to the kitchen. She raked empty bottles from the countertop to the garbage can. She tried to clear her head, but it was like a duck trying to mate with floating debris. The stench of loneliness and addiction swarmed the room, and Odester shook her head as if she were telling herself no. Daddy would understand her. He'd know what to say and how to fix things. She picked up the house phone and quickly hung it up. Daddy was gone. And even if he wasn't, the phone company disconnected the houseline three days ago. Her sisters called her often, leaving messages that they were concerned, but she never called them back.

She splashed water on her face and slipped into rubber flip-flops, then stepped outside for her first trip of the day. The kids across the street played ball in the lot of a vacant house, and their mother yelled for them to come back to their yard. The days when Odester and her sisters hung out until the streetlights came on and walked to the corner store for pig lips and pickles were long gone. These days, kids now had to worry about stray bullets and gang violence. Walking home from school could be a test of survival in Odester's neighborhood. Poverty morphed the neighborhood from hopeful to hopelessness. Families led by single moms or grandmothers raising their grandchildren was common. Underemployment was the norm, and the plight was enough that people who could afford to move had left in droves. To wake up each day and walk through festering despair was depressing. The schools were failing, and the frustrated teachers were underpaid. Two days ago, Odester ditched another treatment program and returned to the litter-laden streets to be among those who wanted to forget their past or numb their pain. She could bury the rumors of being called fast when she was the victim. She gave in to the beast of hopelessness that didn't rest. These days, she woke up to feed a habit so repulsive that she would forget who she was or what she once wanted to become.

Odester paced outside of the liquor store. Her dealer was twenty minutes late and threw off her plans to get high. Then, from around the corner, Hot Rod's car pulled up and she rushed over.

"Hold up." Hot Rod held up his hand, flashing a huge diamond ring on his pinkie finger. "Don't run up to my car like that." He looked around. "You look suspicious."

Odester handed him a handful of crumpled bills, and he gave her a cellophane baggie.

Back at home, she smoked the first rock. Somehow, she'd remembered that she had to do something today. What was it?

Her cheeks sank beneath sallow eyes, and her ashen skin changed her complexion. Her pants and belt were too big, and she hadn't washed her hair in weeks. The house smelled of stale smoke and garbage. She searched the ashtray for another cigarette butt when she saw the graduation announcement.

Shit.

Odester arrived at Opelousas Community College just as Arelia walked across the stage. After struggling in school, just like Odester, Arelia had managed to get her act together and went on to earn her two-year associate degree with plans to transfer to a four-year college. Addie and Marcel had offered to help pay for Arelia to attend a university right after high school, but Arelia struggled with turning in assignments and had to attend summer school in order to graduate. She was a year older than Manon and Phillis but a few years behind them academically. She seemed to be on the right track now.

Odester looked across the auditorium and saw Addie, Clotee, and the rest of the family cheering. Bumpie and his new girlfriend, Esther, were there as well. Odester didn't have time to shower and instead had thrown on a skirt and white button-down shirt. She didn't notice the stain on the front of the shirt until after rushing out of the house. She stood off to the side, fidgeting through another hour of names before the ceremony was over.

The field outside of the auditorium was filled with proud families and enthusiastic graduates who were smiling and posing for photos. Her family was surrounding Arelia, taking photos and smiling with pride. Bumpie looked happy, and Esther looked polished, with her slick ponytail and ruby-red lips. She held a bouquet of flowers, and Odester cursed at herself for forgetting. After today, she promised she was going to clean up and be a good mom to Arelia. Odester wasn't raised to give up. She could make something of her life and still have a decent life. This didn't have to be her fate.

She approached the group slowly. She knew Addie and Clotee were mad by their expressions. She wasn't in the mood for them to judge her today—not in front of Arelia or Esther.

"Glad you could make it, Dette," Clotee whispered.

Arelia looked over at Odester and her eyes widened. She was about to say something when Addie pulled her into a hug.

"Congratulations, Arelia." Addie handed her an envelope.

"Thank you, Auntie!" Arelia looked beautiful in her cap and gown. Odester was proud but couldn't find the words to say it.

"You earned it," Addie said.

Arelia stood amid the family as they snapped pictures and sang her well-deserved praises. She didn't always have Bumpie and Odester's support, but she did well enough in school despite the hard days.

No one dared to look Odester in the eye, as if her addiction were contagious.

Bumpie also handed Arelia an envelope. "I love you, baby girl," he said. "I'm proud of you."

"Thank you, Daddy," Arelia beamed.

"Let me get a photo of you two," Esther offered.

Odester and Bumpie didn't give Arelia many fond memories growing up, and suddenly, the weight of guilt felt suffocating. Odester bit back tears as she stared at her daughter's smiling face.

Most days, she and Bumpie would come home from work and lock themselves in their bedroom, leaving Arelia to fend for herself. Sometimes, Arelia would spend the night at Nadesna's house, but most often she locked herself in her room, waiting for her parents to emerge. The first time their electricity was turned off, Bumpie told young Arelia, "Something's wrong

down at the electric company, but they gone get it fixed soon."
Odester and Bumpie fought about who was supposed to pay the
bill, just like they fought over who was supposed to buy the food.
Then they fought over who started the fight in the first place.
With each passing year, Arelia's relationship with her parents
deteriorated.

"I have to take pictures with friends," Arelia announced
excitedly. "Be right back!"

"Can't believe she graduated college," Bumpie said. He was
awkward around Odester's family now that he had Esther on his
arm. But Addie and Clotee welcomed Esther—she wasn't the cause
of Bumpie and Odester's marital problems. More than anything,
they seemed to be happy that Bumpie was stable for Arelia. The
family knew Odester struggled with dependency, but fortunately
for Odester, Arelia kept the excruciating details to herself—the
strange overnight guests, Odester holing up in her room for hours,
the utilities being turned off repeatedly, and the strange man who
slept on the couch.

"We are going to Mama's house after we leave here," Clotee
said. "You and Esther should come."

Odester shifted her feet. Not only did she have to deal with
Bumpie, but skinny-ankled Esther too?

"We will," Bumpie said after getting Esther's approval. "That
would be nice."

"Good," Clotee smiled. "We'll see you at Mama's then? Around
three?"

"See you then." Bumpie and Esther disappeared into the
crowd.

"Where's Mama?" Odester asked. Anger was brewing with
every second that her family ignored her.

Addie and Clotee exchanged looks.

"Buster took Mama back to the house," Clotee said quietly. "Too hot out here for her."

"Phillis and Manon didn't come?" Odester frowned. "I thought I saw them sitting with y'all in the auditorium."

Addie and Clotee exchanged looks again.

"They were here. Everybody was here. On time," Addie pursed her lips. "Manon and Phillis just left to pick up the cake for Arelia. Everybody else gone meet us at the house."

"Why y'all lookin' at me like that?" Odester looked from one disapproving sister's face to the other.

"Like what?" Clotee said.

"Like I'm a piece of shit. It's my daughter graduating, not y'all."

"Dette, lower your voice," Clotee admonished. "This is Arelia's day. It's not about you this time, okay?"

"Right," Addie said in a hushed tone. "And what have you done in preparation for your daughter's graduation day, Odester?"

"Don't come at me like that, Addie." Odester pointed in her sister's face. "I'm grieving my father."

"You're not the only one who misses Daddy, Odester." Addie tossed her handbag over her shoulder. "You're just the only one who uses it as an excuse to fuck up." She turned to Clotee and said, "I'll see you at the house. I'm not sticking around for a circus."

"Excuse me?" Odester called after her sister. "Who do you think you are to judge me? Fuck you, Adeline!"

"No," Addie said, stepping inches from Odester's face. "Fuck you," she whispered.

"Odester!" Clotee grabbed her sister's arm. "Addie! Y'all cut this out right now. Addie took Arelia to get her graduation dress and she paid for everything. Why are y'all doing this? Arelia is right over there. Don't let her see this."

"I'm out," Addie walked off.

Tears formed in Odester's eyes. "I'm sick of it, Tee. Everybody acting like I'm not trying. I'm trying. You think I woke up and decided to just mess up my life with drugs?"

"Odester, pull yourself together. Your daughter just graduated. Please. Don't let her see you like this. And why would you come here with your shirt all dirty like that?" Clotee said in a calm tone.

Odester looked down as if she had just realized where she was, then shook her arm free from her sister. "I see Bumpie brought his whore." Odester laughed.

"She's not a whore, Dette, and you know it." Clotee failed at smiling.

"Yes, she is!" Odester laughed again.

"Girl, you something else. Let's go find your baby and take some pictures so we can get to Mama's house."

"Fine." Odester followed her sister across campus.

CHAPTER 21
Emersyn 2019

Emersyn placed two lemon slices in a ceramic teacup and curled up on the small couch in her hotel room. After spending the day at Nadesna's house, she was overcome with emotion but also refueled with questions that Phillis never answered. Her family didn't seem like the people Phillis described over the years. They were kind, funny, and she was still trying to figure out why Buster thought she worked for the CIA. She called Phillis.

"Hi," Phillis said from the other end.

Emersyn bit her lip and considered how to approach her mom. Devanie and Buster had asked why Phillis didn't come. Why hadn't Phillis returned in so long?

"Hi," Emersyn said easily. Phillis sounded weak from her last treatment, and Emersyn would tread lightly, but she needed answers. And she needed them now.

"What's wrong?"

"Nothing," Emersyn said unconvincingly. "How are you feeling?"

"I'm fine. A little tired, but fine." Phillis sighed. "Now tell me what's wrong. I know my child, and I know when something is wrong."

"I saw Nadesna today."

"Interesting," Phillis said.

"Ma, I need you to tell me why you left here to go all the way to California."

"Emersyn, you don't give up, do you?"

"Nope. My mama taught me to never quit."

"Fine," Phillis said with a feeble chuckle.

Folks didn't think much about Phillis Chavis's departure from Opelousas over a decade ago. Gen X'ers often migrated to other parts of the country, searching for opportunity, love, or a rational climate. Travis Manning moved to Houston to be closer to his bride's family; William Duggan relocated to Atlanta to work for an airline; and Bessie Smith took her chances at acting in Los Angeles. In 1993, the story was that Phillis moved across the country to attend graduate school at Berkeley. In fact, Phillis moved to California to avoid the shame of being pregnant and single.

Phillis landed in Oakland, California, with two suitcases and twenty-five hundred dollars in scholarship money. She was also pregnant. She never thought she'd have a baby out of wedlock, and even more, she never thought she'd do it alone. She tried not to dwell on what she had left behind in Opelousas and focused on her future in the Bay Area. Her new landlord, Johnnie Pearl Hildebrandt, was shocked to learn that Phillis was from Opelousas.

"Phillis was my great-grandmother's name, dear," Mrs. Hildebrandt said. Her hearing aids didn't work well. Mrs. Hildebrandt boded her time quilting, talking to her cat, and renting the extra rooms to college students.

Phillis settled into her new home, a second-floor bedroom that looked out to the busy street. She needed more space and time to figure out what she was going to do. When she'd first received the letter of acceptance to graduate school, leaving Louisiana and moving to California felt like a pipedream. Now, it was her only option. She had only planned to stay at Mrs. Hildebrandt's until she could earn enough money to get her own place. Phillis started graduate school and landed a part-time job as a personal finance manager at Great Western Bank. Her days were long, and she slept her evenings away.

During her second trimester, Phillis earned enough money to move into a one-bedroom apartment near Lake Merritt. She liked the Bay Area, albeit lonely. She loved the weather and quickly learned her way around. She purchased a crib, a wicker living room set, and she bought a car. When she talked to her mother on the phone, she kept her voice light. "I love it here!" she'd exclaim. "The California sunshine really agrees with me." Truth be told, she was scared and alone. All she knew was that a baby was growing in her womb, and she would do whatever it took to have this baby and love it unconditionally.

Phillis didn't have grand expectations for the Lamaze class for single moms that she signed up for. More than anything, she joined to occupy the time. Each evening after work, she showed up in yoga pants and breathed her way to a better experience in the delivery room. The rail-thin instructor stood before class every week with her bouncy ponytail and gave the participants insight on what to expect during delivery. *You will need to breathe, okay? Don't forget what we learned. These techniques will be essential in the delivery room.* Phillis hardly paid attention, mainly focusing on the dark-haired chatterbox who sat next to her in class.

One day, the dark-haired woman said to Phillis, "I tell my husband I need the class, but I don't. I just need to get out of that house and away from my boys!"

Phillis smiled politely. "I understand."

"I really don't," the woman chuckled.

Phillis followed the stretches and nodded.

"Are you from Oakland?"

"No." Phillis leaned over and placed her hands straight in front of her.

After class, Phillis grabbed her bag and rushed out before the woman could catch up. For the next few weeks, the pint-sized woman sat next to Phillis.

"I'm not single," the woman confided one day. "Men in my culture don't do things like this." The woman pointed to her belly.

"What?" Phillis asked. "They aren't involved in their wife's pregnancy?"

The woman feigned shock, then burst into laughter. "I like you!" she roared. "You have a smart mouth. Just like me. Also, do I detect an accent?"

"My family is from Louisiana."

"Ah, Louisiana. You must be good people then." She extended a hand. "I'm Waris. Waris Khan."

"Phillis Chavis."

Waris was born in Lebanon and attended college in London. She didn't want to marry young like most women in her family. She dreamed of a career and an office and lots of dating. She met Junaid during her junior year of college. Junaid was a strait-laced Muslim with strict tenants and traditional parents. He had a hard time dating Waris and wanted to marry her immediately. "I made him wait," Waris told Phillis. "And he wouldn't touch me. Can you believe that?" After graduation, they wed and moved to the States, where they both dreamed of living. Junaid worked in IT for IBM, while Waris flexed her talents in social work. Once Waris became pregnant, she stopped working and had been home with the kids ever since.

Phillis shared her story of her and Otis making plans to be together forever, and how he reneged because he was seeing somebody else. She also talked about her master's program and shared bits about her family back home.

"Is your mom coming to help you with the baby?" Waris asked.

"I haven't really talked to my mom in a while."

Waris's eyes widened. "What sensible girl doesn't talk to her mom? You must fix that."

Waris was as pushy as she was loving, and Phillis took the woman's advice.

That evening, Phillis called her mom. She couldn't keep her pregnancy a secret any longer.

"How's school?" Clotee said from the other end of the line.

"It's going well," Phillis stammered.

"Are you sure? I don't hear from you much these says. You all right?"

"I'm good, Mama. Just busy."

"Well, don't get too busy for family. Everybody been askin' 'bout you. Thought you'd at least come back for Manon's wedding."

"I ... um ... some of the courses were harder than I expected, and I just found a job," Phillis said.

"You know I'll help you with whatever you need."

"I know, Mama."

"I'm happy you are doing well in school and all, but family is important. Family is everything." Clotee sniffled. "And with your daddy gone on to the good Lord, it's just me now. I miss you, baby. Are you coming to visit soon?"

"Mama, I'm pregnant," Phillis blurted out. There was no other way to share the news.

"Pregnant?" Clotee yelped. "You met a man that fast and got pregnant?"

"Mama, please," Phillis said.

"I know it's a new day and age, but a man should still take care of his responsibilities. Did he propose?"

"Mama, people don't get married because they are pregnant anymore," Phillis said.

"Well, they should," Clotee huffed. "You gone bring him down to meet me?"

"Yes, Mama."

Emersyn Irene Chavis arrived a month after Phillis told Clotee about her pregnancy. Clotee had flown out and stayed for two weeks while Phillis recovered from delivery. Clotee sang to her granddaughter, and Emersyn cooed in her grandmother's arms. Emersyn was a good baby, often sleeping through the night and hardly fretted. Her dark curls shrouded her face, and Phillis spent hours staring and cooing at her. Three weeks later, after Clotee was back in Opelousas, Waris gave birth to Amal Judah Khan.

"Auntie Waris was your first friend here?" Emersyn asked after Phillis finished her story. Emersyn had never heard the story of how Phillis and Waris met. She'd known Auntie Waris her entire life, and to know that she was once a stranger her mom met at a birthing class felt strange, especially after being around her Louisiana family earlier today. Waris and Phillis were such different people. Waris was a traditional homemaker who cooked dinner, cut the edges off her kid's sandwiches, and screamed expletives at her children, while Phillis let Emersyn camp out in her office when she had to work late nights and spelled out curse words until Emersyn reminded her she was a third-grade spelling bee champion. Both were great moms, just different.

But more importantly, Emersyn noticed the discrepancy in stories about Otis. Phillis had told Emersyn that Otis didn't want to be a father, but apparently, she'd told Waris that Otis was seeing somebody else. Then there was the issue of how Grandma Clotee thought Phillis had gotten pregnant by someone in Oakland. Something wasn't right. But Emersyn wouldn't berate her mom now. She still had some digging to do. She'd circle back with her mom to find out what was going on.

"Waris is like a sister to me," Phillis said.

"I see," Emersyn said. "But what about your cousins and aunts? Were they like sisters to you too?" Emersyn knew the answer because Nadesna told her how close Phillis was to her cousins. "Sister-cousins" was what Nadesna called them.

Phillis paused. "What's your point, Em?"

"I feel like you are leaving things out of the narrative, Ma. What happened before you left? Grandma Clotee has three sisters, and nieces and cousins, and you're acting like they don't exist. It doesn't make sense."

"Em, please. I'm not in the mood for this. I hope those people aren't filling your head with nonsense. That's exactly why I never took you around them. Too much drama."

"Actually, everyone is great. Nadesna had a cookout at her house yesterday, and I met a lot of the family."

"I see," Phillis said.

Emersyn felt bad. Phillis was still recovering from her latest chemo treatment, and she never meant to bombard her.

"I know you are resting, Ma. I just have one more question."

"What is it, Emersyn?" Phillis sounded exasperated.

"You told me my father was from Opelousas, but you told Grandma he was from Oakland. Which is it?"

Phillis was silent.

"I need to know," Emersyn implored. "Please, tell me."

"Emersyn," Phillis said in a tone Emersyn didn't recognize. "It's much deeper than you think. We should discuss this in person."

"I'm here, Ma, and I want to know. I'm not a child anymore. Tell me."

"Em, things aren't always as they seem. I don't want you to get hurt."

CHAPTER 22

Manon 1993

"Are you listening?" Manon lay back on the couch in Tate's small but well-lit studio apartment. She was in town for the weekend but came on Thursday instead of Friday so she could spend a night with Tate. It was a nice change from living in the college dorm at Louisiana State University even though her parents had paid extra tuition for her to have her own room. She explained the Pythagorean theorem again, but Tate still didn't understand.

"Yes, but my brain don't work like that." Tate paced the room.

"Why are you so upset? It's just a concept, you'll pick it up. You always do." Manon eyed him. He was agitated or spaced out. Earlier, she had to call his name three times before he responded. "What's going on with you?"

"It's just these tests."

"Nah, I know you. It's something else. What's going on?"

"You got all these expectations of me, and sometimes it makes me feel like I'm not good enough for you."

"Have," Manon stated.

"What?"

"Have," she repeated. "You said I *got* all these expectations."

"See what I mean? Then you want me reading all the papers . . . it's a lot. I just wanna get my degree and get a good job so I can take care of you. I'm a simple man."

"There's nothing wrong with using correct grammar. Daddy

always says if you stay ready, you don't have to get ready. You never know who you will meet, Tate, and if you aren't privy to current events, it will be a bad reflection."

"On who?" he challenged.

"Excuse me?" Manon sat forward and looked him in the eyes. He was enrolled in a community college, and she'd spent a lot of time helping him with his schoolwork and briefing him on what was going on with the world. She even bought him new outfits to wear, but all he did was complain.

"Never mind."

"No, speak your mind," she challenged.

Tate lowered his voice and eyes. "All I'm saying is that your father is different. His parents paid for college, he speaks English and French, and both of his parents went to college. He can dole out that kind of advice because he grew up easy."

"Are you questioning my father's authenticity because he was raised properly?" Manon said.

"That's why I don't like saying anything to you." Tate sighed. "That's not what I'm saying at all."

"Well, it sounds like it."

"I just wonder if you are doing all of this for me or for you."

Manon raised her eyebrows. "And what is that supposed to mean?"

"It means your mom had a birthday party last month and you didn't invite me. Then there was the homecoming party on campus, and you invited your cousins, but you didn't invite me."

"They're my cousins." Manon rolled her eyes. "I just wanted to hang out with them for homecoming. We planned it months ago." Manon avoided eye contact. Tate wanted everyone to know they were dating. She had called Phillis last night because she knew this conversation was coming, but Phillis still hadn't returned her call. In fact, Phillis hadn't returned Manon's last three phone calls, which wasn't like her. Phillis was hanging out with a new guy friend, but it still wasn't like her to go this long without calling.

"Okay." Tate went to the kitchen, and Manon embraced him from behind.

"I love you."

"I know." He turned and looked into her eyes. "But sometimes I wonder why. Because you love me, or because I'm your escape to freedom."

"What does that mean?" Manon raised her voice again.

"Look at you." He waved his arms. "You have to lie to your parents just to spend the night with me. You're a grown woman."

"You know how my parents are. I don't want to hear about putting a man before my education. Sometimes I swear my mom is punishing me for her decisions."

"Is it that you don't want to hear what your parents have to say, or you don't want them to know you are dating an uneducated dude who works odd jobs and was raised by his aunt?"

"Tate, stop." Manon massaged her temples. "Listen, my family is having a get-together in a few weeks. I want you to come with me."

"No, you don't. You want to throw me a bone so I won't be mad."

"Stop it." She draped over him. "You're right. It's time. I love you, and I don't care who knows."

Manon caught a faint reflection of herself in the wall mirror. She looked like Addie and was starting to behave like her. Manon wanted to fold herself in Tate's lap and tell him she was afraid they were making a mistake. Tate would never fit in at her father's country club or at one of his fundraisers. He didn't even own a suit. Yet she loved him so much. She wanted to keep him, and if that meant introducing him to her family, then so be it.

Tate was different from the privileged boys Manon had grown

up with. Predictable boys with nannies, golf coaches, and uncles in high places. In contrast, Tate was from the side of town Manon wasn't allowed to visit as a kid.

"Let's not talk about serious stuff right now." Manon led Tate over to the couch. She had had enough heaviness for the day, and she needed to talk to Phillis about Tate. Something was off with him, and it wasn't just because Manon hadn't invited him to Homecoming.

"I really need to tell you something," Tate said.

"Whatever you have to tell me can wait until later. Let's go to the movies."

Tate stared at her for a few minutes before agreeing. "You are something else. Sometimes I don't know what direction we are going, but I love you."

Manon opened her mouth then closed it. "I love you too."

Tate smiled. "I just want you to know that I appreciate everything you do for me. I know I'm not like the dudes you usually hang out with. But you take your time with me, and you seem to care about me."

Manon leaned in and kissed Tate. He was a good guy, and he liked her for who she was, not for her father's money or influence. She couldn't say that about most of the guys she dated. Tate was real. For once in her life, she would do things on her terms.

"Let's get married," she blurted out.

"Married? Hold up." Tate held up his palms. "It's too soon for all that. I don't got no steady job, and this place is small. I know they say the recession is supposed to end soon, but I don't know."

"Ah," Manon grinned. "Looks who's been reading the business section."

Tate blushed.

"You're right." Manon stared at her hands.

"What's wrong?"

"My cousin hasn't been returning my calls. That's not like her."

"Is that the cousin you always talk about?"

"Yes, she's also my best friend, but she's going to get demoted if she doesn't return my calls."

"Maybe she's busy." Tate kissed Manon's neck. "When you get home, you will probably have a message from her."

Manon gave in to his affection. The man who'd captured her heart wearing baggy jeans and a backward baseball cap. He always walked closest to the sidewalk, opened Manon's door, and waited for her to hang up the phone first after their late-night conversations. He was gentle and kind, but he didn't have a passport and said "frigerator" instead of refrigerator. But even with the things that annoyed her, Manon loved Tate, and she could be herself with him. He wasn't perfect, but he was easy and gave her whatever she wanted. Besides, he wasn't conniving enough to go after her trust fund if she married him.

The next morning, Manon headed to her parents' house.

Addie was piddling around as usual, probably planning another house project that would cost Marcel a fortune. Marcel was in his home office.

"Hey, Daddy." Manon kissed her dad on the cheek and sat across from him.

"Now, here's the real sunshine," he said. "How's my baby girl?"

"I'm good. Going riding this afternoon. Will you come with me?"

"Now you know I vowed not to get on another horse after my fall last spring."

"I know, but please?"

Manon was the only person who could get Marcel Lafleur to change his mind about anything. Even his mother, Manon's sweet grand-mère, didn't have that power. If she did, Marcel would have never married Addie, whom Grand-mère called *sauvage*. Throughout the years, Addie had tried to impress her mother-in-law with her degree, a membership to the Links, and any other accolade Manon deemed impressive. But Grand-mère didn't care about any of it.

"Oh, I see you decided to grace us with your presence?" Addie leaned in the doorway with her arms folded across her chest.

"Hi, Mother," Manon said.

"Did you return Mr. Savant's call about speaking at his youth award ceremony?"

"Yes," Manon said. Addie wasn't much for small talk with Manon. She stuck to her agenda and that was it. Manon had grown used to it and preferred to pretend like it didn't bother her.

"And did you take that suit I bought you to the tailor? The sleeves are too long."

"Addie, let the girl get in here for five minutes before you start in on her," Marcel said. "Besides, if she hasn't done those things, she will have to do them later because we are going horseback riding."

"Horseback riding?" Addie raised her eyebrows. "You said you'd never get on another horse again."

Marcel smiled at Manon. "Well, my sweet baby girl convinced me otherwise."

Addie scowled. "Make sure to call Mr. Savant before the end of the week, Manon." Then she stormed out of Marcel's office.

"Okay, Daddy," Manon stood up. "Let's leave around noon."

"Okay, baby girl."

Manon sauntered into the kitchen and picked up the phone to call Phillis again. This time she answered.

"And where have you been?" Manon seethed.

"I'm sorry," Phillis panted. "I've been working on these grad school applications, and I'm busy with work."

"Hmph, you've been working on grad school applications and working, and you've still had time to return my calls," Manon said accusingly.

"Whatever, Manon. What's up?"

"What's up is I need you and you haven't been around. Is that AJ boy taking up your time?"

"Well, actually, we had breakfast this morning. I like him. I really do."

"I need to meet him."

"He works a lot, but he said I'm the sweetest girl he's ever met."

Manon chuckled. "I need to meet this slick-talking slickster. He might be trying to run game on you."

Phillis sighed. "Not everyone is like Douglas, okay? I'm an adult now."

In high school, Douglas Floyd was Phillis's first crush. He sat with her at lunch every day and helped her bait her fishing pole. She even carved their initials in the oak tree on her property. Phillis was heartbroken when she found out that Douglas had used her to get close to Manon. Manon had kicked Douglas in the balls and told him to stay away from her cousin, and Phillis never spoke to him again.

"I didn't say he was like Douglas."

"You think I'm stupid."

"Phillis, you are one of the smartest people I know. But—"

"But what?" Phillis raised her voice.

"But . . . Aunt Clotee kept you in school and church," Manon lowered her voice. "You don't have a lot of experience with boys."

"And?"

"Can you just meet me at my parents' house later? I'm going riding with my dad. We should be done around six. We'll talk more then."

"I'm seeing AJ this afternoon. I'll drop by afterward if I have time," Phillis said.

"It's the weekend. How can you not have time?"

"Mama wants me to help her with Bingo night."

Whatever Clotee wanted, Phillis always obliged. Phillis was genuinely a good person who did the things her mother asked out of the kindness of her heart. Manon's allegiance to her parents' whims were primarily related to keeping her allowance uninterrupted.

"Fine," Manon said. "Love you, bye."

"Love you, bye."

A few weeks later, after three arguments and two days of Tate not returning Manon's calls, Manon agreed it was time for her father to meet him. Manon had told her father that Tate was coming, but she didn't mention it to her mother. She arranged to have the meeting on an evening when Addie wouldn't be home.

The doorbell rang. Manon heard the chime, and a wave of anxiety washed over her. Now she wasn't sure about Tate meeting her father. Perhaps she had moved too fast. She hurried down the hallway and entered the dining room. She slid close to the door and waited.

"Good evening, young man," Marcel said as he led Tate into the formal living room, where Tate sat on the plush sofa that faced a painted portrait of Marcel, Addie, and Manon as an infant. The Steinway Baby Grand nestled in the corner like a shy child, which hadn't been used since Manon stopped taking lessons in middle school. The matching grandfather clock seemed to tick in sync with Manon's heart. She peeked around the corner, praying Tate had worn something she'd bought him.

Tate's eyes floated across the high ceilings, lavish furnishing, and custom window dressing. She sent him a telepathic message to stop gawking and to sit up straight. The last thing she wanted was for her father to know that Tate had never been inside a nice house before. Maybe it was too late.

"Good evening, sir."

Tate sat on the edge of the loveseat across from Marcel. He was wearing a V-neck sweater over a button-down shirt and khaki pants. He got an A for effort but a C for listening. Manon had told him to wear jeans. She giggled into her hand at Tate sitting there in his preppy outfit, fingers intertwined as if he was waiting to be sentenced. She'd tease him about it later. Now that Tate was meeting her father, Manon wouldn't have to meet him in secret anymore, especially since he'd learned so much. Over the past year, Manon taught him how to use chopsticks, to put a napkin in his lap, and told him to keep up on current events. He wasn't polished, but Manon planned to get him there. The next thing she would do was introduce him to a tailor. Then she'd convince him to transfer to a four-year university to get his degree.

As Marcel made small talk about the first Black homecoming queen at LSU, Manon patted herself on the back. She and Tate just talked about that. Two of her favorite people were finally meeting. It would be perfect if Phillis were here, but she was all bent out of shape about her guy friend standing her up. Manon had to meet this guy who had her cousin all out of sorts. Phillis had always been level-headed, so this guy must be something special.

"Manon is a good girl, Mr. Lafleur," Tate said. He looked tiny in comparison to Marcel.

"Thank you for that confirmation, son." Marcel sat back in his recliner with a cigar between his lips. "Now, what can I do for you?"

"I love Manon, sir," Tate said. "And I want your permission to marry your daughter."

Marcel let the cigar dangle and leaned forward in his chair. He snorted in disbelief. "You see this house, son?"

Tate looked around the room, noticeably this time, and nodded. "I do, sir."

"Do you see the fine clothes my daughter wears? You know about that Friesian she rides and our vacations? The classes, tuition, credit card, that she speaks fluent French?"

Manon squirmed. She never told Tate about the credit card. He complained that he didn't want her using her parents' money on him. She lied and said it was hers.

"So if you come here asking to marry my daughter, I'm going to have to ask if you can take care of her the way I have taken care of her." Marcel always said a man should take care of his family.

"I can do better," Tate said.

Manon put her hand over her mouth again. Tate barely had a job. Mr. Stephens had threatened to fire him if he was late one more time.

Marcel raised an eyebrow. "Better than me?"

"Eventually," Tate cleared his throat. "With all due respect, sir, material things are great. I'm a young cat . . . er, I mean, young man, and I'm working my way up at the trucking yard. I'll make money, sir. That won't be an issue. But I will love Manon. I'll listen to her. I'll take care of her feelings, be honest with her, cherish her, and always be there to support her. To me, those things are more important than anything. I can earn a million dollars, but what would it all mean if I mistreat your daughter?"

Manon covered her mouth.

"She seems fond of you," Marcel said. "And that's my baby girl. I want her to be happy. Since you were man enough to come and introduce yourself to me, I'll trust your word when you say you can take care of her, but promise me one thing, son."

"Anything," Tate said.

"If you find that you can't take care of her, or if you don't want to take care of her, bring her back home, you hear?"

"You have my word."

"I respect you coming here to let me know that my daughter will be with you. I hold you accountable if anything happens to her."

"Yes sir," Tate said.

Manon leaned back and looked at the ceiling. Marcel was one hurdle. He had Manon's best interest at heart. Addie wouldn't be so easy to convince.

CHAPTER 23

Odester 1993

"Dette!" Clotee said, grabbing her sister in a bear hug. Clotee was in Mama's kitchen, cooking as usual. She looked pretty in one of Addie's old dresses that hung down around her shoulders for a change.

Odester put a finger to her lips. "Shh, don't be so loud." She placed a plastic dish wrapped in aluminum foil on the counter next to other bowls and Tupperware of various sizes and shapes. "Who all in there?" Odester peeked into the full living room.

"Just the usual hungry family members that come over every Sunday. Where you been?" Clotee put a hand on her hip. "I been calling you. Mama's been calling you." She squinted her eyes. "Why you so skinny, Dette?"

"Why you pray to a white Jesus who don't care nothing 'bout you?" Odester's voice sounded like gravel. "This why I don't come around."

"Odester! Who are you talking to like that?" Clotee put her hand to her chest.

"Too many questions, Tee." Odester backed down. Clotee loved Jesus, but she could fight. Odester washed her hands in the sink and grabbed an apron from the wall. "What you need help with?"

"You haven't come around. Won't call nobody back," Clotee continued. "Ain't nobody talked to you since Arelia's graduation. Mama has been worried out of her mind. Came by your house the other day, but you didn't answer the door. Of course, I'm going to be excited to see you. And worried. We are sisters, remember? Sisters don't go missing for weeks and not call to check in."

"I didn't know you came by."

"Don't lie, Dette." Clotee wiped the counter like it had offended her.

"Fine. I'm sorry. Just got a lot going on. And you know when I stress, I don't eat or communicate. Now, no more questions."

Odester peeked around the corner again and watched family members gather in the living room. Some were sipping on cold drinks, while others watched television. Two little girls sat on the floor playing with dolls. Odester forgot momentarily that she didn't want to be seen yet. Years ago, she and her sisters lived for these family gatherings—catching up with relatives, listening to old stories, and hanging out with their cousins. Her life wasn't perfect when she was younger, but Earline and Rutherford did their best. They showed up and loved their girls the best they knew how. She felt a pain in her chest thinking about her father. She could picture him walking into the kitchen with pecan candy. He always said it was for everybody, but Odester was the only one who really liked it. Funny how you didn't know what you had until it was gone.

Now, Odester hardly came around the family because she was either getting high or trying to get high. She attended a Narcotics Anonymous meeting last week and left after the Serenity Prayer. Her mind rattled back to that day: a skull tattoo on the back of one man's neck, the empty eyes of another, the lowered head of a woman dressed in all black. On top of everything else, Arelia was hardly home anymore. She spent most of her time at Bumpie and Esther's and recently took a job at Dillard's. She came by last week to drop off the twenty dollars Odester had asked to borrow, but she didn't stay. Arelia promised to come by the following day, but she never showed.

"Peel those sweet potatoes, then cut up some green onions," Clotee demanded, still eyeing her sister as if she were looking for something.

Odester took to her tasks, just like she always did. She peeled sweet potatoes, chopped onions, grated garlic, and cut up sausage. Cooking didn't have the same meaning since Daddy died. She wiped a tear away with the back of her hand.

Clotee reached over her to get a dish towel and smiled. "Good to see you." She kissed Odester on the cheek.

"Oh, now you wanna act like you got some sense." Odester smirked. "Good to see you too. Is Mama in her room? I didn't see her in the living room with everybody else."

"Yep," Clotee said. "She's getting old, Tee. You really need to come around more." Clotee poured oil in a skillet. "So you thought anymore about going back to rehab?"

"Dammit, Tee." Odester slammed her palms against the counter. "I don't need all of these questions." She had almost forgotten she told Clotee she'd gone to rehab. She told her sister she needed forty dollars and lied and said she was in rehab. Odester's way of making up for it was attending that awful Narcotics Anonymous meeting.

"Odester Chavis, you need to stop." Clotee faced her. "Every month, one of us is loaning you money for one thing or another. I heard you lost your job at the motel, and I'm not trying to be mean, but you look a mess. How many times have you worn those jeans? When was the last time you washed your hair, Dette?" Clotee was bossy, but she wasn't a gossip, and as much as she got on Odester's nerves, she trusted her sister. But right now wasn't the time for one of her sermons. Clotee had Jesus. All Odester had was a crippling habit and a family full of disappointed relatives.

"Thank you for the vote of confidence," Odester snarled to hide her hurt. "I don't need you. I can handle it alone."

"Well, that's not possible," Earline said from doorway. "And that's how it should be. We family. And family minds each other business, whether it's for good or bad. That's what we do." Earline's white hair was pulled up into a high bun. If she let it fall, it would hang down her back. Age softened her eyes and left blue rims around the brown pupils. She looked at her daughter's unkempt hair and sunken eyes.

"Mama," Odester said, and flung herself into Earline's arms.

"Hey, Dette." Earline rubbed her back. "You all right?"

"Yeah, Mama," Odester sniffled and shifted her feet. "Just a lot going on."

Earline stood back and looked at Odester. She didn't cry; she was always a fixer and believed in standing tall in the face of adversity. She was a pillar of strength, but Odester wanted sympathy and reassurance.

"I see." Earline sat down at the small kitchen table where she used to feed her daughters breakfast. The yellow tablecloth had seen its share of family potlucks. The brown stain near the edge of the table was from when Addie tried to press Odester's hair and the hot comb fell on the table. The tablecloth had been washed many times, but Mama never threw it away—it carried family memories. Earline said the same thing about the dining room chair with the loose leg, and the floor-model television in the living room that hadn't worked since Nadesna started walking. Instead of getting rid of it, Earline placed a new television on top of the old one.

Odester felt overwhelmed with memories as she stared at her childhood home. What if she hadn't been so defiant against Earline and tried harder in school? What if she never started talking to Bumpie? Addie and Clotee didn't have perfect lives— no one did—but they were living. Working, raising their children, dealing with their marriages, and helping Mama when she needed it. This wasn't the life Odester saw for herself as a young girl. She thought Bumpie was going to make her happy, but it turned out that only she had the power to do that. And she smoked that power away every single day.

Nadesna walked into the kitchen. She was removed from a lot of the drama between the other Chavis sisters because she was so much younger. She spent most of her time with their nieces, as she was closer to their age. But even though she was young, Nadesna had the same nurturing nature as Mama and Clotee. She was never judgmental and was always there when Odester needed her.

"Don't forget you have a family," Nadesna said as she wrapped her arm around Odester tenderly. She was soft and comforting like Rutherford and Clotee. Addie was cold like Mama. "We here for you. No need for you to struggle when you have a family."

"Nadesna is right," Clotee said. "You don't have to go through things by yourself."

"I know." Odester wiped tears from her cheeks.

"Hey, hey!" Addie walked in looking like a million bucks and smelling like fresh air. Her skin glowed from ten days on the beach in the French Riviera. She put a large glass bowl on the counter.

"Oh, Lord," Odester chuckled through sniffles. She didn't want Addie in her business. Besides, this pity party had gone on for too long. She was with family and wanted to try and enjoy herself. "What did you bring, Addie? This doesn't look like cups." Odester examined the contents of the glass dish.

Addie pursed her lips. "Hush, Dette! I don't do cups and plates anymore, remember? I cook now. You know that." Addie hugged Odester and turned up her lip. "Oh, Dette, you are tiny."

Odester plopped back down in a chair, and Clotee spun around from the stove and glared at Addie.

"What?" Addie asked. "What did I say?"

"We 'bout ready to eat?" Earline said. "Your uncle Buster gone eat all my dried shrimp. Better call everybody to say grace so we can eat now that Addie's here."

"The girls are out back," Odester offered.

Clotee gave Addie a dirty look, then leaned out of the back door. "Girls!" she called.

"They are behind the Jouberts," Nadesna said. "I'll go get them."

"Now, what would they be doing behind the Joubert house?" Clotee stood on her toes and tried to look over the fence.

"The same thing we used to do behind the Jouberts," Odester said sarcastically, recalling when she and her sisters would talk and laugh until the mosquitos were too much to bear.

"Tee, leave those young ladies alone," Addie said. "They are not the little girls you used to force into Sunday school. They will eat when they are ready."

"Girls!" Clotee ignored her sisters and yelled from the back door the way Mama used to do. "We getting ready to eat. Y'all come on in!"

"Tee, leave those girls alone!" Odester said, shaking her head. "They good girls, and they are responsible. Especially Phillis. I heard all she does is pray the rosary and teach the youth group."

"You all are right." Clotee closed the door, missing Odester's sarcasm. "I'm truly blessed with that one. My Phillis is so sweet. Ain't worried about worldly things." Clotee raised her hands and jerked her body. "Hallelujah, Jesus," she whispered with her hands still raised in the air. "Whew, y'all feel that?"

"Feel what?" Odester turned up her lip.

"The Holy Spirit. It's in here." Clotee's body jerked again. "Whoo, yes, Lord." She waved her hands again.

"No," Odester said.

"Um, I don't feel anything, Clotee," Addie said.

"Tee, just get this food on the table and stop worrying about those girls," Earline said. "If you raised your daughter right, she won't stray too far from what she learned."

"You're right, Mama," Clotee said.

CHAPTER 24

Manon 1993

The setting sun cast a golden hue across the Jouberts' storage shed where Manon and her cousins gathered. The air was thick but cooler from the quick rain. Manon and Phillis sat on lawn chairs, while Arelia sat cross-legged in the grass in front of a magnolia tree. The Jouberts were old and went to bed early, so the girls were safe and secluded in their backyard.

"Pass me one." Phillis held out a hand and looked across the tall grass toward Grandma Earline's back door.

"Girl, please." Manon flung a leg over Mr. Joubert's lawn chair and blew a smoke ring. "I don't want Auntie Tee coming after me with a crucifix and her Jesus posse for giving you a cigarette. You better get some of this second-hand smoke and chill."

"Whatever." Phillis grabbed the cigarette from Manon. "I'm grown." Phillis tried to fit in with her cousins but couldn't always keep up. She did well in school and was social enough, but she wasn't as outgoing as her cousins.

"Tell that to Auntie Tee." Manon snatched the cigarette back. "She thinks you are still her innocent baby. She told Addie you're still a virgin."

Phillis gasped. "What?"

"Her sweet angel of the lamb." Arelia pulled a small baggie from her purse.

"What's that, Ree?" Phillis asked. "Y'all smoking weed now?"

"You can't hang out with the big girls if you gone act like a kid," Arelia challenged. "Too many questions." Arelia rolled a blunt.

"I'm just surprised y'all are smoking weed." Phillis looked around the group as Nadesna approached.

"Uh-uh, not me," Manon said. "That stuff makes you forget things. I'm having a hard enough time remembering things. Plus, it makes your breath stink."

"Me either," Nadesna said. "I don't like the way it makes me feel. I prefer Jesus juice."

"Me too, but I can't drink at my parents' house." Manon sighed.

"Is your mom still trying to control you?"

"Every little thing I do. And you know my daddy is old-fashioned. He said I should live at home until I get married, so he won't pay for an apartment. So it's get married or go to grad school." Manon took a drag. "But it's getting to be too much. Last weekend, Addie tried to introduce me to one of her friend's sons! Talking about how we would be a power couple. No, thank you, lady. She wanted to be a power couple, and look at where that got her." Manon frowned.

"At least she's interested in your life." Arelia lit her blunt. "My mom doesn't even think about me, let alone try to match me with a husband."

"Aunt Dette is having a rough time, isn't she?" Manon asked.

"Isn't she always?" Arelia folded her legs and frowned. "Especially since my dad met Esther."

"She's still tripping off that?"

"Girl, yes," Arelia said. "I can't stand it. She talks about how he dogged her out after he got clean. She never asks about me or what I'm going through."

"I wish my daddy would move out," Manon said. "We would all be happier. All my parents do is ignore each other at home and pretend to be a couple around other people. My mom calls my dad arrogant, and my dad calls my mom lazy—a match made in dysfunctional heaven. What's the point of pretending in front of people who couldn't care less about your personal life? And if they do care, who cares that they care? I'm just glad I'm away at school so I don't have to deal with them so much."

"Well, none of that is worse than when I had to watch my mom peel my drunk father off the floor and then clean up vomit. God rest his soul." Phillis tried again to grab the cigarette from Manon.

"Ya'll just stay prayerful," Nadesna said. "I know we are all going through something, but that's how life is. Let's be thankful we have each other to lean on and don't have to go through this alone. Besides, y'all got your parents. And give my sisters a break. They are doing the best they can."

"I still think you got it better than the rest of us." Arelia took a hit of the blunt.

"Don't forget," Nadesna raised a finger. "Your grandma is my mama, and she's not as nice and sweet to me as she is to you guys."

"It's funny how four women can grow up in the same house with the same parents and come out so differently," Arelia mused. Her high had set in. "Who knew my mom would end up with dead-end jobs and smoking her life away?"

"Who knew my mom would end up in a loveless marriage?" Manon said.

"Y'all stop it," Nadesna said. "Those are my sisters. And they have been through a lot. All three of them. Addie faced adversities you can never understand, Manon. You think being smart and pretty in that all-white school was easy for her? And Phillis, your mama spent so much time trying to be like Jesus that she missed out on most of her young years. They are doing their best. Give them a break."

"Ah, I keep forgetting you play both sides." Manon blew smoke rings.

"I don't play both sides," Nadesna said. "We are solid for life." Nadesna put her palm up in the middle of the group. One by one, the cousins added their hands palm up, then closed them. "But those are my sisters. They love you guys and are doing their best."

"Solid for life," they all said in unison.

"So, anybody got a man?" Arelia leaned back against the tree and closed her eyes. "Or am I the only one pulling in action?" She gyrated her hips.

"Hush with your little fast-tail self," Nadesna laughed.

"I have a man," Manon said sheepishly.

"Is it that tall boy you went to high school with?" Arelia asked.

"No, ma'am. I don't waste time on those Lawtell boys." Manon draped her waist-length waves over her shoulder. "You guys know that."

"Ah, you mean the boys with argyle sweaters and penny loafers?"

"And all the money they can spend?"

"And daddies who golf?"

"Yes." Manon blew a smoke ring. "I'm over all of that. I met a real man."

"What do you mean you met a real man?" Arelia frowned.

"I mean a man who is brave and different." Manon stood up and raised her hands toward the sky. "A man who isn't afraid to take chances and who lives by his own rules."

"Oooh, does he go to LSU?" Phillis asked.

Manon shook her head.

"Southern?"

Manon shook her head faster.

"Oooh, you met a Morehouse man?" Arelia said. "You better get it, girl!"

Manon shook her head again. "He's not in college. He has other plans."

Phillis's face dropped. Arelia and Nadesna exchanged looks.

"Does Aunt Addie approve of this real man with *other plans*?" Phillis tilted her chin toward her chest.

"Forget Addie," Nadesna chimed in. "What about Marcel? I know he won't approve of some boy with no college education pursuing his princess."

"My mama doesn't know yet," Manon smized. "But Daddy does. I'm going to introduce him to the family at the cookout."

Arelia choked on her weed.

"You done lost your mind," Nadesna said. "You going to introduce your boyfriend to our family and your mama at the same time?"

"Yep," Manon chuckled.

"We haven't talked about this, Manon," Phillis looked worried. Manon had a history of making bad decisions when she didn't consult Phillis. But Phillis had been too busy lately to be there for Manon like she had in the past.

"I know. I called you three times last week," Manon said accusingly.

Nadesna and Arelia watched the conversation unfold. Phillis and Manon were close and shared everything. They never disagreed on anything. Sometimes, it was like they had the same mind. Phillis not meeting Manon's new boyfriend was odd.

"Anyway," Manon pouted, "if I introduce him at the party, Addie can't act a fool. You know she tries to hold her façade of perfection around the family."

"Well, I can't wait." Phillis clasped her hands together. "It will be a little drama, but not too much. And I'll finally get to meet this fellow."

"I don't want anybody to judge him." Manon lowered her eyes.

"Judge him?" Nadesna raised her eyebrows. "We are in the same family, right? There's no room for anyone in this family to judge."

"Just because there's no room doesn't mean it doesn't happen," Phillis chimed in.

"I know that's right." Arelia pursed her lips.

"You sure about this boy, Manon?" Phillis asked. Manon had never been with a guy long enough to get serious.

"About as sure as you are about that new boy you you've been hanging around with for the last few months."

"What boy?" Nadesna raised her eyebrows. "You met a boy?"

Phillis tilted her head. "Yes, I met someone. Just because I don't smoke weed doesn't mean I am not versed in life."

"Anybody who says they are 'versed in life' is not versed in life." Arelia laughed.

"I can't believe you met a boy." Nadesna shook her head.

"I like him," Phillis gushed. "But sometimes he doesn't call me back and goes missing for days at a time."

"Wait," Manon sat up. "You didn't tell me that."

Phillis hunched her shoulders. "Probably because it's embarrassing."

"So, Manon," Arelia grinned "Have you met Phillis's man friend?"

Manon shook her head.

"So, as close as y'all are, you are dating men the other hasn't met?" Arelia frowned. "That's crazy."

"Well, I hope Phillis's friend is into long-distance relation-ships," Nadesna said.

Manon frowned at Phillis. "Long-distance?"

Phillis bulged her eyes at Nadesna.

"Phillis is moving to California for school," Nadesna said.

Manon's eyes widened. "What? What is she talking about? I thought you were still working on the applications."

"A few. But I heard back from Berkeley," Phillis shot Nadesna the side eye. "I told you they offered me more money than the other schools."

"What about the schools in Louisiana?" Manon asked.

"I got accepted into several."

Usually, Manon would be annoyed by Nadesna, who couldn't hold a secret to save her life, but today she was grateful because Phillis hadn't told Manon any of this.

Manon blew a smoke ring. "Then there's no choice. You will stay here in Louisiana with me, right?"

"Come on, y'all," Nadesna said. "Tee's been calling us for a while now. If we stay out here any longer, she will come looking for us."

Manon grabbed Phillis's hand, pulling her back from the group. "Don't go to California," she whispered. "I need you here."

"I won't leave you," Phillis said. "I'll always be here for you."

CHAPTER 25

Emersyn 2019

"Hey," Emersyn stuck an earbud in her ear and stepped into Nadesna's spare bedroom. She'd forgotten to return Matt's call.

"Hey yourself," Matt said. "How's it going down in the bayou?"

"It's going," she said, looking around the tidy room with a lavender comforter and matching sheets. Next to the bed was a large wicker basket that housed photo albums. Emersyn picked up a tattered red one.

"So, is he cool?"

"Typical," she said as she thumbed through the photo album. The pages stuck together, and some of the photos were discolored with age. "Armand thinks he's so beloved that he's above scandal."

"Ah, he's one of those. Did you tell him how things work?" Matt asked.

"Of course I did. It will be fine. I just have to get him to understand I'm on his side. I also have to talk to his wife."

"You haven't talked to the wife?" The concern in Matt's tone was palpable. Emersyn was recently promoted but had worked in public relations longer than Matt. She could do a campaign sweep in her sleep.

"Nope. I'll reach out tomorrow." If Matt was already uneasy about Emersyn's progress, Armand's encumbrance would only worry him more.

"He's hiding something."

"Probably," Emersyn agreed.

"If you need me to come out there, I can," Matt offered.

"I'm on it. I'll give you an update after I meet with her."

As Matt updated Emersyn on the list of SEO experts they received, Emersyn saw a photo of herself with her bangs sticking straight up in the air, and she was flashing her best pre-braces smile. When did her mom send this photo? And to whom? The next photo was of four women sitting on the hood of a sky-blue convertible. She recognized Phillis and Nadesna but couldn't place the other two women.

"Good," Matt said. "He may be correct, but it's best to talk to Armand's wife and get that NDA signed. That NDA is gold."

"Trust me, I know. I'm on it," Emersyn agreed. She would get her signed statement, finish Armand's announcement, and put this case to rest so she could use her remaining time in Opelousas to find her father.

Emersyn waited for Mrs. Gray to open the door. She'd get a brief statement and be out of here in minutes. That was if Armand's assessment of his wife was correct. The exterior of the home envisaged refined Southern extravagance: Greek revival with a white wrap-around porch, an oversized welcome mat, contrasting black shutter panes, and a front yard the size of a neighborhood park. The street was lined with other handsome homes with massive porches and shuttered windows shrouded by beautiful landscaping.

"Emersyn?" a small woman opened the right side of the double doors.

"Yes," Emersyn extended a hand. "Mrs. Gray?"

The woman looked momentarily confused. "Uh, yes."

"Oh, okay," Emersyn smiled. "I thought I had the wrong person for a second there."

Armand hadn't described what his wife looked like. If Emersyn had to paint a picture based on his description, she'd never come up with this familiar gentlewoman with an exquisite complexion and petite frame.

"Do I know you?" Emersyn admired the sapphire cocktail ring on Mrs. Gray's delicate hand. Emersyn couldn't put her finger on it, but she knew this woman. Perhaps from the coffee shop. Maybe the airport.

"Of course you do," Mrs. Gray said with an indiscernible chuckle. "Doesn't everybody in the South know one another?" She tipped her head and studied Emersyn's face. "But you do look familiar." Her bare feet tapped across the floor as she slowly led Emersyn through her home.

Emersyn admired the dentil and batten molding that complemented the oversized windows and high ceiling. The house smelled of ambrosia. Mrs. Gray's kimono swept behind her like a loyal companion, refined and gentle like its owner. Emersyn entered a room with white furniture and a wall bookcase. Emersyn accepted her invitation to sit, suddenly feeling the need to incorporate the etiquette training she'd learned in preparation for her cotillion. *Ankles crossed, chin up.*

"My apologies if it's warm in here. I adore the natural light, but it doesn't do much to keep out the heat. I like it warm." Mrs. Gray put her palm to her chest again. "But I realize a lot of people don't. I can turn up the air if you'd like."

"No, the temperature is fine," Emersyn said. "I actually get cold in air-conditioned rooms, so it's perfect."

"Good. Me too." Mrs. Gray carried the slightest southern drawl, but it was different from most Emersyn had heard so far, more tapered, less intentional. She was like fine china—so delicate you only wanted to bring her out on special occasions.

"So many books." Emersyn recognized book spines and noted Mrs. Gray's penchant for francophone Black writers: Dumas, Mabanckou, Condé.

Mrs. Gray searched Emersyn's face, then her linen slacks and patent oxfords.

Emersyn quickly said, "Thanks for seeing me today."

"Of course. Is this your first time in Opelousas?" Mrs. Gray threaded her fingers around her knee and tilted her head as if to get a better view of Emersyn's response.

"Yes," Emersyn said, pulling out her planner.

"Mrs. Gray leaned in as if she couldn't hear well. "The South is an interesting place," she mused. "Filled with secrets and dark pasts. So, how are things going?"

"Great so far," Emersyn refocused. "I just have a few questions, and I will get out of your hair."

"Sure," Mrs. Gray said.

Emersyn explained the campaign sweep and the need to ensure that all information, past and present, was aligned. "No surprises," she said. "And this must remain anonymous until we announce."

"Of course," Mrs. Gray agreed. "He is a good guy."

"He is." Emersyn's eyes shifted around the room. "But the campaign will be competitive, and my job is to ensure that Mr. Gray is ready."

"Mr. Gray," she repeated. "After all these years, I still can't get used to how well-respected he is in this community. He's made quite the name for himself, you know?"

"I do. It's pretty impressive," Emersyn said.

"Not as impressive as the sacrifice to being his partner while he was getting there." Mrs. Gray's face soured. "But that's another story for another day." She paused again. "You are correct. You do look familiar."

Emersyn spotted a small crystal Baccarat butterfly that sparkled brilliantly against the light. The butterfly had white etching on it. Her mom had a similar one. "That's a beautiful butterfly."

"Please feel free to look," Mrs. Gray offered.

Emersyn held the figurine up to the light. "Nice."

"Yes, it was an anniversary gift. I forget which year. Our initials are on the bottom," Mrs. Gray said.

"My mom has the same one," Emersyn said.

"Your mom does?"

"Yes." Emersyn smiled. "She's back home in Oakland."

Mrs. Gray popped up from her seat as if she'd forgotten something. She stared at Emersyn.

"Is everything okay?" Emersyn asked. She walked toward Mrs. Gray, who moved backward.

"I understand what you need from me, and I will not utter a bad word to ruin his campaign." Mrs. Gray blinked her eyes and placed her hand over her chest.

"Are you okay?" Emersyn asked again.

"Yes!"

Emersyn moved back, startled.

"Yes, I'm fine," Mrs. Gray said again. "I won't say a word until he announces. You have my word. I have another meeting, so you will have to go."

Mrs. Gray ushered a confused Emersyn to the front door. Emersyn didn't get a chance to finish her spiel, but Mrs. Gray wasn't interested.

"Thank you for your time—"

"Thank you, Emersyn," Mrs. Gray said as she closed the door in Emersyn's face.

Emersyn called Armand as soon as she got in her Uber.

"Everything was fine," she explained. "At least I think it was."

"Do you have some time to talk?" he asked.

Emersyn assumed that was what they were doing. "Um, sure," she replied.

"Would you mind stopping by my house? I will text you the address."

Didn't she just leave his house? Things were getting strange, with Mrs. Gray's abrupt dismissal, and now Armand was telling her he lived in another house.

"I know it probably doesn't make sense," Armand read her mind. "But I will explain when you get here. Can you come?"

"Sure," Emersyn said. "Be there soon."

Armand's neighborhood was quiet like Mrs. Gray's but with minivans and basketball hoops instead of Benz coups and sculpted gardens. Here, the fake green lawns sat patiently next to parked cars. His porch was petite and offered two rocking chairs and a small table. Emersyn sniffed a magnolia as a couple passed with their bulldog and put a book in the Little Free Library at the end of the block. Ivy shrouded the sides, almost completely covering the double-hung windows. The quiet roar of southern comfort was as conventional as the blue porch ceiling.

Armand greeted Emersyn at the door. His short, wavy hair looked grayer, and he was wearing faded jeans and a black polo shirt. His dim eyes peered at Emersyn with curious anticipation.

"Would you like anything to drink?" he asked. Meeting at

Armand's house was more comfortable than in Room 202, but Emersyn was still confused.

"No, thank you."

Armand led Emersyn to the library off the entryway's front foyer, and she lingered behind, taking in the décor. Phillis and Emersyn shared a love for interior design. Some Sundays, they would visit open houses to scope out the décor. The black-and-white-tiled entry complemented an Astoria Grand full-length mirror. Emersyn tried not to gasp at the bespoke butterfly coat rack as she stepped over two unopened Amazon boxes. While there were stark differences in Mrs. Gray's contemporary flair and the conventional feel of Armand's home, Emersyn recognized similarities in taste and quality. The office was a turret of wall-to-wall shelves lined with classics: *Native Son, Song of Solomon, Their Eyes Were Watching God, A Lesson Before Dying*. Mrs. Gray and Armand both loved books. Books were mixed on the shelves among old black-and-white photos. Emersyn walked along the bookshelves and fingered the spines of books that held the stories that had an invaluable spot in literary history. One free wall housed a wall shelf and an enormous black-and-white portrait of a man and a woman holding hands. The curved walls were made for attractive decorating options like cherry wood molding, window seats, and modular seating. Emersyn was in heaven.

"Please take a seat." Armand motioned to an armchair and sat across from her in his leather Bergère. He carried the same expression Phillis did when she gave Emersyn the awful news about her diagnosis. But this was different. Armand didn't have anything to worry about.

"Your home is beautiful."

"Thank you."

"So, Mrs. Gray gave me a little insight during my visit today."

"I know I should have told you we were separated." Armand held his hands up in surrender. "It's just been such a sore spot. Some days I feel like we can make it work, and then I talk to her or visit and realize our marriage is over." Armand looked sad. "I know that has nothing to do with you, and I should have been forthcoming. I just think we've tried to hide it for so long, and it was easy to hide it from you as well."

Emersyn cleared her throat, thankful for some clarity. That explained a lot. She decided to put him out of his misery. He could explain their living situation later. "Your wife didn't tell me any of that, but thank you for finally telling me. I can't express enough the importance of full disclosure with me. It's in your best interest."

"I know." Armand clasped his hands together. "So if she didn't tell you we were separated. what did she say?"

"She said you were a great guy. *And* she seems fond of you. She says she won't say anything to ruin your campaign and will keep it confidential until after you announce it."

"What else did she say?"

"Nothing of consequence." Emersyn opted to leave out the woman's odd behavior at the end of their visit. "You're good to go. We can announce! Do you have time to go over some details right now?"

"Absolutely!" Armand said.

Emersyn pulled out her laptop. Finally, she'd gotten a break. The case was wrapping up, which left her a few days to look for Otis. Life was good again.

CHAPTER 26
Manon 2019

There were plenty of stories that Serenity Village was once a prestigious facility with residents that yielded from diplomats, doctors, and the upper echelon of southern Louisiana. Mayor Henry Warren—the first Black millionaire, was a typical resident. Relatives and residents were pleased with Serenity Village's plush single-occupancy rooms, epicurean cuisine, and a top-notch staff that included registered nurses and nurse practitioners. The *Opelousas Gazette* once featured the article, "Serenity Village: An Actual Home Away from Home."

The facility was inspired by mid-century modern principles and included elements of sculptured brass, light wood, and 1940s artwork. The indoor-outdoor concept featured an open lobby, courtyard, and spacious terraces.

"Hello, Mother."

Addie's room was located at the end of the tiled hallway nearest the nursing station. The room was smaller than the others because it was single occupancy. Addie paid for extra privacy and premium food selections.

"Hello, Manon." Addie sat up in bed. Her soft, silver waves were piled atop her head, with a few strands cascading down her pretty face.

"Your mother is a strong lady," the dark-haired doctor with

wire-rimmed glasses said. His lab coat had seen better days, and his nametag was upside down.

"Really?" Manon asked.

"Strong enough to leave here, but she still needs help."

"Like she has to live with someone, or can someone come and help her a few hours a day?" Manon asked.

"Twenty-four-hour presence. She's mobile but still a little weak. I don't want to risk a fall. I prefer to err on the side of caution. After our follow-up visit in one month, I'll make a second determination."

"One month?" Manon exclaimed.

"Is there a problem?" the doctor asked.

Manon gathered herself. "Um, no. A month. I understand."

"Great," the doctor said. "We are waiting for more test results and in-house physical therapy, and she will be ready to go home. I'd say no longer than forty-eight hours. I'll have the nurse bring you instructions since you're here," he said before leaving.

Before the stroke, Addie was the picture of health. She walked every day with her walking group. She was vegetarian and swore drinking water was the proven fountain of youth, and given her looks, she might be correct. The stroke was stress-induced. Addie took over some of Marcel's business affairs after he passed and was overwhelmed. Manon had offered to help and to hire someone to help, but Addie heard none of it. She wanted to do it all by herself, and she did until her body called foul.

"Will I be safe at your house?" Addie grunted.

"Of course," Manon ignored Addie's contempt. "Are they feeding you okay in here?"

"As well as can be expected," Addie said. "Nothing like home-cooked food, of course."

"I'm happy you are doing well," Manon said. "I just wanted to stop by to check in and see how to prepare the guest room."

"That room behind the kitchen?" Addie lifted the side of her mouth.

"That would be the guest room, Mother. Any complaints?" Manon's perfect eloquence dissipated in Addie's presence.

"I suppose not. Well, yes. Change the linen, please."

The nurse gave Manon the physical therapy schedule and advised that Addie should be mobile in a few weeks.

"She's a tough cookie." The nurse winked at Addie. "No neurological damage, but being immobile for so long has weakened her muscles. She will be shopping again after a few more weeks of physical therapy and regular walking."

"Looks like we will be living together again," Manon said.

"Thank you for allowing me to stay with you." Addie fussed with her hair. "Actually, I'll need my own sheets."

Mother and daughter avoided eye contact as if years of turmoil would strangle them if their eyes met. Manon learned from Addie how to cope by avoidance. If she'd known better, her marriage may have survived. Lord knows Tate did everything he could to make the marriage work.

<hr />

Manon 2006

"Babe, come look!" Tate called.

Manon cupped her hands over her mouth and admired the new gazebo. "You did it!" she exclaimed. Tate used a cedar wood frame and mosquito netting to complete their end-of-the-day oasis and final project on their backyard renovation list. He installed the outside firepit three weeks before, and the wicker patio furniture and bar stand arrived last week.

"Course I did." Tate pushed out his chest. "Your man can do anything."

"Yes, you can!" Manon exclaimed. "And just in time for the party."

"Who's on the list this time? Your hot-shot political friends?"

"*Our* hot-shot political friends," Manon reminded him. "And some people from the neighborhood."

"The Stevensons?" Tate teased.

"Linda Stevenson will never receive an invite to my home. I can't deal with people who blame the world for their problems."

"Alrighty then." Tate grinned.

Tate's charm matched Manon's social status and panache. When the couple wasn't hosting parties, they traveled the globe to less beaten paths in Malta, Frégate Island, and Kotor. Manon existed off her trust fund and contented herself in fundraising and gourmet cooking classes. Tate finally graduated from Southern University and worked his way up the union ranks.

"What do you want to do for dinner?"

"There's a new restaurant in New Orleans. We can drive down and spend the night," Manon suggested.

"Nah, I have meetings in the morning. Let's stay home, and maybe you can cook?"

"Cook?" Manon frowned. Manon didn't acquire the skill or interest in cooking. Another way she was like Addie.

"You are something else." Tate swooped her up in his arms. "Forget food. I know something we can work on." He pulled her close.

"And what is that?"

"Making my son."

Manon obliged her husband and let him lead her to the bedroom. He was masterful in bed, tending to her every need carefully, slowly. She reveled in his scent and forgave herself for her deception. Besides, according to her gynecologist, she could get pregnant again any day. *Any day*. Any day she could be carrying life. Any day she could make her husband the happiest man on earth. Any day she could lose the elasticity in her breasts forever.

"Are you okay?" Tate lay across her bare body, tracing his hands across her belly.

"Just thinking about how I never imagined our life would be this good. Addie gave us such a hard time. She didn't believe in you, but you graduated from college . . . twice."

"None of that matters. You believed in me. You believed in us, and that's what got us here," Tate said.

"I know, but I love to rub it in her face. She finally had to eat her words."

"Sweetie, you can't live the rest of your life exacting revenge on your mother."

"Exacting revenge?" Manon bolted up. "I'm not exacting anything. That woman said you'd never be anything. That you would be a blue-collar worker your entire life."

"And if I were, what's wrong with that?" Tate raised an eyebrow.

"It's not like that, and you know it." Manon rolled her eyes. "My mother doesn't like to admit when she's wrong."

"Okay," Tate said.

"What's that supposed to mean?" Manon pulled on a robe.

"Nothing. I just don't care what anybody thinks about me. Neither should you."

"I'm your wife, Tate," Manon spat. "I'm here to defend you when necessary. That's my job!"

"You can't defend me against someone's opinion," Tate said.

"Oh no?" Manon folded her arms. "Tell me more things I can't do. You seem to be so great at that."

Tate held his palms toward the ceiling. "Babe, let's not do this again."

"Do what?" Manon snapped.

"Nothing," Tate sighed.

The last blow-up had sent Manon off to Napa for a week. The time before that, they didn't speak for nearly a month. Their fragile marriage didn't need another fight.

"No, Tate. Speak your mind. You've never had a problem before."

"Whenever things are good," Tate said carefully, "I feel like you find a way to make them not."

"That's absurd."

"Is it? We just made love. I finished the gazebo. I got three promotions in the last year. We're good, babe. We are solid. And you find a way to make anything an issue. I can't keep doing the hot-and-cold thing with you."

"I never asked you to do anything, Tate." Manon tilted her head. "I'm doing the best I can, okay?"

Tate grabbed his robe. "Here we go with the I-have-stuff-going-on-but-can't-tell-you. It's getting old. I'm your husband, Manon. I want to be here for you, and I will be here in any way you need, baby. I just need you to let me."

"It's fine," Manon dismissed. "You know how I get. I probably just need to rest."

"We can't keep going on like this," he pleaded. "Please talk to me."

If Manon knew what to say, she'd tell her husband how sometimes she felt empty for no reason. How her heart sometimes felt like it was going to stop beating from frustration and resentment. She wanted to be happy and enjoy the wonderful life she had, but she couldn't. She was her own unhappiness. How could she explain that? And in true Manon fashion, instead of being vulnerable and explaining to her husband that words failed her, she deflected.

"Don't act like you care, now," she said.

"I'm not doing this." Tate held up his hands as if Manon was going to shoot him. "Life is too good for us to be in this space, Manon. We should be happy." He hung his head and sighed. "But I'm starting to think you don't want that." Tate tied his robe around his waist. "I will use the downstairs bathroom."

"You can sleep down there too," Manon yelled after he closed the door. "Forever!"

CHAPTER 27

Odester 1993

As Odester cut and tied flowers together in Earline's dining room, she listened to her daughter and nieces' conversation in the next room. Seeing her nieces close the way she and her sisters were warmed her heart. Each girl was different, reminiscent of their mom in some unique way, but also similar in beauty, strength, and loyalty. Nothing could tear those girls apart, and Odester rested better because of it.

"Tate didn't come to see me last night," Manon pouted and reached out to Phillis for a piece of tape.

"I'm sure he's just preoccupied," Phillis said.

"Or he's seeing somebody else," Arelia snorted. "I told you about dating them fools from the other side of the tracks," she snickered. "They ain't got no home training."

"Oh hush, Ree," Nadesna chimed in. "All you date is dudes from the other side of the tracks."

"I can handle them though," Arelia said.

"Y'all ready for tonight?" Phillis asked.

It was Earline's sixty-fifth birthday celebration. Odester had been clean since she last visited her mother's house a few weeks ago. She struggled with sobriety, but she used each day as an opportunity to try again. She entered a week-long inpatient program and now attended meetings three times a week. She stopped hanging out with the likes of Peggy and everyone else she knew who used narcotics. She had told Clotee about her sobriety journey, and since then, Clotee had called almost every day to check on her.

Clotee had asked Odester to manage the decorations for Earline's party. Odester tasked Arelia, Nadesna, and her nieces with living room decorations and party favors while she worked on the centerpieces. Manon and Phillis hung streamers, and Arelia and Nadesna tied ribbons around mesh bags of candy.

Odester was happy her daughter and nieces were all together again, especially because she didn't like Arelia's friends. Last week, one of them got caught stealing, and another one just had a baby. Odester had plenty of regrets over the past few years, and one was how absent she was in Arelia's life. All those nights she stayed out late, high as a kite. All those times she couldn't help Arelia with her homework. She had failed her only child. Despite the fact that Odester was now sober, Arelia didn't respect her and rebuffed any of her advice with, "Hm, and how did that work out for you?" Or, "Is that what they taught you in rehab?" Odester worked with her sponsor on ways to communicate with Arelia. Sometimes the techniques helped, but most often guilt overwhelmed her, and she felt like a failure as a mother. Being around her cousins always put Arelia in a good mood, and this time was no different. Odester was pleased.

"I can't wait for everybody to meet my man," Manon said.

"The man with no home training?" Arelia snorted.

"Just because he's not from Lawtell doesn't mean he doesn't have home training," Phillis said defensively. Phillis was so much like Clotee, nurturing and protective. Odester figured that was why Phillis and Manon were so close. Because Phillis nurtured Manon in ways that Addie never did.

"Yes, it do," Arelia challenged. "Them boys from the other

side of town don't know how to act. Straight up. I don't care what nobody say. My daddy from that side of town."

Odester gasped. No one in the family treated Arelia differently, but Odester's conscience ate her alive. Addie had married a man who could pay for Manon to attend college. And years of financial literacy workshops at the church bode well for Clotee, who'd saved enough money to pay off her mortgage and fully fund a college savings for Phillis. Fate didn't provide Odester the same grace. Odester couldn't help Arelia pay for her community college credits. A four-year institution wasn't in the cards before, but now that Odester was clean, she planned to get a job and save enough money to help Arelia continue her education.

"You can't judge a person's character based on where they grew up," Phillis said.

"Sure you can," Nadesna said.

"Regardless," Manon interrupted. "If Tate doesn't have a good explanation for not coming to see me, he can't come to Grandma's party tonight."

"If you ask me, you shouldn't bring him," Arelia said. "You begging for drama."

"Well, thank goodness no one asked you," Manon snapped.

"She might be right, Manon," Phillis chimed in. "It might cause more of a stink than you planned for, catching Aunt Addie off guard and all."

"Yeah, Addie gets crunk." Arelia laughed.

"What are you saying, Phillis?" Manon squinted her eyes.

"Maybe you should tell Addie how serious you guys are first, then introduce him to the rest of the family. This might not be the best way to do it."

"I'm sick of that woman ruining my life!" Manon threw a streamer roll across the room. "I can't do anything!"

"Don't start with them damn white people tantrums," Arelia said. "Go pick up that damn roll of streamer. People gone be here soon, and I don't want to hear my mama's mouth about these decorations."

"Aunt Odester won't say anything to you." Manon leaned back in her chair and peeked into the dining room, making eye contact with Odester. "You have the coolest mom."

"The coolest?" Arelia frowned.

Odester winced. She didn't want Arelia to embarrass her in front of the other girls, as her daughter had a fiery tongue. Odester pursed her lips and continued with the centerpiece without looking up. She lost her daughter's respect, and there wasn't a lot she could do about it. Arelia didn't listen to Odester or Bumpie. She hardly talked to Odester and only called Bumpie when she needed money. Both parents were so consumed with guilt that they catered to Arelia. She loved Addie's fancy clothes and money, so she tended to listen to her, but Addie wasn't her mother.

"Yes," Manon said, looking at Odester with tender eyes. "She's not as demanding as Mama and Aunt Clotee. That's all."

"She didn't mean any harm, Arelia," Phillis said.

"There you go, defending Manon again," Arelia fussed. "And when are you going to tell Aunt Clotee about your man?"

"And that you're thinking about having sex?" Manon laughed. "She needs to know that too."

"Hush," Phillis said. "Mama says I'm supposed to wait until I'm married."

Odester's eyes widened at Phillis. Clotee would have a fit if she knew Phillis was planning to have sex. If Odester learned anything in life, it was to mind her business. That was something Phillis and Clotee would have to deal with. She went back to working on the flower centerpiece.

There was a honk outside and Arelia jumped up and looked

out the front window. "That's for me," she gushed. "Be right back, y'all."

"Arelia, where you going? We need to finish these flowers," Odester said. But Arelia was already out the front door.

Odester hung her head and slumped in her chair. Her eyes welled with tears.

Nadesna walked over to Odester. "You alright, sis?"

"I did the best I could," she said, then released the stream of tears that flowed down her cheek onto her shirt and plopped on the flowers. "God knows I did the best I could."

"I know." Nadesna bent down and hugged her. "I know."

"Awww, Auntie," Manon said. She and Phillis rushed to Odester's side and hugged her.

"You know how Arelia is," Phillis said. "She will come around."

Odester listened to her sister and nieces. She knew what Arelia was like because Odester was the same way when she was that age. She didn't want to listen to anybody, didn't want to follow rules, and felt like the world was against her—all with two loving parents by her side. Odester failed her daughter in ways she'd never be able to forgive herself for. The nights she left Arelia alone while she went out to buy drugs. The times she spent grocery money to get high. Those were things that couldn't be taken back. Scars that couldn't be sutured. Odester deserved whatever Arelia dished out.

Odester wiped her face. "I'm alright, just a little emotional, it being Mama's birthday and all. Y'all finish these decorations."

"It's okay to not be okay," Nadesna said, looking concerned.

"And it's okay to stop being so dramatic." Odester tried to laugh and lighten the mood.

"Okay, Auntie," Manon said. She and Phillis seemed relieved, but Nadesna still wore a frown.

A few hours later, Earline's backyard birthday party was in full swing. The festive décor included string lights along the fence, a table reserved for gifts, and another for desserts. Circular tables were topped with black tablecloths, mosquito-repelling candles, and Odester's flower centerpieces. The hosted bar stood next to the gift table. The DJ spun from a lit table in the corner of the backyard. Clotee and Odester sat in wicker chairs near the kitchen door to limit indoor foot traffic.

"This turned out nice, Tee." Odester leaned back in her chair. "You so good at planning parties."

"Thank you for your help with all the decorations. I couldn't have done it without you, sister dear."

"You welcome, sister dear. But the girls helped me a lot."

"Good," Clotee sighed. "Mama looks so happy."

Earline laughed with some ladies from church. The card and domino tables were in full effect, and a few people were line dancing in the middle of the lawn. Family, neighbors, and Earline's sewing circle friends filled the backyard. Earline walked from group to group, laughing and posing for photos. She prided herself in walking without a cane, but her right knee might debunk that pride any day.

Odester excused herself to take a phone call from her sponsor. Jackie was ten years sober and understood the triggers that stemmed from social gatherings. She and Odester went through a few exercises and talked about the things that had triggered her, like the bar. Clotee wanted to omit the bar, but Odester didn't want to ruin the party for the others. Odester's week-long inpatient treatment was difficult. She couldn't have outside contact for the duration of her stay, and they monitored everything she did. Odester didn't make friends while in treatment. She attended the mandatory group discussions, but she never shared. Even now when she attended meetings, she didn't share.

"If you need to leave, then leave," Jackie said. "Don't force yourself to be strong or put yourself in a position where you might succumb. It's okay to say when you've had enough."

"I think I'm fine." Odester held the phone close to her ear. "It's just that I haven't been this close to alcohol since I left the center. I think I'll be okay." A year ago, Odester would have used a strong breeze as an excuse to have a drink or get high. She'd spent her life blaming others for her issues and making excuses for her dependency.

"Okay," Jackie said. "Know your limits and stick to them."

Just as Odester ended her call with Jackie, Manon entered the backyard with Tate at her side, their fingers intertwined. She walked a few steps in front of him. Her face was filled with defiance and pride, his of uncertainty and fear.

Not many people noticed the couple's entry because Buster had stopped playing Spades long enough to dance with their cousin Pat, who was egging him on. "Drop it low. All the way to the floor." Marcel and Addie sat at a table nearby. Marcel enjoyed the dancing, and Addie enjoyed her wine. Then Buster pulled Earline to the dance floor.

Odester eyed the couple. Tate was the first boy Manon had brought over to meet the family, and he was an interesting-looking fellow in baggy jeans and a Hot Boyz T-shirt. Manon made the rounds introducing him to family members.

"Who's that boy with Manon?" Clotee asked as she emerged from the kitchen with a fresh bowl of punch.

"Her boyfriend," Odester said. "Tate."

"Boyfriend? I declare!" Clotee walked over to Manon and Tate.

"This is my boyfriend, Tate," Manon announced. "Tate, this is my Aunt Clotee."

"Ah!" Manon squealed when she saw Phillis, who was cleaning off the serving table with her head down. She grabbed Phillis's arm and pulled her over. "Tate, this is my cousin and best friend, Phillis. Phillis, *this* is Tate."

Phillis's smile faded quicker than the platter of watermelon she had set on the table two minutes ago. Tate raised his hand to greet her, but Phillis just stared.

"Finally, my two favorite people meet!" Manon squealed.

"Well, now this the first time Manon bought a man to meet us," Buster said as he walked over. "Where you from, young man? And why them pants so big?"

"Oh, Buster stop that." Clotee tapped Buster's shoulder and laughed.

Phillis slipped away from the group and toward the back door.

Odester knew something was wrong. She got up and quickly followed Phillis. "Hey, Phillis. What's wrong?"

Phillis looked like she'd seen a ghost. Her eyes darted to Manon. "Nothing . . . I don't feel well."

"You were just fine." Odester followed Phillis's gaze to Manon. "Is it something with Manon's new boyfriend?"

"No!" Phillis said. "Of course not. I'm just not feeling well."

"Manon, what is this about?" Addie's voice pierced the air. "This is a family event. Not an event for strays."

Odester turned her attention to Addie's tantrum, and Phillis disappeared through the kitchen door.

"Do not speak about him that way." Manon placed her palm on Tate's chest. Tate looked as if he wanted to disappear. His eyes pleaded with Manon.

"Here we go." Buster took a swig of beer. "Rich people problems."

"I will speak any way I want." Addie moved closer to Manon, ice cubes clinking in her glass of sweet tea laced with vodka.

"Not about my fiancé, you won't," Manon said.

Fiancé?

The family erupted. Each family member had differing reactions to Manon's announcement.

"Say what?"

"She marrying the Thuggish Ruggish Bone?"

"There goes the neighborhood."

"I declare!"

"Manon, if you don't stop it this minute!" Addie screamed.

Marcel approached his wife and daughter. "Not here," he said sternly to Addie. Then to Manon, "Let's do this another time, baby girl."

"You coddle her!" Addie erupted. "That's why she's so spoiled and entitled. How dare you march in here announcing your fiancé that your parents have never met!"

"The parent who counts met him," Manon retorted.

Addie slapped Manon so hard that her drink spilled on the front of her dress.

Manon cradled the side of her face with her palm. Her eyes were wide and burning with anger. "You are miserable and mean."

"Hey," Marcel shushed Manon. "I said, not here."

"Not anywhere!" Manon grabbed Tate's hand and pulled him behind her as she stormed out of the backyard.

Everyone was in shock, whispering to each other. Odester hated to see Addie and Manon this way. She and Addie didn't always agree, but having a daughter who was angry hurt your heart and soul. For once, Odester wasn't the cause of the drama. She looked over at Earline, who was on the other side of the huge backyard learning the Electric Slide.

"I hate you," Manon yelled over her shoulder.

CHAPTER 28

Emersyn 2019

A rmand's assistant led Emersyn to his office, where he sat at the computer screen with one finger pressed against his temple. An empty bottle of sparkling water and shrimp fried rice sat clumsily on his desk. His frown indicated he was frustrated with whatever happened in cyberspace.

"Come on in." He waved Emersyn to an empty chair. "You ready?"

"As ready as I can be."

Armand's leadership team would arrive soon. Emersyn would give a brief presentation about campaign management and funding, and then they could file Armand's Notice of Intention which would allow him to fundraise.

"Good," Armand gave up on whatever he was working on. "Shall we?"

Emersyn nodded.

"I'll bet your parents are proud of you, especially your dad. I can tell you are a daddy's girl. Aren't you?"

And there it was. The words that always made Emersyn digress. The words that emptied her soul and left her bare before the world. She was a bastard. The only girl at Templeton Elementary with a borrowed dad for the father-daughter dance; the girl who made flower bouquets for Father's Day instead of a blue card with a necktie. She used to think that she'd feel better if she knew his name. The empty space on her birth certificate left a hole in her heart. "He didn't want to be bothered," Phillis always said. But when you brought a child into the world, you didn't have a choice. You took care of them the best you could. At the very least, you made yourself known to them. Over the years, Emersyn vacillated between anger and sadness. Mad at his absence and indifference; sad about not knowing her roots. Otis McGee might not want to be bothered with Emersyn, but he'd know exactly who she was before she left Opelousas.

"Um," she snapped back to reality. "They are proud."

"I'll bet." Armand smiled, his eyes crinkling in the corners. "If I had a daughter, I'd want her to be just like you."

Emersyn followed Armand to the sleek botanical terrace, where three people greeted them. A sour-faced guy with chubby red cheeks was eating pastries. Next to him was an older woman in a big red bird hat with her short arms folded across her girth. And finally, a frail guy squinted behind his thick-rimmed glasses with piercings and a face tattoo.

"Emersyn, this is my exploratory team, the people I trust and have known for years," Armand clasped his hands together and introduced the group. "This is Beau Garner, my right-hand man." He pointed to the red-cheeked guy. "He has an arsenal of political capital, experience, and politics runs in his blood. Literally."

"Pleasure," Beau popped his lips.

"And this is Jean Pierre." Armand pointed to the frail guy. "Nobody knows numbers and analytics better than he does. Getting him to talk is hard, but he gets the job done."

Jean Pierre nodded. "Nice to meet you."

"And last but never least, Miss Eugenia Beekirk." He put a hand on the older woman's shoulders. "She's the godmother of these parts and one of my biggest supporters."

"That means she's loaded," Beau interjected, still gobbling pastries.

"Pleasure to meet you," Eugenia said in her velvety twang. "Armand is such a dear man. Like a son." She smiled at Emersyn.

"Team, this is Emersyn, PR extraordinaire all the way from California. She's smart, a new associate, and she's here to whip us into shape."

"California," Beau snickered. "You're an associate, and you came down to these parts for a sweep?"

Armand cleared his throat, and Beau looked the other way.

"I thought there were four on the team?" Emersyn asked.

"He's running late," Armand looked at his watch. "He'll be here soon. We can get started without him."

Emersyn handed each a bound packet and shared the campaign strategy roll-out. With the sweep finished, it was time to file and start fundraising. It didn't matter how impressive a candidate was; the campaign funds determined his chances. Jean Pierre never looked up from his computer, and Beau busied himself with a seemingly important particle beneath his fingernail.

"Questions? Comments?" Emersyn asked the team.

"I gotta be honest with you," Beau said. "We're not gonna spend a bunch of money campaigning in areas where people don't vote. And those areas you just mentioned in your presentation—they don't vote."

"I hate to say it, dear, but he's right." Eugenia's hat bird danced in fervor.

Emersyn referred everyone to page four of her packet.

"The last time a Black candidate ran for this seat, ninety-seven percent of the population in the crucial areas voted. So, to your point, Beau, if your average white person runs—which typically has in this district—then you are correct; this group will not vote in high percentages. But when they find out Armand is running, they will. And Jean Pierre, I'm sure you can pair down those numbers, but that's why we have to show them who Armand is. They need to see his face."

Beau rolled his eyes. "I don't know. I mean, we have verbal commitments for contributions."

Eugenia snapped her fingers. "You are right, young lady! I remember that election. Dillwyn Robinson won by a landslide. People are ready for change around here. I like the way you think. And Armand is such a charmer. Once they see him, ooooh-weeee, I know they gonna love him."

"I agree." Jean Pierre jutted his chin forward. "Statistically, people in those areas will come out to vote in margins sixty-eight percent higher when an African American person runs."

Beau sucked his teeth and stared at the pastries. The buttons on his shirt weren't willing to accept another bite, but he took the chance anyway.

The group huddled and discussed strategy when the fourth team member arrived.

"Sorry I'm late, y'all," he said as he rushed over and unloaded his laptop. "Got held up at another meeting."

Emersyn's mouth fell open.

"No worries," Armand said. "Thanks for joining us. Emersyn, this is our communications manager, Rico."

"Cali?" Rico squinted.

"What a coincidence." Emersyn scratched the back of her head. Thank God she'd paid close attention to her outfit today. It was the smartest workwear she owned; her shirt was V-neck instead of crew, and her knee highs were nude. Whew. She recapped the first part of the meeting for Rico before ending the session. Armand took a phone call in his office.

"It's a trip seeing you here, Cali," Rico said outside of Armand's house.

"Yeah, weird," she said. "Such a small world. You are my cousin's best friend and work for the candidate I'm representing,"

"Good meeting in there." Rico nodded his head toward Armand's house. "You really know this political stuff. Very articulate."

"Articulate?" she asked. "Only white people call me that."

"My bad," he laughed. "But seriously, seeing a woman in this space is good. Especially a sista."

"Thanks," she said. "It was nice meeting everyone. Beau is, um, interesting."

She could smell Rico's cologne mixed with something earthy, like he'd burned incense in his house all day. Emersyn didn't have the best luck with the dating pool. Certainly, she had never dated anyone as handsome as Rico. He was what Amal would call "out of her league."

"Beau's a weird cat, but he's smart and knows a lot of people," Rico said with a shrug. "Politics flow through the boy's veins. His grandfather was the governor of Louisiana back in the day, and he has cousins in the assembly and Senate. I heard Beau wanted to go into politics, but he couldn't stop fooling around with that booger sugar."

"Really?"

"Oh, he's clean now. It's been years. But then somebody outed him on the internet. It was wild. Now I guess it's his mission to piss off homophobic conservatives and get liberals elected."

"I see." Emersyn nodded. So Beau was gay and used to snort coke. That explained nothing, but she appreciated all the insight she could get. Armand was tight-lipped about his circle.

"You need a ride?"

"Uber." Emersyn waved her phone in the air.

"Aw, hell naw. Southern hospitality is real. Where can I take you?"

Emersyn accepted with a smile. They walked down Armand's street to the end of the block where Rico's candy-green mustang was parked.

"Wow." Emersyn eyed the shiny car with white interior and trim that matched the outside.

"This my baby right here," Rico said proudly. "Took me years to get her right."

"It's pretty." Emersyn wasn't into cars, but this one was interesting, like it could be in a car magazine. She sunk down into the bucket seat.

"Where to?"

"Downtown."

"You feel like taking a ride? I have to make a quick run."

"Sure." Emersyn didn't mind the extra time with him.

"Cool, I'll show you a lil' bit of my city too." He grinned and his whole face smiled. Rico was more relaxed than in the meeting. He sounded like Lil Wayne with a slow Southern drawl.

They took the interstate and Rico pointed to his old high school, where his grandmother lived, where his cousin was shot, and the woman's house who made the best gumbo in Opelousas.

"You alright?" he asked.

"Yeah, it's beautiful here. People don't seem to be in a rush like they are back home."

"'Cause there ain't nowhere to go," he laughed. "You ever thought about moving to the South."

"No," Emersyn said matter-of-factly. "I'm a California girl. I need to get out for walks and breathe. It's way too hot here."

"That's because you got on all them clothes." Rico looked over Emersyn's outfit.

"Whatever." Emersyn crossed her ankles and lifted her head.

"I like you, Cali." Rico smiled.

"You don't know me," she challenged.

"I know enough." He looked her over again, but this time he wasn't smiling. "I know a good soul when I come across one. You good people."

"Oh, and you can tell that from meeting me once? Look at you, all clairvoyant."

"Ah, you got jokes. I didn't know people on the West Coast had a sense of humor."

"Don't come for my people," Emersyn chuckled.

"I'm not. You gotta admit, y'all do some wacky things in Cali."

"First of all," Emersyn said, "the United States would be nothing without California. You'd have no Google, no Facebook. No social media period. Y'all would perish without us."

"Yeah, but y'all gone sink in the ocean."

"Not before y'all," Emersyn retorted.

"I like you, Cali," he said again.

Their destination was just outside of town on the second floor of a gray building with sleek windows, vertical metal panels, and a flat roof. Emersyn trailed Rico, who took the wooden plank steps two at a time and stopped before a metal sign that said: Vera. Rico disappeared into the dim but exquisite room while Emersyn marveled at riveted bar chairs and the evocative ambiance of a James Bond rendezvous. The bar's yellow backlight inspired discretion and luxury, and African-inspired art adorned gold-splatted wallpaper. Emersyn walked past four round tables. Large pieces of furniture along the back wall blocked the kitchen entrance.

"These are not the lounge seats that we ordered!" Rico's voice carried.

Emersyn peered toward the back of the room where Rico

was talking to a pint-sized but sturdy-looking man whose cheeks flushed beneath his Saints cap.

"All we do is deliver and install, sir," the man said. "If you got a problem with the order, you need to call the company. We can't deliver without a signature. I just need somebody round here to sign so I can leave 'em here."

"Then you won't deliver because I ain't signing," Rico said, trying to keep his calm.

"Please, sir," the man said in a frustrated voice. "This here is the order sheet, and these here loungers match this sheet." He waved the sheet in the air.

"Then the sheet is wrong. And you have these seats blocking the walkway. We can hardly get into the kitchen!"

"Sir, we can install 'em. That's what we came to do, but your people told us not to."

"Because these are not the loungers we ordered!" Rico rubbed his hands over his face and took a deep breath. "Dude, listen," he calmed down. "We reopen in four days. The loungers were supposed to be in today. I need you to get somebody on the phone to assure me that the correct loungers will be delivered and installed."

"I can't guarantee that."

"Hold on a second." Rico pulled out his cell.

"What's your name?" Emersyn asked the delivery person when Rico stepped away.

"Call me Tank, ma'am," he said gruffly. His squat body stood at attention, and he looped his forefingers through his belt loops.

"This is so weird, Tank. I mean that there would be such a big mix-up." Emersyn was in mediation mode. Part of being a good public relations representative was deescalating and resolution.

"Don't know what to make of it, ma'am," Tank replied. "This

here is what the order calls for," he assured Emersyn, who was much more patient than Rico. "I confirmed before I got here, and there ain't but one delivery in Opelousas today."

"Wow," Emersyn said. "It makes even less sense to know you confirmed the order. I'm sure you know your orders."

"Oh yes, ma'am." Tank tipped his tattered cap. "I know my job."

"I'll bet," she smiled. "I remember something like this happened to me before."

"Ma'am?" Tank seemed interested.

"Oh yeah," Emersyn said. "I bought tickets to the Saints game once. Close to midfield, above row 10. I was furious when I went to pick up my tickets, and the agent told me the only tickets under my name were in the three hundred level."

"I'd be pissed fa sho," Tank scoffed.

"Well, I know it wasn't her fault. Kind of like you and the loungers. Glitches in the system happen, you know?"

Tank nodded. "This certainly ain't my fault," he said. "But at least you got to a Saints game," he said. "Been wanting to take my son for years. Can't afford it on my salary though."

"Really." Emersyn looked over at Rico, who was still on a call. "I have a friend who can get you a couple of tickets. Close to midfield above row 10."

"You shittin' me!"

Emersyn shook her head. "I'm not. But I'm trying to help my friend Rico figure out this lounger situation, so I may not be able to get to it today. Maybe some other time."

"You know what?" Tank pulled out his phone. "Let me go make a quick phone call. Sometimes they get these deliveries wrong. Nobody's fault. Definitely not mine, but lemme check. Dem gals in the front office be on them cell phones all the time."

Emersyn ignored Tank's comment and watched him hustle

out to make his call. She wasn't at all surprised when she heard him curse, or when he asked, "How in Sam's hell did that happen? It's dem gals on dem damn cellular devices."

A few moments later, Tank ended his call. "You were right, ma'am," he said. "Gals in the office got the orders switched up. The loungers for Vera are about fifteen miles out. Folks out in a horn-tossin' mood too." Tank looked down and shook his head.

"So crazy," Emersyn said. "Is there any way you guys could just meet up somewhere? Maybe switch trucks?" She hunched her shoulders.

"Lemme check." Tank pulled out his phone again. "Gimmie a sec."

Rico and Tank ended their phone calls at the same time.

"Just talked to the other driver," Tank said. "He headin' this way now. I gotta go meet him and will be back, and my guys will install loungers for ya." He tipped his cap at Emersyn.

"Thank you, Tank. I have a call to make as well." Emersyn winked.

"Sure thing, ma'am." Tank rushed out.

"Tank?" Rico furrowed his brow as he watched Tank hightail it out of the door.

"That's what they call him." Emersyn shrugged.

"So, you bamboozled Tank into admitting he made a mistake and installed my loungers today?"

"Correction," Emersyn held up a finger. "Dem gals with the cellular devices made a mistake."

"What?" Rico was confused.

"Never mind," Emersyn said. "There's no bamboozle in being a decent arbiter. It's my job."

"I owe you, Cali. Big time."

"You owe me nothing except a ride to my hotel. I'm waiting on a call from my mom's doctor."

"Say no more." Rico grabbed his keys, then made a phone call to someone, informing them that they should expect the loungers to be installed today.

"Oh, tell him to get Tank's phone number," Emersyn whispered.

Rico frowned.

"Just do it," she mouthed.

Rico followed instructions.

"What was that about?" he asked once they were back in his car.

"Tank works hard. He deserves to be able to take his son to a Saints game," Emersyn said.

Rico stared at her. "I like you, girl."

CHAPTER 29

Emersyn 2019

O verall, the Opelousas trip was a success. Emersyn was pleased with how the sweep turned out. Mrs. Gray was compliant, Armand's past wasn't too horrible to repair, and she met Rico. She didn't expect much to come of their friendship. Afterall, Rico wasn't the sort of guy she'd take to office parties or wine country, but he was sincere and hadn't stopped thanking her for the loungers. She agreed to meet him for drinks later.

If there was a downside to the trip, it was that Emersyn was no closer to finding her father than when she first arrived. She discovered the last place Otis McGee worked. One afternoon, she approached a guy at Temple's tow yard who recalled the "short, brown fella with the limp."

"That cat could build a car from scratch," the man in an oil-stained overall said. He also recalled how Otis loved pecan candy. "Whew, Otis could eat a pound of pecan candy in one sitting." The man laughed. The facts weren't profound, but every bit of information brought Emersyn closer to her father.

The supervisor, a tender-eyed gentleman in a faded Dickies shirt, shared his accounts of Otis. "Nice fella," he recalled. "Like to gamble, though." He handed Emersyn a piece of paper. "Say you his daughter, huh? This here is the last place I sent his paycheck. Not sure if he still lives there, though."

"Thank you so much," Emersyn said.

With all the running around, Emersyn decided to rent a

car instead of relying on Uber. She sat in the car, recalling her conversation with Otis's former employee, when she discovered her planner wasn't there. As she retraced her steps, she remembered having her planner at Nadesna's and then she'd taken it to Mrs. Gray's house.

Shit.

She called Mrs. Gray.

"Ah, yep. It's here," Mrs. Gray said. "Slipped right between the cushions. It will be here waiting for you."

"Great."

Twenty minutes later, she was at Mrs. Gray's house.

"Hello." A vexed young woman with multicolored fingernails rested her small eyes on Emersyn.

"Hi, is Mrs. Gray here?" Emersyn conjured a smile. She thought Mrs. Gray lived alone. Armand didn't mention anyone else who lived in the house. Maybe she was a niece. Whomever she was, she could use a lesson in manners.

"What?" Beady Eyes turned up her lip.

Emersyn hadn't stuttered and wondered why this personal security guard clad in Shein and Givenchy acted as if she hadn't heard what Emersyn said.

"I asked if Mrs. Gray was around?" Emersyn used her sweet voice. "I was just here the other day."

"Look," Beady Eyes cut Emersyn off with a palm. "We don't give money to solicitors. And we already believe in Christ, so you can leave."

"I'm not asking for money," Emersyn's voice was even. "I just need to speak to Mrs. Gray."

"Emersyn?" Mrs. Gray appeared behind the ill-mannered door monitor, looking majestic in a black cashmere lounge set and furry pink slippers. Loose amber waves framed her face.

"Hi," Emersyn waved.

"I told her—" Beady Eyes began.

"That's enough for now, thank you." Mrs. Gray dismissed Beady Eyes, who watched open-mouthed as Mrs. Gray welcomed Emersyn inside and led her down the hall.

"All safe." She handed Emersyn the planner. Mrs. Gray stood with her hands on her hips and her head slightly twisted to the side.

Emersyn's eyes floated to the Baccarat butterfly. It was similar to the one her mom said an old friend had given to her. Phillis never gave Emersyn details, but she kept it perched on her nightstand in her bedroom. Almost instinctively, Emersyn's eyes drifted to the photo on the mantle. She saw the picture from a distance during her last visit, but this time she was close enough to see the faces in the photo. Emersyn's eyes hadn't failed her. Her heart raced, and sweat beads formed under her breasts.

"Do you mind if I smoke?" Mrs. Gray asked.

Emersyn hardly heard Mrs. Gray's words as she stared at the photo. Four young women sitting on the hood of a sky-blue Cutlass convertible stared back at her. Suddenly, Emersyn was short of breath.

"This butterfly . . ." Emersyn's heart almost beat out of her chest.

"Yes?" Mrs. Gray shifted her eyes.

"I've . . ." Emersyn stammered. "I've seen one like it before."

"Of course you have," Mrs. Gray wrinkled her brows. "Neiman's sells it."

"This photo." Emersyn pointed to the photo on the bookshelf.

"My cousins? Yes?" Mrs. Gray looked concerned.

"You're the woman on the end."

Mrs. Gray walked toward Emersyn and examined her face. "You've seen this photo before? Where?"

Emersyn nodded. "At my aunt Nadesna's house."

Mrs. Gray took in a sharp breath and put her hand over her chest as if she discovered something she suspected. "You're Phillis's daughter." Her statement was matter of fact, but her eyes searched for the truth.

"I am, but I feel you knew that before now."

"I didn't." Mrs. Gray extinguished her cigarette in an ashtray. "I mean, I suspected it. Though it makes sense now. Nadesna has called me several times this week. Now I see why. And the resemblance." She shook her head. "How could I have missed it?" she said more to herself than to Emersyn.

Emersyn was confused. "Why did you let me think you were someone you aren't? You knew I thought you were Mrs. Gray."

"Hold on. I didn't lead you to think anything," she advised. "And I am Mrs. Gray. It seems that my dear husband never told you my first name."

Emersyn felt like an idiot. How could she explain not knowing her client's wife's first name?

"My name is Manon Lafleur Gray."

Suddenly, another realization hit Emersyn. "Does Armand know we are related?" She should have just disclosed this from the beginning. This could be a catastrophe if Paul Bricks found out.

Fuck!

"That I don't know," Manon said. "We don't talk much these days, as I'm sure he probably told you. How much do the two of you talk?"

"He's my client. We talk every day."

"You guys talk about anything personal at all?"

"I'm not sure what you are getting at. Armand is my client, and we talk about things related to the case." Emersyn stared at the photo again. "So, you and my mom were close when you were younger?"

Manon nodded. "We're cousins, so yes."

"Why did you stop talking? Why haven't I heard of you before coming here?"

Emersyn was crossing the line of professionalism, but she couldn't shake the feeling that Phillis was hiding something. Phillis always referred to her family members as toxic and made Emersyn believe they were better off without them. However, the more Emersyn learned about their family, the more she realized Phillis was misleading her. But why? Why keep Emersyn away from the only family they knew? They were decent people. No one was perfect, but they were good people. Now, she was standing before one of her cousins who was also her client's wife. Her head started to throb. She should have never come here under false pretenses. She should have let one of her team members manage this case and leave her personal aspirations out. Now she'd made a complete mess, and once Armand found out Manon and Emersyn were related, he'd tell Paul, and Emersyn was probably going to lose her job.

Manon stared at Emersyn like she was trying to discern the truth. "That's a complicated question." She tilted her head again, as if she were trying to decide how much to say. "Phillis was the only person who understood me," Manon said, looking at the photo. "She had the purest heart of anyone I knew. She kept me grounded." She stared at the picture as if she were talking to the people in it. "She was the only person that I felt truly had my back. I trusted her completely. Told her things I didn't even tell my daddy."

"What happened?"

Manon blinked and looked up at the ceiling. "Sometimes . . . you think you know a person and discover you don't. We never know what we're capable of until our back is against the wall."

"I don't understand," Emersyn admitted.

"The truth is between your mom and me. But we both have to

be willing to tell it. I haven't spoken to my cousins in years, but we used to be best friends. Can you believe that?" she said, as if she weren't expecting a reply. "Relationships are about trust and reciprocity. If you don't have trust, you don't have a relationship."

Emersyn took a gamble. Her career could rest on what she was going to ask next, but at this point, it couldn't hurt. She would have to ask Phillis about her relationship with Manon, but there was something else she needed to know. If Manon and Phillis were so close back then, Manon must know Emersyn's father.

"Do you know a man named Otis McGee?"

Manon finally met her gaze. "Otis McGee?" She scrunched her lips to the side in a way that seemed out of character for her. "Yes, I do," she said in a trance. "He was a nice guy, rough around the edges, but who am I to judge?" She chuckled. "He and Tate worked together at the trucking yard, but Tate earned his degree and worked his way up in the trades. Otis didn't have the same ambition. Last I heard, he still worked out at a truckyard. Why do you ask about Otis? I doubt he'd affect the campaign. I'm sure he doesn't even vote."

Emersyn's heart raced. "So, he's still here in Opelousas?"

"He's still around, as far as I know," Manon said.

Emersyn was at a crossroads. She'd worked hard to reach this level of success. Men doubted her because she was female, and their counterparts questioned her because she was Black. She'd learned to hold her temper, soften her tongue, and use her wits to get everything she wanted for her clients. She was one of the most sought-after in her field. But she felt incomplete. Even if Otis outright rejected her, she'd be content to just meet him.

"Otis is my father," Emersyn said.

"Who told you that?" Manon said quickly.

Emersyn frowned. That wasn't the response she expected.

Maybe one of shock or curiosity, but Manon's tone was accusatory, maybe even disbelief.

Manon stared at Emersyn, looked at the photo, then back at Emersyn.

"I see." Manon ran a finger across her chin. "Otis's ex-wife used to live near the mall. I don't have her phone number, but here's her name." She scribbled on a piece of paper and handed it to Emersyn.

"Thank you," Emersyn sighed. "Can we keep this between us?"

"I wouldn't have it any other way," Manon said.

Emersyn stared at the name. An easy internet search would yield everything she needed. Phillis would be angry when she found out, but she'd have to get over it. This was Emersyn's journey. She knew people who had never met their father and they turned out fine. She, too, fared well without a paternal figure. But all her life, something was tugging her toward finding her father. There was something about him that haunted her. Something inside of her couldn't shake the feeling that Otis wasn't just a deadbeat who wasn't interested in raising a child. So far, Phillis hadn't been honest, which meant there was more to his story, and Emersyn was determined to find out what it was.

CHAPTER 30

Manon 1994

"**A**re you ready," Gwen asked as she and Manon sat outside of Tate's apartment complex. Gwen was Manon's maid of honor and supportive of the last-minute errands and Manon's anxiety attacks.

In a few hours, Manon would become Tate's wife. No one would ever accuse Tate of being the man people expected Manon to marry. Her parents sent her to the best schools, and they entertained families with eligible sons with similar backgrounds as Manon. Addie never pretended to like Tate, but Marcel respected his daughter's decision and her husband to be. As long as Manon had her father's approval, she wasn't concerned about Addie, who would always find a way to be unhappy. Tate wasn't pedigreed, rich, or well-connected, but he was the kindest, most gentle man she'd ever met, and he loved her for who she was. She loved the way he made her feel, and in return, she loved him the best way she knew how. She softened his rough edge, introduced him to people, and helped him expand his vocabulary. There was no mistaking the affinity between the two, and each was fond of the other.

Manon sighed and looked at the building where she'd spent so many nights in secret. "As ready as I ever can be."

"Okay, good," Gwen said. "Go grab whatever you need so you don't have to spend another night in this dump."

"G, stop it. He worked hard to get here. He wasn't handed a

lump sum of money from his parents and sent off to find himself. He worked to help his aunt and worked his way through school."

"I'm sorry. I'm not trying to come for your man. I'm just saying the guy in the overalls over there pushing the shopping cart is making me nervous. So is the dude standing on the corner—so go grab your shit and let's go."

"Oh," Manon mocked Gwen. "Says the woman who loves working with people from varying socioeconomic backgrounds and underrepresented communities."

"I never said that," Gwen said quickly. "And if I did, it's some shit my mom made me say. Now, leave me alone and go get your shit."

Manon poked her tongue out in a playful manner and hopped out of Gwen's Mercedes.

Manon grabbed the mail from the mailman and climbed the stairs to Tate's second-floor apartment. They'd shared so many memories here when they first started dating. Manon's parents wanted her to stay at home from college when she came to town, but Manon stopped telling them when she came home to avoid fights. Most of the time, she would come home a day or two earlier and hang out with Tate first. Tate's one bedroom was their love nest, where they studied, watched movies, and got to know one another better. Manon hated the way his feet smelled, and Tate hated Manon's hair in the bathroom sink. When they argued, Manon packed her bag and threatened to leave. Most often, Tate stopped her, but sometimes he called her bluff. They loved hard and fought harder.

Manon took one last look around Tate's apartment and left her key on the counter. It took her two weeks to get Tate to agree to hire somebody to clean the place. "I'm not scrubbing this place down," Manon had demanded. "We can get somebody to do it, or you can do it yourself." Tate wanted his deposit back, and Manon agreed to pay for the cleaners. Both were happy.

She dropped the mail on the counter. In her haste, a handful of mail fell to the floor. When she picked up the pile, the handwriting on a white envelope stood out. As kids, Manon and Nadesna teased Phillis for her bubble-like cursive. Her *i*'s were so fat they looked like *o's*, and her *s*'s were constantly mistaken for the number eight, just like on the envelope. The return address was Berkeley, California.

Manon opened the envelope.

Dear AJ,

I don't know if this letter will find you single, married, or living with regrets. Nothing has changed since I saw you with Manon at my grandmother's birthday party. At first, I had so many questions for you, but in the end, all that matters is that you lied and betrayed me, my best friend, and my entire family. I can never show my face to them again. I am so ashamed of being played for a fool. I loved and trusted you. Unfortunately, you chose to take both my love and trust for granted. The worst parts of me thought about not contacting you, but the sensible part knew I couldn't do that and live in peace. I cringe to think what kind of man dates two close cousins. But I digress.

In my haste to love you and give you what I thought you wanted, I neglected to protect myself in the most basic ways. I'm carrying our baby. I know we will never be together, but I felt it was only right to let you know. Below is my contact information. If I don't hear from you, I know where you stand, and I (or the baby) will never bother you again.

Phillis

Manon covered her mouth with her hand to conceal her wails of grief. When she sobered, she looked at the letter again.

AJ.

Armand Jackson Gray. This was Phillis's boyfriend? This was the boy she'd been talking about all along? Manon recalled the night she introduced Tate to the family and Phillis disappeared. How vague and distant Tate was after they left Grandma Earline's house that night.

Her thoughts raced. Did he know that Phillis and Manon were related? He told Manon that his birthname was Armand, but everyone called him Tate after his grandfather. She took several deep breaths and tried to recall the interactions between Tate and Phillis. No, that wasn't possible. If Tate knew Manon and Phillis were related, he would have never shown up to the party. That wasn't Tate's way. She refused to let her mind drift to the unreasonable.

Manon had so many questions that needed to be resolved, but all of her family and friends were waiting for her pending nuptials. Her father would be disappointed and hurt that his baby girl was hurt. She stared at the letter for a few more seconds before she crumpled it in her hands. Poor Phillis. She never had a real boyfriend before, and Manon could only imagine how she felt when she saw Tate—AJ—at the family party. Certainly, she had to feel betrayed. How awful for her to find out that he was two-timing her and dating Manon. She blinked back angry tears. She would have to deal with Tate later.

But what hurt the most was Phillis's absence. They were cousins. Best friends. They'd been through so many things together. How dare Phillis disappear and move to California with no conversation or explanation? That was the ultimate betrayal.

Manon felt her face getting hot. Men would come and go, but family was forever. This wasn't Phillis's fault. But instead of working it out, Phillis took the cowardly way out and ran without so much as a goodbye. Why would Phillis respond this way? Now it made sense why Phillis hadn't called since leaving for California.

Manon stuffed the crumpled letter and envelope into her purse. Right now, on the day of her wedding, it was easier to allow herself to focus on her anger at Phillis for leaving rather than Tate for his betrayal.

"What's wrong with you?" Gwen asked when Manon returned to the car.

"Huh?"

"You look like you've seen a ghost. What the hell happened in there?"

"Nothing. Just drive."

"You sure? Are you having second thoughts? Because if you are, we can take off and go down to Galveston and have a—"

"Drive, Gwen," Manon directed.

The ride to the church was silent except for Gwen sighing in exasperation at Manon's strange behavior. Manon couldn't wrap her head around the situation. She tried to understand why Phillis didn't come to her. If she truly didn't know that Tate and AJ were the same person, then why run away? Something wasn't right, and since Manon didn't have answers, she landed on her own conclusions. There would be hundreds of people expecting a wedding ceremony today. Manon was getting married, and all of the Opelousas elite would be present. There was no way she could cancel the wedding. Addie would have Manon's head on a platter.

Manon walked into the church, dazed and confused. Her mind drifted from canceling the wedding, to how hurt Phillis must be, to her own broken heart. She didn't know how she was going to look Tate in the eye. Manon shook her head to focus, but it was as if she was drifting in and out of reality. She barely recalled getting her makeup done or her cousins helping her into her wedding dress. She shook her head when she heard someone talking.

"So, Phillis really isn't coming to your wedding?" Arelia asked, straightening Manon's veil.

"What made you ask that?" Manon asked sharply.

"Um, 'cause you're getting married soon and Phillis ain't here. I'm just asking, dang. What's wrong with you?" Arelia snapped.

"Nothing," Manon sat back in her chair and let Arelia and the makeup artist finish getting her ready.

Clotee had told the family that Phillis was traveling from California to attend Manon's wedding. So far, she was a no-show. Manon was hurt, then frustrated, and then angry. She grew tired of pestering Clotee and didn't understand how Phillis could abandon her on such an important day.

But now she knew.

"I don't care," Manon said. "The people who are supposed to be here are here," she declared. She stared at herself in the dressing room mirror. This was supposed to be the happiest day of her life, but it felt like the worst day. She couldn't cancel the wedding of the year, and she couldn't let Addie have the gratification that Manon had made a bad decision in marrying Tate.

Manon's chest pounded as the pipe organ reverberated through St. Benedict's, where every seat in the chapel was filled. The more Addie involved herself with the wedding planning, the more the guest list grew. Manon didn't want a big wedding, but here they were, and soon, everyone in the sanctuary would stare at her with admiration and pride.

Manon couldn't focus. She envisioned Phillis and Tate together. When had it happened? How? And how did she miss the signs? She closed her eyes, hoping when she'd open them it would all be a bad dream. She couldn't walk down the aisle to marry a man who was also in a relationship with her best friend and cousin. Her father was waiting outside the door to grab her arm and lead her to the man who was supposed to take care of her for the rest of her life. She should have been filled with joy and excitement, but all she wanted was a hug. Assurance that everything would be okay.

Manon tucked Grandma Earline's blue handkerchief into her slip. The pearl-encrusted gown with sheer scalloped sleeves lay across her body like a second skin. She looked as radiant as the women in the brides' magazines she subscribed to. She felt empty and lost, wishing the last twenty-four hours had never happened.

"Stunning," Gwen put her hands over her mouth.

"I agree," Arelia bounced her daughter, Devanie, on her shoulder. "You look beautiful."

"Gorgeous," Nadesna sniffled. "You're the prettiest bride ever."

Manon refocused on her reflection. She would soon become Mrs. Armand Gray in true Southern Belle style thanks to a surly wedding planner who chain-smoked and snapped her fingers when she couldn't remember something. "What's the name of that designer?" *Snap Snap.* "He always wore the hat with the feather in it?" *Snap, snap, snap.*

"Thank you." Manon tried to muster up some excitement on what was supposed to be the most important day of her life. Soon, she would be a wife. Like Addie, she'd have high tea and rotating brunches, and complain about window dressings and housekeeper woes. On the outside, everything in her life appeared to be coming together, but that was far from the truth.

"Now, here's the real sunshine." Marcel held out his arms, and Manon sank into them.

"Don't mess up your makeup!" Nadesna warned.

"Let's give her a few minutes with her daddy," Gwen said. "See you on the other side, Manon."

"You ready?" Marcel looked into Manon's eyes. She wanted to escape in his arms and make all the confusion disappear. The bitterness with Addie, the betrayal from Phillis and Tate. The burden of marrying a man who couldn't be trusted. But how could she walk away with a room full of people who were waiting for the "wedding of the year"? Addie would have Manon's head on a Waterford platter.

"I'm ready, Daddy." Manon took a deep breath and looped her arm through her father's. People from every stage in her life were in the sanctuary: elementary school teachers, Manon's dressage trainer, ballet instructor, family, sorority sisters, and her hairstylist.

Months before she was engaged to Tate, she was looking for a stamp in her father's office. Manon wasn't a snoop and wouldn't have given the manilla envelope a second chance if her name wasn't written across the front. Most documents were about property parcels and some other stuff Manon didn't understand. The next set of documents was Marcel's trust. He was generous and would provide Manon with a trust fund that she would receive at one of two milestones: when she turned forty or when she married. If she wasn't married by the time she was forty, she would receive the money in increments. But when she got married, she would receive all but twenty percent of it.

Marcel leaned toward her. "You ready, baby girl?"

Manon blinked. People loved to love. Weddings brought people together and gave hope and a reason to feel good. Manon put one foot in front of the other. She caught warm smiles and approving nods through her veil as she slowly passed each row. Aunt Clotee's perm rod set looked pretty, and Addie's sweeping updo was divine. Aunt Odester looked sober and healthy. They were gathered to wish Manon well in her next life stage. Everyone she loved was there. Everyone except for Phillis.

Tate waited at the altar with the minister and the wedding party. He looked straight ahead, jaw clenched. She held her father's arm as she walked down the aisle. Her legs felt weak. She closed her eyes, and when she reopened them, she was standing before the minister and Tate, the same minister who'd christened her as a baby and blessed the food at her high school graduation dinner. He was older and broader now, but he seemed just as jovial as ever.

"You alright, baby girl?" Marcel asked quietly. His brow furrowed.

Manon nodded.

"Who gives this woman to be wed to this man?" the minister's voice boomed.

Manon blinked.

"I do," Marcel released Manon to Tate.

Tate moved next to Manon and whispered, "You look beautiful."

Manon spent her life being appropriate and polite and an overachiever. Her primary mission was to avoid embarrassing Addie. Tate wasn't the ideal husband, but he was the first man who loved Manon unconditionally. Addie had shuddered the first few times they all went to dinner together. She questioned his background, his father, and even his mental health. "Has anyone in your family ever been institutionalized?" Addie asked Tate once. Manon couldn't fail. Failing meant Addie was right, and she'd never let Addie be right. This marriage would work. And because she chose Tate against their will, she couldn't fail. That letter was gone. No one knew about it.

"In sickness and in health," Tate said.

Tears streamed down her cheeks as the minister turned to her and said the vows.

"Manon?" the minister said.

Manon blinked. "Huh?"

"Repeat after me."

"You okay?" Tate leaned in and whispered.

Manon repeated the minister's words, tears still streaming. Tate smiled and squeezed her hands. Could this man, who said he loved her so much, be a two-timer? The father of her little cousin's baby. Even if she didn't know who Tate was initially, she should have said something when she found out. But no one knew about the letter. If Phillis wanted to run away and hide her secret, Manon wouldn't reveal it.

Tate squeezed her hand again.

"I do," Manon said.

CHAPTER 31
Odester 1998

O dester stared across the church parking lot as people walked, heads down, hearts heavy. She longed for the days when she and her sisters sat on the front porch eating crawfish and dreaming out loud. Nothing mattered except for school, chores, and who got the most time on the phone. Odester could have been nicer to Addie, and she could have helped Clotee more with Nadesna, but hindsight was twenty-twenty. Everyone wished for another chance at something: relationships, career choices, eating habits. Hell, some people would have paid more attention to their homework. There was a myriad of things that could change the course of someone's life if there was a such thing as a do-over. She wiped stray ash from her cigarette off her black dress and slipped off her pumps.

As much as she disliked Bumpie, she was thankful for his family who helped cook and serve today. To Bumpie's people, family was in the heart, not the relationship. The tassel from her high school graduation cap hung from her rearview mirror. Where did she go wrong in her life? Why had she taken the most difficult path possible? Her heart was broken into pieces again. She took a drag of her cigarette and let tears stream down her face.

Aunt Jerutha, who drove down from Houston with Julius, spotted Odester sitting in the car. Odester hadn't seen Aunt Jerutha since Rutherford told her he didn't think she should marry Julius—something about him being too young and not having a job. Odester didn't remember all the details, just that Aunt Jerutha stopped coming around. But funerals brought families together during the worst time. Emotions were high, and overwhelming sadness kept you from enjoying relatives you hadn't seen in years. Somebody always made potato salad that caused an argument, and there were never enough obituaries to go around. Odester put four obituaries into her bag. She wanted to give two to her coworkers, and she'd keep the other two for herself. She wiped her face as Aunt Jerutha approached her car.

"So good to see you." Aunt Jerutha leaned in Odester's window and hugged her.

Julius awkwardly waved a hand. "My condolences," he said.

Odester smiled enough to be polite but not enough to elicit conversation. There was nothing to discuss. Besides, if Daddy didn't like Julius, neither did Odester. She accepted a hug from Aunt Jerutha, who walked away when the smallest talk didn't bud.

Odester extinguished her cigarette and looked for a breath mint in her purse. When she pulled out her wallet, a small white pill was lodged in the corner. The last time she used this purse was at Rutherford's funeral and when she abused pills. She got out of the car and headed toward the church.

"Hey, Auntie," a voice came from behind. Odester jumped and dropped the pill in the grass. She was planning to throw it away, but dropping it was just as well. She looked up and did a double take. Phillis looked so much like Clotee it was almost scary. Even the way she walked, swaying one arm higher than the other, was like Clotee. Years ago, Phillis had moved to California for some graduate program. But did a graduate program stop you from ever returning home for a visit?

"Oh, Phillis." Odester embraced her niece and burst into tears all over again. After a few long minutes, she released her.

"Everything was so beautiful." Odester wiped her face. "You did a good job. Your mother was so proud of you."

"Thank you." Phillis was small like Clotee, but she had wide hips and a shorter torso.

Odester started crying again. It was exhausting to have your heart torn out of your body and replaced with missing pieces. Until she saw Phillis, she didn't think she could make it through this day. Losing a parent was an inexplicable feeling, one that Odester knew all too well. Years later, she was still grieving her father. She'd moved on, but the pain never stopped, and she knew it would be similar for Phillis.

"Why are you out here? I think they want to serve us food now. Plus, it's getting hot." Phillis fanned her face.

"I can't eat, Phillis," Odester said, not remembering the last time she ate a full meal. She hadn't seen Phillis since she arrived from California three days ago because Phillis was busy arranging the funeral and figuring out what to do with Clotee's belongings. The poor girl had lost both of her parents. Willie Earl's demise was different because they mourned him for years. Clotee once said she lost her husband to drinking long before she lost him to death. But Clotee was the picture of health. Losing her was different.

"I know, but at least try." Phillis put her arm around her.

"How are you so strong?"

Phillis sighed. "I'm not. I miss her so much. The grief is so overwhelming that sometimes I can't think straight. Maybe I'm strong. I don't know." Phillis looked off into the distance. "Maybe I'm numb. The only thing I'm sure of is that life will never be the same."

Odester grabbed her niece again. "It's okay," she consoled her. "Let it out."

"I came out here to check on you," Phillis sniffled.

"That's what family is for," Odester said. "We are here to help one another, not to be separated. My sisters and I have been through a lot, but we help each other. We deal with our issues together. We may fight or speak for a long time, but we don't walk away."

Phillis wiped her face again. "Yeah."

"I saw Manon in the service. First time I've seen her in a good while."

"What do you mean?" Phillis furrowed her brow. She wore the same look Clotee did when she found out Odester was pregnant with Arelia.

"She doesn't come around. Hasn't come around the family much since she got married." Odester waited for a reaction. Something happened between Phillis and Manon, and the family skirted around it long enough. It was time to find out the truth.

Phillis opened her mouth, then closed it and opened it again. "That doesn't make sense."

"You and I agree. After Manon married Tate, Manon clung to her marriage. She came round for birthdays and special occasions. Then the visits became less frequent. Now we hardly see her anymore. And it ain't like she married up the way Addie did. That fellow is just a regular guy. Not good enough for her, if you ask me."

Phillis studied Odester's face. "You don't know why she stopped coming around?"

"No." Odester lit another cigarette. "Do you?"

"What y'all out here doing?" Nadesna and Addie walked up. Nadesna always had terrible timing, but today she looked broken, with her arms draped across her body and puffy, red eyes. When Nadesna was little, she had nightmares, and Odester would come into Nadesna's room and tell her stories about four sisters who would travel the world together one day. She would describe a beautiful location, and Nadesna would fall asleep. As Odester recalled those stories, she realized that day would never come.

"Just talkin'." Odester was annoyed by her sisters' interruption. She looked over to see Phillis's reaction. There was none. She was so much like Clotee—genuine, those eyes that seemed like they could see right through you, and she never let on how she felt. If Odester knew Phillis like she knew her sister Clotee, Phillis would never open up now that there was an audience.

"I needed a break," Phillis said. Her curls were pulled back, separated by a middle part.

"Don't we all." Addie tossed her short bob. She was the only sister who preferred straight hair. She was also the only one who wore designer clothing and had a manicurist who made home visits. "I appreciate the church's gesture, but I'm not hungry. I'm not too fond of repasts. They are like parties for the deceased, and that doesn't seem appropriate."

Today wasn't the day for Addie's haughty attitude, but Odester didn't respond. They were all hurting, and hurt people tended to get on one another's nerves when they gathered together.

"It's tradition." Odester lit another cigarette. "But I feel you. I'm not in the mood for socializing either. And I don't know who made that mac and cheese, but I wouldn't dare eat that."

"Dette, please put that out." Addie turned up her nose. "I just lost one sister. I don't need to lose another one to lung cancer."

And they wondered why Odester didn't come around. Just like when they were kids, Addie and Clotee were always telling her what to do and how to live her life.

"I got one life to live, and I want to live mine with cigarettes. Least it ain't crack."

Addie jerked her head away and looked at Phillis. "I heard you have a little girl. Why didn't you bring her?"

"Yes." Phillis cleared her throat and shifted her eyes. "She had school. I didn't want her to miss it."

Odester extinguished her cigarette and waited for Phillis to say more.

She didn't.

"What's her name again?' Odester asked. "Tee told me, but I forgot."

"Emersyn."

"Such a pretty name. Tee said she real smart."

Clotee talked about her granddaughter all the time. She had visited California a few times but stopped when her headaches became too extreme. "Just not feeling well," Clotee told Odester just before canceling the last visit. By the time the doctors diagnosed her, the tumors lit the imaging screen like fireworks on the Fourth of July. Clotee promised to tell Phillis about her illness, but she never did.

"She is really smart. Thank you," Phillis said. "Just wish I would have come back home more often."

"You didn't know your mom was ill," Addie rationalized. "If you had, I'm sure you would have come home more, dear." She put a hand on Phillis's shoulder and rubbed for a few seconds. That was probably the most affection she'd shown anyone in a long time.

"Even if she didn't know Clotee was sick, she should have come home more," Odester said. She couldn't hold her peace. She was happy to see Phillis, but she'd seen her sister hurting over her only daughter not coming home more often to visit.

"Dette, give her a break," Nadesna said. "She just lost her mother."

"And I lost my sister," Addie said. "She was the only one who took up for me." She dabbed an eye with a monogrammed handkerchief. "She was a saint. Don't ever let anybody tell you differently. Your mom was a saint."

"Yes, she was," Manon said as she approached the group. She glanced at Phillis. "She held honesty and family values in high esteem. There will never be another like her."

Phillis averted Manon's stare. Odester watched the exchange with intrigue. She would never forget the look on Phillis's face years ago at Earline's birthday party before leaving for California.

"I have to go, but I wanted to tell you the service was beautiful," Manon said. "And Aunt Clotee was one of a kind. I love her so much."

"Thank you." Phillis nodded. "And thank you for coming."

"I will call you later." Manon kissed Addie on the cheek and hugged Odester and Nadesna before leaving.

"Manon," Odester called out. "We are heading over to Clotee's to help Phillis clean out a few things. You wanna join us?"

Manon turned and looked at Phillis. "I don't think that would be the best idea."

Phillis, Odester, Addie, Nadesna, and Arelia met at Clotee's house when the repast was over. The house was neat and organized, just the way Clotee kept it.

"Oh girl, I remember this hat!" Arelia held up a purple fedora. Her daughter, Devanie, was asleep on the couch. Odester didn't know who Devanie's father was, and she had no idea Arelia was even in a relationship when she got pregnant. She just came over one day and announced that Odester was going to be a grandmother. Fortunately, Odester was a better grandmother than she was a mother, and she babysat her beautiful grandbaby often.

"Tee always said she felt like Jackie-O in this hat!" Nadesna laughed.

"She sure did." Phillis smiled. She separated Clotee's things, packing a box of items she wanted to ship back home.

"How long are you staying?" Arelia asked.

"I'm leaving tomorrow," Phillis said. "I have to get back to Emersyn."

"I still can't believe you have a daughter," Nadesna clasped her hands together. "I always imagined you traveling the world with one of those tiny dogs on your lap. Not a child."

"Yeah." Phillis folded one of Clotee's quilts. "Life is funny that way."

"Ain't that a trip?" Arelia leaned in. "But what's a trip is how our girls are close in age like we are and like our moms were."

Phillis nodded and smiled.

"And what's even more of a trip is how you and Manon stopped talking."

"Ree, stop being messy," Nadesna said from across the room.

Odester looked on but kept quiet. She wondered the same thing.

"I'm not messy." Arelia folded a sweater and put it in a pile. "I want to know what happened." She focused on Phillis's face. "We all do. Y'all were best cousins, and now y'all act like you don't know one another."

Phillis continued folding.

"Tell me." Arelia stood up. "Is it because you were jealous of her getting married? Was she jealous you went to graduate school? Tell me."

"Ree, stop it!" Nadesna warned.

"Yeah," Odester chimed in. "That's enough."

"Don't tell me what to do." Arelia ignored Odester. "After Phillis left town, nothing was the same. Manon stopped coming around. Aunt Clotee was depressed. I just want to know what happened. Is that too much to ask?"

"Don't listen to her," Nadesna said to Phillis.

Phillis stood up. "I'm going to ship this box home. That pile over there is for the taking if anybody wants anything. The movers will come to get the rest tomorrow, and the property manager will take over from there."

"You still leaving tomorrow?" Odester asked.

"Yeah." Phillis shifted her eyes. "I need to get back."

The next day, Phillis left, and it would be years until she returned.

CHAPTER 32

Emersyn 2019

Rico looked delectable in a suit with no tie. He sat two drinks on the table—his garnished with lime, and Emersyn's with sugar around the rim. "I'm glad you could make it," he said.

"I'm glad you made time." She looked around the packed lounge. Vera was famous among mixed-age groups. A line formed around the bar, and a tall woman in a sparkly red dress crooned from the corner. Emersyn ran her finger around the base of her glass.

"What's bothering you, Cali?" Rico had the same eerie instinct that seemed to be part of Opelousas culture. "Something is going on. You helped me, so let me be here for you."

She thought about canceling tonight's date, but she liked Rico and could use someone to talk to. Emersyn's plan to not mix business with pleasure crashed around her, and she didn't know what to do. She sipped her crafted Lemon Drop and disclosed her visit with Manon.

Emersyn took a deep breath. "So, Armand told me about his wife, but we both referred to her as Mrs. Gray. It turns out she is my cousin."

"Wait. What? How? Mrs. Gray is your cousin?" Rico shook his head. "Why would Armand lie to you?"

"Technically, he didn't," Emersyn said. "I didn't dig beyond her married name because I didn't think I needed to. It's complicated, but I don't think he intentionally lied. Something is missing; I just haven't figured out what it is. Mrs. Gray is hiding something as well. I can feel it."

"Why don't you ask him?"

"I thought about it," Emersyn said.

"I think you should, before she does." Rico signaled the waitress to bring another round even though he hadn't finished his first drink. "But how can he be married to her and not know she's your cousin?" Rico scrunched his face together. "Didn't y'all have family gatherings?"

Another good question.

"It turns out Manon is estranged from the family and hasn't talked to them in years. And I never met her. She said she felt like she knew me when we first met, but she figured it was a coincidence."

Rico shook his head. "But if Armand knew you were trying to contact her, why wouldn't he give you her full name?"

"I don't think he wanted me to talk to her," Emeryn said. "But I think more than anything, he was worried she would have said something to ruin his campaign, and he didn't want to risk that. I also think she has health issues. She tries to hide it, but she walks with a limp."

"Damn," Rico said. "I've never seen her at any of Devanie's family events. She was always nice to me. Before she dropped off the scene, everybody wanted to be friends with Armand and his wife. They were the power couple in this town."

"What do you mean, before she dropped off the scene?"

"Did she tell you about the car accident?"

Emersyn shook her head.

"All I know is her recovery was slow, and they both disappeared from the social scene for a while."

"Wow." Emersyn listened intently.

"Yeah, I heard the doctors said she wouldn't walk again, but she started progressing slowly. Armand started to engage socially more over time, but she never re-emerged. I heard she's in a wheelchair, but from what you're sayin', that's not true."

"No, she's definitely not in a wheelchair," Emersyn said as she recalled Manon ambling through her house.

"I also heard a rumor that her face is disfigured too. Is that true?"

Emersyn shook her head and sipped her drink. "Not at all."

Armand claimed that he and Manon had an amicable split, said they didn't talk much but were otherwise civil. "She's stubborn like her mom," Armand had said. These phrases all had new meanings because these people were Emersyn's relatives. Manon's mom was Addie, who was sisters with Emersyn's grandmother Clotee.

"Does Armand have a girlfriend?" Emersyn didn't see the relevancy in the question, but nothing made sense right now, so she should find out all the information she could. She also had to find a way to tell Armand that she and Manon were cousins. As of a few hours ago, she didn't know they were cousins, so technically, she wasn't hiding anything.

"Nah, I never heard him talk about anybody. I have heard him mention a girlfriend from back in the day. I think he is still in love with Manon."

"Really?"

"I think so. Armand is a good-looking cat, successful, and nice. Those older ladies are always hitting on him. But he doesn't respond. I heard he used to be a player back in the day, but from what I can tell, those days are over for him."

"That's sweet that he still loves her. I wonder why they can't work it out."

"Who knows? Anything could happen when you have been

together as long as those two have. That won't be my story, though." He pulled Emersyn's eyes into his.

"It won't?" Emersyn temporarily forgot her woes and lowered her eyes. Amid the chaos, Rico had been a great distraction. Handsome, a good listener, and smart. If she had known that all she had to do was come to the south to find a man, she would have done so years ago.

"Nah," he looked deep into her eyes. "I got one marriage in me. When I find my queen, she'll have to put up with me until God calls one of us home." He bit his bottom lip, and Emersyn crossed her legs.

"How 'bout you, Cali? You wanna get married one day?"

"I hope so. I don't want to be alone for the rest of my life. It's just my mom and me. After watching my mom for so long, that's not the life for me."

"I feel you. What about kids?"

"With the right person," Emersyn said.

"I like you." He studied her face.

"I like you too." Emersyn rocked in her seat. He leaned closer and pulled her chin in his hand.

"We have a problem up front," a mousy girl with a high ponytail interrupted.

Rico sighed and pulled back. "What's wrong, Marsha?"

Marsha explained about overbooked reservations and an angry party of ten that was there to celebrate a birthday.

Rico scoffed. "I'm sorry, Cali. I have to handle this."

"No worries. I've taken up enough of your work evening. I have to go anyway." She got up. "Are you interested in coming to my aunt's house on Sunday? It's my farewell Sunday dinner."

"Farewell dinner?" He put a hand over his heart as if someone had injured him there.

"Yeah, I gotta get back home. My mom needs me, and I have

to get back to work. I want to settle all this drama with my family in my remaining days here, though." Emersyn still didn't tell him about Otis. The number Manon had given her didn't turn up anything. She was back at square-one.

"Aw, man, I was hoping you'd be around a little longer. I wanted to get to know you better," Rico said. She looked up into his eyes and took tiny breaths. He was the most beautiful man she'd ever seen. She could hardly believe he was interested in her. Back home, no man this fine had ever given Emersyn a second look, let alone want to spend time with her.

Rico pulled her chin up with his finger and kissed her gently.

Emersyn took a deep breath.

"Was that okay?"

She looked around. "It was perfect," she whispered. "But you have to get to work."

"Right." Rico put his hand over his heart again.

"Will I see you on Sunday?" Emersyn asked. "At my aunt's?"

"Your big shindig before you go home? I wouldn't miss it for the world, Cali."

CHAPTER 33

Manon 2019

People walked in and out of cooling tents, nibbling on pork ribs, pecan candy, and ordered daiquiris from a hosted bar. The local band, the Dazz Brothers, played smooth seventies soul, and a few courageous folks cut a rug. Manon sipped a daiquiri and bobbed to the zydeco music.

"I love this music," Emersyn said.

Manon invited Emersyn to the fundraising event at the last minute. She didn't like the way things had unfolded the night before. Emersyn had nothing to do with Manon's relationship with Phillis. Emersyn was a beautiful and smart girl. Manon imagined being there for her milestones growing up, like she and Phillis always said they'd do when they had children. Manon still grieved her relationship with Phillis. Gwen was a good friend, but no bond touched the bond she and Phillis once had. That was a bridge to cross another day, but for now, Manon wanted to make amends with her younger cousin.

Emersyn had Tate's eyes and crooked forefinger. She nodded her head to music the way he did. Manon's stomach fluttered. Emersyn was the child Tate had always wanted. He wanted a son, but Emersyn's spirit, determination, and drive would have made Tate a proud father. She took Emersyn away from Tate by hiding Phillis's letter the way she almost took Leonard from his family.

All Manon had wanted to do was to protect Leonard. His parents were drunken, negligent, and irresponsible, leaving

Leonard unattended so often. Manon had hid diapers in a small drawer in the pantry for the days when he'd come over soaking wet. She also had his favorite snacks: Goldfish crackers and Dixie Cups. The last time he came over, she'd foolishly wondered if it would be possible to keep him. His parents were fighting in the street the night before, and Leonard stood on the porch screaming, a binky hanging from his mouth. The next day, he walked up to Manon's house, and she had led him inside where he gawked at the wall art—*red, blue, yellow*—she said, pointing to the colors. Manon followed him around her house with a bowl of grapes, and he'd turn to grab one, then continue to explore his surroundings.

Leonard had silky chocolate skin and knotty hair. It was much coarser than Manon would know how to manage. She imagined getting it all cut off so the texture was unnoticeable. Maybe she'd get him one of those do-rags Uncle Buster wore. And she'd have to get him all new clothes. The ones he wore were tattered and smelled like urine.

Manon had bathed him and dropped a small yellow ball she'd picked up at a street fair in the tub to keep him occupied. Leonard loved the bath. He cooed, splashed, and threw the ball in the air. "Yaaaay!" he'd repeated after Manon. "Yaaaay!" She'd scrubbed his little brown body, tattered from falls and scrapes while he was unattended. *How could two people neglect their child?* she'd wondered. Manon only considered motherhood because of Tate, and unfortunately for him, her body couldn't hold a baby. In that moment, Manon believed Leonard was a gift from God. He was her chance to prove she had maternal instincts and would be a much better mother than Addie. Leonard's parents didn't care, and Tate would understand. She fell into a deep daydream where Leonard opened presents under a huge Christmas tree.

"Everybody step back," a voice had boomed from outside.

Manon had wrapped Leonard in a towel and lathered him with lotion. After dressing him, she gave him a piece of pecan candy and walked out to the front porch. A group had gathered across the street. Leonard's stupid parents were probably fighting again. But when Manon looked closer, she saw his parents talking to the police. She tried to step back into the house, but Mr. Genessa saw her. Manon hiked Leonard up on her hip and strolled over.

"What the fuck?" Leonard's mother wailed, and she yanked him from Manon's arms. She glared at Manon. "You stole my baby!"

The cop pulled Manon to the side. "Ma'am, how did the baby get inside your house?"

He got in the way he always did. He walked over while his inept parents did whatever drunken meth heads do during the day.

"He walked over." Manon had folded her arms across her chest. "He always does." All she did was give him grapes and a bath. "I lost track of time."

"I need to tell you something." Manon scootched closer to Emersyn. The Dazz Brothers mellowed the music to smooth jazz.

"Of course," Emersyn said. She was so kind. Manon felt horrible for how she'd upended this girl's life, but she didn't understand what Phillis did. If Phillis knew Tate was Emersyn's father, why did she tell him that Otis was the father? Otis could barely string two sentences together. It didn't make sense. This moment wasn't about Phillis's fallacies; it was about Manon. She needed to atone for the last thirty years and forgive herself. She needed to be free of the damage and trauma—most of it self-inflicted.

"Tate and I lived separate lives for years," she began.

She then explained how they'd tried to conceive over and over, but it never happened. It was her fate for being a horrible person.

"You're not a horrible person," Emersyn corrected. She sounded so much like Phillis.

Manon sipped her daiquiri as she told her story. "One night, we had this big fight. I . . . um . . . said some awful things and Tate left the house. Later, I decided to go to a friend's house because I needed to clear my head and didn't want to be home when Tate returned." She paused and looked down. "When I arrived at my friend's house, she didn't answer the door, so I went around and entered through the backyard—something I always did. When I was inside, I noticed wine glasses and music. I figured she had company. When I turned to leave, I saw her and Tate sitting on the couch."

"You don't have to tell me this," Emersyn said.

"It's okay," Manon said. "Anyway, they both turned and saw me, and I rushed out of the house. Tate chased me, but I made it to my car and locked the door. He wanted to explain, but I didn't want to hear it. I couldn't. Not at that time. And as luck would have it, Opelousas weather did its thing and a huge thunderstorm erupted. I knew I shouldn't drive—not with the heavy rain and my mental state—but I had to get out of there. I felt betrayed, used, and I was mad. Tate begged me not to drive. He kept saying that even if I didn't want to talk to him, just please don't drive. But I did anyway. Halfway down the street, the tires hit something, and I tried to control the wheel as a car was heading toward me. But I couldn't get control. The last thing I remember is a long honk. The next day I woke up in the hospital."

"I'm so sorry."

"Don't be," Manon said. "I think that fight was the end for us, but we couldn't admit it. We were the *it* couple, powerhouses in the community: beauty, brains, money. People thought we had it all. But in reality, we had nothing. It reminded me so much of my childhood, when I'd shrink within myself with depression. My entire life has been predicated on having everything and nothing. We didn't make time to fix the things that were wrong because we were so busy with the façade, and when we did try, it was too late."

"That's an incredible story," Emersyn said. "You are a strong woman. I'm sorry things didn't work out with you and your husband. That must be so hard."

"Men, you can't live with them, you can't kill them," Manon laughed.

"My mom says that." Emersyn looked into Manon's eyes. "In fact, she said it recently about her oncologist when I tried to hook her up with him." Emersyn chuckled.

"Oncologist?" Manon sat up. She couldn't bring herself to say the words. All these years of secrets and silence and grudges, and for what? In that moment, all she cared about was Phillis. Her best friend and cousin. The person who had had her back when no one else did.

"Cancer." Emersyn finished Manon's sentence. "Found a tumor last year. It's been tough, but as I said, she's so strong. Just like you. Can I ask you a question?"

Manon nodded.

"What happened between you and my mom?"

"Do you want to know the truth?"

Emersyn nodded. "I do."

"Your mom and I have unfinished business. We were both too proud to clear the air, but we should have done it so long ago. The truth lies between the two of us, and not until we reconcile that truth can I tell you what happened. Because I don't completely know myself."

Emersyn looked confused but didn't press. "Are you coming to Nadesna's on Sunday?"

"I don't know," Manon answered honestly. "She invited me. I have a lot to work out with myself before dealing with my family.

There was a lot of hurt and betrayal, and I don't know if I'm ready to be around all of them. I'll let you know."

"I'm sure they would be happy to see you. I'd love to see you there."

"You're a sweetheart, Emersyn."

"Thank you." Emersyn blushed.

"You remind me a lot of your mama."

"Yeah, I wish she came, but she doesn't want to come back. I've tried for years."

Manon looked away. She ruined three lives. "I'm sure she has a good reason. Probably not even her fault. How did that address work out for you?"

"For Otis's ex-wife?" Emersyn frowned. "Another dud. I'm leaving in a couple of days, and I think I'm going to give up. Maybe I'm not meant to know my father. Maybe this is part of God's grand plan for me to have a testimony to share with some other fatherless adult woman."

"Don't be sarcastic. Everything will come out in due time."

"I used to think so, but now I doubt I'll ever find him."

"You'll find him," Manon said. "I promise you."

CHAPTER 34

Odester 1998

T he Meadows, a one-story recovery center located along the Airline Highway, was serene with white walls, strict staff, and mediocre food, though the banana pudding was worth noting. The program was voluntary, so there were no fences or extra security measures. Residents endured limited phone time, group and individual therapy, and daily meditation.

Odester was one week into the program and ready to burst at the seams. She had a rough night last night, but one of the other patients, a small woman with thick glasses named Annalise, helped her.

"Don't walk out that door," Annalise warned Odester. "If you do, you will hate yourself, and you will have to start over again."

Odester didn't care about starting over. She wanted to relieve the pain. She missed her daddy. She missed her sisters, and she wanted a relationship with Arelia, who hardly came around. Why had her world turned upside down? After an hour of back and forth with Annalise, Odester went to bed, but she didn't sleep.

But today was a new day. She sat in the group circle and waved to Annalise. Today was her last day in the program. Again. But this time, she swore she wouldn't be back.

"I want to thank everybody here for supporting me." Annalise wiped tears from her face. "I couldn't have done it without you. And thank you, Timothy, for keeping it real with me," she said to their group counselor. "I'm ready this time, y'all. I'm ready to be a mother and a wife again. No more letting addiction control my life."

The group clapped, and they indulged in pastries and coffee to celebrate. Odester approached Annalise.

"So, this is it, huh?" Odester smiled. "I'm proud of you."

"Thank you. I'm proud of you too," Annalise said. "I know you struggle with the past, but we can't keep dwelling on that. Focus on the now. Your daughter needs you now, and so does your granddaughter. Forget what you did and who you were, and just be the beautiful person you are now."

Odester hugged Annalise. "You've been a good friend. Thank you."

"Chavis!" someone called. "You have a visitor."

"Looks like this is goodbye," Annalise said. "Take care of yourself and call me anytime."

Odester approached the front lounge area where guests visited. Arelia promised to bring pecan candy today, but Odester wasn't holding her breath. Arelia was a no-show the last three times she'd promised to visit. Odester suspected it was Nadesna checking in on her again. But when Odester arrived in the lounge area, she was surprised to see her visitor.

Bumpie sat on the edge of the red and yellow sofa that didn't match the other décor in the room. He was looking down at the floor but stood up when Odester walked in. He rubbed his hands together. "How are you?"

Odester looked around. Was Arelia parking the car? "I'm good," she looked toward the door. "It's just you?"

"Yes." Bumpie cleared his throat. "Just me," he motioned toward the sofa. "Can we talk?"

"Sure." Odester sat down. It had been a long time since she and Bumpie had a real conversation, and as she sat next to him, she noticed how different he looked these days. It seemed like the older he got, the better he looked, but maybe it was just that he had started taking care of himself. Clotee always said, "Can't nobody clean you up like Jesus."

"How are you?"

"I'm as good as can be expected, but I'm sure you know all about that."

"Yep," he sighed. "I did my share of time in one of these. A couple of times."

"But you are fine now," Odester noted.

"One day at a time. I still struggle sometimes, but I know turning back is not an option. You . . . um . . . are looking well."

Odester had seen better days but appreciated Bumpie's compliment.

"Thanks. Bumpie, what are you doing here?" Odester wanted to know. Small talk was never her forte, especially not with Bumpie.

"I know we've been through a lot. I also know I met you when you were young. Some might say too young. You were vulnerable, sweet, and beautiful. I just want to say I didn't take care of you the way I should have. I didn't respect or love myself, so I couldn't respect and love you the way you deserved. And for that, I'm sorry."

Odester quickly swiped her cheek.

"You were good, Odester. Just as smart as your sisters. Just as deserving of a good life, and I didn't give that to you. I know I can't change the past, but we can move forward from here."

He handed Odester a tissue from the table.

"We can't change the past, but we can fix our relationship. We can be cordial."

Odester broke down. She cried until she had no more tears. She mourned her daughter, wept for her father, and mourned for the life she never had. Life wasn't supposed to be this hard. She had come from a solid home, with parents who cared and sisters who would do anything for her. How had she ended up being such a horrible mother? And now her daughter was running the streets doing only God knows what. It broke her heart. After a rocky childhood, Arelia seemed to have overcome the odds. She'd even gone back to school for her associate degree. But she ultimately succumbed to a life of darkness.

"You are right," she said when she gathered herself. "I blamed you for not making me happy, but I know now that my happiness comes from me. Not you. And as a result, Arelia suffered."

"I should have helped you more when I moved out," Bumpie said. "I should have given you money so you didn't struggle as much. I'm sorry."

Odester learned in group therapy that to move forward, you could never look back. She also knew that forgiving Bumpie was more freeing to her than it was to him. They lived their lives and made their mistakes, but now they were able to support the only good thing that had come from their union.

"I forgive you, Bumpie. And I'm sorry I couldn't be the person you needed. We had some rough years, but you decided to clean up and tried to bring me with you. I fought you on that, and for that, I'm sorry. And yes, we can make it better so we can be here for Arelia. She needs us."

"No need to apologize. You may not believe this, but you were the best thing that happened to me. Back then, I was broken by all the stuff happening at my mom's house. Being around you and your family reminded me that life could be good when you have a family. We all struggle, but when you don't have to struggle alone, that's what's most important."

Odester always admonished Nadesna for visiting. But this wasn't the time to be prideful and embarrassed because she needed her family. There was no need to travel rough roads alone when you didn't have to. Odester suddenly felt light.

"Thank you for coming, Bumpie."

"Thank you for loving our daughter," he said. "She will make it through this just like we did."

CHAPTER 35

Emersyn 2019

Nadesna stirred collard greens and checked the oven as guests arrived. She invited family and friends to celebrate Emersyn's last night in town. Nadesna's backyard was almost full. Cousin Pat and Fred shared a table with another couple, and Buster made daiquiris at the bar. String lights offered a festive silhouette, and mosquito candles provided minimal protection. Rico made eye contact with Emersyn from across the backyard where she talked to a few new relatives. Rico seemed to notice Emersyn's new tank dress was different from her typical business casual. He toasted Emersyn and she walked over—curls bouncing, skin glowing, and smiling.

"Hey," she said.

"Hi," Rico scanned her new look. "You look great."

"Thank you." Emersyn blushed. "Thanks for coming."

"Told you I wouldn't miss it." Rico licked his lips, and Emersyn could have died. But she didn't. Instead, she perspired a little more.

"I see Uncle Buster got you going with the drinks."

"Yeah." His eyes bore into her. "Did I tell you how great you look?"

Emersyn blushed, but before she could respond, Devanie grabbed Rico and Emersyn's hand. "Soul train line! It's a Chavis tradition."

Emersyn didn't inherit the Chavis rhythm but got in line

anyway. Rico helped her out of her two-step comfort zone and helped her sway her hips from behind. When it was their turn, he held her waist, and they swung through the line to a myriad of cheers:

I see you, girl!
California style!
Get it, cousin!

They swung through the line twice more when Rico pulled her into him.

"Dance with me. Just me."

"I can't dance." Emersyn looked around. "You saw me out there."

"Come on, have a little fun." He snapped his fingers. "Just get into it." The music slowed and Rico pulled her in closer.

"I can't believe I'm leaving tomorrow night," she said as they swayed in tandem.

"Are you coming to Armand's announcement?"

"Yes. I'll head out after."

"Good. That means I'll get to see you again." Rico smiled and pulled Emersyn's eyes into his.

"Thank you," Emersyn blushed when something caught her eye.

Rico followed Emersyn's gaze across the yard to a woman wearing a head wrap.

Emersyn rushed across the yard with Rico at her heels.

"Mom?" Emersyn touched Phillis's arms and face and hands, as if she couldn't believe she was there. "What are you doing here?" She studied Phillis carefully. Her skin color appeared normal. "Are you okay? You flew here by yourself?" Emersyn tried to process her mom's presence. Had she flown into town alone? Emersyn tried to contain the flood of emotions that threatened to overwhelm her. What about treatment? She wanted to drag Phillis inside and get her questions answered.

"I'm fine, Em." Phillis's face tightened. It was the same expression she wore when she received the cancer diagnosis. She had walked into Emersyn's apartment and asked her to sit. Emersyn didn't like the expression back then, and she didn't like it now. What on earth would make Phillis fly all the way to Louisiana?

"You flew by yourself?" Emersyn asked again. Maybe something happened to Waris, and Phillis didn't want to tell her over the phone.

"Is Auntie Waris okay? Amal?"

Nadesna emerged from the house with sweet tea and plastic cups.

"Phillis?" She squinted her eyes as if she were seeing things. One of the teacups dangled from her hand. "Is that you?" Tears welled in Nadesna's eyes. Rico took the sweet tea and cups, and Nadesna draped her body across Phillis.

"Oh my God, Phillis. I can't believe it's you."

Emersyn watched the interaction with a furrowed brow and complete confusion.

"Hi, Nadesna," Phillis muttered. "It's good to see you."

"It is a gift from God to see you." Nadesna covered her mouth with her hands before turning to Emersyn. "Emersyn, did you know your mama was coming? What a surprise!" She grabbed Phillis again.

"Is there a place we can go inside and talk?" Phillis looked around. "Before I see the family, I wanted to talk to Emersyn."

"Of course," Nadesna said. "Everybody is out there partying anyway. Nobody will notice."

Emersyn squeezed Rico's hand to let him know that she was okay before following her mom and aunt inside.

"Nobody will bother coming in here," Nadesna said, standing at the door of her den. Then she closed the door behind her.

"I loved it here," Phillis said after Nadesna was gone. She slowly paced the room. "My cousins were like my sisters. No, they were my sisters. We did everything together. We had different issues in our homes, but we were always there for one another. Our bond was unbreakable. My grandmother would hold Sunday dinners every week, and my aunts and cousins showed up. We would eat and cook and dance. It was always a good time." Phillis paused and looked off into the distance.

"Why did you let me believe things here were so awful?" Emersyn asked.

"Because I was ashamed." Phillis sat down on the couch. "I was always the good girl in our cousin group. Nadesna was older than us—and technically our aunt—so she always tried to boss us around and tell us what to do." She chuckled. "And Ree was always in trouble."

"And Manon?" Emersyn locked eyes with Phillis.

Phillis cleared her throat. "Manon was smart. Much smarter than any of us, but she didn't apply herself. Aunt Addie stomped on her self-esteem a lot when Manon was younger. I always reminded Manon how much she had to offer."

"So you two were close?"

"Yes. She was my best friend." Phillis sat down on the recliner.

"What happened?"

"Before I left for California, I met a boy. It was during the summer. He was nice, but I didn't expect much. I was struggling about where to attend graduate school because Manon didn't want me to leave."

Emersyn scrunched her toes to quell her growing anxiety.

Phillis smiled. "He was nice . . . this boy I met that summer. First guy who paid me any attention besides wanting me to tutor them in calculus. Most boys were intimidated because my mama scared everybody off with her religious talk." Phillis chuckled. "But this guy didn't know Mama or my family. He was from across the river, which was different because we knew everybody in town. He was nice, funny, and believed in me. Before I knew it, I was in love. I've never loved a man the way that I loved him. Even until this day," Phillis said.

"What happened?"

"At the time, Manon was dating a guy named Tate. We both agreed we'd introduce our new boyfriends, but we were both so busy, and we didn't make it happen. Finally, Manon decided to introduce her boyfriend at Grandma Earline's birthday party."

"Okay?" Emersyn tilted her head.

Phillis took a deep breath. "It turns out that Manon's boyfriend Tate was the same man I was dating, though he went by AJ."

"Wait. What?" Emersyn furrowed her brow. "You and Manon were dating the same guy at the same time and didn't know it?" She sat down across from her mom.

"Yes. He was dating both of us. Manon knew him as Tate, and I knew him as AJ. I never found out if he knew we were cousins before the night Manon introduced him to the family."

"So then what happened?" Emersyn's eyes widened.

"Nothing." Phillis took a deep breath. "After Manon introduced him to the family, I never spoke to him again."

"You didn't tell Manon?"

"No. And when I think about it now," Phillis sighed, "I should have. It would have been so easy. I didn't do anything wrong. But back then, I felt so consumed with guilt, and I was so ashamed about being duped by him that I just buried my head in the sand and took the first opportunity I could to leave town. The master's program at Berkeley was the perfect excuse."

"But why? You didn't know he was dating Manon." Emersyn scrunched her nose.

Phillis pushed herself forward in her seat and looked into Emersyn's eyes. "I slept with him."

"I see," Emersyn said. "But you didn't know, Mom. It wasn't your fault."

"We have to be accountable for our actions. No excuses," Phillis said.

Emersyn was still confused. Her mother was right, but there was more to it than just accountability. Emersyn learned that Grandma Clotee set disciple-level standards for her only child, and it took a toll on Phillis. The longer Emersyn was in town, the more she learned about her mom. She was the consummate perfectionist and harder on herself than anyone because that was how she had been raised. It seemed there was no room for error or to be human. Emersyn felt bad for Phillis, but she still needed to know about her father.

"So, is that when Otis came into the picture? Once you got to California?" Emersyn stared at her mom for a reaction.

Phillis opened her mouth and closed it. She looked at the photos on the mantle. She was never at a loss for words. Tears welled in her eyes as she stared at Emersyn.

"Mom, please tell me how Otis came into the picture. I can handle it, I swear. I've been preparing myself for this for years."

"Otis never came into the picture, Emersyn. I . . . um . . . thought I was protecting you from getting hurt, but I've done the opposite."

"I don't understand," Emersyn said.

"Tate was the first and only person I'd slept with at the time."

Emersyn felt as if a ton of bricks hit her. Her pulse quickened, and her hands were suddenly sweaty.

"What do you mean?"

"Em, I'm sorry," Phillis said.

"You slept with Manon's boyfriend?" Emersyn asked.

"Yes."

Emersyn stared at her mom, then said, "Otis McGee is my father, right? I've been looking for him."

"Looking for him?" Phillis raised her eyebrows.

"Yes, Mom. I've been looking for him. I have a right to know my father."

"Emersyn."

"Mom, I know you have a lot to explain to Manon and you want to get things straight, but I have to do this. I need to find Otis. I need to meet my father. And you can't stop me this time. I won't let you."

"Tate—Armand Gray—is your father." Phillis blinked. "Not Otis. I made that up."

Emersyn gasped and sat back. She felt weak. *Armand? The man I've spent the last nine days with and who got on my nerves seven of those days? Armand Gray is my father?*

Emersyn was beside herself. She'd never been betrayed by anyone on this level. She quickly stood up and paced the floor, backing away each time Phillis reached out to her. She recalled the different scenarios she imagined about meeting her father. The research. The tears and feeling of abandonment. The way she trusted her mother's judgment and story about her father for so long. It didn't make sense. Emersyn shook her head for clarity and couldn't stop.

"What do you mean you made that up?" Emersyn raised her voice.

"Oh, Emersyn." Phillis stood up and extended arms.

"Stop it." Emersyn held up a hand. "Don't touch me. None of this is about me." She shook her head. "None of it!"

Nadesna crept back into the room. "Y'all alright in here?"

Phillis wiped her cheeks and smiled. "I don't know, Nadesna."

"Oh, Phillis, what's wrong?" Nadesna rushed over and wrapped her arms around Phillis. "Is everything okay?" She stroked her back.

Emersyn watched the dynamic. The irony that Nadesna felt sympathy for Phillis after everything that had happened. Emersyn had always respected Phillis and sometimes put her on a pedestal. Her mom was a survivor, a strong woman who raised a daughter on her own because her toxic family couldn't be trusted, and her baby's father didn't want to be bothered. But it was all a lie. Emersyn's entire existence was a lie. This wasn't the woman Emersyn admired and respected.

Phillis glanced at Emersyn, who quickly looked away. Emersyn didn't disrespect her mother, and she didn't want to tonight, but she was beside herself with emotion. That was why Phillis flew all the way down here. She knew Emersyn would find out the truth, and she wanted to cover herself.

"Anything I can do?" Nadesna asked.

Emersyn folded her arms across her chest and waited for Phillis to respond.

"I don't think so," Phillis said, still looking at Emersyn.

"Okay. Well, it's so good to see you, Phillis. We missed you. Now, I didn't tell anybody you were inside. I promise. But I can't keep folks out of the house much longer. Somebody will find out you are here. Best to get on out there before folks start coming in here." Nadesna looked from Emersyn to Phillis again. "And give us all a chance to breathe."

Nadesna was right. There was plenty of family here, and they would have to uncover the rest of the story later. For now, Emersyn was bombarded with more questions. If Phillis never told Manon she had dated Armand, why was Manon angry with Phillis?

CHAPTER 36

Manon 2019

"Are you ready?" Dr. Task's hair disappeared in her virtual background.

Ready was an overused word. She wasn't sure if she was ready for Addie to come live with her. She wasn't sure if she should come clean about Emersyn's identity, or if she could face her family again once they found out what she'd been hiding. Just a year and a half ago, she had the full function of her legs, a husband, and the grand appearance of contentment. Now, all she had were buried secrets that were bursting the seams of her conscience.

"I don't know." Manon adjusted her laptop. "I thought I let a lot of things go from my past, but now I realize I hadn't let anything go. I buried my issues instead of dealing with them."

"We talked about how your parents liked to pretend everything was okay when you were a child. How do you think that affects you now?"

"I don't know," Manon said. "I think I learned to do the same thing. I remember my parents having horrible fights in the car on the way to various events, and when we entered the room, they pretended like everything was fine. It never seemed right, but I began to fall in line with it too. I'd see my mom crying in the bathroom at home, but when someone asked how she was, she was always 'fine.' Everything was always 'fine.' But in reality, we were barely a family anymore. I think I learned by example."

"Say more," Dr. Task prodded.

"Well, my marriage, for example," Manon said. "Tate and I didn't have to end up this way. We could have made things work. But I was more focused on keeping up appearances when I should have focused on my marriage. I wasn't honest with him or with myself. And he tried so many times." Manon wiped a tear from her cheek, recalling Tate's frustration at not finding a solution. He'd suggested therapy. He'd apologized. He'd tried new things. Sex was incredible; he hit her spot—every single time. But it wasn't enough. "I didn't reciprocate. I couldn't love him because I couldn't love myself."

"Why?" Dr. Task probed.

Manon shrugged again. "Because I'm so fucking consumed with guilt and presentation that the inner me is all fucked up, and I don't want to take time to fix her. And until she is fixed, I can't be in a relationship . . . any kind of relationship."

"Wow." Dr. Task nodded. A slow, methodic nod that suggested pride in leading her patient to the still waters of insight and accountability.

"I know, right?" Manon chuckled. "I'm healing over here." She wiped her cheeks.

"You are," Dr. Task said. "Seems like you are ready after all."

"I might be ready for Tate." Manon raised a finger. "Addie is a different story."

"Okay. Why?"

Manon took a deep breath. Why? So many reasons, but one thing stood out more than the rest.

"I'm afraid of failing her," Manon finally said. "I've always been afraid of failing her. It's why I never tried hard at anything. Nothing I ever did was good enough. She constantly pushed me to do better—jump higher, stretch longer, stand up straight, sit down slowly. I could never measure up, so I stopped trying."

"Do you ever think her pushing you was more about her than it was about you?" Dr. Task asked, and Manon nodded. "Tell me what you know about your mom."

That is easy, Manon thought. Addie was cranky, strong-willed, couldn't cook, loved her sisters, kinda liked Marcel, and tolerated Manon. Easy. But as she thought about it, there was more.

"My mom was smart," Manon said. "My aunts are always telling me how she was smarter than everyone in school. In town, even. She always dreamed of going to law school, but she got married and then got pregnant with me."

"Let's pause right there." Dr. Task held up a hand.

Of course, she'd want to pause here to explore how Manon ruined Addie's life. Manon already knew that. She saw it in Addie's eyes the day she ran in from school to share the news of an academic award. Addie had pursed her lips and said, "Good job. Now go and fold your clothes in the laundry room."

"Could it be that your mom regretted her decision to forego law school and pressured you in your accomplishments because she didn't want you to live in the same regrets she did?" Dr. Task asked.

Manon hunched her shoulders. Anything was possible, but should regret stop you from loving your daughter? Telling her she was intelligent and capable? Maybe even hugging her sometimes? Supporting her when she was sexually abused? Seemed like that would be covered in Mom 101 classes. Was it that hard?

"I don't know."

"Do you think your mom loves you?"

Manon recalled the time she fell in a mud pile before a dance competition, and Addie drove forty-five minutes to find Manon another leotard. The leotard didn't match the other girls' uniforms on Manon's dance team, but Addie convinced her that she was the star of the show. Then there was the time Addie banished Manon to her room for spilling red Kool-Aid on the counter. Addie was a mix of good, impatient, and wicked.

"Yes. I think she loves me."

"And could it be possible that she's doing the best she can?"

"What do you mean?" It was Manon's turn to put her finger to her lips.

"I don't know. What were your grandparents like? Were they doting and encouraging, or did they push your mom and aunts to excel? You talk about how smart your mom was. Somebody must have encouraged her."

Addie didn't talk much about her childhood. Manon learned about Addie's younger life from her aunties when they were in the kitchen cooking. Grandma Earline was always sweet to Manon. She loved to rub her fingers through Manon's hair and always said Manon looked just like the "girls back home."

"I don't know," Manon responded.

"Manon, why did you stop communicating with your family?"

The elephant in the room just sat on the bed and crossed his huge ankles. Dr. Task was on a roll today, uncovering Manon's trauma and bad decisions.

She stopped communicating with her family because she was ashamed of her secret and her failed marriage. She was also mad at herself for allowing selfishness to drive her to foolish decisions. Unearthing that secret would threaten the livelihood of so many people and tarnish her reputation. Could she do that? Could she tell everyone the truth about everything?

"Manon?"

"Huh?" Manon furrowed her brows. "What did you say?"

"Why did you stop communicating with your family? And I ask that question with the intention of revisiting it next week. Our time is almost up here today, but I want you to think about why you aren't communicating with your family and how you can fix it."

All her life, Manon went after what she wanted, and she wanted everything. Her trust fund. She wanted to be married to get out of her parents' house. And she wanted her life to appear perfect. But all along, she'd been miserable. Tate was a good man. He wasn't perfect, but neither was Manon. Instead of meeting him where he was, she belittled him and distrusted him during their marriage. She should have confronted him about Phillis and gave their marriage a real chance, or she should have just let him go.

Addie was less than seventy-two hours from moving in. Addie was hard on Manon and made it her life's mission to keep up appearances, but she did the best she could. She loved Manon in the best way that she could, but now it was time for Manon to deal with all the anger and frustration. She was releasing it to free herself from the prison that kept her from happiness and from her family.

"I know what to do." Manon took a deep breath.

"Really?" Dr. Task raised her eyebrows. "What?"

"Tell the truth," Manon bolted up. "I have to."

After her meeting with Dr. Task, Manon headed east on the 182 Highway. She drove out of the gossipy Clos Du Bois to a part of town she hadn't visited in years. She drove past the shanty homes and empty lots until she reached a small beige shotgun house. She kissed the cross around her neck, walked up the rickety stairs, and knocked on the tattered wooden screen door. The door rapped against the doorframe.

A woman in a house coat and two gray plaits made her way to the door. Her two front teeth stood alone in her mouth, and her forehead creased.

"May I help you?"

"Hi," Manon cleared her throat. "Are you Tulip? Tulip Dupree?"

"That's me." The woman squinted at Manon. "Who you?"

"My . . . um . . . my name is Manon Lafleur." Manon reared her shoulders back, expecting an outcry or barage of accusations. Instead, the woman frowned more.

"And how can I help you?"

"I used to live in Clos du Bois across from Leonard's family."

"Leonard?"

"Yes, I believe he's your grandson."

"Oh, Leonard! Bless his heart. Yeah, you know Leonard. You wanna to come on in?"

Manon opened the screen door after Tulip removed the hook.

Tulip's house was tidy. The living room doubled as a bedroom. There was a mock fireplace against the wall with a queen-sized bed next to it. A small loveseat was stuffed between the foot of the bed and the window, and a floor-model television sat near the door. Across from the bed was a regular-sized sofa. It was cramped but tidy.

Tulip sat across from Manon and frowned as if she couldn't see her.

"My grandson, Leonard, lived here for a while, you know. My son couldn't get it together. I told him not to date that gal. I never trusted her. But you know men." Tulip grinned, revealing her remaining front teeth. "They like them red bones, and this gal, she was a red bone." Tulip slapped her knee. "I don't know how Leonard turned out so Black, like midnight."

Manon nodded and noticed photos of Leonard on the mantle. After all these years, her heart fluttered.

"Anyway, that gal wasn't mother material, and after they moved from your neighborhood, they dropped him off here. Said they had to work and never came back."

"What do you mean?" Manon asked.

"They just never came back. I enrolled Leonard in school, and he lived with me until he was a grown man. He got caught up in them streets, though. I was too old to keep up with him. I feel so bad. Them streets got him."

"What do you mean?" Manon's heart pounded. What had happened to her sweet Leonard?

"Drugs." Tulip looked off into the distance, shaking her head. "Just like his daddy. Such a good boy and got caught up."

"Where is he now?" Manon sat on the edge of her seat.

Tulip opened the small nightstand that doubled as a side table, pulled out a piece of paper, and handed it to Manon.

It was Leonard's obituary. Manon caught her breath and blinked hard. Leonard was dead. The boy she could have saved had succumbed to the life she had tried to save him from years ago.

"What happened?" Manon's voice was barely above a whisper.

"I don't know, baby." Tulip looked down. "Some folks said he owed the dope man money. I don't really know 'cause he used to always tell me the dope man was gone kill him if he didn't pay. Course that was just a way to get me to give him money. But I guess that one time, he was telling the truth." She shook her head. "Shot him in the back of the head."

Manon could hardly contain herself, so she stood up, dropping the obituary to the floor. "In the back of the—"

Tulip stood up. "I know who you are. My son and his messy wife told me about you. I didn't remember your name until you said it, but now I remember. You was good to my grandson. I overheard that raggedy daughter-in-law of mine telling one of her friends how much Leonard liked you. She also said if you wasn't so snooty, she might have let Leonard stay with you. If you feeling bad about Leonard, don't. He wasn't your responsibility. He was ours and we failed him."

Manon couldn't conceal her emotions any longer. She cried for all the years she held in her secret. She cried for Leonard's life and cried that she couldn't save him.

"I should have kept him," she muttered between tears. "He needed me."

"He needed his parents, and they failed him. You gave him the best you could for the time you had him. And he was a sweet boy. I would have tried to keep him too. But I ain't mad at you. Leonard ain't mad, and neither was my son. We 'preciate your concern for Leonard. Be at peace, baby. And if you came here to apologize, don't. No need."

CHAPTER 37

Odester 2019

O dester laid out her kitchen rugs on the front porch to dry. She opened the screen door and let Phillis inside.

"Hey, Auntie." Phillis kissed Odester's cheek.

"Come on in." Odester closed the door and turned up the window air-conditioner. "Let me know if it gets too chilly in here."

Phillis stood at the mantle and looked at the photos. She picked up the one of her, Manon, Arelia, and Nadesna posing on Manon's convertible.

"Those were the good old days, weren't they?" Odester asked. "I couldn't keep up with y'all. Prettiest girls in St. Landry County. And the smartest."

"I suppose." Phillis sat on the couch.

"Can I get you something to drink?"

"I'm okay for now. Where's Arelia? She wasn't at Emersyn's party, and Nadesna said she doesn't see Ree much anymore. She's still in town, right?"

Odester sighed and sat down. "Yes, she's still in town, but Nadesna right. Arelia don't come around the family much."

"There seems to be a lot of that going around," Phillis snorted. "Guess it's a family trait."

"Arelia don't come around because she struggles with addiction issues, like me. Guess you can pass on good traits and bad ones too."

Phillis nodded.

"I imagine you've seen me drinking most of your life and probably seen me pass out a time or two. It took me a long time to admit I had a problem and get help. Now I'm hoping the same for Ree."

"What, um, kind of addiction," Manon scrunched her face. "Alcohol?"

"Among other things. I don't know all of what she does. I hardly talk to her anymore. She gets angry with me when I won't give her money, which is never anymore, so she's sworn me off. I can't get her to take my calls or anything. Only way I know she's alive is through Devanie. My poor grandbaby has seen so much. I'm surprised she turned out as well as she did. She's not well though. Pours herself into work like nothing else matters. She's trying to escape."

"Oh, Auntie, I'm sorry."

"No need for you to apologize, you didn't do anything. They say we all pay for the sins of our fathers, and in this case, I guess Ree is paying for mine." Odester looked down at her hands.

"Addiction is nobody's fault. It can happen to anyone at any time. Don't blame yourself." Phillis moved close to Odester and folded her hands into hers.

"Thank you," Odester said. "You were always a sweet girl, just like your mama. We used to tease her for dragging you to church so much, but she wanted the best for you. She loved you more than anything in this world."

Phillis wiped a tear. "Thank you for saying that. Is there anything I can do to help you? To help Ree?"

"Well, right now all we can do is pray. She hardly comes around and won't speak to anybody unless you are offering her money. But for now, I want to know how you are. I couldn't believe it when Nadesna told me you were in town. I didn't make it to Emersyn's party because this gout got the best of me this week, but I'm glad you came. We didn't think you would ever come back."

"Yeah." Phillis looked at the photo again. "Neither did I. But at some point, we all have to face our pasts. And it's time for me to face mine."

"Have you seen Manon?" Odester asked.

Phillis shook her head. "No, I wanted to make my rounds and talk to everybody. Manon is on the list, but I will see her last."

"Good. I don't know all of what happened between you two, but we are family. We've been through some rough times, but we need one another to survive. Whatever happened between you and Manon is over. Family over everything. You are in town, and you might as well make it right while you have the opportunity."

"You are right, Auntie," Phillis said.

"And is everything else all right?" Odester looked at Phillis's small frame. "You healthy and all?"

"Yeah," Phillis said. "I'm fine."

"Okay," Odester said.

"Actually, I'm not," Phillis said. "I'm battling cancer and have been undergoing chemotherapy."

"Oh, Phillis." Odester pulled her into a hug.

"It's scary and hard, and I worry about Emersyn because she's been taking care of me. If something happens to me, she will be all alone. She needs to know her family," Phillis sobbed.

"Hush now," Odester said. "The good Lord won't let anything happen to you. Not right now. And Emersyn is among family now. We will never let her go, just like we never let you go. Even after all these years. You hear me? We will never let either of you go."

Phillis sobbed until she had no more tears. "I miss Mom."

"I know you do. I miss her too. Clotee was the light of my life. Always encouraged me. She would get on my nerves with all those damn scriptures, but they come in handy now. I remember all of them." Odester chuckled.

"Thank you, Auntie."

"No need to thank me. You remember your mama taught you to make gumbo?"

Phillis nodded. "Yes."

"Well, family is like roux. You mix a lot of different things together. Some match and some don't. But after it simmers, it all comes together perfectly."

CHAPTER 38

Emersyn 2019

Emersyn had reasonable expectations for this trip. She figured the sweep would go well because political sweeps were her jam. She knew she and Devanie would hit it off and perhaps she'd click with a few family members. Whether or not she would find Otis was always a crapshoot. And while she didn't know what would happen, she knew heartbreak was a possibility.

But things turned out well so far. Emersyn was thrilled to meet her extended family. The Chavises were chaotic and loud, and some of their conservative beliefs were cringeworthy, but they were hers. This was her family, the people she shared DNA with. Every time she interacted with them, she looked for similar traits among them. Some of them shared the same features; others had the same laugh. And they were family, no matter what their differences were. That was what Emersyn wanted more than anything. She was even close to convincing Buster she didn't work for the CIA, and Nadesna taught her how to make a lemon icebox pie. Finally, she had a place to come visit for the holidays and to send gifts and greeting cards. Finally, she had a family. Things weren't perfect, but they were good . . . until Phillis arrived.

After Nadesna summoned Phillis to join the rest of the family earlier that evening, Emersyn eased out the back door and returned to her hotel where she could process the news about her father. She'd spent her entire life feeling alienated and incomplete. In all the ways she didn't resemble Phillis, Emersyn wondered if she were like her father. Whenever a doctor asked if she had certain medical conditions in her family's history, Emersyn always felt like she was being dishonest. She had a father—everyone did. But rather than allowing Emersyn and Armand the opportunity to have a father-daughter relationship, Phillis had stolen that in her selfish efforts to hide from her own secrets and guilt. How could she? The person she trusted more than anyone—her shero, her best friend—had betrayed her. Were there more lies? Could Emersyn trust her mother ever again?

Emersyn hadn't responded to Phillis's text messages since leaving Nadesna's. She wasn't ready for the conversation yet. She still had to process everything that happened. Not only tonight but throughout the years. She recalled all the times she cried in her mother's arms, asking why her father didn't want her. All the years of therapy and feeling unwanted. All these years, Phillis had watched Emersyn struggle as she withheld the truth.

She lay on the bed in her hotel room staring at the ceiling. The two glasses of Chardonnay weren't working, and it was too hot to work out. She probably should have suspected something was amiss about the story of her father long ago. She wholly trusted that her mom was being honest about Emersyn's paternity. That wasn't a lot to ask for a child who earned straight A's her entire life and always followed the rules. But no, instead of being honest, Phillis lied, and now Emersyn was left to pick up the pieces of her life, and it didn't feel good.

Emersyn grabbed her cell and mindlessly scrolled through social media. For the first time, she saw herself among the family members on Devanie's posts. There was a photo of her smiling next to Buster and another of her with her arms wrapped around Nadesna. So this was what it felt like to belong. The evening's events clouded Emersyn's feel-good moments.

There was a knock at the door. She hadn't ordered another glass of wine, but anything was possible given her current state of mind. She opened the door.

"Hey," Rico said.

"Hey." She closed the door behind him. Sweet Jesus, he was beautiful standing there with his eyes full of concern. The ironies on this trip were uncanny.

"Are you all right?" He studied her face for a few seconds, and she fell into his arms.

Nothing was all right. She was worried about her relationship with her mom, worried about her job since it was just a matter of time before Armand found out she was his daughter.

"I'm sorry I left you at my aunt's house," Emersyn sniffled. "I just—"

"Don't apologize." He wiped the tears from her cheeks. "I'm here to support you, not for an apology or for you to explain anything. We can talk or not. I just want to be here with you." He led her to the small sofa near the window and pulled her close.

"I just can't wrap my head around this," Emersyn said after she told the story to Rico. "How could my mom lie to me for so long? She made me think something awful happened when she was here, but she left for reasons that had everything to do with her and nothing to do with our family. She kept me from them for years."

"We all make mistakes," Rico reasoned. "I'm sure she had a different mindset all those years ago. I'm not making excuses, but I do think you and your mom need another conversation. Maybe a few more conversations about this."

He was right. Emersyn still had a lot to process and even more questions. "Thank you for being here." She rested her head on his shoulder.

"No place I'd rather be, Cali." He rubbed her back. "Sometimes people do things they think are protective but are harmful," Rico explained.

"I'm glad you came." She looked up at him.

"Is that right?"

"Yes."

"Can I do anything for you?" His throaty voice was measured, and he did that thing where he pulled her eyes into his.

"I think I'm okay. What happened after I left Nadesna's?"

"I don't think most people knew what was going on," Rico recalled. "I think between your uncle Buster's drinks, the food, and music, most folks were just having a good time. People were still drinking daiquiris when I left, and your mom and aunt had just come to the backyard.

"I guess it's nice to know my life's downfall didn't stop people from having a good time."

Emersyn held her head between her legs to stop the thoughts from swirling so fast. She'd have to explain all of this to Armand. Opelousas was too small for her to pretend that none of this happened. She snuggled against Rico. His hand rested comfortably on her thigh, and she squirmed closer until she was nuzzling his neck.

"Emersyn." Rico was breathless.

"Hmm?" She reached up and kissed him.

"Mmm," he moaned as Emersyn glided her legs across his body and unbuttoned her shirt. "Emersyn," he murmured. "Are you sure?"

"Yes." She removed her shirt.

He looked at her, and Emersyn instinctively covered her chest with her arms. What was she thinking, taking off her clothes in front of a man who had such a beautiful body?

He pulled her arms back and slowly kissed her cheeks, then her neck. "You're beautiful."

He picked her up—something no man had ever even tried to do—and carried her to the bed. He kissed her all over, stopping at her sweetest spot.

A few hours later, the room was dark and silent. Emersyn was curled up in Rico's arms, feeling on top of the world.

"Wow," Rico said as he played with a strand of her hair.

Emersyn smiled and buried her head in the pillow.

"Don't act shy now," he joked. "You weren't shy earlier."

"Don't do that!" Emersyn shrieked.

"Ah, I see you are one of those who like to keep your freakiness a secret."

"Rico, stop." Emersyn covered her face again.

"Fine." He smiled. "It's been a helluva week."

That was an understatement. Emersyn was so accustomed to masking her feelings for fear of being hurt. But against her best mind, she felt something for him. His delicate charm and rough exterior were a gift from God himself. She smiled with her eyes to show her appreciation. She still wasn't ready to talk to Phillis, who sent a text saying she would be staying in Opelousas a few more days. She didn't have another doctor's appointment for two weeks, so Emersyn didn't worry about her mom staying.

"Been a hell of a week," Emersyn repeated.

"No doubt," Rico said. "You're tough, though. I like that."

"Oh, you like that Cali swag?"

"I like it." He reached for her hand. His eyes were gentle, but his jaw was tight. He wasn't the same guy who ran communications for the campaign, or the guy all the ladies swooned over at Vera. He was also her friend. "I like you."

"Thanks. This was a tough case," Emersyn said.

"I agree." Rico watched Emersyn. "But you did an amazing job."

"Thank you."

"So, you're leaving soon, huh?"

Emersyn nodded, and Rico put his hand over his heart. "I am," she said. "But Oakland is only a plane ride away."

"Is that an invitation?" He leaned closer to her, and she smelled his cologne.

"Absolutely." She kissed him on the lips. "But before I go, I have one more thing to do."

"That's right." Rico said. "Are you ready?"

"Does that matter?" Emersyn tried to laugh.

"I guess not," Rico looked into her eyes, and Emersyn's heart fluttered.

The next morning, Emersyn and Rico stood among a crowd in front of a local coffee shop as Armand prepared to declare his candidacy. He stood behind an oak podium shrouded with microphones. His self-assuredness raged beneath dark eyes and a white Son of Opelousas T-shirt. His tone rose when he spoke about poverty and lack of job opportunities and dimmed when he mentioned Aunt Hattie, who helped him become the man he was today.

Armand's candidacy announcement was one of the top successes of Emersyn's trip. Clad in a black Theory suit, wearing mascara and light concealer—makeup tips from Devanie—Emersyn sipped coffee as she watched her client in action.

"I was fortunate enough to have multiple chances at success," Armand explained to the group. "As a businessman, as a nephew, as a friend, and, yes, as a husband. But if someone hadn't given me another chance, there's no way I would be here today. There's no way I would have the courage or desire to help others if my aunt Hattie hadn't taken a chance on me."

He spotted Emersyn in the crowd. "Everybody makes mistakes, but success comes when people are given a second chance." He looked back at the crowd. "We falter in our judgment, and people will hurt us, but I challenge us to look at the core of the person who has wronged us. Did their action come from a place of ill-intent or someplace else? Is this district deserving of another chance? They may not have an aunt like I did, but they have us! Do our little Black boys and girls deserve an opportunity at greatness? I say yes! And so should you!"

The crowd erupted.

He was good.

Emersyn held Rico's hand as Armand continued. "I beat a system that wasn't designed for me and many others. Remember that to get somewhere, you have to come from somewhere." He paused. "I met a sweet older lady in West Monroe the other week. She raised five grandchildren by herself. Three of them are developmentally disabled. They are all professionals now, but they wouldn't have been if they were never given a chance. Just because something doesn't appear to be good doesn't mean it's not, my friends."

The crowd nodded—some enthusiastically, others pensively.

"People have counted Opelousas out, but we are good!" Armand revered each attendee, taking his time to explain his platform. "I'm not here for the money. You all know my portfolio. And I'm not here for power. I'm here because I was given a chance to make it, and I want to ensure we all get the same chance!"

More cheers from the crowd.

"That's why I'm running to represent this great district," Armand continued. "To ensure we all get a chance to get a piece of the pie. To make sure everybody has an aunt Hattie experience and to keep our hope alive and burning. Are you with me?"

There was more eruption from the crowd. Signs filled the air, and some people gathered around Armand.

"He's good, isn't he?" Emersyn said. Armand was shaking hands and posing for photos with babies. He was a natural.

"He is." Rico smiled. "And I'm sure it had everything to do with your guidance."

Just then her phone rang. It was her mother. "I have to take this," Emersyn said, and she stepped outside.

"I know you're upset with me, but I wanted to tell you that I'm proud of you, Em," Phillis said. "So much has happened, and you remained professional and got the job done. Most people wouldn't have been able to handle it. You're strong."

Emersyn blinked hard. She didn't feel strong.

"I'm going to stay for a few more days," Phillis said. "I think I need to spend more time with family."

"I see." Emersyn nodded. She didn't know if she should be happy or worried. Phillis hadn't been home in years. She worried about leaving her mom alone, but she had to get back to the office. "Are you sure? I can get time off, and we can come back in a few weeks."

"I'm fine," Phillis said. "You go back to work. It's my week off from chemo, so I might celebrate with a daiquiri."

"Enjoy your time, but be sure to rest," Emersyn said. "I know Nadesna will take care of you."

"I love you," Phillis said.

"I know." Emersyn hung up the phone feeling both happy and sad. It would take some time to process everything that had happened. Her phone beeped, then beeped again. Emails and texts were flooding her inbox.

Armand's assembly announcement had made it to Bricks and Associates, and Paul reeled with pride.

"I knew you could do it!" Paul's text read.

Emersyn scanned the congratulatory emails. They "knew she could do it" and called her a "team player." She finally proved herself worthy. There were more hills to climb, but there were always glass ceilings to break. But she was up for it. She was a Black woman with clout and took it as seriously as her family relationships. She had a lot to learn, but she was willing to do the hard work to reach the pinnacles of success.

She opened Paul's email about a new client—a presidential candidate in New York. Emersyn's chest heaved, and she suppressed a scream with her hand.

Bricks had a long way to go in promoting women, but this was a damn good start.

CHAPTER 39

Manon 2019

Manon dreaded today but was ready for the possibilities as she sat on the back porch. Heavy rain revolted against eighty-degree weather, making Bordelais Drive feel like a sauna. Manon saw a new red ant bed in the yard and took note to tell Pierre. In high school, Manon carelessly stepped on a red ant bed and still had scars from the incident. She blew a smoke ring, slipped her feet out of her sandals, and crossed her legs. Emily waved from across the yard, pushing her boys in the tire swing. Looked like the older boy had survived Miss Genessa's alleged curse. Manon waved back.

"Well, I guess that's it." Celeste stepped outside with a Dior tote in one hand and her final check in the other.

"Yes, thank you so much for everything, Celeste." Manon stood to hug her former employee.

"Thank you, Miss Manon. I learned so much from you. You are literally the coolest old person I know."

It was the best compliment Celeste could give. Manon was determined to stop depending on things and people to keep her afloat. Celeste was the first person she cut off the list, but she did so gracefully. The Opelousas Society needed a new clerk for their board, and Manon had recommended Celeste, who wasn't the most qualified but had potential, and the executive director of the Society owed Manon a favor.

"I'm excited for this next chapter for you."

"And I will look for you at some of these events you had me RSVP to," Celeste chuckled.

"Deal." Manon smiled. She'd miss the pampered princess from the West Coast, but all mediocre things must come to an end.

"I'll lock the bottom lock and leave my key on the kitchen counter."

"Thank you, Celeste."

Celeste handed Manon the laptop. "It's all yours." She nodded toward the kitchen. "And good luck," she whispered. "I'll let myself out."

"I appreciate that," Manon said.

Celeste disappeared through the back door. For the first time in a long time, Manon sat back, sipped coffee, checked email, and paid her bills. Manon didn't like change, so her biggest challenge wasn't paying bills and responding to emails; it was adjusting to the differences in her life. Her marriage, the changes to her physical abilities, and learning to accept accountability.

The most significant adjustment was Addie. Since leaving Serenity Village, Addie resided in the guest room next to Manon's kitchen. Manon and Dr. Task worked diligently on Manon's reparenting of herself. Manon had chosen to live life on her terms. The old Southern theories of marriage, gender roles, titles, and self-sacrifice were exhausting. Manon didn't care if she showed up to an event with no one on her arm or if she took out her own trash. The standards set by her family were suffocating, and poor Aunt Clotee had died trying to live up to those standards. She cooked, served, cleaned, and took care of Willie Earl until the day he died. She sacrificed her entire life for Willie Earl and Phillis. It was a noble thing to do, but she died never doing anything for herself. Manon wasn't going out like that. She was going to break the cycle, starting with herself.

"Good morning," Manon walked into the guest suite where an

oversized fiddle leaf fig dominated one corner of the room and a small desk occupied the other. A small chair faced the sliding glass door and provided a view of the backyard. The room was perfect for houseguests to rest, lounge, or work.

"Good morning." Addie was sitting up in the queen-sized poster bed with white plush bedding, reading a book. Her eyes were bright, and her mood was tolerable so far. Her loose waves were pulled into a high bun, and her dark eyebrows accented her delicate features. Since Addie arrived yesterday evening, she and Manon drank coffee, tiptoed around complex subjects, and avoided confrontation. This morning, Manon brewed coffee, cooked breakfast, and ensured Addie's pillows met her standards. All Addie had to do was recuperate and ring the bronze bell Manon had given her.

"Is there anything else I can get for you?" Manon asked. She took the empty plate from Addie's bedside. She'd eaten all of her breakfast; that was a good sign.

"Was that Community Coffee?"

"Yes, Mother. What was wrong with it this time?"

"Nothing," Addie said. "It was good, thank you."

It was only a cup of coffee, but Addie's trivial approval might as well have validated Manon's entire life.

"You're welcome." Manon smiled.

The slur in Addie's speech was almost gone. The discharge nurse from Serenity Village said Addie should be able to return home within a week with a daily visit from the home health nurse. In the days preceding Addie's release, Manon followed Dr. Task's advice and wrote Addie three letters. Each letter represented something that hurt her. The first letter was about protection, the second was about respect, and the third was about acceptance. Manon had grown prideful during her developmental years and spent a lot of time protecting her feelings. She learned to master the art of keeping her heart at a distance to avoid heartbreak. Sometimes it worked, but most of the times it didn't. The letters to Addie removed any emotional barriers Manon had tried to build. She was honest, vulnerable, and in one letter she was ten years old again. The hurt and betrayal she'd felt when Addie didn't stand up for her after the sexual assault had created a gap in Manon's heart that she didn't think could ever be mended.

Last night, mother and daughter sat in this room and small-talked for hours. Addie didn't mention the letters, and Manon refused to bring them up. She had written and delivered them prior to Addie's release from Serenity Village. Manon almost expected Addie to not come and stay with her after reading the letters. Perhaps they would spend the next part of their lives just as dysfunctional as the last. Addie would have to meet Manon halfway, but if she didn't, Manon prepared herself for that possibility as well. She was still pressing forward on her personal journey to understanding the value of kinship and forgiveness.

"You said you're having company today," Addie said. "Are they still coming?"

"Yes," Manon said.

"Do you have a few minutes?" Addie patted the bed, motioning for Manon to sit next to her. Manon obliged. Addie removed her reading glasses and placed her hand on top of Manon's.

An unexplainable emotion sparked in Manon at Addie's touch. Of course, Addie touched her all the time as a kid—little tugs at her hair when she combed it, pulling her arm when she walked too slowly, obligatory hugs in front of family, but nothing tender or comforting. It was a small gesture, but it warmed Manon's heart, and tears rimmed her eyes. It was a feeling she'd longed for all her life. To feel accepted by her mother. To feel good enough.

Addie looked down at their hands and blinked tears away. "The first thing I want to say is thank you. Thank you for letting me stay here. Thank you for being the woman you are. And thank you for your strength."

Well, that did it. Manon openly let the tears stream down her cheeks.

"When I was young, all of these people—some that I didn't even know—had these grand expectations of me." Addie blinked hard and tilted her head up. "I remember going to church with Mama and Daddy one Sunday, and someone introduced me as the future Supreme Court Justice. Mama was always telling people about how I was going to save our community when I graduated law school. My sisters were jealous of the attention, but I hated it. I hated the expectations that were set for me. I didn't think I could live up to them.

"When I met your father, it was the first time I felt safe and protected, like I had someone to look out for me and who didn't expect anything. Somewhere along the way, I got stuck. I couldn't bring myself to study for the LSAT or apply to law school. I let people believe it was because of your father. Your father liked taking care of me and didn't have a problem with me being home, but he would have supported me if I wanted to go back to school. That was the kind of man he was. And when I got pregnant with you, it was even easier to run from my fear. I was afraid and insecure, and I took it out on you. You were feisty and rambunctious and smart, and you constantly reminded me of how much I'd lost of myself."

"Oh, Mama." Manon's tears burned her eyes. "Why didn't you—"

Addie held up her hand. "When you came home from camp that year and told me what happened to you, I remembered how I felt when one of my uncles did the same to me. I was young, but I remember it like it was yesterday. My father's relationship with his brother deteriorated. Hell, my father stopped talking to his family because of it, which caused him great distress. Whenever I saw one of my relatives on that side of the family, even as an adult, they would look at me with contempt, as if I had done something wrong. I was just a little girl at the time, and I wasn't at fault. But it still brought great shame to me and my family."

Addie pulled a tissue from the box next to her bed. "I didn't want the same for you, Manon. I thought you would suffer the same fate if I brought that accusation out. And I knew if your father found out, he was going to war with anybody and everybody until he got a resolution for you. The thing is, there is no resolution in that. At the time, I thought I was protecting you. Now I know I was wrong." Addie lifted Manon's head and looked into her eyes. "I should have protected you. I should have fought for you. I'm sorry. I'm so sorry."

Manon's weeping was uncontrollable. For every tear she shed, the resentful moments and feelings of worthlessness and abandonment left her. She knew what happened wasn't her fault; she just didn't know why Addie had responded the way she did, but now she knew. She leaned over and fell into the bend of her mother's arms and wept some more. Addie rubbed her daughter's back and didn't hold back tears.

"I am so sorry, Manon. So sorry." Mother and daughter embraced.

Manon sat up, and Addie handed her a tissue.

"I'm going to look like a swollen-eyed fool when my guests get here." Manon tried to laugh.

"You could never look like a fool." Addie lifted her daughter's chin. "You are a success, Manon Lafleur, as a woman, a wife, a cousin . . . and a daughter. You've done well for yourself."

Addie held her tighter.

"Manon, I'm sorry you had to carry this alone."

"I understand, Mama. When the expectations are high, we do

what we have to, and when we don't know what to do, we simply do the best we can. I don't know everything that was going on in your mind, but I choose to believe that you did the best you could by me. I choose to believe that you didn't intend to damage me."

"I didn't." Addie cleared her throat. "I swear I didn't intend to hurt you. The backlash from my uncle was so awful. When you told me what had happened to you at the camp, I was so angry and hurt. I wish I could have protected you. Even though you didn't do anything wrong, there's a shame that comes from being sexually abused that I didn't want for you."

Manon looked up and wiped her face. "Thank you for saying that. I can't say I would have handled things the same way if it were my daughter. I have carried the shame with me all these years because I buried it deep. But the person I am today and the person I want to become forgives you and will try to understand."

Addie nodded slowly. "You hush now." She rubbed Manon's back. "We all make mistakes, and you are trying to make yours right, and I'm trying to make amends. You are doing things I should have done to heal and move on from my experience."

"Hopefully others feel that way," Manon admitted. "Tate is coming over."

"You make sure to hold your head up," Addie said. "We are all doing the best we can."

Manon jumped when the doorbell rang.

"Are you going to be okay?" Addie asked.

"Yes. I got this. I have to make things right. If I'm ever going to have peace, I have to do this."

Manon closed Addie's door and walked down the hall, her silk kimono trailing behind her like a support system. Her legs shook with each step.

"Please come in," she said, opening the door for Tate.

They hadn't spoken since the argument the other day, and his other attempts to talk were sent to voicemail. Tate followed her to the great room, where he hovered near the door. He looked at her suspiciously.

"What is this about?" He stood with his hands at his waist. Manon forgot all the sweet, clever things she'd practiced. Instead, she pulled a manilla envelope from her desk and handed it to him.

"What's this?" Tate looked at the envelope.

"Divorce papers," Manon said. "All signed and ready to go." She'd heard the term *soulmate* many times in her life. She wasn't sure she believed there was such a thing, but if there were, she knew Tate wasn't hers. He was loving, handsome, and hard-working, but he was no longer her person. If she dared to be honest with herself, he never was. It was possible to make a marriage work if you were patient, accountable, and communicated. But making a marriage work didn't mean happiness. Manon didn't want to be married just to say she was married. She wanted a complete life with love, partnership, respect, and where she was able to be herself. Tate was a good man, but he had issues and wasn't perfect, not by far. But even in growth and forgiveness, Tate wasn't the man for her, and she could finally admit that.

"I don't know what to say." Tate tucked the papers back into the envelope.

"Say it will be amicable." Manon shrugged. "You know I don't like drama."

"Of course." He looked into her eyes. "I'd never do anything to hurt you," he said.

The doorbell rang. "Just a minute, Tate," Manon said as she excused herself.

She opened the front door and smiled at Phillis and Emersyn. It was the first time she'd seen Phillis since Aunt Clotee's funeral. She resisted the urge to throw her arms around Phillis's frail frame, beg for forgiveness, and tell her how much she missed her.

Phillis had aged gracefully. Her black strapped maxi swept the top of her sandals. She was thin, but she looked good. Phillis furrowed her brow and hesitated before crossing the threshold. Manon noticed Emersyn did the same.

"Thank you for coming," Manon said as she led Phillis and Emersyn into the great room.

Tate stood up when the three women entered the room. His mouth gaped open. "Lily?"

Phillis shifted her eyes in suspicion. "What's going on?" she asked, lifting an arm protectively toward Emersyn.

"I haven't seen you in years." Tate shook his head in disbelief.

Manon watched Tate's body language. He stared at Phillis the same way he did when he saw her at Grandma Earline's party all those years ago. Back then, Manon didn't notice it the way she did now. He'd loved her back then.

"I came to visit family," Phillis said as if she were giving a presentation. She was still so poised. It was one of Manon's favorite things about Phillis. She could always talk Manon into being rational. "And to check on my daughter." She smiled at Emersyn, who smiled nervously.

Tate did a double-take. "Emersyn?"

"Yes," Phillis said proudly. "Emersyn is my daughter."

Tate furrowed his brow at Emersyn. Emersyn twisted her mouth but didn't back down from his confused stare.

Manon cleared her throat. "I called the three of you here for a reason."

"Wait." Tate held up his hand. "I'm sorry, Manon, give me second. Emersyn, your mother is Phillis?"

Emersyn nodded.

"We're cousins," Manon cleared her throat. "As I said, I called the three of you here for a reason. Please, everybody, sit down."

Tate looked confused but finally took a seat, not taking his eyes off Emersyn. Phillis and Emersyn sat next to each other on the couch.

"I don't want to continue to live a lie," Manon shared. "I want to live a life free of secrets and drama."

Manon took a deep breath. This was the moment she had been waiting for.

"Phillis, I know about you and Tate. I know you two dated when he and I dated," Manon said.

Phillis sighed. "You know I'd never hurt you, Manon. I swear didn't know AJ was Tate."

"I know." Manon nodded slowly. "It took me a long time to realize it, but I know you'd never hurt me. And for the longest time, I couldn't figure out why you would leave town so suddenly. Now I know it was because you were pregnant."

Tate's eyes widened, and Phillis's mouth fell open in shock.

"I found the letter, Phillis," Manon said. "On the day of my wedding, I went to Tate's apartment, and I found the letter you sent to him. I destroyed it."

"Wait. What letter?" Tate shook his head in confusion.

"You never saw the letter?" Phillis asked. "I wrote to you. I told you that I was pregnant with your child."

Tate stood up. "What?" He shook his head again. "Pregnant? I never saw the letter. I figured you didn't want anything to do with me after finding out about me and Manon."

"But we slept together," Phillis lowered her voice, as if she were still ashamed.

"It was only once." Tate raised his eyebrows, then looked down as if he regretted the comment.

"I know," Phillis said.

"You got pregnant?" Tate squinted his eyes as he struggled to understand what was happening, but he couldn't make sense of it all. He hunched over and looked at Emersyn. Tears welled in his eyes. "Emersyn?" he whispered.

Phillis nodded. "When you didn't respond to my letter, I thought you didn't want anything to do with us . . . with Emersyn."

Tate walked over and placed a hand on her shoulder. "Phillis, I would never, ever have left you that way. I loved you. I was young and got caught up. I couldn't give you what you needed, but if I had known you were pregnant, I would have been there for you and our child."

"I didn't know," Phillis said. "When I saw you that night with Manon, I realized you were a liar and a cheat. I wrote the letter about my pregnancy out of courtesy more than anything. When you didn't respond, it just cemented my opinion about you."

Tate held up his hands. "But I never saw the letter. I didn't know. I—"

"I know," Phillis said.

Everyone looked at Manon, who was watching the scene unfold with tears in her eyes. She'd hurt so many people to escape her own hurt back then. She'd broken up a family. She recalled how lonely she felt without Phillis in her life, and how hard she cried on her wedding night. She'd told Tate she was starting her period, but it was more than that. Through the years, she sold herself the narrative that Phillis had deceived her, and if she wanted to keep her baby a secret, Manon wouldn't tell. It was the only way she could justify what she did. But that lie was like closing a surgical incision with a Band-Aid. And poor Emersyn didn't deserve any of this. Dr. Task told Manon she would experience extreme guilt and reminded her to be gentle with herself.

"Why, Manon?" Phillis asked. "Why didn't you let him see the letter?"

"I was selfish, young, insecure, and I wanted to do anything to get out from under Addie. My wedding day was hard. I almost didn't make it down the aisle. There were so many times that day when I wanted to cancel the wedding and call you, Phillis. I wanted to talk about it all, explain my side and let you explain yours. But in that moment, the wedding, the guests—everything seemed bigger than me, and I forced myself to go through with it. I can't tell you all how sorry I am," Manon said.

Tate winced and clenched his jaw.

"I'm so sorry, Tate," Manon said. "What you did was dishonest and hurtful, and this secret has destroyed our marriage because I could never let myself forgive and forget. And with every year that passed, the secret morphed into something I no longer recognized."

"You told me you didn't have family here," Tate said to Emersyn.

"I was trying to keep business and personal life separate. Guess I blew it," Emersyn said. "I didn't intertwine the two, not knowing I was doing so just by representing you."

"It's not your fault," Tate reassured her. "None of this is your fault. Don't apologize. And as family, this matter stays between us. No need for anybody outside of the family to know. You follow me?" He still looked at Emersyn, who was visibly relieved.

"Thank you," she said.

Manon felt droves of guilt. She had not only taken Emersyn's father away from her, but she had stripped away Tate's opportunity to be a father.

"I was young, stupid, and insecure too," Tate said to Manon. "I never thought I was good enough for you, Manon. I wanted to be, but I always feared I wasn't. Something about how you looked at me made me know I'd never be able to give you everything you wanted. But that didn't stop me from trying."

"I know," Manon agreed. "I know."

Tate turned to Phillis. "You were the confidence booster I needed. You were kind, supportive, and honest. I needed everything you were giving me. I had no intention of us being anything but friends. I didn't expect to fall for you the way I did."

The room was thick with tension and curiosity.

"I was going to tell you about Phillis that night of your grandmother's party," Tate said to Manon. "But when I saw Phillis and connected the dots, I knew it was over for Phillis and me. I figured she would have told you, since you two were so close, but after a while, I realized she hadn't told you." Tate looked at Manon intently. "I didn't want to lose both of you. And when Phillis left town, I didn't see a need to tell you. So, yes, I was seeing both of you, but I swear I didn't know you were cousins. I swear to you."

Phillis scoffed, and Manon felt sorry for her. Clotee had raised Phillis to be the pillar of integrity and morals. Phillis had very little room for error, much like Manon, except Phillis was guided by her mom's Christian morals. How awful she must have felt to be pregnant, unwed, and alone as a young woman.

"I didn't say it was a good reason," Tate said to Phillis. "I'm merely telling my side of the story."

He walked over to Emersyn. "If I had known your mother was pregnant with you, I would have been there every step of the way. Every single step of the way. You are a wonderful young lady, and if I have any regrets in all of this, it's that I wasn't able to be there for you growing up."

Emersyn blinked hard a few times.

"But if you let me, I swear I'll be here for you in every way I can for the rest of my life. I know it won't be easy, and we will have to adjust, maybe even go to counseling. I don't care. I will do whatever it takes. I just need the chance."

Manon studied Emersyn. The way her lip trembled, the way she regarded her mom for approval. The speculation in her eyes.

Manon silently prayed for a resolution, not to ease her own guilt, but because the three of them deserved it.

"It's . . . um . . . a lot," Emersyn sighed. "A whole lot. I don't hold anything against you Armand . . . Tate—"

"It doesn't have to make sense right away, Em," Phillis said lovingly. "Search your heart before you decide anything. Your happiness and peace are what matter most. You didn't create this mess. We did." Phillis pointed to herself, Manon, and Tate. "So you take the time you need."

"Yes," Tate said quickly. "Whatever time you need."

Emersyn hoisted her bag on her shoulder. "I need to get going," she announced.

"I will come with you." Phillis stood up.

"No." Emersyn held up her hand. "I heard what I needed to hear, and I have to process it all. I need some time by myself. I can take an Uber and leave you the car if you'd like."

"I can take you back," Manon said to Phillis, expecting her to decline.

Phillis stared at Emersyn before saying, "Sure, Manon. Thank you."

"I've created quite the mess," Manon said after Emersyn left. "It's all my fault."

"Don't play victim, Manon." Tate whirled to face Manon. He was angry. It was rare to see, but there he was, nostrils flaring, shoulders reared. Who could blame him?

"She's apologizing," Phillis said defensively. She turned to Manon and said, "All these years without my family have been hard. And now, it's even harder. I don't want any more negativity and resentment to build. I'm so mad at you for what you did, Manon, but you are family, and I forgive you. I have to. Not just for you, but for me as well. It may take a while for our relationship to mend, and perhaps it will never mend to even close to what we were as young women, but we have to do what we can. Life is too short."

Manon fell into Phillis's thin frame. She remembered the times when she cried to her cousin about everything that had plagued Manon in the earlier part of her life. Phillis had always been her rock, often putting Manon's needs before her own. Phillis was kind and loved Manon unconditionally. She'd felt so betrayed by Phillis's disappearance. But it was her fault their relationship had come to an end. Instead of reaching out to understand what had happened, Manon had built a wall of contempt for Phillis that she held on for too long.

"I'm so, so sorry, Phillis," Manon sobbed.

"I know." Phillis rubbed Manon's back and caught Tate's eyes across the room. "We all make mistakes. It's how we make up for them that matter."

"I should go," Tate said.

After Tate was gone, Manon composed herself. "I'm happy you are back. So is Addie."

"How is she?" Phillis was guarded but calm. "I heard about her stroke."

"She's here recovering," Manon said.

"With you?" Phillis scrunched her nose.

"Yes, I know she'd love to see you."

Manon held Phillis's hand. "I want to try to be friends again. Not just relatives, but friends."

Phillis took a deep breath. "Let's just take it one day at a time."

"Agreed," Manon said, and she led Phillis to Addie's room.

CHAPTER 40
Odester 2019

O dester prepared dinner with chrome dials, utensils that required an instruction manual, and pots shinier than jewelry. Most of it was new because Manon didn't spend much time in her kitchen. The family gathered at Manon's for Sunday dinner—the first ever at Manon's house. Addie was faring better each day. She sat at the counter deveining shrimp.

"Dette, make sure you check the temperature," Nadesna said over Odester's shoulder.

Odester playfully nudged her baby sister away. "Nadesna, don't micromanage me. I know how to cook. Been helping Clotee all my life."

"She sure did," Addie chimed in. "While you were still playing with dolls."

Nadesna sucked her teeth. "You are defending her?" she accused Addie.

"Just saying," Addie chuckled. "I'm doing what I was assigned to do. Nothing more."

"I helped Tee cook sometimes too," Nadesna scoffed.

"Mmmhmm," Odester teased. "Sure you did."

"Tee was the best cook ever," Addie said. "I miss her so much."

"Me too," Nadesna said. "She was like my second mama."

"Always telling us what to do." Odester faced the stove to hide her tears. The hardest part of her recovery was dealing with grief. In the past, she'd numbed it with drugs and alcohol so she didn't feel the pain, but now the pain was very present, and she had to learn how to manage it in healthy ways. Being here with her sisters was a good way to cope. They had their differences, but they were family, and through it all, they supported Odester the way family should. They didn't talk about Odester and make her feel small. They loved and supported her, and they helped Arelia when Odester couldn't. Family wasn't perfect, but it was just what Odester needed.

"Dette, you over there crying?" Addie asked.

"I am." Odester faced her sisters. "I miss her."

"I know you do. It's okay to miss her." Nadesna pulled her into a hug. "She's always gone be with us, Dette."

"Remember that time when Mama and Daddy went to New Orleans for the weekend and Tee caught you and Bumpie in the backyard?" Addie laughed.

"Oh my goodness." Odester rolled her eyes and laughed. "She made me get on my knees and pray for forgiveness."

"Are you serious?" Nadesna raised her eyebrows.

"Yes," Addie and Odester said in unison.

"She said Dette was being attacked by the lust demon," Addie said.

"Aw, shit, y'all in here crying?" Buster walked in wearing a Saints cap and holding an empty cup. "Or is y'all laughing? What's going on in here? Where the sweet tea at?"

"Buster, get on out of here trying to pretend you want some tea. We all know you got that pint of vodka under your chair." Nadesna quickly looked at Odester.

"It's fine." Odester smiled. "Y'all can mention alcohol in front of me. I won't fall off the wagon because I hear the word *vodka*. Relax. But I want to know why y'all are acting like I can't cook?"

Odester put a hand on her hip. "Addie is the one with the cooking deficiency."

"Don't put that on Addie. We know Addie never had to cook," Buster said. "'Member that time Tee asked you to watch the greens while she ran to the store?'"

"Oh my God!" Addie screeched. "And Dette let the water boil out and burned the greens."

"Shole did," Buster laughed.

"Get on outta here, Buster," Odester said. "Coming in here with them old stories. Don't make me talk 'bout you and that gal from South Forty-Fifth with that missing front tooth."

"Now, there you go, Dette. Can't have fun round here." Buster laughed.

"Buster, you just go on in there and change that music," Addie said. "I don't like that hip-hop music or whatever you're listening to. Put on some Marvin Gaye."

"This is the jam." Buster tapped his foot and snapped his fingers. "Ain't nobody listening to Marvin Gaye, Addie. This here is what they call trap music. Better learn about it." He swiveled his hips.

"You need to learn about leaving those young girls alone," Nadesna chuckled. "The only one who gone get trapped is you. Over there, snapping your fingers to rap music like a fool. Don't even much know the words. Now, put on some Marvin Gaye like Addie said."

"It's trap music," Buster corrected. "Not rap." He disappeared to the living room with a fresh glass of tea.

"Sound like y'all having a good time here." Esther peeked into the huge kitchen. "Anything I can help with?"

Odester looked over at her sisters. Nadesna grabbed something from the refrigerator, and Addie peeled shrimp as if her life depended on it. They were no help. Another part of Odester's recovery was accepting Bumpie's new life, which included Esther. Inviting them here today was a big step. But did the woman need to be in the kitchen with her and her sisters too?

"Actually, there is," Odester finally said. "It looks like that dispenser needs to be refilled with iced tea. Buster drank most of it. Can you refill it, please?"

"Sure!" Esther grabbed the crystal dispenser. "This is beautiful." She held the dispenser up in the air.

"There's a sink behind that wall." Odester pointed. "And the ice is in the deep freezer in the garage."

"Two sinks!" Esther's eyes widened. "This is a fine house."

"Yes, it is," Odester smiled proudly. "Belongs to my niece."

"Well, look at God," Addie whispered after Esther left. "Never thought I'd see the day you'd invite Bumpie and Esther to a family event."

"One thing at a time, one day at a time," Odester recited.

"You talked to Ree?" Nadesna exposed the elephant in the room.

Odester sighed. She hadn't heard from Arelia in weeks. Thinking about her daughter was like pouring alcohol on an open wound. The last time Arelia had called, she'd asked Odester to send for an Uber. The thought that her own addiction lifestyle had initiated Arelia's spiral into drugs was hard to reckon with. Odester had many demons. Sometimes, she lay awake at night imagining what Arelia was doing, praying she was okay, and asking God for forgiveness.

"Not lately. Praying she okay though."

"She called Manon the other day," Addie offered. "She asked for money. Manon agreed to give it to her if Arelia agreed to meet in person."

"Did she come?" Odester's eyes widened.

"She did," Addie said. "Manon said she looked okay. A little small, but okay."

"God is so good," Nadesna said.

"What number did she call from?"

"She asked Manon not to give it to anyone." Addie lowered her eyes. "And Manon promised not to."

"Well, least we know she's okay, and she's in touch with Manon," Nadesna offered.

"Dette," Addie said. "She's going to be fine. She's a fighter just like you and so strong. She will get through this."

"We all will," Nadesna said.

Odester walked over and hugged Addie. "Thank you for saying that," she whispered."

"Now, go cook before you burn the entire meal," Addie said as she wiped her tears.

A burst of laughter emerged from the living room. Manon, Phillis, Emersyn, and Devanie were engrossed in conversation.

"How's Devanie doing?" Addie asked.

"Ah, my granddaughter is a blessing from God." Odester folded her hands together. "Checks on me all the time, and she works hard. She don't talk too much 'bout Ree. I know she lets Ree spend the night sometimes, but I don't pry. If she wanna talk about it, she will, but I don't press her."

"That's gotta be hard on her." Nadesna looked over at her niece, who was laughing at something Emersyn said. "Good to see her and Emersyn bonding."

"Me too," Odester said. "Emersyn is so sweet. She's so much like Clotee. And Phillis and Manon seem to be doing okay."

Addie nodded. "Manon says they are trying—both guarded, but they're trying."

"They've been through a lot."

"They have," Nadesna said.

"Maybe she and Phillis will have a relationship again, maybe not. But they are together in the same house, talking civilly, and being family. That's enough for now. We've had enough division in this family to last a lifetime."

"Y'all heard anything about Emersyn and Tate?" Odester whispered to her sisters.

"I haven't," Nadesna said.

"I haven't either," Addie said.

"Devanie said Emersyn and Tate were supposed to have dinner before Emersyn went back to California, but Devanie doesn't know if the dinner happened," Odester said.

"I think they are going to be fine," Addie added.

"Yeah, they seem fine, but that might not be the case. People thought Ree was fine. Thought I was fine, but I wasn't. Just because someone appears fine doesn't mean they are."

It wasn't long ago when Addie didn't attend family functions. If Odester remembered, there was a time when Addie couldn't be bothered with the rest of the family either. Only time would tell how things would go. In the meantime, all the family could do was pray.

"What's up with you and Mr. Clyde?" Nadesna joked.

"Clyde is my friend." Odester blushed. "That's all. Now, don't go trying to make something out of nothing. I'm way too old to be sweet on some old man."

"Hm, okay," Addie laughed. "I think you probably should share that memo with Clyde because he's sweet on you."

"No, he's not."

"He certainly is," Nadesna chimed in. "He can hardly focus on what Buster and Bumpie are saying because he keeps trying to walk past this kitchen to look at you."

"Ya'll need to stop. Nadesna, you are too much. He's just my friend."

"It's okay to have a man like you, Dette. You are not too old, and it's not too late to be happy." Nadesna chuckled.

Odester put a top on the roux and turned the fire down to let it simmer just as the doorbell rang. She wiped her hands on her apron when she heard Manon call out, "Ree's here!"

Odester put down the spoon and stood in the kitchen doorway as Arelia walked down the hall toward her. She looked skinny, and her eyes were sad, as if she needed a hug.

"Mama." She fell into Odester's arms and wept.

"Mama's here, baby."

About the Author

Tamika Christy was born and raised in Oakland, California. Her passion for writing developed at a young age. Drawing inspiration from her own experiences, she has a unique talent for creating relatable characters who come alive on the pages of her books.

Through her work, Tamika tackles essential and timely themes such as mental health, addiction, self-love, and the complexities of family dynamics. She sheds light on these topics with sensitivity and depth, sparking conversations and fostering a greater understanding of the human experience.

Tamika's ability to empathize with her characters and breathe life into their stories has garnered her a dedicated following of readers eagerly awaiting each release. With each page, turned, she leaves an indelible mark on the literary world, captivating audiences with her depth and dedication. Stay tuned for her upcoming projects.

Other Books
by Tamika Christy

Frenzied. Overburdened. Stressed. Overwhelmed. These are just a few ways to describe college senior Anaya Goode's life. Add to this no career prospects following a looming graduation, and Anaya quickly finds herself drowning in the chaos of her own life.

Her family and friends demand much of Anaya, and she's struggling to balance herself in the mire. Facing an onslaught of grief, complex relationships, and a life that is full of deafening noise, Anaya must find herself, and maybe even true love and redemption, amid old traditions and new beginnings.

Book 2 in the Anaya's World series.

Things are looking up for Anaya Goode after the deaths of her brother and mother. She is the youngest (and highest paid) executive in Alameda County. She is in an adoring relationship with the love of her life, her natural twists are on point, and she runs a six-minute mile. What else matters?

When Anaya is tasked with leading negotiations for the most significant development agreement in County history, her world unravels. If the antics of inept officials and her micromanaging boss aren't enough to drive Anaya mad, she discovers that her ex-boyfriend Jeff is commissioned as a consultant on the development agreement. Anaya hasn't had contact with Jeff since their messy break-up six years ago.

As negotiations for the development agreement intensify, an internal scandal threatens Anaya's reputation—and her job. Amid bureaucratic indecision and public outrage, Anaya leans on Jeff for support, and unresolved feelings resurface.

As Anaya questions her steady relationship, her extended family's perception of her as Goode matriarch puts her in the middle of every aunt's and cousin's problem. She is tired of serving as supplemental income to her scripture-quoting, ever-pregnant sister, and would love to burn the imaginary pedestal her family has perched her on. Can she see her work and family commitments through and still maintain her love life—and more importantly, her sense of self?

Ripe with witty dialogue and relatable characters, "Never Too Soon" offers a look into complicated relationships and haunting pasts, and shows the importance of the familial ties that bind.